BLOWBACK

JAMES P. SUMNER

BLOWBACK

First Edition published in 2020 by Both Barrels Publishing Ltd.

Copyright © James P. Sumner 2021

Editing and Cover Design by: bothbarrelsauthorservices.com

ISBNs:

978-1-914191-24-4 (Paperback)

Visit the author's website: jamespsumner.com

About damn time, right?

BLOWBACK

ADRIAN HELL: BOOK 8

1

_____

Okay, before you say anything, I just want to clarify this wasn't my fault. I didn't ask to be in this situation. I certainly don't *want* to be in this situation. The situation just kind of found me.

As these things invariably do from time to time, I guess.

The two guys standing in front of me aren't especially impressive in any way. They're both shorter than me. Neither are as broad as I am. They're dressed the same—black tank tops beneath colorful short-sleeve shirts, which hang open above loose-fitting jeans. Too much jewelry around their necks. I see they have *some* muscle. It's the sinewy kind that pulses and tenses along the arms, signaling fitness and a modest strength comparable to their frame.

One of them is talking. A lot. I don't understand him because he's speaking Japanese.

That's not an exaggerated metaphor for the fact I can't tell what he's saying. He's *actually* speaking Japanese. For

I

the last two years or so, I've been living in Tokyo. I share an apartment with Ruby.

I know, right?

But it works. We're both happy, which is great considering everything that happened prior to moving out here. Don't get me wrong, we're not... y'know... *together*. We just live together. Which is totally different. There's nothing—

You know what? Never mind. This probably isn't the time to get into all that.

The guy's still speaking Japanese, and I still don't understand a word of it. Normally, I would. Like most people nowadays, I have a little piece of tech called a Pilot, which is an earpiece that translates most languages into English in real-time. But I wanted a little peace and quiet and a couple of drinks tonight, so I left it at the apartment when I came out to the bar.

However, given this guy's body language and the look on his face, I reckon I can catch the gist of what he's saying. He's scowling and gesturing sharply with his hands. He also keeps pointing a finger near my face—which, I swear to God, I'm going to break if he doesn't stop. He's purposely flexing, rolling his shoulders and twisting his head to crick his neck every few words.

All textbook behavior designed to intimidate.

Yeah... good luck with that.

His friend is scowling at me too, except he's not saying anything. Instead, he's holding his nose, trying to stop the bleeding.

Now *that* was my fault.

Look, here's what happened. I was sitting on a stool at the bar, right? I had a beer in my hand. It's called Asahi. It's all I've drank since I moved here. I'm not sure how I survived without it. Beats the hell out of Bud. It was lovely and cold.

The glass bottle felt like ice, and the condensation dripped onto the counter with each mouthful.

Anyway...

I heard a commotion behind me. Now, this place is pretty loud. Music—and I use that term in its loosest possible sense—was blasting out, and it was busy without being overcrowded. There's enough going on that if I could hear the commotion from where I was sitting, it had to have been something pretty intense.

So, I looked over my shoulder and saw a girl. Whether she was old enough to be in a bar, I honestly couldn't say. Here, the legal drinking age is twenty. If she were too young, it wasn't by much. Eighteen or nineteen, for sure. She wasn't a local. Maybe not American but definitely not Japanese. She wore a skirt that barely covered tomorrow's laundry and a top that showed more than it concealed. Her skin was a dark tan, her hair black with tight curls. She was attractive, if you like that sort of thing.

There were two guys standing in front of her. The same two standing in front of me now. The one doing all the talking and gesturing had his hand on her arm, gripping it tightly just above the elbow. He was trying to drag her toward him. She was screaming and struggling to move away. The other guy looked on, laughing.

I turned away. Took another gulp of my beer. Tried to ignore it. Figured it was nothing to do with me. I was out for a quiet night. Tokyo is an amazing place, breathtaking at times, but it has its dark side too. I'm not saying it's right, but things like that happen. It's how the place works, and most people accept it. It's rarely safe to get involved. Everyone is just looking out for themselves.

But then I looked around again, just in time to see the first guy slap the girl across the face. He used the back of his

3

hand. The crack was loud. The music stopped. Onlookers gasped.

That was when I resigned myself to the fact that I'm not *most people*. That whatever was going on had suddenly become everything to do with me.

I've seen and done a lot of shit in my time. Some of it good, most of it questionable at best. I've spent the majority of my adult life doing bad things for profit. I like to think of myself as a nice person, but I'm not naïve enough to think I'm a good one. I'm certainly not a hero.

That said, for as long as I can remember, I've never stood for anyone doing wrong by people who don't deserve it. There's already so much shit in this world we can't do anything about—there's no reason you can give me that justifies purposely making it worse.

So, I got to my feet. Pushed my way through the crowd of slack-jawed locals holding cell phones. Moved toward the three of them and, without breaking stride, stepped between the girl and the two guys. No hesitation. No doubt. Just did the only thing in that moment that made any sense to me.

I heard her whimpering behind me. I heard the quiver in her breathing. It told me she wasn't sure if her situation just got better or worse.

The guy on my left was the taller of the two. He stopped laughing almost immediately. He looked surprised, clearly wondering who I was. The guy on my right, who had been grabbing the girl's arm, had already begun posturing up, seemingly unconcerned with who I was, focusing instead on how I could dare think of inter-rupting his fun.

I looked them both in the eyes, holding each gaze for a long beat. Then I stared more intently on the guy who had slapped the girl. I smiled at him, nodded a greeting, and said, "*Kon'nichiwa*, dickbag."

The taller guy made the first move. He was fast but nowhere near fast enough. He started to throw a punch, but mid-swing, I took a small step to the left and whipped the heel of my palm into his face, finding the gap he had left in the process.

Rookie error. You always keep your guard up, even when you're attacking.

His punch never connected. Never even came close. I broke the thin cartilage in his nose. He staggered back, stumbling into the booth behind him.

The other guy wasn't happy about it, understandably, but did nothing except posture some more. I saw the restlessness in his stance. The hesitation. He didn't want to lose face, but having just seen me handle his friend with very little effort, he wasn't in a rush to attack me and risk the same thing happening to him.

Which it would have.

He was beaten before the fight could begin.

I glanced back at the girl, told her she was safe, and that she might want to call it a night. She understood me, thankfully. She nodded, turned, and made her way out through the crowd, who all kindly parted to give her space.

And here I am.

See? How is *any* of this my fault?

The guy with the busted nose takes deep breaths through his mouth, boring a hole into me with his beady little eyes. He won't make another move. He's learned his lesson. This other guy's still thinking about it, but I'm not in the mood to wait around and see if he finds his balls in the next couple of minutes. My drink's getting warm on the bar.

I gesture him away with my hand. Shooing him as a

master would his slave. Dismissing him as if he's nothing. "You're done. Leave while you can still walk unaided. I see you again, you wake up in the hospital. Clear?"

There's a moment's silence. I roll my eyes. Of course, that wasn't clear—he can't understand me.

I have another piece of tech, called an Ili. It's a tiny microphone-slash-speaker... thing that works in the opposite way to the Pilot. It translates whatever I say into another language and broadcasts it in a robotic voice. Most people have Pilots, which negates the need for anything else, but sometimes it's useful to have the option. Just in case.

But my Ili is sitting on the side in my apartment, next to my Pilot.

Oh, he's started talking again. Started waving his finger near my face again too.

I can see I'll have to rely on the universal language.

No, not mathematics. The other one.

I grab a hold of his finger and wrench it back, feeling the delicate bone snap at the second knuckle. He yells out in obvious and justifiable pain. I push the finger back further, forcing him down on one knee.

"Don't be a *baka*. Use your brain. Walk away."

I like that word. *Baka*. It means *idiot*. I've picked up some of the language while I've been here. Mostly just the essentials—how to order beer, how to insult someone... that kind of thing.

He finally shuts up, choosing instead to nod his head rapidly and hold his other hand up in apology.

I smile down at him. "There's a good *baka*. Now get your ass outta here."

I let him get back to his feet. His friend grabs him as they run toward the door, scrambling through the crowd, looking back at me for fear of being followed.

I take a deep breath. It helps calm the flow of adrenaline and subdue the rage.

I look around the bar, ignoring the shocked expressions on everyone's faces, habitually checking for any additional threats. I see nothing. After a moment, the music starts up again. The crowd turns away. The cell phones are slid back into pockets.

My work here is done.

I make my way back over to my stool. Sit down heavily. Wearily. Take a long, satisfying pull on my beer, emptying the bottle. I shake it at the barman, who nods and brings me another one. He flips the top off the bottle as he places it in front of me. I take a grateful gulp and tip the neck toward him.

"*Arigatou*, man."

That means *thanks*.

I let out a tired sigh.

Tokyo. Got to love it.

2

Ruby and I live in the penthouse building of an exclusive apartment block on the outskirts of Chiyoda City, over-looking the Sumida River. It's one of the wealthiest districts of Tokyo and central to most conveniences. Personally, while money isn't an issue, I would've preferred something a little more low-key, but Ruby was insistent. I learned long ago that unless I have a strong opinion about something, there's no sense arguing with her.

It's spacious. Five rooms spread across two floors. The main elevator runs up all thirty-seven floors from street level and opens on one side of our living room. For security, you can only select our floor by inserting a key and entering a six-digit passcode first. There's a thick, solid oak door on the opposite side of the room that leads to a short hallway and stair access. We never use it—it's permanently locked with enough bolts and latches to make the security guard at Fort Knox jealous—but it's there in case of emergencies.

The living room is open plan with minimal furniture. A nice sofa, table, TV, and a white, fluffy rug that Ruby insisted on buying to give the place some character. The walls on either side of the living room are glass, offering stunning, panoramic views of the metropolis below. The kitchen is at the back. A counter runs almost the full width of the cooking area, leaving a gap wide enough to walk around at either side. High stools surround it, positioned so your back is to the living room. Beside it, stairs head up to the bathroom and two bedrooms. Ruby's is the larger of the two. She asked for it, and I didn't care, so it's hers. She has an en-suite, so the main bathroom is predominantly mine.

I'm sitting at the counter, elbows resting on the surface, drinking what passes for coffee in this part of the world and reading an American newspaper on my tablet. The world is borderline normal again in a lot of places. Nice to see some things don't change, though. In between the politics and financial news is an article about a new celebrity baby named Kiwi-Diane. I shake my head. That's child abuse. Imagine shouting that name across the schoolyard when the lunch bell rings? Poor kid. Doesn't stand a chance.

Schultz's re-election campaign is in full swing. Good for him. The guy deserves a second term. He's been instrumental in the re-envisioning of Texas. Not easy to re-build an entire state from the ground up. Especially one that size. But he's having a damn good try. His efforts are going to sew up the election for him. His campaign wrote itself. The number of jobs he's created, the strengthening of the country's relationship with Mexico... it's a no-brainer.

There's still a small number of the population not happy with him, though. There's been rioting up and down the country recently, protesting Schultz's new vision for America. Now I'm all for freedom of expression, don't get me wrong. I know from experience that the guy isn't always the easiest person to deal with. But he's a good man, doing what he genuinely believes is best for the people of his country. What really pisses me off about the people rioting is that they're doing so because they preferred things when Cunningham was in charge.

The guy was a fucking terrorist!

Ah, whatever. I'm not getting worked up about it. I'm six thousand miles away for a reason. I'm done caring what goes on in the White House anymore.

Still, it's nice being able to say you have the president on speed dial. Not that I call him. We haven't spoken since... y'know... that day in Arlington. Figured he wouldn't want a semi-famous retired assassin on his phone logs.

I take a final mouthful of coffee and lower the cup onto the counter. As it nears the surface, my hand starts to shake. Nothing too drastic but a noticeable tremor. I place it down with a bang and repeatedly clench my hand into a fist. Goddamn thing hasn't been right since I damaged the nerves a couple of years back. It healed as well as could be expected, but I still get a few twinges now and then. GlobaTech's surgeon said it's normal and that it shouldn't interfere with my everyday life.

Yeah... unless you're a hitman, in which case not being able to hold a weapon steady is a real pain in the ass. I might be mostly retired nowadays, but I like the option, y'know?

I move around the counter and open a drawer on the opposite side. Take out a foil-backed sleeve of prescription painkillers. Push two tablets out.

I stare at them for a moment as they rattle to a standstill on the counter.

Screw it.

I push a third one out.

That should keep me going. It usually does.

I swallow them with a glass of water and pick up a sponge ball resting on the side nearby. I start squeezing it gently. I was given this as an exercise to keep my hand flexible. The doc said to only do it when the shaking starts. It stretches out the tendon, helping it settle. I move over to the sofa and sit down heavily on the soft leather cushion. I sink into it, let my head fall back, and close my eyes as I continue my exercises.

My mind wanders. It does that thing everyone's mind does when left to its own devices. It starts thinking about one thing, and then runs away in whatever direction it feels like, leading me to think about all sorts of other things I initially had no intention of thinking about.

I think about my hand. Then I think about what happened after I injured it. I think about the kind of person I was. The situation I was in. The fallout. The people I've lost.

War wounds. Scars both physical and mental, serving as a constant reminder of all the shit I went through to get *here* —my third attempt at a new life. You would think I'd be an expert at it by now, but the truth is, this is the first time it's truly felt like it's working.

The first time, way back when in Devil's Spring, was perfect. I had a bar, a dog, a gorgeous woman who was crazy about me. It was everything I ever wanted. It ticked all the boxes. Problem was, it was *too* perfect. It's as if my mind rejected it because it felt unreal. It was too far removed from my old life. The sad, horrible truth was that it only served as a beacon, summoning everything I was trying to escape from to come and take me back.

Eventually, it did, which didn't end all that well for anyone.

The second time wasn't really my choice. It felt like it was at first, but that soon changed. I ended up destroying that life myself. The whole experience left me feeling toxic. Like I was poison to anyone around me. That I was destined to be alone, for the sake of everyone else.

Things got a little dark for me after that. I remember looking in the mirror one morning and seeing a reflection of myself from thirteen years ago staring back. The same tired eyes that had lost their shine. The same burdened soul that struggled with losing everything it held dear. Back then, had I been alone, I'd have been dead inside six months. Either by eating my own bullet or choosing to live recklessly enough that I ate someone else's. But I survived for one reason and one reason only.

Josh.

He stuck by me, put up with my shit and misery, and dragged me through the dark until I could walk unaided into the light.

When I saw that same guy in the mirror that morning, I panicked. I thought, after losing Josh, I'm going to end up traveling that same road, on the same journey, heading for the same destination. And this time, he wasn't there to save me.

Except I didn't.

This time, I saw it coming, and I asked for help. The time I spent in therapy helped me realize that asking for help isn't a weakness. It doesn't take away from who I am. I'm still the most dangerous assassin alive. I know it. The kind of people who used to hire me know it. My peers know it. If anything, help gives me strength. It allows me to still be that person, even though I've got some shit to deal with. And let's face it, without wishing to turn things into a pissing contest, I'm confident in saying the amount of shit

I've had thrown at me these last few years tops anything most other people have on their plate. It's understandable I'd find it difficult coping at times. I'm a professional killer by nature, by design... but I'm still human.

So, I made it through. It wasn't easy, but I did it. I got through the dark times because of Ruby. We've made one hell of a team these last couple years, and as much as I never thought I would say this, I'd be lost without her. I like to think she feels the same way, but you never quite know with her. She's in character as much as she isn't, and while she's always honest with me, I'm pretty sure she masks a lot of her emotional and psychological issues by being *Ruby*. By turning the volume up and hiding behind the crazy noise. But that's who she is. It's what works for her, and it takes nothing away from the fact she's always had my back.

So, third time's a charm. We moved to Tokyo and decided between us what kind of life we want to carve out for ourselves over here—similar enough to what we know that we won't feel lost but different enough that we feel as if we're starting over.

It's been working well. We—

"How come you never let me squeeze your balls like that?"

I open my eyes. Speak of the devil.

I lift my head. "Morning, Ruby."

She appears in front of me wearing a short, silk robe, loosely tied, barely covering her breasts. Her long, tanned legs are almost completely visible, suggesting small or absent underwear. She decided to go blonde about six weeks ago. I'm still not sure it suits her, but as I've said, it's best not to comment sometimes. She still turns heads everywhere she goes, so she must be doing something right.

She arches an eyebrow as she looks me up and down. "Rough night? You look like shit."

"Thanks. No, it wasn't rough or late. Just a few quiet beers."

She sits down beside me, crossing her legs. "Where'd you go?"

"That place near the shrine, just across the river."

"Cool. So, no trouble then?"

I turn to her. "Why d'you ask?"

She shrugs. "Because you have some impressive Louis Vuittons under your eyes. Plus, you seem far too relaxed, suggesting lethargy more than comfort. I know you can hold your drink, so my guess is you're suffering from an adrenaline hangover. Figured you got into something last night."

See why we're such a good team?

I roll my eyes. Rest my head back and stare at the ceiling again. Can't resist a smile. "Yeah, just a couple of assholes hitting on a young girl. One of them slapped her, so I stepped in. Wasn't a big deal."

Ruby gets to her feet and moves around the back of the sofa. She leans forward and kisses my forehead. "You're a true gentleman, Adrian."

I hear her padding barefoot across the wooden floor toward the kitchen.

"Coffee?" she shouts over.

"Just had one. But thanks."

"I'm heading out later. You need anything?"

I think for a moment. "No, I'm good. Going anywhere nice?"

She pauses. "Nowhere specific. Just running a few errands."

I don't reply. A couple of minutes later, she disappears back upstairs.

Ruby and I came to an understanding when we moved in together that we will always be there for each other, for anything, no matter what, but we will each live our own lives. No question or judgment. We respect each other's privacy and typically spend more time apart than together.

However, I've... kept my eye on her, shall we say. Not in an intrusive way. I'm not spying on her. I'm not prying into her life. I'm looking out for her, the same way a big brother would look out for his kid sister. It's instinctive, whether she needs it or not. I don't feel like I'm crossing any lines. Besides, it would surprise me if she hasn't done the same thing. We know each other too well.

We've never spoken about it, or even admitted it to one another, but we've both chosen to stick to what we know. By that, I mean we're both working contracts from time to time here in Tokyo. It's not a full-time thing—not for me, at least —but it keeps us on our toes, and we would likely go crazy otherwise. A new life doesn't mean a completely different life. We're keeping things familiar, just changing our outlook on it all.

I felt bad at first. As if I was betraying her loyalty and support by picking up old habits. But when I realized she was doing the same thing, I just laughed. It only served as proof we're the ideal company for each other at this stage of our lives. I'll always remember what Josh said after he met Ruby for the first time. He said she was a female me. That we were each a side of the same coin. He was right. As he was about most things.

So, by *running some errands*, she means seeing a man about a job.

Which reminds me.

I check my watch.

I'm late.

I get to my feet, tossing the ball onto the sofa as I walk over to the sideboard by the stairs. I pick up my Pilot and place it in my ear. I drop the Ili in my pocket, just in case.

Good to go.

I move to the bottom of the stairs. "I'm heading out. See you later."

"Be good," she shouts back.

I grab the keys from the table by the elevator and press the call button.

I've got to see a man about a job.

3

My hands are dug deep into my pockets. The collar on my jacket is turned up against the wind. It's not usually warm in these parts this time of year, but it's been colder than normal the last couple weeks. It was fifty degrees yesterday. Doesn't feel much different today.

The streets of Tokyo are almost schizophrenic. At night, they pulse with life and vibrancy, bathed in neon and drenched in culture. Markets and pop-up restaurants attack your taste buds. Clubs and bars assault your senses with lights and music thumping so loud the sidewalk shakes. But when the sun rises, the city transforms into an overcrowded petri dish of urgency and introversion. Tall, crumbling buildings form borders around the narrow streets, trapping people like rats in a maze. Small cars shuffle along to a soundtrack of blaring horns. Sidewalks are crammed with people who want nothing more than to get where they're

17

going without having to look at anyone. Everywhere is shrouded in a light haze, a mixture of social disdain and pollution.

It's like nothing I've ever seen before.

I like it.

I twist my torso left and right, leading with my shoulders as I thread my way through the crowds, walking with unhurried purpose. It took me a while to get to grips with the landscape here. Not just the streets, but the city itself. Its structure and inner workings. Tokyo isn't a city; it's a metropolis—an amalgamation of cities and towns, split vertically down the middle. In the east, what we would call a city is known as a ward, and there are twenty-three of them. Chiyoda, where I live with Ruby, is in the heart of Tokyo's financial district. Consequently, it's a richer area than most. Property is more expensive, and the cost of living is high, but the place looks fantastic.

Our apartment overlooks Koto, which lies just across the river. That's where I'm heading now. It's another of the larger wards but one that's steeped in tradition. Shrines and gardens are scattered throughout, and the overall tempo feels as if it's a few notches below where I now call home. It's a more modest way of life. People aren't as wealthy, but they're probably more welcoming than those who are used to the hustle and bustle of true city life. Restaurants aren't places of extravagance; they're small, one-story buildings, filled with the smell of hundred-year-old recipes being prepared by the great-grandchildren of the people who created them.

While I've adapted to life in Chiyoda, I feel far more comfortable in Koto.

I've been walking for almost twenty minutes. The sound

of the busy streets fades away as I cross over the bridge. The dull hue is replaced by a warmth of color, which helps me forget the gradually declining fall temperature.

My errand involves meeting one of the few people I've allowed myself to befriend since moving here. Ichiro is maybe ten years older than me. Easily a hundred times *crazier*. He's always chuckling to himself, even when he's not saying anything. It's as if he's constantly telling a joke in his head. His skin is tanned and mottled, his head bald and wrinkled. A thin, gray beard stretches down to his chest. He's always smoking a long pipe with God-knows-what inside it. At first glance, he looks as if he belongs in a temple. He even wears prayer beads around his neck.

But his appearance is deceiving. In his day, Ichiro was a feared member of a Yakuza family and served as one of their most dangerous enforcers. Now he spends his retirement running a noodle bar and working as a go-between for people looking to find employment in the global network of underworld activity that reaches this far east.

Maybe that's why I got to know him. That similar approach to life. Both looking to start over. Both wanting a change, but both sticking to what we know. Kindred spirits. We occasionally meet for a drink, usually as a welcome accompaniment to whatever business we're talking at the time. Neither of us speak at length about our pasts. Neither of us need to. He knows all about me. Most people do, even all the way out here. And the fact he not only survived the life he had but was able to leave it behind him says all I need to know about him.

His noodle bar is situated on a corner plot across from the park that divides the rural and modern areas of Koto. The street it's on serves as a kind of DMZ for the ward. The whole place is Yakuza territory. The left, stretching back to the river, belongs to one family. The park and beyond belongs to another. But this street—*his* street—is holy ground for the rival factions. A show of respect for who Ichiro was and is today.

I push the door open and step inside. A wave of gentle heat and incredible aroma greets me. A low counter runs the full length of the right wall, serving as an open cooking area. A line of chefs hunch over huge woks, tossing noodles, meat, and vegetables expertly before ladling it into small cardboard tubs for the line of impatient customers. A handful of tables face the counter, but few people sit inside to eat.

It's always busy in Ichiro's place.

I idle near the door, scanning the crowd. My eyes rest on the doorway behind the counter, covered by hanging beads, leading to the kitchen area in the back. Standing just inside, seemingly in conversation with someone out of sight, is Ichiro. I recognize his outline. He steps out into the restaurant and looks around, surveying his small kingdom. His gaze falls to me. He nods and chuckles, signaling me over to him. I signal back with a slight wave. I reach the far end of the counter, and he lifts a section of it, allowing me to walk through.

He pats my shoulder as I pass him, still chuckling. "Adrian-san. Always pleasure to see *Shinigami* here." He gestures me through the beads. "Come. Come. We talk. We drink!"

I step through, past some more staff and into the storage room on the far side. He follows me, closing the door behind us. The room isn't huge, but it's spacious enough for his stock. Metal shelving lines both sides. Piles of wooden boxes haphazardly litter the floor.

We walk to the far wall, and I side-step, allowing him to pass. About halfway up is a panel, roughly seven inches by ten, which lights up momentarily when he places his palm against it. A loud beep sounds, then a section of the wall clicks open with a hiss, revealing itself as a door to a hidden room. Ichiro pulls it open and ushers me inside.

This office is where he conducts the part of his business that doesn't revolve around teriyaki sauce. A large painting of a samurai hangs on the wall facing the camouflaged door, above an old desk with a laptop and a lamp standing on it. He moves around it and sits in a worn leather chair. I sit opposite, shuffling in the creaky, wooden seat until I find some level of comfort.

Ichiro claps his hands together, grinning wide. "Good to see you again, Adrian-san."

Despite having the luxury of technology to bridge any language barriers, it's still nice to interact with someone who speaks the same language. Sort of.

I smile back. "You too, my friend. Business good?"

He nods. "Good enough. The client was impressed with how you handled last job."

About a week ago, I took a small contract to kill a man who was sleeping with the client's wife. Initially, I had turned it down. Domestic disputes don't warrant a bullet from me. Ichiro had understood but had asked that I give him twenty-four hours to investigate, as the payout seemed unusually high for a job that appeared so mundane. I had no problem with that. Saved me doing it. Anyway, it turned out the guy sleeping with the client's wife was also known to sleep with other peoples' wives. And their daughters. Regardless of age. Or consent.

Six hours after Ichiro gave me that information, the guy

was found hanging from the ceiling fan in the rented apartment he took his conquests to.

Staging a suicide isn't difficult. We all know the different ways of doing it and what they're supposed to look like. The hard part is making sure no one *knows* it's staged. If you're fortunate enough to have a target who is weak and spineless, as I was, the task is made much easier. I simply aimed my gun at him and explained that if he didn't commit suicide, I would make him suffer to such an extent, his mind would give up trying to comprehend it. He noosed himself up real good. All I did was kick the chair out from under him.

No evidence I was ever involved. Easy.

I shrug, trying not to appear modest. "It was a simple enough contract."

Ichiro laughs. "*Shinigami!*"

He claps again. I roll my eyes.

Shinigami is a nickname he gave me the first time we met. My reputation preceded me when we were introduced, and it's what he called me. At first, I figured it was some kind of informal greeting, but I later found out the rough translation is God of Death, or Grim Reaper, to give it its western meaning. It was said with tongue firmly in cheek, but it stuck, and now it's our little private joke.

I wave a dismissive hand, keen to change the subject. "You said you have another job?"

He nods. "Yes. Yes. But first..."

He opens a deep drawer on his left, then takes out a decorated porcelain bottle and two small matching cups.

Sake.

I breathe out a reluctant sigh.

Great. This shit is lethal!

He uncaps the bottle and pours two measures. He takes

one and passes the other to me. Raises his cup in a silent toast. I reciprocate, and we both slam it back. The flavor burns my throat. A combination of sweet and savory. The spice of the alcohol is offset by the hint of apples.

I suck a painful breath in through my teeth, grimacing as the oxygen stings my mouth. "How do you drink this stuff?"

Ichiro chuckles, slapping the surface of his desk with his hand. "Considering you so dangerous, Adrian-san, you can be real pussy!"

I roll my eyes again. Smile politely. "Thanks. So, this job?"

He packs the sake away. "Yes. Client asked for you specifically."

"Repeat business?"

He shakes his head. "No. Just word..." He makes a snaking motion with his hand. "...traveling around."

"Okay. Lay it on me."

He spins the laptop around. There's an image of a man, maybe my age. Short, dark hair. Narrowed eyes. A thin, curled line for a mouth. Wide jaw. Full cheeks.

"And what's this guy done to deserve me?"

"Nothing." He points to the screen. "He is client."

I raise an eyebrow. "You know I don't like knowing who's hiring me, Ichi. All I care about is who they send me after."

"I know, but client wants to give you job in person. Insisted I arrange meeting."

That's weird. Usually, the people who hire me prefer to distance themselves from the transaction. To minimize exposure and liability. Same reason I distance myself from them.

I can't think of many reasons why anyone wouldn't take that precaution.

"Who is he?"

"He is Santo, a *kyodai* for the Oji-gumi family."

My Pilot translated the information in my ear, but it didn't need to. I have a basic understanding of how the Yakuza works. A kyodai is a mid-level member of a family. He outranks the foot soldiers on the streets but answers to the lieutenants and advisors, who themselves speak directly to the head of the family.

That explains why he's not interested in distancing himself from the contract. He's high enough up the food chain that he's practically untouchable. He simply doesn't care.

"I'm not familiar with the Oji-gumi," I say.

He chuckles. "They are biggest Yakuza family in all the wards. Nothing happens they don't know about."

I look away.

Wonderful. That's what I was afraid of.

I've always turned down anything that might involve me with or obligate me to Yakuza business. Hard to avoid completely, but if necessary, I only take low-level work. Nothing with any potential implications. I'm not here for riches or glory. I'm here to keep busy. I want things nice and simple.

I look back at Ichiro. "Not interested, sorry. You got anything else?"

His expression hardens. "Adrian-san, it would cause great offense to turn down a request from someone like Santo. It would not look good on you."

I shrug. "My reputation will survive, I'm sure."

He shakes his head. "Not your reputation I'm concerned with."

"Yeah..." I take another deep breath. "But still, I don't want to get involved in anything too high-profile. You know I don't take jobs from known Yakuza. Just say I'm not avail-able or something. It'll be fine."

Ichiro thinks for a moment before nodding. "Okay, Adrian-san. I will handle it."

"Appreciated."

"I... heh... I do have one other job, if you interested? It's from independent source. Local. As low-level as it gets."

I nod. "That sounds better. What is it?"

"A young man fell in with bad people. He turned up dead." He places two fingers to the side of his head and taps his temple. "Executed. The parents want justice, but police do nothing. The father now seeking revenge instead."

A sadly familiar story. Like I said, Tokyo can be a dark place. If you're not careful, it will eat you alive.

"How much are they offering?" I ask.

Ichiro checks his screen. "Three million yen."

"Which is...?"

He checks again. "A little over twenty-six thousand, U.S."

"That *is* low-level..." I think for a moment. "But if I'm honest, I'm a little bored, so what the hell. Who's the target?"

A wide, almost maniacal grin creeps across Ichiro's face. His eyes come to life with excitement.

My eyes narrow. "What?"

"Oh, you gonna like this, Adrian-san." He starts chuck-ling to himself as he spins the laptop around for me to see.

I stare at the screen for a moment before frowning. "I don't understand. That's the guy who wants to meet me about the Yakuza job I just turned down. You're supposed to be showing me the target for this new job. Seriously, Ichi, I keep telling you to lay off the sake before lunch, man."

His chuckle becomes a laugh, deep and loud, from the gut. "*Shinigami*... it is same man! Potential client is also someone's target!"

I lean forward in my chair. "You're kidding?"

"No! Crazy, right?"

"Well, you would know..." I mutter with a smile before sitting back and folding my arms across my chest. The cogs inside my head are turning, suddenly alive with dreadful purpose.

"What I say, Adrian-san? You got to love this, no?"

He starts laughing to himself.

I run a palm over the stubble covering my jaw and throat, lost in thought as my mind analyzes a million different outcomes.

"Okay," I say after a few moments. "The set-up is obvious, right? My concern is, can I take out this Santo prick without screwing myself over and becoming a target for his family?"

Ichiro's chuckling subsides. He strokes his long beard thoughtfully.

"It is valid concern, yes, Adrian-san. There is always risk."

I nod. "Big risk for that level of payday..."

He nods back. "Yes. But I know you. You will take job."

My brow arches as I smile. "Oh, will I now?"

"Of course!" He leans back and starts laughing again. "You know how I know?"

I shrug. "Enlighten me."

"Two reasons. First, it is stupid idea. Most people... logical. Say no. But you crazy... see that as challenge."

I scoff and look away, silently cursing to myself at how accurate that statement was.

"And second," he continues, "you see struggle of family who lost son. You do what is right." He taps his own chest, then points at mine. "You are burdened with heart,

Shinigami. You are master of this world. Yet, you do not belong in it. You are better than it."

I hold his gaze as his words sink in.

That's probably one of the nicest things anyone's ever said to me. And probably the most serious thing Ichi's ever said to me.

Finally, I get to my feet. "Okay, accept the father's job, then confirm the meeting with Santo."

Ichiro stands and nods. "Consider it done, Adrian-san. Tell me... how will you ensure Santo is removed without retribution?"

I shrug. "Not sure yet. That's the fun part."

He chuckles as he hands me a piece of paper with an address and time written on it. I take it from him, then shake his hand. I leave his office. Make my way through the back, out into the serving area. The line of people is still taking up most of the space inside. As I lift the counter, I feel a hand on my arm. I look around and see one of the chefs standing there, smiling broadly. He's holding out a box of food with a plastic fork sticking out of it.

I nod a thank you, take the box from him, and head outside. The temperature is a shock to the system after the heat of the noodle bar. I set off walking back down the street, heading for the bridge. I tuck into the food as I navigate the steady stream of people flowing both ways around me. It's tasty and does a good job of warming me up.

For a brief moment, I wonder if I've just made a colossal mistake. But then I think about what that father must be going through, wanting justice for his son. Sure, his son made some bad choices. But haven't we all? His decisions shouldn't have been punishable by death. The way I see it, I get to do right by a family that deserves it, and I get to make a dent in a Yakuza family without getting directly involved with them.

I just need to figure out how to take Santo out at this meeting without leaving a trail that leads his friends back to me.

I smile to myself.

Easy.

4

I toss the empty food container in a trash can and check my watch. I'm not meeting Santo until twelve, so I may as well grab a coffee. No sense in heading all the way back to the apartment only to come right back out again.

The effects of the hot noodles have worn off, and I'm becoming more aware of the low temperature with each step. I cross the bridge, back over into Chiyoda, and the wind's stronger over the water, adding to the chill.

The noise of the city ahead rises slowly, as if someone's turning the volume up a notch every couple of seconds. It's welcoming. Helps me feel anonymous. Invisible to the world. My very heartbeat is drowned out in a sea of humanity and machines.

When I first moved out here, with little more to my name than my ill-gotten gains and my newly acquired freedom, I felt self-conscious. Like a celebrity. A spotlight constantly shining on me. Not in a vain or egotistical way, of course. But after everything this world had endured, coupled with some unfortunate and completely fictional PR, my face had become somewhat synonymous with bad news. Even President Schultz publicly clearing my name did little to change that. If anything, it made me even *more* recognizable.

But as with most things, the spotlight soon moved on. Fame, if you can call it that, is a notoriously fickle thing, and once the global dust had settled, I quickly became yesterday's news. Ruby had asked how I felt about that, suggesting I liked the attention.

No idea what could've made her think that...

But I answered honestly and said I was glad to be just another face in the crowd again. In my line of work, it's how things should be.

It takes me almost fifteen minutes to reach the coffee place. In much the same way that western civilization is fascinated by its eastern counterpart, the culture over here also pays tribute where it can to the westernized approach to things.

Take this café, for example. It looks like the type of place you would expect to see in a cultural U.S. city. Somewhere like San Francisco or New Orleans or Seattle. It has beads hanging just inside the door. The aroma of ground, roasted coffee beans greets me like an old friend as I step inside. Posters cover the walls, advertising music and events. A huge, complicated-looking machine sits behind the counter that, by some miracle, *actually* produces coffee—which isn't half bad, if I'm honest.

Of course, it's not perfect. After all, this is only Japan's interpretation of a trendy café. Where you would expect to hear the acoustic guitar and dulcet tones of an aspiring singer, or the spoken angst of a troubled young poet coming from the corner, here you have giggling teenage girls screeching into a karaoke machine. As a professional killer, I can confidently say I have never witnessed anything be murdered quite so completely as Don McLean is being right now.

I come here often, and while I'm not on speaking terms with the staff beyond a polite greeting, they recognize me and wave as I enter. With the aid of my Pilot and Ili, I order a large black coffee, which they kindly offer to bring over to me when it's ready. I nod a thank you and head over to a round table in the corner, next to the window. I sit with my back to the wall, which gives me a full view of the place, as well as the street outside, with the added bonus of being able to see anyone who approaches me.

Old habits.

A waitress brings my drink over after a few minutes. I take a grateful sip. The three girls committing verbal homicide in the corner finally relinquish the microphone and move over to a table on the opposite side of the café, where they each poke a straw into a large iced coffee and begin chatting animatedly.

The rest of the patrons are mostly individuals minding their own business. One elderly couple are reading newspapers. A handful of people call in for a coffee to go, but otherwise it's a calm, subdued atmosphere.

I check my watch.

Just under an hour until my meeting.

I'm worried I'm over-complicating the situation. I'm a firm believer that if something seems too good to be true, it usually is, but is this meeting with Santo *really* so difficult? He thinks I'm coming to see him to discuss the contract he has to offer. And I think it's safe to assume that from his point of view, my acceptance of this offer is a foregone conclusion. A mid-level Yakuza boss like him would only get directly involved with a hit if the target was important. He'll be desperate to impress those above him in his family's hierarchy, which is likely why he asked for me personally. So, he has no reason to suspect I'm there for anything else.

Which means I'll have the element of surprise.

I reckon he'll still have some protection. He'll bring muscle—maybe two or three guys, as a way of emphasizing his reputation and asserting his overall dominance of the meeting. That's fine by me. Let him have his fun. It won't change anything.

The only thing I need to worry about is taking him out without making it look like a hit. It needs to be scrappy, messy, rushed. It needs to look as amateurish as possible.

I'll be fine.

Ichiro was right—this isn't the kind of job I could just pass up. Getting to someone like Santo would've been borderline impossible, but the fact he offered himself up on a plate is a stroke of good fortune rarely seen in my line of work. I get to take out a high-ranking piece of shit, remove the main obstacle of such a job while retaining the challenge, and do right by a struggling family. So long as I keep my name away from any of it, this should be a good day at the office.

I take another sip of my coffee.

I have a good feeling about this.

11:23 JST

Second cup of coffee finished. Time to go to work.

As I get to my feet, the door opens. The swish and the clack of the beads rises and settles as a young woman steps through. Her dark hair is tied up in a bun. Her clothes are casual and loose. She has a backpack slung over one shoulder. A student, maybe? As she turns to walk toward the counter, I catch a brief look at her face. Her skin is tanned, olive. She's walking as if she's on edge. Hunched, protected, but her eyes remain alert. She looks familiar, but I can't immediately recall from where.

I head for the door. She snaps her gaze to me as I near her. I see her double-take. She steps toward the counter but hesitates, turning to look at me once more. As I draw level, she reaches out with her hand to stop me.

"Ah... hey. Hi." She smiles. "Sorry, you... you probably don't remember me."

The moment she said that, I remembered where I knew her from. She's the girl I helped in the bar last night. She looks very different without her make-up and party outfit on.

I hold up my hand. I'm not sure why. Maybe it was a subconscious gesture to keep her at bay. Maybe it was an attempt to shake her hand as a greeting. Whatever it was intended to be, it ended up being a weird, awkward wave.

"Hey. Yeah, of course I remember you. How are you?"

Her smile broadens. "I'm fine, thanks to you. I... I was hoping I would see you again. I didn't get a chance to thank you for what you did."

I shake my head. "No need to thank me. I'm just glad I was there to intervene. Looked to me like your night wasn't about to get any better."

She looks away, as if she's ashamed. "Yeah, those guys were jerks. They bought me a couple of drinks, and they both seemed nice enough, y'know? Then they wanted me to leave with them, go back to their place. I said no. That's when one of them got aggressive."

"I saw. I wasn't going to sit there and let some punk treat a woman like that."

Her cheeks flush. "I'm really grateful. Could I... ah... maybe buy you a coffee?"

I'm pretty sure my cheeks just flushed too.

I smile as I take a small, involuntary step back. "That's kind of you to offer, but I gotta be somewhere. Sorry. Maybe another time?"

She nods. "Sure. You come here often?" She bites her lip and looks away momentarily. "Oh my God, that sounded like such a bad line! I'm sorry, I didn't mean..."

I chuckle. "I know what you meant. It's okay. And yeah, almost every day."

"Okay. Okay, well, maybe I'll see you around?"

"Yeah, maybe."

"Bye... ah... sorry, I don't even know your name..."

"Adrian."

She extends her hand. "Mia."

I shake it gently. "Nice to meet you."

"You too."

I leave without looking back and find myself hoping it didn't appear I was running away from her. Seriously, what the hell was *that*? Why was I acting like some pubescent teenager?

Maybe because you just got hit on by one?

What? No, I didn't!

Hey, listen to your old pal, Satan, all right? That chick was totally into you. She offered to buy you coffee, for Christ's sake!

We were in a café...

So? She was flirting with you.

She's a kid!

She's old enough to be in a club...

And young enough to be my daughter.

Whatever, man. Your loss.

Hey, you're here to help me kill people, not give me advice on the opposite sex, all right? Shut it.

...

...

...

I hate myself sometimes.

I turn the collar of my jacket up and hunch against the cold as I take in a deep breath. A faint plume of air forms in front of my face as I exhale.

So, I handled *that* badly. But what was I supposed to do? She's more than half my age, easily. I can't have a coffee with her... jeez.

Anyway, right now I have more important things to worry about. I check my watch and set off walking.

Showtime.

5

The building in front of me stretches up to the gray clouds, holding its own against the towering skyline of Chiyoda. Across the street, behind me, is a park. Beyond that is the expressway. The street itself runs right through the heart of the financial sector. The buildings on either side of the one I'm looking at are both reputable banking firms.

It's not uncommon for Yakuza families to hide their criminal activities behind the doors of legitimate ones. It used to be that only the richest and most powerful families did this, simply because they were the only ones who could afford to. Nowadays, I think most outfits do it. It's the new normal.

I walk toward the revolving doors, which are turning slowly in the cylindrical, metallic frame, wedged between panes of tinted glass. I shuffle through and step out inside a spacious lobby. It's just like every other I've seen before—a desk over to the right with women sitting behind it, tapping away on keyboards and talking animatedly into headsets; chairs and sofas to the left, with a scattered collection of people in business dress, presumably waiting for an appointment; a strip of waist-high security gates running the width of the space between, with two desks, one either side, each manned with security personnel...

...and two men in dark suits walking toward me with guns poorly concealed inside their jackets.

Christ. I barely made it through the front door!

I stay where I am. Hold my hands loosely out to the sides, palms open. I'm not armed. I want them to know that. I've trained myself to feel comfortable not always having a gun on me. Not so long ago, I wouldn't go anywhere unless I was prepared to shoot someone on a moment's notice. But I feel those days are behind me. Now, I'm confident enough that I don't need a gun to kill someone on a moment's notice.

I hope.

The two men stop in front of me. Look me up and down. Both hold their jackets loosely with one hand, probably to counter the weight of the guns they have holstered underneath. The one to my right utters something in Japanese. I glance to the side and lower my head slightly, allowing him to see the Pilot in my ear, giving myself time to process the translation.

Arms to the sides.

I shrug and oblige. He reaches out and professionally pats down my arms and body. He steps back and assesses my legs. Satisfied, he nods to his partner, who, in turn, says something to me.

This way. Mr. Santo is expecting you.

They head back the way they came. I follow, through the security gates, past the bank of elevators, and toward a single door sunken into the left wall at the end of the wide corridor. The first guy steps through. The second holds the door for me in a gesture I figure is half courteous, half precautionary.

Concrete steps spiral counterclockwise before me. Sandwiched between them, we descend. One floor. Two floors. Three. We push through another door, identical to the one above, and emerge in the underground parking lot. It appears almost full. Cars are parked perfectly in their spaces, hoods forward, patiently waiting for their owners to return like oversized metal dogs. I look around, noting the lack of variety in the makes and models. Nothing out of the ordinary. Nothing I'm concerned with.

Yet.

The guy leading the way points to his left. We head in that direction and around a corner to another section. Large concrete pillars are positioned at the end of every fourth space. Parked alone, nose-in along the near wall, is a black sedan. Tinted windows. A man dressed identical to my escorts stands guard next to the passenger's rear side. As we approach, he sidesteps and opens the door. His movement is fluid and practiced.

A man wearing a light-gray suit climbs out. He's maybe five-eight. On the heavier side of two hundred pounds. His face is exactly as I saw it in the picture. His eyes permanently laced with suspicion. His skin mottled and tight over his slightly inflated features. His mouth curled to a thin sneer, suggesting arrogance and entitlement.

Kon'nichiwa, Santo.

He stands tall and straightens his jacket. Takes in a deep breath, swelling his chest and broadening his shoulders as best he can. Looks me dead in the eye and smiles. "It is an honor to meet you, Adrian Hell."

I'm taken aback by how good his English is. Well-spoken. Unbroken tone and pronunciation. Not what I was expecting at all.

Now for the part of all this I hate—the acting.

I bow very slightly, careful not to take my eyes off him. It feels like the correct thing to do. "The honor is mine. I'm flattered you would ask for me directly."

He waves his hand dismissively. "I'm sure you're used to it, a man of your caliber and reputation..."

I don't like small talk, but I need to let this play out for now and wait for my moment. He thinks I'm here to discuss *his* job offer, after all.

I smile politely. "You'd be surprised."

He clears his throat. "I asked our mutual friend, Ichiro, to arrange this meeting. I trust it's not an inconvenience?"

"Not at all. A little unorthodox, maybe, but I've spent my life going against the grain, so I never take issue when someone else does the same, y'know?"

He nods. "Indeed. The reason I wanted to meet in person is because this job is of a... *delicate* nature."

I nod. "Most hits are."

"We of the Oji-gumi do not trust many people. Trust leads to complacency, which leads to death."

"No arguments there," I agree, shrugging.

"I hope I can rely on your discretion?"

I raise an eyebrow. "That goes without saying, Santo. There's a reason you've heard of me. Nobody does this kind of thing better."

He holds up a hand. "I meant no offense. I am simply a cautious man."

Yeah, and you clearly think you're more important than you are too... asshole.

The way he's talking, you would think he was running the whole family. What a douchebag.

"No offense taken." I glance at the three men standing in a loose triangle, surrounding me. I figure there's at least one more in the car. "I only ask the same of you. I pride myself on my independent work, and it's important to me that no one sees me as being affiliated with one particular family over another. I'm sure you understand?"

He nods. "Of course. You are a much sought-after talent, Adrian. I do not wish for your livelihood to be affected, in the same way I have no desire for anyone to learn how I choose to handle certain problems. The only people who know about this meeting are attending it. Apart from Ichiro, obviously."

Bingo! That's exactly what I was hoping he would say. If no one knows he's meeting with me, there is even less chance of any suspicion being directed my way when he's found dead. I know I can trust Ichiro not to say anything if pressed too.

Game on.

"All right, then," I say. "What's the job?"

He clears his throat. "Another family's operation has begun to interfere with one of our own. We need that to stop."

I frown. "I'm not here to take down a Yakuza business venture…"

He shakes his head. "No, of course not. We want you to take out the head of the family. That way, *all* business ventures will cease."

What?

He said that almost casually, as if he'd just remembered something he should've written down on his list of chores. *Pick up a loaf of bread while you're out… oh, yeah, and kill that Yakuza boss while you're at it.* Fuck that! I'd have the entire Japanese underworld gunning for me! He can't be serious?

I try to suppress a laugh of disbelief, but it slips out.

"Santo, with all due respect, you can't be serious?"

He smiles back, but there's no humor in it. His eyes stare blankly ahead. No emotion.

"You are the best there is, are you not? After what you have... accomplished in your career, surely this would be child's play?"

Ah, flattery—the most transparent form of compliment. I need to keep this conversation going a little while longer. I just need one of his guards to get within reach...

"You're right, this *would* be child's play, compared to, say, killing a sitting president... or assassinating someone on the steps of the Vatican... but that's not the point. It's still not easy. And I'm not stupid. One of the golden rules of this business is you never let your ego get in the way of a good kill. I don't need flattery. I don't need a confidence boost. And I certainly don't need an entire Yakuza family hunting me. Santo, your world revolves around honor and respect and tradition. What you're proposing would betray all of that, and if anyone comes looking for answers or revenge, it'll be me who gets thrown under the bus."

He frowns, casting a glance at the men to his left. "Are you saying you are refusing the job offer?"

I take a deep breath. I have to play this just right...

I nod. "Yes, I'm afraid I am. I'm grateful for the opportunity and flattered to be asked for personally. I certainly mean no disrespect to you or your organization, but I'm not the man for this. Sorry."

I hope that wasn't too much. I'm trying to guide the situation, nudge it in the right direction to create the type of opening I need. But so far, it's been much more civilized than I expected.

"No need for apologies, Adrian. I understand and respect your decision."

Really?

I nod. "Appreciated."

He holds up a hand. "However..."

There we go.

"...I need you to understand *my* situation before you commit to anything."

Pretty sure I just *did* commit to something. I said no. But never mind. This could be the chance I'm looking for.

I gesture toward him. "Please..."

He takes a step closer. "Are you familiar with the Oji-gumi, Adrian?"

I shake my head. "Not really. I've only been in town a couple of years, and I've stuck to low-level work, mostly. I know the name but little else."

"The head of our family, Akuma Oji, is a powerful and proud man. He adheres to a strict code. He embraces tradition. Considers himself a samurai, in many ways. The man we want removing is Tetsuo Kazawa. Have you heard of *him*?"

I nod. "Only because I worked a job for his family about ten months ago. His father founded the Kazawa family. Tetsuo took over when he passed away. Four, maybe five years ago?"

"You are correct, Adrian. You see, Tetsuo personally killed someone who worked closely with one of our larger business interests. Sliced his throat from ear to ear in his bed. It wasn't an intentional slight on our family. We know that. It was simply an unfortunate coincidence. Yet, we cannot ignore such an act, no matter how much fate intervenes."

"Which I completely understand." I shift my weight from one leg to the other, growing restless and more concerned with how my current situation is unfolding. "But I—"

"Tetsuo, it seems, is running an organ trafficking ring behind the doors of a legitimate courier service. He killed our friend because he had a buyer for a heart, and he happened to meet the criteria."

"And that's wrong on *so* many levels, but—"

Santo steps closer. But I don't want him this close. I want one of his bodyguards this close. He's no use because he won't be armed.

"Such a venture is an insult to God," he continues. "And to the tradition and code our family is built upon. The tradition and code we believe *all* Yakuza should be built upon. It is our responsibility to not only send a message but to stop this atrocious business."

I sigh. "Yes, I completely agree. Things like that shouldn't happen. But—"

"Akuma Oji himself passed the responsibility of dealing with this to me. Naturally, I want it done properly, with minimal disruption to our business and our great ward. I'm sure you understand that someone like Akuma Oji cannot be left disappointed? The consequences of failure do not bear thinking about."

I clap my hands together. "And I wish you all the best in your endeavors, I do. But I'm *really* not the man for the job."

Santo laughs. "You are too modest. You are the perfect man for this job. You will be compensated, of course. With great risk comes great reward, after all. Does one hundred million yen sound enough?"

My eyes widen again. A hundred million? Jesus! That's almost a million bucks. That is a *lot* of money for one contract. I'm struggling to think of a time when I was paid anything close to that for one job. Still, it changes nothing. I have plenty of money. More than I could ever spend. Not more than *Ruby* could ever spend, given half the chance, but still, it's plenty for me.

Focus, Adrian.

"That's... ah... that's a very generous payday, Santo. But my answer remains no. I'm sorry."

His expression hardens. He moves closer again, standing mere inches from me. "Adrian, I took you for a smart man. I thought, here is someone who has survived his profession longer than almost anyone else. Here is someone who has carved out a reputation so impressive, the very mention of his name creates fear among criminals across the globe. Yet, for a smart man, you make stupid choices."

I shrug. "Yeah... so I'm told."

"You would turn down such a lucrative payday? For what? Pride?"

I let out a short sigh. Not directed at Santo, or this conversation. Just a general, involuntary show of frustration. He's so close, I can smell the piss-water he uses as cologne. I could easily grab him now. Snap his neck. Except that wouldn't do me any good, because I would then be exposed to three, maybe more, armed bodyguards. So, if I grabbed him, I would need to use him as a human shield to get out of here. Or, at least, until I secured a weapon of some kind. Which is pointless, because I need to kill him, not take him out of here with me.

I need one of his guys to get close.

I think for a moment.

...

...

...

The guy on my left, just behind Santo, has a hand on the gun inside his jacket. The two on my right, my escorts, don't —they're standing loose, arms by their sides. The first guy might get a shot off before I move, but Santo's partly blocking his view of me, so I have a potential window there because he would likely hesitate before pulling the trigger.

I could grab the guy nearest to me, use him as a shield while I take out his gun and shoot the other two. Then I could incapacitate him and be ready for whoever gets out of the car. Three down easily enough. Perhaps a fourth or fifth, if need be. That would leave me, armed, and Santo. He won't do shit. He's a mouthpiece, nothing more. He'd probably shit his pants before the other guys hit the ground.

Straightforward enough.

Didn't even need my Inner Satan to figure it out.

Of course, there are a million things that could go wrong. But I've got to do it. The longer this conversation goes on, the harder it will be. It's risky. It's arguably stupid. But it's the only way. I need to be fast. Precise. Uncompromising.

I sigh again.

I'm getting too old for this shit. I know I say that a lot, but this time I *really* mean it!

With no warning or preparation, I lash out at Santo with a strong left hook. It connects exactly where I intended—on the right side of his face, flush on his chin. The blow took everyone by surprise. As soon as I see him begin to stumble toward the two men who brought me here, I lunge the opposite way, grabbing the guy to the left with both hands. One around his throat, the other around his wrist, preventing him from reaching for his gun.

JAMES P. SUMNER

I spin him around, putting him between me and the others. I glance past him, over his shoulder. The two guards have caught Santo, stopping him from falling to the ground. Good. That means their hands are full, which buys me valuable seconds.

I release my grip of this guy's throat and deliver a short jab to his nose, designed to disorient more than hurt. It stuns him. I push him away, reaching inside his jacket as I do, feeling for the butt of his handgun. As he flies away, the pistol draws itself, and I'm left holding it, aiming at the gathering in front of me.

So far, so good.

I hear a car door opening. Must be someone in the passenger seat.

Need to be quick.

I take a deep breath. Hold it.

My eyes dart in all directions, assessing the task ahead of me, programming the required movements into my brain.

I breathe out and fire three times, quickly snapping to a new target after each round.

Within seconds, all three guards drop to the ground, hitting the concrete with a dull thud. Santo is sent sprawling away from them.

I see movement in my peripheral vision. I spin left, weapon raised and ready. Another guy appears on the opposite side of the car, a look of shock on his face. I pull the trigger, putting a single round into his skull. He drops backward out of sight. A thin cloud of crimson mist slowly evaporates in his wake.

After quickly surveying the scene, I'm happy that everyone except Santo is dead, and there's no one else around. No witnesses. I couldn't even spot any security cameras, which I thought was strange at first, but then it made sense—if this is a Yakuza-owned building, they would have a ton of physical security, but no video feeds... nothing that could be used as evidence against them.

I pace slowly over toward Santo, the gun held loose by my side. He's crawling away from the car on his stomach, like a cockroach desperate to avoid being stomped on.

"See, here's the thing," I say to him as I draw level. "I haven't been *completely* honest with you."

I reach down and grab the back of his suit jacket, hoisting him up to his feet. He yelps with fear, like a dog who knows he's disobeyed his master. I move in front of him and begin walking, forcing him to back-peddle. His eyes are wide. His lips are quivering.

What a piece of shit.

I keep walking him backward until he's pressed up against the car. I scratch my brow with the barrel of the gun.

"Yeah, the reason I can't take your job is because I'm actually already working one," I explain. "A young man fell in with the wrong crowd. He was blinded by the allure of being a badass, ended up in over his head. A head that soon got a bullet stuck in it—y'know what I'm saying?"

He nods hurriedly.

"This guy's old man, he wants justice for his boy but wants it the right way. So, he calls the cops. Problem is, the cops do nothing. Why would they? A kid gets killed in some bullshit Yakuza drama... it ain't worth them getting involved. Hell, they've probably been paid to ignore it anyway, right? The father's distraught. His diplomacy turns to anger. His desire for justice becomes a thirst for revenge. And so..." I gesture theatrically to myself. "...here I am."

Santo's expression becomes torn. His eyes are still laced with fear, but his brow is furrowed with apparent confusion.

"W-what do you mean?" he asks. "I don't understand."

I place the barrel of the gun slowly against his forehead.

"I mean, this kid who was killed... *you* killed him. Maybe not personally, but if you didn't pull the trigger, you gave the order to whoever did, so you're accountable."

The gravity of the situation seems to dawn on him.

"I'll... I'll double—no, triple whatever they're paying you to kill me! I'll give you anything you want. Please don't kill me! Please!"

I smile. "The problem you have, Santo, is that I'm not here for the money. You offered me a hundred million yen. This kid's father is offering me three million to kill you. That's everything he has. Do you know what? I might even do it for free. After spending some time with you, I see killing you not so much as a job but as a civic duty."

He drops to his knees and clasps his hands in front of him. Praying. Begging. He looks up at me with tears in his eyes.

"No, please! I'll give you anything you want. You don't want money? Fine. What else? Women? Drugs? A new house? Anything! I can get you anything you want, just please, d-don't kill me!"

I shake my head. "That's possibly the saddest thing I think I've ever seen."

"W-what? No! Please!"

I place the barrel of the gun gently against his temple and step back, straightening my arm and creating enough distance that I should avoid getting any blood on me.

"Consider this a courtesy, Santo. I never usually offer an explanation to people in the same situation you now find yourself in, but it actually *matters* to me that you understand why today is the last day of your life. You exploited a young kid. You took a son away from his mother and father. And speaking as a father who once lost their child, let me tell you... that's a real piece of shit thing to do."

I pull the trigger. The single gunshot echoes around the garage. His head smacks against the door of the car before he falls almost gracefully to the ground. A thick spray of blood now adorns the side panel. I quickly look around to make sure no one is here.

I'm clear.

Using the sleeve of my jacket, I wipe down the pistol butt and place it inside Santo's grip, being careful not to step in any blood. I shot the side of his head on purpose. The angle, coupled with the fact he's now holding the gun, could create the argument that he killed himself. It's weak, I know. Hardly my finest work. But given no one knew he was here except me and this bunch of corpses, I figure at the very least, it will add to the mystery a little. Whoever investigates might buy it, or they might not. But one thing's for sure—no one will come looking for me.

After a final check to make sure there's no visible blood on me, or any of my DNA near the scene, I turn on my heels and walk briskly toward the exit. I climb the stairs and step out into the foyer by the elevators. I slow my pace, relax, and walk out of the building, disappearing into the bustle of another busy day in Tokyo without looking back. Without thinking twice about what I just did.

A job well done.

6

I'm slumped on the sofa in my apartment, my head resting back against the cushion as I stare up at the ceiling. My legs are outstretched, resting on the coffee table in front of me.

After leaving the parking lot, I went back to see Ichiro, to let him know I had completed the job. He said he would inform the client and transfer the funds into my account by the end of the day. I told him to only charge ten thousand, U.S. I couldn't in good conscience let the guy bankrupt himself for wanting justice for his son. Hopefully, now he'll have some closure.

Ichiro told me again that I'm too nice to be an assassin.

Never thought I would hear someone say that. Maybe I'm mellowing in my old age...

This moment right here is the calm *after* the storm. My mind is no longer engaged. The adrenaline is no longer flowing. Aside from the habitually constant state of self-preservation, I'm about as relaxed as I could ever be. A mixture of relief, satisfaction and exhaustion that only comes after completing a job.

It used to be, back in the day, that a feeling of guilt—or, at the very least, an effort to justify my actions—accompanied these feelings, but nowadays I don't concern myself with such trivialities. I accepted who I am and what I do a long time ago. So long as I can look myself in the mirror at the end of the day, I'm good.

As I sit forward and reach for my coffee, I hear the elevator approaching. A moment later, a loud ding signals its arrival. The doors slide smoothly open. Ruby steps out and smiles at me.

She's dressed for a night of partying, despite it being the middle of the day. Short skirt, heels, tight top, bare midriff, skimpy jacket. She's holding three bags from a designer clothes store.

I shake my head, trying to hide a smile. "How are you dressed like that in this weather?"

She shrugs as she totters past me toward the kitchenette counter. "What? It's not *that* cold, you big pussy."

I roll my eyes. "So, your errand was shopping?"

She stoops to take her heels off, using the counter for balance. "You sound surprised..."

"I guess I forget sometimes you're just a normal woman."

She straightens, dropping her shoes to the floor, causing a loud clatter. She tilts her head as she stares at me. "And what's *that* supposed to mean?"

Uh-oh.

"I... ah... I just mean... it's not a bad thing, by the way. I think you're great. I just meant..." I sigh. "A little help here?"

She holds my gaze for a few moments before allowing a smile to creep across her face. "You are *so* easy!"

I let out a low whistle of relief. "Thank God."

She scoops up her shoes and bags. Starts up the stairs.

"I never get bored of doing that," she says without looking back.

I run my hand across my face, rubbing my eyes in the process. "Well, that makes one of us. Listen, when you're done up there, I've got something I wanna talk to you about, okay?"

"Okay," she shouts down.

I sit back again, resuming my absent scrutiny of the ceiling as I think about what I'm going to say to her. The job today, it... I don't know... it just made me think about what I'm doing. What I'm making of my life here. I mean, I'm happy. As happy as I can be after everything I've been through, anyway. I certainly have no regrets. But I think I need to tell Ruby I've been working contracts in my spare time. I'd just feel better not hiding it from her anymore.

Maybe I'm feeling sentimental after that last job. I felt for the father who hired me. Sure, his boy made some poor life choices, but that isn't justification for killing him. I know what the guy must be going through. It's one of those situations that kind of gives you that *life's too short* feeling, which is likely what's got me all bothered about Ruby not knowing I'm still working.

But at the same time, I know she's working contracts too, and the fact she hasn't told me doesn't seem to be bothering her...

I let out a heavy breath.

Maybe I'm just being a pussy, like she said.

Don't be so hard on yourself, man. You're just exploring your human side for once.

I smile. For years, I've relied on my Inner Satan for moral guidance. Not the healthiest of choices, admittedly, but now there's more of a balance inside me. See, that wasn't my Inner Satan just then. It was my Inner Josh. The angel to my devil.

It helps.

A couple of minutes pass. I hear Ruby walking downstairs. She sits next to me on the sofa, wearing yoga pants and a tank top. Both gray. Both tight enough to show me there's nothing underneath.

She raises an eyebrow. "What?"

I compose myself. "I've... ah... got something I need to tell you."

She puts her hands over her mouth. "Oh my God! You're not pregnant, are you?"

I frown. "Huh? No!" I glance down at my stomach. Run a hand over my abs. "Do I look it?"

She chuckles. "Jesus, Adrian! You're extra sensitive today." She puts her hand on my shoulder and leans close. "Is it that time of the month?"

I brush her hand away. "All right, will you knock it off?"

She sits back, laughing. "Okay, okay, I'm sorry. What's up?"

She's worse than Josh ever was!

I take a moment to compose myself. I want to word this right, so it doesn't look bad.

"Since we moved here, I've been working contracts. Nothing big. Not on a regular basis. Nothing like that. But I've been taking jobs to, y'know, keep busy."

She nods slowly. Patiently. "I know."

"You do?"

"Of course, I do. Same way you probably know I've been doing the exact same thing. I'm not an idiot, Adrian. What, you think you figured it out, but I couldn't?"

"Yeah, fair point. Not sure why I thought you wouldn't already know and understand."

She puts a hand on my knee. "It's because you're an idiot."

"Oh, well, now you've patronized me and made me feel bad, everything's okay…"

She shifts in her seat, turning to face me, crossing her legs like she's meditating. "Was that what you wanted to tell me?"

"Yeah," I say with a nod. "I took a job today and… I don't know, it just got me thinking. I realized I wasn't happy with not being honest with you."

She smiles. It's kind. Genuine.

"I appreciate that. What was the job?"

"A father wanted justice for the man who killed his son. They fell in with the wrong crowd and got themselves dead as a result."

"Shit. Yakuza?"

"Yeah. Some prick named Santo, from the Oji-gumi family."

"Ooo. I've heard of him!"

"Really?"

"Yeah, he was a… what do you call it?"

"Kyodai?"

"Yes! One of those! How did you manage to take out someone that high up in a Yakuza family? They must've had some heavy protection, right?"

I take another sip of coffee.

"Funny story, actually. My guy originally offered me a job that Santo had taken out himself. He apparently wanted to give me the job in person."

Ruby nods. "Makes sense. Harder to say no face-to-face. Plus, what does he care? He's a Kyodai, right?"

"Exactly. So, I told him to decline the meeting, which he

said he would do. Then he offered me another job—the one I took. When he said Santo was the target..."

"You accepted the original meeting request and used that as the set-up? Very nice!"

I smile. "Yeah, funny how it all came about, really. But it worked out."

"Did you listen to Santo's job offer before you killed him?"

"I did."

"And? Where you not tempted by it?"

"For a moment or two, yeah, I guess I was. He wanted me to take out the head of a rival family who had killed one of their own as part of his organ trafficking ring, or something."

Ruby grimaces. "Organ trafficking? That sounds grim. So, wait... he wanted you to kill the head of a Yakuza family?"

I nod.

"That would be impossible."

I shrug. "Nothing's impossible. But I admit it would have been difficult."

"What was he offering you?"

I glance away. She's going to hate me for this.

"A million. U.S."

Her jaw drops slightly. No words fall out.

Never seen her speechless before. It's nice.

"A million dollars?"

And we're back.

"Yup," I confirm with a nod.

She slaps my leg.

"And you *turned it down?*"

"Hey! And yeah, of course I did. Even that amount of money wouldn't have been worth it for a job like that. And it's not like we need it. We have all the money we would ever need."

She sighs. "No, Adrian, *you* have all the money *you* will ever need."

"What are you talking about? What's mine is—"

"Don't say it, all right? Look..." She shifts in her seat, almost like she's squirming. She's fidgeting with her hands and looking anywhere except at me. "I don't feel comfortable living off your bank balance. I never have. I'm grateful, obviously—please don't think I'm not—but I sometimes feel like a kept woman, and that's not me."

I raise an eyebrow. "Okay, how many bags of designer clothes did you just walk in with again?"

She punches my arm. "Hey, fuck you—I'm being serious!"

I wince at the blow as I look at her. This is perhaps the most honest and vulnerable I think I've ever seen her.

"Okay, I'm sorry."

"Why do you think I've been working my own contracts on the side?"

"Honestly? I figured you hated retirement, like me."

She shakes her head. "No, Adrian. God, no. I'd give anything for the quiet life. I'm working to earn my own money. To pay my way. Because as generous as your offer is to support both of our new lives, I don't feel right taking from you."

Now it's my turn to feel awkward and uncomfortable.

"Is this... is this one of those times when you're pretending just so you can mock me for being nice?"

Her eyes narrow and she raises her fist again.

I hold a hand up. "Okay, okay, it's not. I'm sorry." She relaxes. "I had no idea you felt this way. Why didn't you say something sooner?"

She shrugs and looks away again. "I don't know. I wasn't sure how, I guess. I didn't want to appear ungrateful. I think what we have here is amazing. The life we've made for ourselves is working, and... I didn't want to ruin it."

I lean toward her and put my hand on hers. "Hey, you wouldn't have ruined it by being honest with me, Ruby. This right here? This is nice. It's good to be normal with one another every once in a while. I mean, I spent most of my life with Josh, so I'm no stranger to jokes and a friendly exchange of insults. But you don't have to hide behind that all the time. Not with me."

She stares at the floor for a long couple of minutes, then finally turns to look at me. Her emerald eyes are wide and misty. They never fail to mesmerize me, even now.

"I'm going to say something to you now," she says. "It's not going to be easy for me. So, under no circumstances are you to ever mention it again or hold it over me in any way in the future."

"Okay..."

She sighs, steeling herself. "When you came for me in Stonebanks, I was... in a bad place."

I smile. "Well, it was an insane asylum, so... yeah, I would say so."

She rolls her eyes. "I meant personally. I felt as if life was spiraling uncontrollably away from me. I'd done some things I wasn't proud of, but they paid the bills. I guess staying there was more penance than an elaborate attempt at security."

I nod quietly, allowing her to speak.

"But when you showed up in my room, I kinda freaked out a little bit, which meant I retreated further into character and... well... stayed there."

I frown. "Why?"

She lets out a heavy sigh. "Because you're *you*, Adrian. You're a goddamn rock star in this business and I was... y'know... fangirling a little bit."

I feel my cheeks flush. "Really?"

"Yes, really. I was nervous putting on my crazy woman act in front of you. That's probably why you saw through it. I tried to play it cool, but it was hard. I never would've thought we'd end up here. Together. You're my hero, my celebrity crush, my brother and my best friend all rolled into one, you... handsome, irritating... kind... violent asshole."

"That's very nice of you to say," I reply, unsure how to react. "But that isn't a reason to feel like you can't accept the life I want to share with you."

She smiles at me. "You're a good man, Adrian. After Schultz confiscated what was left of the twenty million you paid me to help you take out Cunningham—which I understand he had to do—I was forced to start over. I promised myself I would never rely on anyone else again. That I would make my own way, y'know? I get the circumstances that brought us here are exceptional, but that doesn't change the fact I feel bad leeching off you."

"Ruby, you're not leeching off me. I'm offering this life to you, which I honestly think is a great deal, given I have company that I enjoy and can trust in return."

"I just want to pay my own way, that's all."

"Okay. I respect that."

I watch her for a moment. I can imagine how difficult that conversation must have been for her. I'm certainly not offended by what she's said, and I don't for a second think she's being ungrateful.

I take a breath. "I'll tell you what. From now on, we're upfront with each other about the work we're doing, and I won't make a big deal about the money. You do what you feel you need to, and I'm here if you need help. Sound fair?"

She looks me in the eyes. I see her defenses completely crumble away. I see all the craziness disappear back inside the dark recesses of her mind. I see *her*. Vulnerable and feminine. Her lips curl slightly, forming an innocent smile.

"That's really sweet, Adrian."

She leans over and throws her arms around my neck. I feel her breasts pressing against me, which I'm trying to ignore. She buries her head into my shoulder and squeezes. I put my arm around her shoulder, reciprocating her embrace. After a moment, she lifts her head. Her face is mere inches from mine. Her chest is still against me. I feel her breathing quickly.

I move away slightly. This is getting a little weird.

Hang on.

Is she... is she going to kiss me? I can't tell. Feels like the right moment if she wanted to. And it's not like there hasn't been the odd moment, here and there, over the last year or so. I mean, it's a natural thing, and we're both in the same place. Both close. Our friendship was forged in extraordinary circumstances, which makes a strong bond. But I've... *we've* always laughed those times off. We both know it would complicate an otherwise uncomplicated and happy way of life. Neither of us want that.

She traces a finger around my shoulder. "So, I was thinking..."

I swallow hard. "Yeah...?"

"How would you feel about..."

"Go on..."

"Maybe... working together?" She moves away. Sits back on her heels again. "I mean, if people knew I was working with you, I would get *way* more job offers! Plus, your name would justify charging more money. That way, I would be earning my own way in no time! Obviously, you would get a cut. I was thinking maybe fifteen percent? But I'd definitely feel better about things if I was earning good money, y'know? It would really... are you okay? You look kinda pale."

I'm staring blankly ahead. For some reason, I'm trying desperately to remember the lyrics to a song I heard a while back. Or the final score of the basketball game I caught some of the other day. Anything, really, except what just happened.

I turn to her. Nod. "Uh-huh. Yeah. Fifteen percent. That works for me. Gonna be great teaming up."

She claps excitedly and springs to her feet. "You won't regret it! This is gonna be so cool—it's been *forever* since we worked together! I'll get us a job first thing in the morning."

She disappears back upstairs. I'm left alone on the sofa, taking deep breaths.

I hate her.

7

───────────

After our heart-to-heart earlier, Ruby suggested we celebrate our newfound working arrangement by going out tonight. I thought she meant for drinks, but it turns out there's a street racing meet somewhere—which is a cultural phenomenon consisting of fast, over-priced, tricked-out cars, young people, and loud music. It's not exactly legal, but it's well-organized. A haven for Yakuza activity too.

Sounds like my idea of hell, if I'm honest. But it's very much Ruby's scene, and she's excited, so I figure it won't kill me to step outside my comfort zone. Consequently, she's spent the last hour and a half in the bathroom, preparing for tonight. I'm standing in my room, staring at my closet, wondering what to wear.

I spend way too much time with her.

It's not as if I'll be out of place. I'm hardly a stranger to any aspect of the criminal underworld. But I don't want to draw too much attention to myself. It's risky for me going to any gathering involving people and business of a question-able nature because I'm inviting the world to see me, remember me, and ultimately link me to something that might happen later. I need to blend in.

Unfortunately, I'm not a twenty-something street racer with a sense of fashion. I'm a forty-seven-year-old semi-retired hitman, and unsurprisingly, I dress as such. I may as well show up ringing a bell and wearing an A-board that says, "I'm going to kill you!"

I let out a deep, weary breath.

"Got nothing that matches your new shoes and make-up?"

I roll my eyes and glance over my shoulder. Ruby's leaning against my doorframe, apparently fresh out of the shower. She has a towel wrapped around her, and she's dripping on the carpet. There's a wry smile etched on her face.

I look back at my closet. "I just want to do this right. Get the right look, y'know? I don't want to show you up or anything."

I hear her padding toward me. A moment later, she's by my side. "You're cute, do you know that?"

I shrug. "Yeah..."

"Asshole," she says, laughing. "Go casual. Jeans. T-shirt. Sneakers. You'll be fine."

"What makes you so sure? Go to a lot of street racing gatherings, do you?"

She shrugs. "I've been to more than you. Trust me."

"Uh-huh. And what are you wearing tonight?"

She turns to me. Grins. Pinches my cheek with a damp hand. "Something that's gonna stop traffic."

"Well, given where we're going, that sounds very counter-productive, if you ask me."

She pinches my cheek like an auntie embarrassing her favorite nephew before leaving my room smiling.

I continue staring at my less-than-diverse collection of clothing and sigh.

It's going to be a long night.

20:45 JST

I took Ruby's advice. Plain black T-shirt, dark blue jeans, and white sneakers. My brown leather jacket is unfastened, although I suspect it'll be freezing when we step outside, so that might change. It's looking a little worse for wear nowadays. But then, aren't we all? I love this jacket. I've had it a long time, and it's seen a lot of shit. Can't bring myself to replace it.

Beneath it is a shoulder holster, strapped tightly to the left side of my torso, just below my armpit. Cradled inside it is my gun—a custom Smith and Wesson SW1911. The barrel and frame are stainless steel. The grip has a laminated wooden finish, engraved with a yin-yang symbol. I thought that was more prudent than a devil, now that I have opposing voices of reason.

I've added a two-inch extension to the barrel, making it seven inches in total. It adds a couple of grams to the overall weight, but the resulting boost in accuracy is off the charts. Plus, it looks all kinds of badass.

As much as I loved my twin Berettas, I found the combined weight of them in the holster at my lower back was taking its toll. I'm trying to stay healthy, and wearing something that was damaging my long-term mobility wasn't a smart choice. The shoulder holster works very well, and having a single gun makes moving around much easier. The only downside is that I moved from having two nineteen-round guns to having one nine-round gun. That's a serious drop in ammo capacity. Luckily, I don't use it that often anymore, and not having to carry two weapons around with me means I have room to carry a couple of spare magazines and a suppressor, so it's not all bad, I guess.

I'm standing by the elevator, waiting for Ruby. Pacing back and forth in front of the doors. I'm a naturally restless and impatient person. I hate waiting around for anything. If there's somewhere I need to go, or something I need to do, I'd rather just do it.

I turn as I hear the clacking of Ruby's heels on the stairs. I see her shoes first as she descends slowly. Then her legs. Then—

Holy...

...

...

...

...shit.

She's standing at the bottom of the stairs, looking at me. She's wearing a dress. It's black, with a white stripe running up each side. It has a strap over one shoulder, and it's clinging to every inch of her body in just the right way to show off her impressive figure. It's long enough that it covers her under-wear, although if I were her, I'd be careful bending down for anything. It has a high enough neckline that it doesn't show any cleavage, but I'm guessing she's wearing one of those bras underneath that pushes everything together, because the twins look a lot bigger than they did an hour ago. Her legs look deceptively long, probably because of the black heels she's wearing. The whole outfit makes her look as tall as I am, even though she's about five inches shorter. To finish the look off, she has a small black bag with a long gold chain resting over the shoulder that's not covered by the dress.

She glances at the floor. Shimmies her dress down a little, for all the good it does. She brushes her hair behind her ear and looks back at me patiently. Perhaps expectantly, like she's waiting for me to say something. But, honestly, I don't have any words for how amazing she looks. In fact, I've just realized... I'm not even breathing!

I gasp in a quick breath and shake my head, cursing myself for staring.

She looks... *incredible*. Never mind stopping traffic— she'll stop hearts walking down the street looking like that! And I stand by what I said before. Ruby and I... it's purely platonic. Mostly. I'm not saying I don't look at her and see the appeal, but I don't have any feelings toward her beyond friendship.

At least, I'm pretty sure I don't.

The life we have, co-habiting together, suits us both just fine. Sure, she flirts a little. Okay, a *lot*. And by flirting, I mean she often wanders around naked just for the sheer amusement she gets from making me feel uncomfortable. But that's just her. That's how she's always been, and honestly, I barely notice it anymore. I'm—

Bullshit.

What? It's true.

As your own personal devil, I'm fully qualified to call bullshit on everything you just said.

Screw you. Josh, back me up here, man.

I hear his hearty, British chuckle echoing through my mind. It brings a brief smile to my face.

65

I agree with Satan. You barely notice when a beautiful woman walks past you, naked? Bullshit, mate!

Great. I have two voices in my head, and if that wasn't enough to make me sound crazy, I'm being bullied by the pair of them!

I've been standing here a while. So has Ruby.

Yeah... I should say something.

I run a hand over my head. "You, ah... you're gonna freeze going out in that, y'know?"

...

...

...

I swear I just heard the slap of both my inner voices face-palming themselves.

She smiles and walks over to me. The sound of her heels on the floor resonates around the apartment. She stops beside me and kisses my cheek. "The whole time when you weren't talking was a much bigger compliment, but I appreciate the effort."

She moves past me and hits the call button for the elevator. I close my eyes briefly and smile to myself before joining her.

I glance sideways. "Seriously, Ruby, you're going to freeze out there without a jacket or something."

She shrugs. "Surely, you would offer me yours if I got too cold?"

I raise an eyebrow. "Would you want it?"

She looks me up and down before pinching the material of the sleeve and rubbing her thumb over it. After a moment, she shakes her head. "I'd rather have hypothermia."

"Gee, thanks!"

The doors slide open and we both step inside. She hits

the button for the first floor, and the doors glide gently together again.

She looks at me. "Tomorrow, we're going shopping. You need a better wardrobe."

I roll my eyes but say nothing. We both smile as a relaxed silence descends.

...

...

...

Hang on a second.

I turn to her. "There's no way you've fit your gun in that purse..."

She shakes her head. "No, I haven't."

"And there's no way you're not packing..."

She nods. "Correct."

I look her up and down. Scratch the back of my head. "Uh..."

She throws her head back and laughs. "Assuming there's no drama tonight, you'll never find out where I'm carrying it." She shrugs. "Then again, if you're lucky... maybe I'll show you anyway."

I stare ahead. "God help me."

8

The raucous atmosphere is intoxicating, if a little overwhelming. The roar of expensive engines competes with the bassline thumping from the speakers at the DJ station. Portable floodlights bathe the scene in a near-white fluorescence. There must be a couple of thousand people here, easily, all drinking and dancing and laughing, admiring the cars... and the people driving them. Guys are leaning casually against their vehicles, surrounded by women as if they're celebrities. And it's the same with the women. The female drivers I've seen are lapping up the attention from interested men.

It's all a little over-the-top for my liking.

We're roughly fourteen kilometers south of Chiyoda, in the Shinigawa ward. The meeting place is a wide storm drain, sunk between two freeways. It acts as an overflow conduit for excess rain to prevent flooding. Not sure how much use it gets here, at least in the meteorological sense.

It's getting some use tonight.

One of the girls serving drinks explained that the race circuit leads out of here, across the street into the stadium that hosts dirt bike racing, once around that and back out, over the bridge, along the freeway adjacent to the river, and back down into this overflow road.

Sounds exhausting, if you ask me.

Ruby's loving it, walking around as if it's her home away from home. Her aim to stop traffic seems to be working too, which I'm sure she's happy about. Most guys we've seen while navigating the crowds have almost broken their own necks turning to look at her as we walked past.

We both have our Pilots in our ears and our Ilis on standby. Both have a drink. I tell you, regardless of it not being my thing, this event is well put-together. Shame it's illegal. People could make a fortune for promoting things like this.

Ruby nudges my arm. "You okay?"

I nod back. "Yeah. Just taking it all in. You?"

"I *love* this place!"

I smile. "I bet you do."

She pinches my cheek. Gently slaps it. Then skips ahead, kind of half-dancing to herself in her own little world. I shake my head in the way a parent does when looking at their child as they enjoy themselves in a way you can't understand.

I'm just happy she's happy, I guess.

I should try to make the most of the night. The music's not to my taste, but it's a good atmosphere. Full of positive vibes. At the risk of sounding like an old man, it's good that so many young people can still come together and enjoy themselves in a world so devoid of goodness. Everything we have endured in recent years, yet here I am, surrounded by some of the happiest-looking people I've seen in a long time, giving a collective *fuck you* to the world and all its shit. There's something admirable about that.

I move into the crowd, twisting my body to thread myself through the narrow gaps between people, aimlessly wandering until I find somewhere to get another drink. This bottle's nearly done.

I break through the crowd and come to what probably passes as the pit lane at these things. I count ten cars in a line, each with their hoods and trunks open, engines running. A shiny red Mitsubishi Evolution with white decals catches my eye. Resting against the driver's door is a guy wearing board shorts and a pullover hoodie. His arms are folded across his chest. He has a woman on either side of him, linking him, laughing.

He's maybe twenty-five. He's just a kid, yet he looks like a king. I imagine a lot of men would be jealous of him. Personally, I don't see why anyone would want that much attention drawn to them.

I feel a hand on my shoulder. I turn around to see Ruby, grinning, dancing on the spot, having the time of her life.

"Having fun?" she asks.

I smile. "Sure."

She stops dancing. Tilts her head slightly. "You hate this, don't you?"

I laugh. "No, I don't. I promise. I just... I guess I just don't understand it. Take this guy, for example." I gesture to the Mitsubishi driver. "I don't see the appeal of making an attraction out of yourself like that."

Ruby looks at him. Her eyes light up.

I frown. "What?"

She smiles at me. "Lunchtime."

"Oh, seriously? He's, like, young enough to be your son."

She scoffs. "So? A girl's gotta eat. Maybe you should try having some fun every once in a while. Then you wouldn't be so uptight all the time."

"Hey! I'm not uptight..."

She raises an eyebrow. "Really?"

"Whatever." I look over at the driver again. "He seems pre-occupied, anyway."

She moves close to me and traces a finger down my chest. "Yeah... how much would you care to bet I can occupy him better?"

I look her up and down. A valid point.

She sees me staring and smiles, then starts walking backward away from me. "You gotta believe it, Adrian. You gotta *own* it. Now, if you'll excuse me, I need to go show those twenty-something, anorexic, wannabe pieces of arm candy how it's *really* done."

She turns and struts away, gliding effortlessly through the crowd toward the Evo driver. She's walking like a model, each step slightly crossing over the opposite leg. It's as if she knows I'm looking. Which I'm not, by the way.

Okay, maybe I am a little.

Along with every other guy here.

I have to hand it to her—she knows how to work a crowd. She pushes to the front and walks straight toward him. I'm maybe fifty feet away, with a clear view of what's happening. The two girls have stopped laughing. They're looking at Ruby, their faces contorted with shock and disgust.

Talk about territorial!

She steps in close to him. Traces a finger over his shoulder.

Poor guy. He has no idea.

I see him shrug. Smile. Lean in close, whispering something to her.

Oh yeah... he's *definitely* interested.

Ruby giggles exaggeratedly, then looks at the other girls in turn. Shoos them away with a condescending gesture. Their expressions haven't changed, but they're leaving.

To be fair, *I* wouldn't mess with Ruby, so I'm pretty sure they won't.

She takes him by the hand and moves him slightly away from the car. Then, keeping her legs straight, she leans forward and rests her arms on the door as she looks inside. He checks out her ass before doing the same, pointing at things, talking to her.

Man, she's good.

Bet the guy can't believe his luck. I mean, the two ladies who were with him before were attractive, but compared to Ruby, they're—

"Adrian?"

Huh?

I scan the crowd around me, confused.

Could've sworn someone just said my name.

I feel a tap on my shoulder.

"Adrian?"

I spin around. Holy shit...

Mia!

My eyes pop wide with involuntary surprise, and I immediately curse to myself over how badly I hid my reaction just then.

What's she doing here?

She's smiling awkwardly, wearing a similar outfit to what I saw her in last night at the bar.

I need to be cool. Stop worrying about interacting with her.

"Hey... Mia, right?"

She nods. Her smile broadens, perhaps happy I remembered her. "Yeah. I didn't expect to see you somewhere like this."

I shrug. "Yeah, it's my first time. Thought I'd see what all the fuss was about, y'know? What about you? Come here often?" I momentarily close my eyes, cursing myself. "Sorry, I didn't mean to steal your line..."

There's a moment's silence, then we both laugh.

She briefly touches my elbow with her hand. "I know what you mean. And yeah, I come to a few meets like this. I'm here with a girlfriend, Verity, but I lost her. She's probably off flirting with a driver or something."

I glance over my shoulder at Ruby. "Yeah, I know how that goes."

She looks away. I watch her. She's nervous. Her eyes are darting in different directions, like she's accessing every corner of her brain, searching for something else to say. After a moment, she looks back at me and smiles again. It's a nice smile. Happy. Innocent.

"So, do you race? Or are you just here for the music?"

I chuckle. "Music? Is that what this is?"

She laughs. "Not your thing?"

"Nah, I'm more of a rock and roll kinda guy. Give me some AC/DC any day."

She frowns. "Who?"

I arch an eyebrow. "Are you kidding me?"

She holds my gaze for a long moment before her smile finally breaks. "Yeah. I almost had you too!"

I roll my eyes. Smile back. "Well played."

"So, do you want to grab a drink or something? I owe you one, after all. I mean, it won't be coffee, but..."

"I'm good, thanks. I'm—"

Ruby's just appeared next to me. She shifts her gaze between me and Mia. She smiles.

Oh, no.

She links my arm. "Aren't you going to introduce me to your friend?"

Please, no.

This is going to go one of two ways. She'll either have an enormous amount of fun at my expense, where she tries to make me look and feel as uncomfortable as possible, or she'll get really protective and aggressive and likely terrify the poor girl.

She extends her hand to Mia. "Nice to meet you. So, how do you know my husband?"

Mia's eyes grow wide. The color starts to leave her cheeks.

I take a deep breath.

It appears she's chosen option one.

"Ruby, be nice," I say with a disapproving glare before looking at Mia. "Relax. This isn't my wife. She's just a good friend. Kinda like a sister. An *annoying* little sister. You'll have to forgive her terrible sense of humor."

Mia relaxes. Closes her eyes for a moment in silent relief.

Ruby casually hits my shoulder. "Spoilsport."

"Sorry. This is Mia. Remember I told you I got into something in the bar last night? Well, this was the young lady being harassed."

"Ah, I see," she says, nodding slowly as she moves beside Mia and puts an arm around her. "Sorry, honey. I'm an acquired taste." She gestures to me with her head. "He's a nice guy, ain't he?"

Mia still looks a little nervous but nods and smiles sheepishly. "Yeah, he is. I was just saying I owe him a drink."

I wave a dismissive hand. "You don't. It was the least I could do, under the circumstances."

"But I really want to say thank you. And this is, like, the second time we've bumped into each other today. It feels like fate, or something."

She giggles awkwardly. I notice she's avoiding making eye contact with Ruby though.

Ruby looks at me. "Twice in one day, huh? That's a personal best for you, isn't it?"

I shake my head. "Wow. Really?"

Ruby steps back over to me and sighs loudly. "Ruin a girl's fun, why don't you?" She looks at Mia. "Sorry, but could I borrow my charming, handsome, rich, big brother figure for just one second?"

I frown at her.

Mia grins and nods. "Sure." She looks at me. "I'll be around, okay? Come find me."

She turns and disappears into the crowd. I make a conscious effort to not watch as she walks away. I take a deep breath and turn to Ruby. "What the hell was that?"

She shrugs. "What? Just trying to help..."

"Well, I don't need your help."

"I can see that. You are *so* in there!"

"What? No! She's just a kid, Ruby. Come on..."

She shakes her head. "She's young, but she's not a kid. I reckon twenty... maybe twenty-one."

"That's what I figured last night, which is too young."

"Oh my God, Adrian. She's good-looking, *clearly* into you, and you could easily play the whole 'saved her ass' card to seal the deal. Let's face it, if ever there was someone who needed to get laid, it's you. I was just trying to help facilitate the situation, that's all."

"Okay, look, I get that in your own... special way, you're

75

looking out for me, but I don't feel right taking advantage of a young, impressionable, naïve woman, all right? I don't need to get laid *that* much."

She shrugs. "That's debatable."

"Jesus, Ruby. Knock it off, would you?"

Dammit.

I can feel myself growing impatient, and that came out a little sharper than I intended.

Ruby takes a step away. Looks at me for a moment. Places her hand on my shoulder. "All right. I'm sorry, Adrian. I went too far."

"No, it's fine, honestly." I pause. "Sorry for being a dick about it."

She smiles. "You weren't. This one's on me."

"Okay."

"Forgive me?"

I nod. "Forgiven."

"Good. Listen, my new friend has invited me to a party at a nightclub in the city after his race. D'you mind if I check it out? I'll see you back at home later. Or tomorrow morning, whatever."

I raise an eyebrow. "You still hungry, then?"

She smiles. "I'm a big girl, Adrian. I can handle myself."

"I know. It's just..."

I trail off because her next conquest is walking toward us, flanked by two of his friends. He seems to be ignoring me. Understandable, I guess. Stood next to Ruby, I'm probably invisible.

"What?" she asks.

"Your main course is here with a couple of sides. He doesn't look pleased."

She looks around and smiles at him.

"Say nothing," she hisses to me discreetly. She quickly

turns on her Ili and reaches for the driver's hand. "Hey, sweetie!"

He doesn't speak English, but my Pilot translates his reply:

"Hey, baby. Where'd you go? Who's this fool?"

She ignores his comment. "He's just a friend. Don't worry about him. Why don't you and your friends show me around? I would love to see some more cars. Maybe grab a drink..."

I can tell he's listening to her because he's smiling and nodding, but he's staring right at me. For a brief moment, I worry he's recognized me, but I dismiss the idea as paranoia just as quickly. He's most likely just eyeballing me to look tough in front of Ruby.

Oh, the fun I could have!

He gestures to me with a flick of his head. *"What about you, old timer... you like racing cars?"*

Ruby puts a hand on his chin and slowly turns his head toward her. "I told you, sweetie. Ignore him. I barely know the guy. He's a friend of a friend, y'know? I'd much rather be getting to know you."

He brushes her hand away.

That tells me two things. First, this idiot is probably affiliated with a Yakuza family. Somewhere like this, the odds of not meeting someone in the Yakuza are slim anyway, but no normal guy pushes someone like Ruby away just to look tough. Having her come onto you is like winning the lottery. It's all the reputation boost you will ever need. But he clearly has a greater need to protect his image, and for me, that confirms he's Yakuza. Nothing is more important to them than reputation and respect.

Which leads me to the second thing. This guy's going to try baiting me into a fight. The fact I'm standing here with the woman who just spent time flirting with him is all the justification he needs. He'll now be thinking he's entitled to her, and my being here is a threat to that. And if you're Yakuza, you can't let something like that slide. You can't let an apparent threat, no matter how great or small, go unpunished. He has two friends and a large audience, which means he won't stop now until I'm made an example of.

Which poses a problem for all concerned, because I'm nobody's example.

I turn on my own Ili and smile. "No, I don't see the appeal."

He laughs. *"Why not? Too scared?"*

His friends join in with the joke. Ruby's trying to subtly urge me to keep my mouth shut and not ruin her evening. I reckon she's come to the same conclusions I have. But the damage has been done.

I shake my head. "I don't do *scared*, sorry. I just know my limits. See, to me, fast cars are like beautiful women..." I pause to gesture to Ruby for effect. "They both look great, but if I ever got inside one, I wouldn't have a clue what to do. Sometimes, you just gotta know when you're in over your head. D'you understand what I'm saying?"

I smile at him. I know he probably won't fully comprehend the meaning of what I just said, but that's okay. Every now and then, you just need to entertain yourself. I glance across at Ruby. I can see she's trying not to laugh.

He doesn't look impressed. He cracks his neck. His smile fades. *"Fuck you, old man. This is my world, you understand?"* He gestures over his shoulder to his car. *"Me and that beast over there... we run these streets. Now, your girlfriend's with me. You should fuck off before you find out exactly who I am."*

His friends square up to me beside him. The three of them are lined up, staring me down like I'm something they would scrape off their boot. I don't know why the idea of Ruby leaving with these assholes is bothering me, but I would never intentionally sabotage her night. She's clearly happy, so that's good enough for me. However, if one of them so much as sneezes in my direction, all three are going to wake up in a bucket.

Ruby steps in close to him again, putting herself between him and me. She snakes a hand around his neck and kisses him on the lips. "Hey, baby... forget him, okay? Why don't you take me for a ride? I would *love* to get inside the beast!"

I fight every inexplicable urge I have right now to look hurt or disappointed. Instead, I focus on controlling the white-hot flashes of anger burning away beneath the surface, urging me to rip his throat out.

I take some deep breaths, allowing my entire body to fill up with air, extinguishing the fire. I let them out with heavy, begrudging sighs.

He stares at me over her shoulder and smiles. Doesn't say anything. In his position, after that, he doesn't need to. He just won this little confrontation in style.

The only issue I have with it all is that I had to let him.

The three of them turn their backs on me. Ruby moves to follow but quickly turns to me.

"Thank you," she says.

I roll my eyes and sigh before giving her a slight smile. "Don't mention it."

She gestures behind me with a flick of her head. I turn and see Mia and another young woman approaching. I look back at Ruby.

"Maybe you should think about getting something to eat yourself..." she says with a smile.

Before I can reply, she joins her new friends, linking the

driver's arm as they disappear into the crowd, absorbed into a world I have no wish to understand.

Ah, she'll be all right.

I turn just as Mia and her friend reach me.

"Hey again," I say with a smile.

Mia beams. "Adrian, this is my friend, Verity. Vee, this is the guy I was telling you about. From last night."

Her friend smiles at me. She's about the same height as Mia. She has striking blue eyes and an easy smile. Dressed nice but a little more discreet than Mia. She extends a hand, which I shake.

"Nice to meet you," she says. "Mia hasn't stopped talking about you."

I feel my cheeks fill with color. Mia playfully slaps her friend's arm.

"Vee!"

They both giggle.

"You having a good night?" asks Mia.

"Yeah, it's okay. Not really my thing though. My friend's just bailed on me. Turns out spending time with a driver is more appealing than spending time with me."

She hesitates. "Who... who was she again? A friend? Sister?"

I smile. "She's a friend. We've known each other a long time. Been through a lot. We're like family."

"Ah, I see..." She steps closer. "Well, I... ah... I don't think it sounds more appealing."

Oh, crap.

Go for it, man. For the love of God, go for it.

Thanks, Satan. Josh?

I'm with him, mate. You deserve it. Live a little.

I take a breath.

Screw it. There's no one here to judge me anyway.

"How about that drink?" I say casually.

Mia beams.

Her friend smiles. "Mia, I'm gonna go hang out with some people by the cars, okay? Leave you to it."

I nod to her. "Nice to meet you, Verity."

She holds her drink toward me. I tap it with mine.

"You too," she says. "Have a nice night."

Mia moves to my side and links my arm as her friend walks away. She leads me through the crowds to the makeshift bar area near the entrance.

Habitually, I look back over my shoulder, checking to see if I can get eyes on Ruby, make sure she's okay. If I'm honest, right now, I'm not sure who I'm more worried about—her... or me.

9

October 18, 2019 — 07:17 JST

I'm leaning against the doorway of my bedroom, wearing
jogging pants and sipping coffee, staring at Mia as she lies
peacefully in my bed. The sheets are covering most of her
body. She's on her side, with an arm tucked beneath a
pillow. Her chest is rising and falling slowly.

I didn't sleep with her. It just wasn't the right thing to do.
Both voices in my head shouted at me a lot last night, but
this was one of those rare times where I didn't listen to
either one of them.

We had a few drinks at the race meet, stayed for the first
race, and then left. I offered to walk her home. She
suggested coming back here for another drink. We did.
After the drink, she kissed me. I kissed her back. Couldn't
help it, really. But I stopped before it went any further. Aside
from her being more than half my age, it just didn't feel
right. I told her she was welcome to stay the night and that
I'd take the sofa. She understood. She was pretty great about

it, actually. I thought she might be offended or something, but she was fine.

I spent most of the night sat wide awake, staring at the ceiling, trying to figure out what the hell is wrong with me. I imagine most guys in my position would have simply enjoyed the company of an attractive young lady. Ruby said I should. The internal sounding board that has guided me through so much of my life agreed. Yet, I couldn't bring myself to do it.

And it wasn't until three o'clock this morning that I realized why.

I'm not weighing myself down with guilt about my wife and daughter. Not anymore. I avenged their memories and laid them to rest. I love them, and I always will, but I've finally moved on with my life, as they would undoubtedly want me to do.

But there's no getting away from the fact that if my daughter *was* still alive... if my baby girl was still here... sweet Maria would be twenty years old right now. Those paternal instincts never leave you, even if your child does, for one reason or another. It's not Mia's age in relation to mine that's the problem. It's the fact she's the same age as my daughter would've been. I can't do it. I just can't.

I leave her sleeping and head back downstairs to get dressed. I throw on my clothes from last night and sit down heavily on the sofa, staring at the floor for a few minutes. Then at the ceiling. I let out an impatient, restless sigh and move over to the window. It's not dark, but the dull, early morning haze hasn't shifted yet. The sun isn't high enough to illuminate the gray clouds from behind.

I look down at the sprawling mass of humanity below me until my eyes glaze over. Minutes pass by like seconds until my gaze re-focuses. My mind engages, zeroing in on a subconscious thought deemed important enough to distract me with.

Ruby didn't come home last night. She texted me a little after midnight to say her main course had won his race, and they were heading to a club to celebrate. She ended the message by telling me not to worry or wait up.

Maybe she's right. Maybe everyone's right. Maybe it's time I stop being so reluctant to enjoy the spoils of my ill-gotten gains, embrace the fact I'm in my twilight years as an assassin, and start living a little.

Yeah... maybe take a trip somewhere. Japan's a big place —plenty to see outside of Tokyo. Maybe Ruby will want to come with me?

"It's an amazing view."

Mia's voice startles me. I look around to see her standing at the bottom of the stairs, smiling. She's wearing one of my shirts, which drowns her. Her toned, olive legs are crossed right over left. While she isn't as tall as Ruby, she's not short —maybe five-four or five-five. Her hair looks straight and neat. It's possible she tidied it up before coming downstairs. I don't know.

She pads barefoot toward me, stopping at my side and looking out of the window.

"You sleep okay?" I ask her.

She nods. "Yeah, thanks. Your bed is so comfortable! And your apartment is amazing. The rent must be crazy for a place like this."

I shrug. "I wouldn't know... I bought it outright."

"Really?"

I shrug again. "Yeah. It's no big deal. I do all right for myself. Coffee?"

Her eyes are wide. Her lips curl into a disbelieving half-smile. "That'd be great, thanks."

I walk over to the kitchenette and grab a mug from the cupboard. As I move to close it, my hand starts to twitch. I feel the pinch inside and stare at my appendage as I slowly lose control of it.

Goddammit, not now!

I open the drawer beside me. Take out the painkillers and pop three tablets out of the small, foil-backed sheet. I shove them quickly into my mouth, swallowing them dry. I grimace as one sticks momentarily in my throat, but I force it down. I lower my arm to my side, slowly flexing my hand, willing it to stay still. It's uncomfortable without causing much pain, but once the spasms subside, it aches for hours.

It frustrates me more than anything, and I do what I can to subdue my unjustified anger as I continue making Mia's coffee. I put my right hand in the pocket of my jogging pants and pick up her mug with my much steadier left. I turn to walk over to her, but she's already at the counter, sitting on one of the stools, leaning forward slightly on crossed arms.

"You okay?" she asks.

Seeing her there made me forget myself for a brief moment. I must've been so distracted while taking my meds, I didn't hear her walking over.

I smile and gently slide the hot coffee toward her. "Yeah, I'm good. You want sugar or cream?"

She shakes her head. "As it comes is fine, thank you."

"You drink coffee as it should be drunk... I like that."

She laughs. "Typical guy." She picks up the mug in both hands. Blows gently and takes a sip. "So, what's with the pain meds? Everything okay?"

I glance at my right hand, despite trying not to. "It's... ah... it's an old injury. Still gives me a little grief from time to time. Nothing to worry about."

She takes another sip of her drink. "So, tell me. Where did you live before moving to Tokyo?"

I move around the counter and take a seat beside her. "I moved around a lot with work. I was lucky enough to see a lot of the world."

"Was? You're a little young to be retired, aren't you?"

She smiles and nudges my arm playfully with hers.

I shrug, fighting the rush of color in my cheeks. "I worked as a consultant. The money was great, but after 4/17, my... my industry changed. As did most things, I guess. I had enough put away that I didn't need to worry about things for a while, so I took the opportunity to move away, enjoy being in one place for a change."

The official line. The practiced lie. Effortless and believable.

I return her gesture of a playful nudge, arm to arm. "What about you? What brings you this far east?"

She goes to speak but stops herself, opting for a sip of coffee instead.

"I'm studying while I'm travelling. Killing two birds with one stone while I'm young enough to get away with it."

"Nice. What are you studying?"

She looks at me. "Psychology and journalism. I've always wanted to know why people do the things they do, y'know? And I figure the world should know about what really goes on around here. Especially nowadays."

I nod. "I can appreciate that. Lot of people doing a lot of weird shit. And even more people wanting to read about it. You come to Japan on your own?"

"Yeah. I knew a couple of people over here, but I don't see them much."

"What about your family? Must be hard being away from them?"

She shrugs. "I don't have much, to be honest. I never knew my dad, and my mom passed away a few years ago."

"Shit... I'm sorry to hear that."

She shrugs again. "Thanks. She left me some money that I couldn't access 'til I was eighteen. I used it to come over here."

"Well, you sound like you're doing okay. Takes confidence to live your own life. Good for you."

She grins at me but says nothing.

"Listen, Mia... about last night..."

She puts her hand up. "You don't have to say anything, let alone apologize. It was fine last night, and it's still fine this morning, I promise. It's, ah... it's the age thing, isn't it?"

I smile an apology. "Kinda, yeah."

"Well, look... for what it's worth..." She spins in her seat to face me, then stands and leans in close. Her lips brush my ear. "It's not a problem for me. Y'know, if you ever change your mind."

She sits back down, still facing me. Her foot rests against my leg.

What the hell is going on?

I must be insane. Mia's gorgeous, and I don't get the impression she's looking for a future husband or anything. I have my reservations and reasons, but maybe I'm thinking too much about it. I mean, let's be honest. It wouldn't be the first time I've shot myself in the foot by overthinking, would it?

I keep telling myself I've turned over a new leaf. That I'm different now. That I've learned from my past. I knew Josh better than he knew himself, and he would've said the same about me. That's why I'm able to visualize him as part of my conscience. Deep down, I'm honest enough with myself that I know exactly what he would say to me in any given situation. Yes, his moral compass was sometimes as questionable as mine can be, but he'd slap me senseless if I could have this debate with him right now.

He would question if I was just using the fact my daughter would've been the same age as an excuse. A way of sabotaging a chance for myself to be happy because of some misplaced sense of guilt, or a feeling that I don't *want* to be happy because, based on past experiences, when I am, things usually go wrong soon afterward.

I reach out and take hold of her hand. Look into her hazel eyes. They're bright, full of life.

I take a breath, steel myself. "Mia, I hope you don't think I'm being an asshole about... whatever this is?"

She smiles. "I don't."

"And I definitely didn't intervene the other night for any reason other than it was the right thing to do."

"Oh, God... of course. I know you didn't, and I'm eternally grateful."

"I can't deny you're attractive..."

Her cheeks fill with color.

"...and I'd be lying if I said I didn't want to... y'know... spend time with you."

She gets to her feet again. Moves in close again. Moves her hand so her fingers are interlaced with mine. "Then what are you waiting for, Adrian?"

I shake my head slowly. "Y'know what? Absolutely nothing."

I move my head toward her. I hear her hold her breath. She closes her eyes, tilts her head. I move to—

My ringtone blasts out in the silence, jolting me from the moment.

We look at each other and smile. We shake our heads playfully, and she sits back down.

I get to my feet. "Sonofabitch. Sorry, I should get that."

She picks up her mug and smiles. "It's okay."

I look around the room, trying to find the damn thing.

It's on the arm of the sofa.

I stride over for it, but it stops ringing the moment I pick it up. I look at the screen. Missed call from Ruby.

I'd best call her back. Make sure she's okay.

I unlock the screen, but as I do, I hear the elevator hum and rattle into life. I look over. The display above the doors is counting up.

Looks as if Ruby was just letting me know she was back. Knowing her, she probably wants a hand with her bags... some emergency shopping on the way home.

I turn to Mia, who's spun around to face me, mug in hand. "That was Ruby. I'm guessing she's on her way up now."

Mia smiles again. Shrugs. She looks cute.

"No problem. Raincheck, yeah?"

I nod. "Yeah, definitely."

My phone beeps. I frown. Look at the screen.

A message from Ruby?

I unlock the phone and open it up.

I stare at the screen, stunned to silence.

The message simply reads: *911*.

My mind explodes, creating a mushroom cloud of questions and hypotheticals inside my head. I take a deep breath. The first step in a process engrained in my subconscious—a result of over two decades of training and experience. Like editing an audio file on a computer, I'm tuning out the background noise. Silencing the unnecessary words.

It takes me all of two seconds to filter out the panic and focus on what I know, and what I need to know.

I know Ruby's in trouble. My spider sense is going

haywire. See, *911* is our agreed code for *get your ass over here, I'm in deep shit*. It's easy to type in a hurry and is about as unambiguous as you can get in a text message. It isn't used lightly, which means she needs me. Right now.

There are, however, a couple of issues. First...

I look over at Mia. Her expression has changed. She's frowning. Confused. Concerned. She can tell something's not right. But she doesn't know me. Not really. She doesn't know who I am or what I've done, and I would very much like to keep it that way.

I turn around and stare blankly at the display above the double doors.

Twenty-eight. Nine more floors to go.

The second issue is, if Ruby's in trouble, who the fuck is in my elevator?

10

I have a gun stashed in the kitchen. Y'know... for emergencies. That's the nearest one to me right now. My gaze is torn between the ever-climbing number above the elevator and the look of bewilderment on Mia's face. It's been changing gradually over the last couple of minutes from confusion to concern, presumably based on the look on mine.

Thirty-two.

Five more floors. Maybe twenty seconds, if I'm lucky.

I need to make a decision.

The elevator is obviously not an option. We could make it out the door and into the hall, but I have to assume even the most half-assed attempt to take me out in my own home would still have people covering the stairs. Sure, I could fight my way out, but the hallway and stairwell are narrow, with fewer opportunities for cover if needed. Plus, I have Mia's safety to think about.

Mia.

This isn't fair on her. In fact, this is *exactly* why I didn't want her getting too close. My life, no matter how well it seems to be going, will invariably turn into a shit-show for anyone else in it. Is that cynical and negative of me? Probably. But you have to admit, I have a point. Bottom line: she doesn't need to know who I really am, what I'm capable of, and what kind of life I lead.

Unfortunately, it doesn't look as if there's any avoiding that now. The sensible option would be to stay right where we are. It's a huge, open space. There's cover available behind the sofa or kitchen counter if needed. Mia can disappear upstairs. Whoever steps out of that elevator won't make it past me.

Speaking of which... I need to prepare for *who* this could be. Ruby's Yakuza boyfriend from last night? No, he's a nobody. Even if shit *had* gone sideways for her, there's no way that little prick would take her out.

Retribution for the Santo job yesterday?

Unlikely, but it's the only thing that makes any sense right now.

Shit.

Shit, dammit, shit, shit, fuck...

Thirty-six. One more floor.

I turn to Mia as I move behind the kitchen counter. I gesture her toward me with my hand, holding it out for her to hold.

"Hey, come here a sec, would you?"

She does.

I try to stand casually, leaning on the counter, with both hands facing the living room, as she shuffles a little awkwardly beside me. I slowly move my right hand to my side, blindly reaching for the handle to the drawer where I keep one of my 1911s. The spare, just in case. I'm still fast. The drawer will be open, and the gun will be out, aimed, with my finger on the trigger in less than two seconds. Plenty of time to take out a bunch of assholes stupid enough to think coming for me in my home is a good idea.

Thirty-seven.

The elevator dings as it arrives on our floor. My right hand grips the handle. My left wraps gently around Mia's wrist, ready to move.

"Adrian, are you okay?" she asks. "What's going on?"

I shake my head slowly. "Nothing. Just do as I say, all right? I'm not—"

The doors slide open.

I begin opening the drawer.

One man steps out. No visible weapon. He looks around the apartment, a genuine look of awe on his face. His old, leathery face is obscured by a long, thin, gray beard.

I frown. "Ichiro?"

I relax my grip on the drawer and Mia. Walk around the counter to greet him.

"What are you doing here?"

His gaze is momentarily drawn to Mia. He shrugs. "Can a man not visit with his friend?"

His smile is broad and genuine.

I raise an eyebrow. "Um, sure he can..."

I move closer to him, distancing myself further from Mia. We're only inches apart, standing close to the open elevator doors.

"Ichi, what are you doing here?" I whisper. "How do you know where I live? And how did you access the private elevator without my keycard?"

He chuckles quietly. "You insult me, *Shinigami*." He looks around the place as he talks, to remain discreet. "I wasn't aware you had company. And such attractive company, at that..."

"That's... ah... that's not what it looks like."

He looks at me and beams. "No need to justify yourself to me, Adrian." He playfully slaps my cheek a couple of times. "If ever someone needed *sekkusu*, it's you, my friend."

He walks toward the counter, with his arms wide to greet Mia.

I close my eyes and shake my head slightly to myself.

Sekkusu means sex.

Seriously, why does everyone think I'm in dire need of getting laid?

He embraces Mia, laughing. She still looks confused but a little more relaxed. She's smiling and looking at me over his shoulder, silently asking me what the hell is happening.

I couldn't tell her if I wanted to.

I walk over to join them. As nice as it is seeing Ichiro, I don't have time for this. Not right now.

"Mia, this is my friend, Ichiro. Ichiro, this is Mia."

He steps back and places his hands on her cheeks. "Mia! Mia, Mia, Mia... you have the appearance of... angel from Heaven. It is pleasure to meet you."

Her cheeks flush a little.

I roll my eyes and place a hand on Ichi's shoulder. "All right, *Casanova*, take it easy."

He steps back, chuckling.

I look at Mia. "Would you mind giving us a minute?"

She nods, smiling, appearing more relaxed than before. "Of course. I'll... ah... I'll go freshen up."

She quick-steps upstairs.

I lean back against the counter. Fold my arms across my chest. Stare at Ichiro as Ruby's message replays over and over in my mind.

"Listen, now isn't a good time, Ichi," I say to him. "But you being here can't be a coincidence. What's going on, man?"

He looks around, as if worried he'll be overheard.

"Your friend. She in trouble."

I nod. "I know. I just found out. How do *you* know?"

"Word travels fast, *Shinigami*."

I frown again. "How fast, exactly? I received a text message from her about ten minutes ago. How could you possibly have found out and got here in that space of time?"

He chuckles. Not with humor. With awkwardness. Almost with apologies. "Word travels fast for *me*. You... I'm afraid you are a little late to party. Your friend in trouble the moment she left last night's race."

"What? With that street racer? How do you know about that douchebag?"

Ichi frowns. "That *douche... bag...* works for Kazawa."

"The guy Santo wanted me to kill for him?"

He nods. "Ruby in bad place, *Shinigami*. Real bad place."

"Why? Where is she? And what—wait a minute... you said Ruby. How do you know her name?

He shakes his head with mild disbelief. "You are too slow! She comes to me for work, just like you."

My eyes pop wide. "*You're* her contact?"

"What?" he says, shrugging. "She asked for discretion, same way you did. I am man of my word."

I don't know if she knew we had the same contact or not, but that would explain her reluctance to tell me.

Not that it matters right now.

"Whatever. What do you know that I need to know, Ichi?"

"After race, she was taken to Golden Tiger. It is nightclub owned by Kazawa."

"And she's being held in there? I find that hard to believe. I don't think there are enough men on this planet to make her do something she doesn't want to."

He shakes his head. His mouth forms an uncharacteristically grave line amidst his beard. "Not in the club... beneath it."

A sudden explosion of dread goes off deep inside my gut. "And what's beneath it?"

He looks away. "Another type of club. A very bad place. A place where they torture... they film... they sell. People pay good money to go there. To take part. To purchase."

"Sonofabitch. Purchase what?"

Ichiro's mouth tenses to form a grave line. "Organs, *Shinigami*."

I stand straight. Take out the gun from the drawer without hesitating. I check the mag. Check the safety. Tuck it at my back, covering it with my shirt.

"Where is it?" I ask him.

He shakes his head again, more urgently this time. "No. No. This isn't somewhere you just walk in off the street. Even at this time, it will be full of Yakuza—foot soldiers... street dealers. It is big operation for Kazawa. You won't make it through door."

I place a hand on his shoulder again and smile. Partly to offer comfort. Mostly because I feel sorry for him that he should have so little faith in me.

"Watch me."

"Adrian. Seriously..."

"Ichi, if anyone has harmed so much as a single hair on Ruby's head, I'll reduce this entire city to rubble just to make sure that nightclub and everyone inside it are nothing but a memory."

He holds my gaze for a long moment, then places his

hand on top of mine, patting it gently. "You know what? I believe you… you scary, scary bastard."

I nod a silent thank you and move to the bottom of the stairs. A moment later, Mia steps into view, dressed as she was the night before.

"Listen, I gotta go," I call to her. "I don't want you to think I'm—"

She waves me away, smiling as she descends toward me. "I figured you probably have something important to do. It's fine. I should get going anyway." As she steps off the final stair, she moves close, leans up, and kisses my cheek. "We should do this again."

I smile. "Yeah, we should."

She moves past me, heading for the elevator. She turns and glances over her shoulder. Waves at Ichiro. "It was nice to meet you."

He chuckles. "The pleasure was mine, sweet angel."

She disappears inside, and the number above it begins to count down as she heads for the first floor.

I turn to Ichi and roll my eyes. "Will you knock it off? You're making me look bad."

He directs his chuckle at me as it graduates to a belly laugh. "You may be *Shinigami*, but you still have much to learn when it comes to women."

I shake my head as I grab my jacket off the back of a chair, heading for the elevator. "I swear, if you call me 'Daniel-san,' I'm going to shoot you."

I take my Pilot from my jacket pocket and place it in my ear. I have the Ili too, in case I need it. Although, I suspect there won't be much need for me to talk where I'm going.

Ichiro appears beside me. "All the crane kicks in world cannot help you now."

I shrug the jacket on and tap the gun at my back, for

97

reassurance. It's fully loaded. Eight rounds, plus one in the chamber. No spare mags to hand. Nine bullets mean the first nine people I see are already dead. If there's more, I'll reach down their throats and tear out their fucking lungs.

We stand side by side, watching silently as the display reaches zero. After a long minute, it begins counting back up.

I look over at him. "Ichi, I wouldn't ask you to help me. I wouldn't want to put you in that position."

He nods solemnly. "I know."

"So, please don't think you have to or anything."

He turns to me and smiles. "I don't. And I'm not going to. I like my life. No intention ending it today, or watching you commit suicide, you crazy American asshole."

I nod and smile back, then resume staring at the display, waiting for the elevator to reappear with growing impatience.

"Fair enough."

A couple of minutes later, the lift arrives. The doors slide effortlessly open, and I step inside. Ichiro follows. I hit the button for the first floor, and the doors close again.

I'm coming for you, Ruby. Just hang in there.

I'm coming.

11

Ichiro was kind enough to drop me a couple of blocks away from the Golden Tiger. His car was... interesting, in that it wasn't so much a car as it was a giant roller skate with two doors. I folded myself into the passenger seat, where I sat for over twenty minutes with my knees practically pinned to the side of my head.

Still, it was quicker than walking here, and time is very much of the essence.

I'm standing across the street from the club, which occupies a large corner plot opposite. A huge neon sign hangs lifelessly above the red doors. It's hard to make out what image it displays during the day, when it's not glowing. I'm guessing it's a tiger.

The clouds are low and gray. Slivers of dawn remain, giving the world a dull hue. The wind rushes purposefully around me, but I stand relaxed, ignoring the low temperatures it carries with it.

I take deep, slow breaths.

The old me—the me from a couple years ago—would already have kicked that door down and started shooting at whatever moved inside. I would be seeing the world in a blood-red haze, thinking of nothing except getting Ruby out of there safely.

And don't get me wrong, it's taking a considerable amount of effort and self-control *not* to do that. But the new me—the *sensible* me—knows that isn't the right move. At least, not yet.

The city is already teeming with life. Sidewalks are shoulder-to-shoulder as far as the eye can see in all directions. Traffic is congested. The circles I move around in notwithstanding, general gun crime is almost non-existent in Japan. If bullets start flying now, every police officer and news reporter in a fifty-mile radius will be on my ass faster than I can blink. And just like that, the me who, not so long ago, was the most wanted man on the planet will suddenly be back in the spotlight, for the same reason I was the first time. Except this time, there's no public presidential pardons to bail me out.

So, if I'm going to save Ruby and make sure our new life is still here for her to get back to, I need to think of another way of playing this.

Aww, our boy's all grown up!

Shut up, Josh.

Y'know, you could always take out the first few guys with your hands... keep it all nice and quiet until you're further inside, where your gunshots won't be heard.

You're not helping, Satan.

I stare over at the building until my vision blurs. I've always known I have a habit of overthinking, despite my history of acting impulsively. In an effort to stop being both a walking contradiction *and* a bullet magnet, I've found calming my mind puts me in this almost meditative state, so I see things clearly. I've always stayed detached from my job in an emotional sense, but it's as if this detaches me *physically*, giving me a better view of the task at hand.

Seriously, dude, when did you learn that?

Josh remains a sarcastic pain in my ass, even when he's part of my subconscious.

I don't even know. It just kind of came to me one day that it might be a better way of doing things.

It's only taken you twenty years. I can't believe you waited until I was dead...

Seriously, will you shut up? I'm trying to concentrate.

All right, keep your panties on! Jesus...

I roll my eyes to myself and re-focus.

Ichiro said Ruby was being held underneath the night-club, so underground... maybe two levels. There will be a protected entrance inside, guarded so that not just anyone can access it. That makes sense. But wouldn't there be another way in or out? It's the same with my apartment—we have the stairs as well as the elevator, for emergencies. Wouldn't this place have an additional way of getting out, if for no other reason than health and safety regulations? It might be an illegal, Yakuza-run torture porn club, but I doubt Tetsuo Kazawa would want his rich, piece of shit customers trapped down there in the event of a fire.

So, where would that other exit be?

I scan along the street, away from the main entrance of the club. The building stretches almost half a block away to the right. It's separated from the next building along by an alley that I can just about see from where I'm standing.

I think we might have a winner.

I pick my spot and jog across the busy road. I slow to a

casual stroll, dig my hands into my jacket pockets, and amble past the club. I gaze absently around as I pass. I spot two security cameras—one above the entrance and one further along, facing the entrance to the alley.

That's not ideal.

It's easy enough to obscure my face from it, but you should always think worst-case. The worst case here is someone's watching the feed from that camera right now. That same someone will see the figure of a tall man turning into the alley at the back of their nightclub before nine in the morning. The worst case is that the someone monitoring the security feeds is as paranoid as I am. Which means seeing me will set alarms bells off, and I'll be greeted by an army of Yakuza before I even discover if there's an entrance down there or not.

I approach the entrance to the alley. Time to make a decision. I need to be smart, but I can't forget Ruby's in there somewhere, enduring God-knows-what from these assholes.

...

...

...

I walk past the alley without hesitation. Just another pedestrian, navigating the sea of humanity, on their way to who-knows-where. I reach the end of the street and turn left.

Plan B.

The building on the next corner is a restaurant. It's modest in size compared to some but one of the finer places to eat, judging by the look of it through the window. It's not open, but I can see movement inside. Cleaning staff, maybe. Or the owners.

The back way out of this place should put me on, or

near, the alley at the back of the club. I'm sure there'll be another camera around the back, but if I'm coming out of the restaurant, anyone watching might not worry as much.

I step into the shallow doorway and tap on the glass. It takes me a couple of attempts, but finally, someone inside looks over at the door. I smile and wave innocently. It's a small, older woman, wearing an apron and rubber gloves. She shakes her head and gestures with her hands, presumably telling me they're not open yet.

I give her the thumbs up, still smiling, and gesture her over to the door.

Come on, lady. I need a break.

She totters toward me, looking impatient. Stops next to the glass on the other side of the door. Repeats the gesture she just gave me.

I tilt my head to the side and tap a finger to my Pilot—the new universal gesture to show someone you have the means to understand them. I quickly turn on my Ili too.

"We... closed!" she yells through the glass.

I nod slowly back. "I know. I... I left a bag here last night. Can I please get it?"

She holds my gaze, frowning.

...

...

...

She nods and unlocks the door.

Showtime.

I don't have an awful lot of time to play the part and talk my way through, so I'll opt for a more assertive approach.

I step inside and immediately take her hand and begin shaking it.

"Thank you. This means a lot," I say in an overly happy tone. I maneuver around her, into the restaurant. "It'll be in the back, I'm sure. I won't keep you—I'll just go and get it. I won't be a moment. Thank you again. This really helps!"

And with that, I let go and walk briskly through the place, ignoring the décor completely as I head behind the counter and into the kitchens. I hear her shouting after me, but I don't look around. I navigate the cooking stations and the piles of trash bags and make a beeline for the service door, which I'm hoping leads—

Bingo!

I step out into the alley I walked past moments earlier. I'm almost at the opposite end of it. I glance to my left and see people crossing the entrance on the street. To my right, a couple of dumpsters stand haphazardly against a wall, maybe ten feet away. A dead end.

Farther along the opposite wall, heading away from me, I see two doors. The first is a set of double doors with a small canopy above them, shielding a security light. There's a camera positioned above it and to the right, pointing directly at them. That will be the normal way out of the club, or maybe a more discreet entrance for select clientele.

I think the door I want is the one a few meters beyond that. I can just about make out the top corner of it at the bottom of a narrow set of stairs attached to the wall that descend into apparent darkness. There aren't any railings or barriers protecting the gap and the stairs, which is perhaps why I didn't spot it on my way past before. I see two more cameras—one to the left of the stairs, facing them so you can see the face of anyone who walks down them, and one on the wall opposite, attached to the side of the restaurant. I'm doubtful it's theirs, as it's also facing the stairs. I imagine the restaurant owners didn't object too much when asked if they could install the camera there.

That's *definitely* my way in, but I can't see any way of

actually getting inside without being picked up by at least two cameras.

Goddammit.

For all I know, I could be standing directly above Ruby right now. I'm so close, it's infuriating.

I'm telling you, man... just rush the place. You'll be fine!

My ever-helpful Inner Satan.

He might be right, though. At least going in the back way would give me some element of surprise, compared to kicking down the front door.

Honestly, what would Ruby do if she were me right now?

...

...

...

She'd strut in there, naked as the day she was born, and slaughter everyone without hesitation.

Well, I'm not getting naked for anyone, but...

I whip out my 1911, flick the safety off, snap my aim steady, and fire three rounds in quick succession. All three security cameras pop, fizzle, and smoke as they're destroyed. The suppressor did a decent job of keeping the noise down, and the bustle of the busy streets beyond the alley will take care of any travelling sound.

Six rounds left.

I walk hurriedly toward the stairs and descend them with careful steps. I pause at the door. It looks solid. I have to assume it's locked.

Now that three cameras have been disabled, whoever's inside likely knows I'm coming. Or, at least, that *someone* is coming. If I were them, my money would be on whoever it is coming through this door right here, which means once this opens, it's game on.

I take a deep breath, steeling my nerves and feeding off the rush of adrenaline.

In for a penny...

I raise my gun, glance away, and fire a round just above the handle. The lock pops and the frame splinters. The door rocks on its hinges, creating a gap maybe an inch wide. I step back and blast it open with a sturdy boot. With my gun raised, senses heightened and battle ready, I move inside.

...in for a pound.

12

The narrow corridor ahead of me is lit by crimson bulbs, stationed intermittently along the walls behind a thin glass shade. The walls, along with the floor and the ceiling, are all dark. Perhaps not black but close to it in this low light. It's like whoever designed this place went through the checklist of requirements for a stereotypical lap-dancing bar and made sure they ticked every box.

There are three doors along each side, with a set of double doors at the far end, barely visible in the ambience. I doubt I'll be lucky enough to find Ruby in one of these rooms near the exit, but you never know. My gut says I need the doors at the end, but I'll check each of these rooms as I pass anyway.

I take slow, cautious steps down the corridor, my gun held low and ready. I approach the first door on my left and wrap my hand gently around the handle, listening for any movement inside.

...

...

...

I hear... I don't know. I hear *something*. Not voices but muffled sounds.

I check my watch.

This place can't still be open, surely?

I hear something else too. Movement. Delicate footsteps. I can't tell if it's from inside the room, or...

Behind me!

I spin around, levelling my gun so it's aiming right between the eyes of—

"Mia?"

My mouth drops open slightly. Mia's standing in front of me, close to the wall, with an expression on her face like a puppy standing next to a freshly chewed shoe.

"What the hell are you doing here?" I hiss.

She looks away momentarily. "I... ah... I followed you. I'm so sorry!"

"Jesus! Why?"

"Because! I... I want to be a journalist, remember? My instincts were telling me you were caught up in something. When your old friend came to your apartment, I saw the change in you. Like something was wrong. I was... I dunno —curious, I guess."

I lower my gun, suddenly aware I'm still aiming it at her.

"Mia... you need to leave, okay? Right now. This isn't the type of place you should be in. And I'm not the type of guy you should be following."

"Yeah, I... I see that." She swallows hard. Her eyes are focused on anything except me. "Why do you have a gun?"

I hesitate, frustrated that I failed to hide this part of me from her.

"Look, I guess I do owe you some kind of explanation, but now isn't the time, all right? You remember Ruby, my friend?"

She nods.

"Well, she's in trouble. I'm here to make sure she's okay."

Mia frowns. "What kind of trouble?"

"The worst kind."

"But... this is just some crappy nightclub. How much trouble can she—"

"This crappy nightclub is owned by the Yakuza. And the bit of it we're in right now isn't where you come to drink and dance with your friends. This is where rich, powerful assholes come to do horrible things to innocent people. And someone brought Ruby here."

She puts her hands to her mouth and gasps. "Oh my God! Shouldn't we call the police or something?"

I shake my head. "The police won't care. Chances are, the people who own this place have paid them off anyway."

I look back at the way I came in. Thinking about it, I can't send her out there on her own. There's no way whoever's here doesn't know someone's coming. There could be anyone waiting out there. I hate to admit it, but right now, she's probably safer with me.

I put my hand on her shoulder. She flinches for a second but soon relaxes.

"Mia, it'll be okay, I promise. But now you're here, it's too dangerous to send you away on your own, and I can't leave until I have Ruby. So, you're gonna have to stick with me."

She nods hurriedly. "O-o-okay."

"You've gotta stay quiet, stay behind me, and do exactly what I say."

She nods again.

"And..." I let out a heavy breath. "You might see me do

things that aren't very nice. But I swear to you, I'm not a bad guy, okay?"

She looks away, then puts her hand on my arm. "I know. You're a good person, Adrian. You saved me the other night. Now you're going to save your friend. Whatever you do, it's okay. I understand. You're a... hero."

She smiles innocently.

I smile back, uncomfortable and embarrassed.

"I'm... ah... I'm a lot of things, Mia. But I'm not a hero. Now come on. The sooner we find Ruby, the sooner we can get out of here."

I move to the door and slowly turn the handle, not wanting to startle whoever might be on the other side of it. My grip tightens around the butt of my gun. I glance down at it for reassurance. The suppressor's in place. I know it's still holding five rounds.

I don't know why I'm so hesitant to push the door open. I guess I don't want to find Ruby in a bad way. Or worse. That said, from what Ichiro told me about this place, who knows *what* I'll find in here. I don't want to expose Mia to anything too...

I let out a short breath.

Come on, Adrian. Man the hell up already.

"Wait here," I whisper to Mia. "Don't make a sound."

I slowly push the door open and step inside.

...

...

...

The room's empty.

There's a bed in the left corner, nearest the door. There's some kind of weird... I don't know what it is—a *structure* in the opposite right corner. It's wooden, with leather restraints in various positions.

I honestly don't want to know.

The noise I heard is coming from a large flat-screen TV mounted on the opposite wall, playing an X-rated movie. I stare at it a moment, frowning.

What *is* that woman doing? What's that she's...

My eyes snap wide as I realize what I'm looking at. I quickly turn around and leave, closing the door behind me.

I'm pretty sure that was a horse.

I shake my head.

I'm not going to un-see *that* image for a while!

Jesus...

"Are you okay?" asks Mia.

I nod. "Yeah. Don't go in there."

Her expression changes. She looks bemused. "Okay..."

I open the next four doors, alternating right, then left. Each one is as empty as the first, with similar devices set up in them. One even had a video camera on a tripod aimed at a bed.

I'm outside the last room on the left before the end of the corridor.

I feel an involuntary shudder travel along my spine.

Seriously, this place is fucking weird.

There's still no sign of life. More importantly, there's still no sign of any heavily-armed Yakuza foot soldiers trying to kill me. Maybe I was worrying about nothing, and nobody was monitoring the security cameras?

I grab the handle and push open the sixth door. At least I haven't seen—

"What the fuck?"

Did I say that out loud? I definitely *thought* it.

In front of me is a man and a woman on a bed. Both turn and look over.

Yeah... I said that out loud.

Shit.

The man is short, overweight, and naked. He's wearing a leather balaclava that obscures everything except his eyes and nose. He's on his knees, holding what looks to be some kind of whip with a purposely frayed end. The woman is also naked, with a gag ball strapped around her head, resting in her mouth. She's on all fours in front of him. I hear her whimpering. To my left is a computer with a webcam set up, aimed at the couple.

I step inside the room. Now I'm nearer to them, I can see the woman's body more clearly. She's very petite, probably mid-thirties, with long dark hair.

"Holy shit..."

Her back is shredded. Flesh has been stripped away, and thin streams of blood flow freely from the open wounds.

I glance at the man, then at the computer, quickly putting two and two together in my head. My guess is people are paying to watch this guy flay this poor woman alive. For a *very* brief moment, I consider the possibility that this is staged in some way. That the woman is a willing participant. That perhaps this is all an act designed to con sick bastards out of the fortunes they likely don't deserve.

But one look at the woman's face tells me that's not the case. The tears are real, and the fear and defeat in her eyes tells me she most certainly *isn't* willing.

I look at my gun again. Then back at the man. Then at the gun once more.

I should save the bullets.

I tuck it behind me and stride over to the bed. Without slowing, I step and thrust my right boot as hard as I can into the side of the guy's head. He flies into the wall, grunting and moaning from the impact.

I move quickly, aware that everything that's happening is

probably being streamed live across the internet. I yank the bedsheet off and throw it over the woman. I remove the gag and take a moment to wrap the blanket properly around her. She's shaking, terrified.

"It's over now," I say, letting my Ili do the work as I try to offer some comfort. "Get out of here, okay? Fast as you can."

She scurries off the bed and huddles in the far corner, staring at me through tear-filled eyes.

I look over at the man, who's just starting to move again.

"And you, you twisted sonofabitch…" I rip the mask from his head, revealing his sweaty, ugly face, and grab the whip he dropped when I hit him. "Let's see how *you* like it!"

I wind up and smash the whip across his face. The leather is tough and thick. The crack echoes around the room. I hear the instant tearing sound as the flesh on his face splits in multiple places. He goes to scream but passes out before the sound can pass his lips. He falls backward on the bed, lying sprawled out and unconscious on the blood-stained sheets.

His face is a mess.

There are five long, deep horizontal slices across it. It looks as if he's been mauled by a tiger. The skin is shredded and covered in thick blood. His brow is split open, and his left eye is bulging unnaturally—stained red from, I'm guessing, a burst blood vessel.

Don't think I'd be very good at this bondage thing. I hit people way too hard.

I regard him for a moment, giving myself a chance to find an ounce of humanity inside me to perhaps feel some compassion for him.

…

…

…

Nope. The piece of shit deserved it.

I hear a loud gasp behind me. I turn to see Mia standing in the doorway, her eyes wide with shock. A hand clasped to her mouth.

That isn't ideal, but there's little I can do about it now. I don't know how much she saw. I'm guessing enough, judging by her reaction.

I walk over to the computer. I lean forward and flip both middle fingers at the camera. "Get off on *that*, you sick bastards."

I upturn the desk, sending the equipment crashing to the floor. I stamp down hard on the camera as I make my way out of the room, ushering Mia out ahead of me.

"I told you to stay out here," I say to her, my hands on her shoulders.

Her eyes are still wide and watering. "I wanted to see... you just... what was that man doing?"

"Nothing you should concern yourself with. Now look— this isn't a nice place, and to make sure I find Ruby and get all three of us out of here safely, you *gotta* do what I say. If I ask you to stay outside the room, stay outside the goddamn room. Okay?"

I feel bad being so firm, but it's for her own good. I can concern myself with the repercussions of her seeing this side of me later. Right now, I just need to keep her safe.

She nods silently. Her face relaxes. She blinks rapidly and stares at the floor.

"Good."

I look over at the poor woman in the corner and gesture to the door with a nod. "Go. Get out of here."

She scrambles to her feet and runs past us, through the door and back along the corridor. I watch her until she disappears outside.

Satisfied she's safe, I look back at Mia. "Now come on."

We approach the double doors at the end of the corridor. Seeing that back there has put me in a real bad mood. The kind of bad mood that silences the sensible part of my brain. The kind of bad mood that uses ammunition to make a point.

An image of that woman flashes into my mind. I see her huddled beneath the blanket, broken and defeated, her body torn and vulnerable. Then I see Ruby, and I'm forced to picture her the same way.

I take out my 1911 again. I grip it so tightly that I feel the color pulse from my knuckles.

No voice of reason is going to stop me now. The time for strategy and diplomacy is over.

"Keep behind me," I say without looking around. "Once we're through these doors, find something to hide behind and stay there."

I don't wait for a response. I kick the double doors in front of me, sending them flying open. They both slam against the walls on either side. I step over the threshold and quickly take in the layout of the inner sanctum. It's a large, open space, almost circular, with doors on all four compass points. I'm standing in the south doorway. At the center is a raised oval platform, possibly used as a stage. There's a pole in the middle of it.

The walls are adorned with a host of... equipment. Everything from sex toys to power drills, baseball bats with nails through the end to flamethrowers, swords to screwdrivers... all on display like some sadistic museum.

Ichiro wasn't kidding about this place.

The north and west doors are closed. The east doors are open, and a man in a suit is standing by them, just inside this room. He's staring right at me, frozen to the spot with a look of confusion and fear on his face. He appears young. His skin is unblemished, his dark hair styled, his suit freshly pressed. Perhaps a new member of the family, eager to make a good impression.

His body language suggests he just spun around, alerted by my indiscreet entrance. The fact he's guarding those doors suggests that's probably the way I need to go.

Sucks to be him right now.

I snap my arm level and squeeze the trigger, aiming on instinct. The bullet finds its mark, as I knew it would. It burrows its way into his forehead and explodes out the other side, splashing a cocktail of gray matter, thick crimson, and bone fragments across the wall. His body falls backward almost instantly, landing just out of my line of sight behind some seating near the open doors.

Four rounds left.

I glance behind me. Mia is ducked behind a booth, shaking quietly.

I make my way across the room, moving counterclockwise around the oval stage, toward the east doors. I turn to head through them and see light shining through a crack in the door ahead, at the end of another, much shorter corridor.

Let's just hope I—

There's movement behind me. Multiple pairs of footsteps rush into position. I hear the mechanical sound of weapons being primed.

—didn't attract any attention.

I turn around slowly.

Well, shit.

Many years ago, I acquired the ability to absorb huge amounts of information from a split-second look. I have a highly functional short-term memory, which is very useful in situations such as this one. I knew there were guns before I turned around because I heard them. Therefore, I know I have no more than a couple of seconds to run through potential scenarios and make decisions that will determine whether or not I'm alive at lunchtime.

In the first second, I count eight hostiles—four from the north doorway to my right, and four from the west doorway straight ahead of me. They're all wearing matching suits, identical to the one on the dead body at my feet. Some of them have ties, others have an open neck. Best guess, they work at the club.

I also count eight handguns. Now, I'm no mathematician, but given I have four bullets in my gun, some would argue the odds aren't exactly in my favor.

The final second was spent planning my attack. I see no option for defense here. There's no cover except where Mia is, and I don't want to attract attention to her. The corridor behind me has no doors besides the one at the end, so I can't turn tail and run down there—I wouldn't make it three feet. My only option is to attack. I consider maybe five alternatives before settling on what I'm going to do.

I take a deep breath. And another.

Here goes nothing.

13

I run toward the group directly ahead of me. Three or four steps into my sprint, my right arm is up, pointing sideways. As I draw level with the other group by the north doors, I open fire. Four rounds in quick succession.

No one's reacted yet. I gambled on nobody considering I would be stupid or crazy enough to run at them.

It paid off.

The group was huddled together in the small space by the doors, so they were sitting ducks. I didn't commit more than a glance in their direction as I fired. I know I dropped two of them for sure. Maybe a third, but he could've just been reacting to the gunfire. I'll check in a moment.

As the hammer thumps onto an empty chamber, I discard the weapon and jump. I'm moving at a good speed and get significant height as I push off. Bracing for the impact, I bring both feet up, dropkicking the closest guy to me in the group by the west doors. I make a solid connection with his chest, and he flies back into his colleagues.

I hit the floor hard. I force myself down and take the brunt of the impact on my shoulders. The air is temporarily jolted from my lungs, but I don't have time to worry about trivial things like breathing. I roll toward the oval stage, onto my front, and push myself upright as quickly as I can.

The group by the west doors are scattered across the floor. The guy I hit dropped his gun. I scoop it up and take aim at the north doors, taking a valuable second to catch my breath and reassess the situation.

I hit three of them. The fourth is about to shoot at me.

BANG! BANG!

I put two in his chest. He collapses lifelessly to the floor.

I spin to face the remaining group. The guy whose gun I'm holding is almost vertical again. I step toward him and slam my elbow into his temple. It's a solid connection, and his legs buckle as consciousness rushes from him. As he falls away to the floor, I take aim and fire another two rounds, putting a bullet in each of the chests of the next two guys in the group.

They tumble to the floor and sprawl awkwardly over one another, restricting the movement of the fourth guy. He manages to get a couple of shots off. Thankfully, despite such close quarters, the bullets whizz a few inches over my head.

Still, that was pretty close...

I fire two more rounds, aiming first at his legs, then at his shoulder. The first round shatters his kneecap, and he drops to the floor. The second clipped his collarbone—a clean hit, through and through. Neither is life-threatening, although that one in his knee is going to hurt like a bitch for a long time.

I think that's everyone.

I turn a slow circle, checking for survivors. No one's moving. I walk over to my discarded 1911 and retrieve it.

"Enough!"

Uh-oh.

I straighten and look at the east doors ahead of me.

Shit.

The driver from last night is standing there, flanked by the same two ballsacks he had with him at the race meet. Ruby is next to him. Her dress is dirty and torn. Her face is bruised. The driver has a knife to her throat.

The world freezes. I stare at Ruby, forgetting everything else around me. Her legs are shaking. Not through fear, but through the effort of being upright. Someone's done a real number on her. When I find out which one of these pricks it was, I'm going to make them wish they were never born.

"So, it's true. The man himself is here."

Huh?

I look to my right, back over at the doors I kicked open with...

"Mia!"

Another man has appeared there, wearing a dark suit, a shirt, and no tie. His black hair is spiked. He has three men with him. All dressed casually. All holding handguns.

I recognize him immediately.

Tetsuo Kazawa.

He's standing behind Mia, who's hugging herself and whimpering. His hand is on her neck, keeping her firmly in place. He's tall, maybe an inch shorter than me. His broad frame is detailed by sinewy muscle, visible through the dark, fitted outfit he's wearing. The unblemished skin on his face is covered by the makings of an equally dark beard. His mouth forms a perpetual smirk, borne of arrogance and privilege.

I glance back at Ruby before stepping toward Kazawa. I make it two paces before he produces his own gun and aims it at me.

"That's far enough, Adrian Hell."

I stop. Hold my hands out to the sides. I look at Mia, desperate to make eye contact with her. To reassure her she'll be okay. But her eyes are closed. She's crying.

"Drop your weapons," orders Kazawa.

With little choice, I do.

"This is turning into a very profitable day, isn't it?" he continues, laughing to himself.

I shrug. "I think that depends which side of the gun you're standing on."

"Ko is a bright young man. Ambitious. Driven. When he brought your lady friend here last night, he saw potential. She is a... *fine* specimen, wouldn't you agree?" He pauses to chuckle to himself. "She will attract many buyers for her beautiful parts."

I look back at Ruby. Then at the driver. Now I know his name.

"It's Ko, right?" I ask him. "Did you do this to her? Did you lay a beating on her? Or did you get someone else to do it for you?"

Ko laughs, turns his head slightly, revealing an impressive bruise just below his ear.

"This bitch put up a hell of a fight... it took all three of us to put her in her place!"

I look at Ruby again. She smiles weakly. I nod to her.

Good for you, kiddo.

"That's good to know," I say to Ko. "Now, when I kill all three of you, at least you'll fully understand why."

Ko and his friends laugh. Then he buries his fist in Ruby's stomach. She keels over, coughing, but the other two guys hoist her upright without a moment's reprieve.

She looks at me. "Would you please... not antagonize... the Yakuza?"

"Sorry," I say, shrugging. Then I look back over at Kazawa. "And as for you, you should let the girl go before you get hurt."

Kazawa laughs. "You know who I am, right?"

"I do. Believe it or not, yesterday, somebody tried to hire me to kill you."

His expression changes. It's subtle, but he fails to mask his concern.

"Really? Who?"

"Relax. I killed him."

He lowers his gun. Smiles. "How kind."

"Yeah, I'm a real saint. Listen, seeing as you technically owe me one, how about you let the two ladies go? Keep me instead? What do you say?"

Kazawa pauses. His eyes narrow.

Is he... is he considering it? That would be a stroke of good fortune. Sort of.

He thrusts Mia away from him, sending her stumbling forward. I step to catch her. She collapses into my arms. I hold her up, place a hand on her cheek, and tilt her face toward mine.

"You're safe now, Mia. I promise."

I drag her behind me, making sure my body is between her and the two groups of men at my ten and two respectively.

Kazawa gestures to Mia. "I let *her* go. Your other friend, she's mine. I already have buyers lined up. She will perform. Then she will be dissected."

"You want her, you gotta go through me."

He smiles. "Oh, I intend to. You see, the only reason she is still alive is because I knew you would come after her. Your dear Ruby was kind enough to confirm Ko's suspicions about who you were. Your reputation and predictability precede you. He proposed we use her as bait. Like I said— smart boy."

Behind me, Mia grips my arm. She moves to my side.

"Adrian... what's he talking about? Why would these people recognize you?"

I curse silently to myself. "It's nothing, Mia. A case of mistaken identity. Nothing we can't resolve."

Kazawa steps theatrically toward me, gesturing with his gun like a conductor heading an orchestra.

"Oh! Oh! This is too good!" He points the barrel at Mia. I step back in front of her. "Your little friend... she doesn't know who you are, does she?"

He moves the gun, so it's resting against my forehead. I stand my ground. Stand tall. Fuck him.

"Tell her," he says.

"No."

Uh!

Christ, that hurt...

Kazawa just jabbed the butt of his gun into my temple. The movement was fast. I barely saw it.

The gun's back against my head.

"Yes," he says.

I close my eyes.

Dammit.

"Fine." I turn to Mia. "The truth is... this guy right here? Smallest dick in Tokyo. I swear to God, it's like a thumbtack."

Gah!

I drop to one knee as Kazawa smashes his gun into the back of my head.

Totally worth it.

"You think you're funny, Adrian?" he asks.

I look up at him. "Well, it made me laugh..."

He drags me up by my collar. Holds me so I'm facing Mia. Puts the gun to my head.

"Tell her who you are, or I'll kill you where you stand," he says. "Fuck the profits."

I believe him.

I look at Mia. I stare into her innocent eyes, full of youth and promise. And fear. I take a deep breath. I don't know why, but her finding out who I really am is harder to deal with than I imagined it could be.

"Mia, I... I'm not who you think I am."

She frowns. Her gaze shifts to Kazawa, then back to me. "W-what do you mean? Adrian, what's going on? Who are you?"

I sigh. "The truth is, I'm out here in Tokyo trying to retire. I'm an assassin. Or, I *was*."

Behind me, Kazawa laughs. "But not just any assassin. He is the world's *greatest* assassin. Tell her, Adrian. Tell her what you did!"

I grind my teeth with frustration. Man, I want to knock this asshole's head clean off right now.

"You remember when President Cunningham was killed?"

Mia shrugs. "Of course. Everyone does..."

"Well, it was me who killed him."

She steps back, recoiling from me. "W-why would you even say that? I don't like this, Adrian. I want to leave!"

"I'm sorry, Mia, but it's true. The guy was the mastermind behind 4/17. He needed to be stopped. I'm the best killer this world has ever seen. It was my responsibility."

She sinks to her knees, covering her mouth with both hands. Her eyes bulge in their sockets. I think she might be hyperventilating.

I look back at Kazawa. "You happy now?"

"Very!"

I take a step toward Mia. "Are you okay? I'm sorry if you—"

"Who else have you killed?" she asks.

The question takes me by surprise.

"Uh..."

"Come on. Tell me! If you're supposedly this great assassin, or hitman—whatever you call yourself, who else have you killed? How many lives have you ended?"

"Honestly? I've killed a lot of people, Mia. I'm not proud of it, but I'm not ashamed of it either. It's who I am. Everyone I've killed had it coming, for one reason or another."

She gets to her feet and walks toward me. "Says who? You? Who are *you* to decide who should live or die? You're a fucking murderer!"

There's genuine, heartfelt anger in her voice. Her eyes are alive with venom. She's almost hysterical. And I can't say I blame her. She's young, and this is a lot to process, especially under these circumstances. She must be terrified. Adrenaline will carry her through this. At least she's forgotten the danger she's in right now, which is a blessing. But thanks to Kazawa, she now knows the real me...

And she hates me for it.

Still, I guess I'd rather have her hate me than try to deal with this shit.

I turn away from her and stare at Kazawa. Over his shoulder, I see Ruby. Her face is contorted with sympathy.

"I did what you asked," I say to him. "Now let her go. She has nothing to do with this."

He smiles. "Oh, I don't know about that."

Huh?

I look back at Mia. She's—

"Ah! A-a-a-a-ah! Uh! Shit!"

Oh my God! I'm flat on my back... I'm—

Hnnn! Hnnn!

My muscles... all of them... spasming...

I flail involuntarily on the floor. I have no control of my limbs. The pain is excruciating... every inch of my body is in shock.

What the hell was that?

...

...

...

The sensation subsides, replaced by a throbbing ache. I look up. Mia's standing over me. She's holding a... a... what *is* that? A taser?

What the fuck?

"M-Mia...? What are you... what are you doing?"

She's glaring down at me. The hatred is still there, but the fear has gone. Her eyes are dead, yet somehow alive at the same time.

I really don't understand what's happening right now.

...

...

...

Christ, even the voices in my head were shocked silent by that.

Mia steps over me. I fight against the leftover feeling of pins and needles and roll over. Push myself up to one knee. I look up at her as she...

She's kissing Kazawa!

And I mean, they're *really* going at it.

I look over at Ruby. Her expression mirrors my sentiments. She's frowning, possibly vomiting in her mouth, unable to believe what she's seeing.

After what seems like an eternity, they part and turn to face me. Mia crouches in front of me. Grips my chin with one hand and lifts my head, so I'm staring at her. There's something in her eyes. Something... primordial, burning within them. A malice of such intensity, I honestly don't recall ever having seen it before. Even in myself.

She spits in my face.

I see the punch coming but can do nothing to stop it. She lashes a left hook into the side of my head.

I eat every bit of it. It hit me so hard, I didn't even register the impact. I just opened my eyes and found myself flat on the floor again.

I push myself up on all fours. Try to gather my senses. Try to figure out what's going on.

I hear shouting. I look up to see Ko and his two sidekicks dragging Ruby into the center of the room. They're tying her to the pole, her arms above her head.

"I'm gonna rip your balls off, you little prick!" she yells.

Ko laughs and slashes the back of his hand across her face. The crack is loud and hollow. It echoes around me. The three of them check her restraints and step away, moving to Kazawa's side.

I bring one knee up, trying to stand, testing my balance. Kazawa, Ko, and his men are laughing among themselves.

Laughing at me. If I could get my ears to stop ringing, my vision to unblur, and my muscles to stop twitching for long enough, I'd beat the shit out of each one of them.

Where's Mia gone?

I turn to look behind me.

Ooof!

There she is.

Jesus! That felt like...

She crouches in front of me again. Bangs her fists together menacingly. She's wearing a set of brass knuckles on each hand.

Yeah, *that's* what that felt like.

"I've been waiting a lifetime for this, Adrian," she says.

She kicks me hard in the side. My ribs feel intact, but they're not happy. I roll away from her, hitting the side of the stage where Ruby's tied up.

Mia's on me in a heartbeat. She grabs my collar with both hands and props me up against the stage by Ruby's feet. She's deceptively strong. My head lolls back as I struggle to stay conscious. I look up at Ruby. She's talking. Probably yelling. But I can't hear her. It's as if someone hit the mute button on the world. She's staring at me. There's panic in her eyes.

I manage to lift my head. Mia's mounted me, kneeling across my stomach. Her hand wraps around my throat.

"You've had this coming for five... *fucking*... years!" she screams. Her words sound distant and shallow.

I try to protect myself, but my arms are numb and heavy. She rains down lethal blows, one after the other. My body, my chest, my face...

I felt the first couple.

The world keeps blinking out of existence and back again.

...

...

...

I see flashes of her face, twisted with primal rage. I see spurts of blood fly after each punch. I assume it's mine.

I'm... I'm done.

...

...

...

"Wake up, you bastard!"

...

...

...

"Wake! Up!"

...

...

...

My eye snap open. I lurch to the side, coughing. I spit blood out. A lot of blood. The bitter taste of copper lines my mouth. I feel my face, wondering why I can't open one of my eyes. Given how swollen it is to touch, I'm guessing it's been punched shut.

I take a deep breath, which instantly makes me yell out with pain.

Maybe my ribs took more damage from that kick than I thought.

I rest back against the stage again. My good eye is only half open. I can just about see Ruby. She's crying. And shouting.

Groggily, I roll my head around, so I'm staring at Kazawa. Mia is beside him. She's smiling. But it's not a happy smile. It's a sadistic smile. I've seen the same look before in the eyes of soldiers on a battlefield. A bloodlust that can't be satisfied.

That young girl—the one I saved from two assholes in a bar... the one I nearly slept with last night—has just laid a beating on me that was borderline inhuman. I've never been taken apart this badly in my life. I'm convinced I'm about to die.

I need to know...

"W-why?" I ask.

Mia walks toward me. She leans over with her hands on her knees, as if she's addressing a child.

"I'm not surprised you don't remember," she says. "You've been through a lot these last few years. But what's about to happen to you has been a long time coming, Adrian. All those nameless faces of the people you've killed... they might mean nothing to you. But one of them meant a great deal to me. You reap what you sow, you sonofabitch."

I try to speak but just cough up more blood.

...

...

...

Ugh! I wipe my mouth. Stare at the thick, dark stain on my hand.

Shit.

I relax back against the stage. Stare blankly into Mia's eyes.

"I don't... I don't remember. I'm sorry. Mia..."

She buries a fist into my gut. Pain explodes across my entire midsection, but my body's too broken and tired to react.

"My name isn't Mia. It's Miley." She pauses, as if waiting for me to suddenly figure out what all this is about. "Miley

Tevani. Five years ago, almost to the day, you killed my mother. And now, I'm going to destroy your legacy, your name, your reputation, your body... and *then* I'm going to kill you."

She straightens. Winds up a right hand. I see the lights reflect off the brass knuckles as her fist flies toward my—

14

??:??

Consciousness doesn't so much wash over me; it kind of trickles... like a broken faucet. My body is paralyzed from head to toe, yet, somehow, I can tell I'm upright. The only thing I can feel is my head. Not my face—just the base of my skull. It's like a police siren and a nightclub's bassline had a baby, and it's just repeatedly stabbing me in the brain.

I need to focus. Assess.

What do I know?

Well, I'm alive. Just about.

I hurt everywhere.

...

...

...

Okay, that's not a great start.

What do I *need* to know?

Where am I?

What happened?

What's going to happen next?

...

...

...

I have no idea.

What can I remember?

My head lolls forward, too heavy for my neck to support. I start coughing. Feel thick, syrup-like blood form on my lips. I spit it out.

I remember Ruby. That asshole driver from last night had a knife to her throat.

I remember being beaten. Badly.

I remember Kazawa.

I open my eyes.

Ah!

...

...

...

Shit.

Okay. I open my *eye*. The right one doesn't want to open, apparently, and who am I to argue?

This room looks familiar.

It's one of the ones I searched on the way in here with...

Mia.

She's standing in front of me. There's a weird smile on her face. It's as if she's bemused and pissed at the same time. She's changed her outfit too. She's now wearing a black leather catsuit and knee-length combat boots.

It's as if she's a completely different person.

Flashbacks of the beating she gave me flood into my mind. Even the memories hurt. Instinctively, I lunge for her, but I don't move. I look to my sides. My arms are tied to whatever's keeping me upright. Out to the sides, like a cross.

Uh-oh.

I look down and realize my shirt has been removed. My ankles are bound together, strapped to the same device my body and arms are. I look like I'm being crucified.

A sadly ironic way to go, by all accounts.

"Hello, Adrian."

Her voice is calm. Her tone like ice. Her eyes stare through me like I'm nothing.

I try to speak, but all I manage is a low, mumbling noise I hope sounded sarcastic.

"Just so we're clear," she says. "Today will be the last day of your life. I need you to understand that. I need you to *believe* that."

I nod slowly. I actually do.

"Good." She paces away idly, as if she's on a stroll through a meadow. She spins to face me as she reaches the computer that's set up on the other side of the room. "I can't begin to tell you how long I've waited for this moment. It's all I've thought about for the last five years. Do you have any idea how long that is to fixate on one thing? It's a lifetime, Adrian."

I take a breath. Cough out some more blood. Try to find words.

"W-who are you again?"

She smiles patiently. "Miley Tevani. You killed my mother, Dominique. And now, I'm going to kill you."

I frown. It hurts to even think, but this is important.

Dominique Tevani...

...

...

...

Jesus! That's the assassin Wilson Trent hired to kill me. God, that was... what? Five years ago? So, Mia is...

I shake my head.

"Y-you got it all wrong, Mia. Miley. Whatever."

Her eyes narrow. "Is that right? This should be good. Please, enlighten me."

I take a few shallow breaths, steeling myself for the upcoming effort of talking coherently.

"First of all, I technically didn't kill your mom. She was hired to kill *me*, but she couldn't—she respected me too much. Then the guy who hired her must've kidnapped you for leverage, leaving her no choice. Me and your mom, we beat the crap out of each other, yeah. But I didn't kill her. She had me dead to rights. Someone else shot her to save me."

Her expression changes. Her brow furrows. Confusion. Anger. Doubt.

"I went after the guy who hired her because he killed my family," I continue, on a roll with a newfound surge of strength. "My wife. My daughter. He slaughtered them in our home to get to me. So, I killed him. Took down his entire empire. And not for nothing, I rescued *you* in the process. You were just this young, scared little kid. Couldn't have been more than fourteen at the time. If that. A friend of mine took you to a hospital in a chopper. I had no idea who you were until right now."

She walks slowly toward me. She seems distant. Lost.

"Miley, I know you're hurting. I know you're angry. But your beef isn't with me. Or with my friend. Your mom was a good person. And a good assassin. Her blood was on Wilson Trent's hands. And I got him, kid. I got him for both of us."

Her hand disappears behind her back. It reappears holding a small flick-knife.

Oh, f—

"Ah!"

She glides close to me, sliding the blade effortlessly into my stomach. Pain erupts throughout my body. I fight to stay awake. To stay alive. Pressing her body against mine, she leans in, on her tiptoes so that her lips are next to my ear.

"I don't believe you."

Miley steps away, leaving the knife in my body. I glance down at it. Blood is pumping from the wound, but I think she managed to avoid anything vital. It's not fatal, just agonizing.

Whether that was skill on her part or luck on mine, I honestly can't tell.

I watch as she moves over to the computer again. She works the keyboard, then adjusts the webcam so that it points directly at me. I see the feed on the screen. I see myself, helpless and immobile. I look on the brink of death.

She puts on a mask that was beside the screen. It covers her eyes, like something you would wear to a masquerade ball. Or like Catwoman. But not the good kind. The Halle Berry kind.

She looks over at me, tilting her head ominously as she stares.

"Normally, this club broadcasts a very specific type of show across the dark web," she explains. "It's available only to people willing to pay the high price this content is worth. It also operates its own online auction, open to people searching for organ donors, who are prepared to do whatever it takes to secure what they need. Understandably, these attract a certain type of... clientele. But today? Oh, Adrian! Today is different. It's special. Today, a unique broadcast will air live online—in the public domain, for all to see! The feed will hijack news outlets and blog sites all over the world."

What's she talking about?

The urge to remove the knife from my body and throw it at her consumes me, overshadowed only by the frustration at the fact I can't.

"M-Miley... you're insane. Stop this."

She races over to me, grabbing my throat and leaning close, baring her teeth like a rabid animal.

"*I'm* insane? Really? After everything *you've* done? After all the lives you've taken without so much as a pause for breath? If *anyone* is insane here, Adrian, it's you! You're a psychopath! You deserve this!"

The effort it's taking to stay awake right now is frightening. I struggle to focus on her face, to stare into her eyes behind the mask. I don't know what to say to her.

I force a smile. "I... I know."

She recoils slightly. "What?"

"I agree with you," I say, smiling wider. "I *do* deserve this. I've done... terrible things in my life. I've lost everything because of the choices I've made. But I've... I've also done some good. I'm no saint. If there's anything waiting for me after this life, it's more likely to be red and warm than white and playing a harp. But I'm not sorry. Not for one damn bit of it."

She's hesitant. Uncertain. She can't look away but is struggling to make eye contact. Her hands are restless. She—

My head snaps to my left as she lands a heavy blow to my face.

"Fuck you!" she yells. "You will confess your crimes to the world, and then you will be executed in front of it."

She returns to the computer. Clicks a button. A red light flashes on the screen. She steps back, moving in front of me and positioning herself to address the camera. I see the gun tucked at her back. She stands with confidence. Her legs straight. Her hips cocked to the side. She could be a supermodel.

"For too long, this world has been held hostage by criminals," she begins. "Killers. Rapists. Psychopaths. Terrorists. The very essence of what's wrong with humanity. As a society, we have endured suffering unlike any generation in recent memory. Each day, thousands of murders, sexual assaults, and robberies go unpunished across the world. But on a much larger scale, all of our lives have been affected by unimaginable tragedies. 4/17. The Cunningham assassination. The Vatican attack. Prague. Texas."

She begins pacing back and forth in front of the camera.

"But those atrocities could've been averted. Every single one of them. You see, the truth is, everything bad that's happened to this world in recent years is nothing but a consequence of one man's life. The aftermath of his actions. Of his decisions. You all know him. The current U.S. president pardoned him on national television, despite his own admission that he assassinated their predecessor. But now, with help from my associates, I will finally bring him to justice, for the whole world to see."

She steps aside, gesturing to me theatrically.

"Ladies and gentleman, I present to you... Adrian Hell."

Looks like I'm ready for my close-up.

I stare right down the camera. I don't do or say anything. I see the feed on the screen. There's a counter next to it, showing how many people are watching this right now. My vision's blurry, but there's well over forty million.

The power of the internet, eh?

Miley moves to my side. She toys with the handle of the knife that's still sticking out of me, tapping it playfully with a finger.

"Now... I wanted to make sure everybody sees this. Sees

that justice *does* get served. In a world where shoplifters get ten years in prison for holding up a convenience store, yet pedophiles get two years for raping a child, I feel it's important to renew people's faith in the concept of consequence. The courts of the world don't have the guts to do what's right anymore. They're too concerned with appearing politically correct to actually punish anyone. So, I've taken it upon myself, as a victim of this man's crimes, to do what even the U.S. government couldn't. Kill Adrian Hell. And I will do it live!"

Oh, shit. This isn't good.

Where's Ruby? I hope to God she's okay. I hate that I can't protect her.

This is a real crappy way to go...

"But first, let me deal with any concerns you might have."

She paces slowly back toward the camera, obscuring me from view. She leans forward, staring right down the lens, acting as if she's talking to a child.

"For those of you outraged at the moral ambiguity of what I'm doing, I say this—fuck you. I lost years of my childhood because of that piece of shit behind me. What I've done to him, and what I'm *about* to do to him, is horrific and violent and the worst kind of wrong. But do you know what? I don't care. I make no apologies for any of this. The right thing isn't always good. It isn't always the nice option. And I own that."

She shifts to the side, displaying me to the camera once again. I feel my head sag forward. The effort needed to hold it up no longer justifies the benefits of doing so. I'm beaten and tired.

"You see him?" she shouts. "He actually thinks all the shit he's done is right! That he should be allowed to get away with it because of some misguided moral compass. That's the very definition of a psychopath! He's one of the worst mass murderers in history, and he deserves to die. But no one seems to want to punish him for his crimes. Well, I do. And I will."

She marches back over to me. I feel her place a hand on the back of my head. The other on my forehead. She lifts me so that I'm staring right into the camera.

"But before I do, he is going to confess his crimes to the world."

I smile.

She hits me.

"Confess!" she screams.

I look at her and smile wider. "No."

She yanks the knife out of my gut and slams the blade down into my right shoulder.

A cry of pain builds in my throat, but I can't let it out. The agony is so intense, I'm not sure I can...

I...

Can...

...

...

...

Oh, Jesus!

A wave of nausea hits me as a foul stench hits my nostrils. I snap awake to see Miley waving a small vial of something hideous in front of my face, presumably to bring me round after blacking out.

"Ah! What the hell?"

She tosses the vial aside, then grips my face, squeezing my cheeks together.

"Tell the world what you've done, Adrian. Or I will!"

"Go... for it..."

She releases a guttural roar of frustration and anger before hitting me in the face again.

The blow rattled something loose inside my head. A hidden cache of clarity and focus buried deep beneath the constant explosions of pain.

All I have to do is stall her.

While I never claimed to understand even half the shit Josh used to say to me, I know enough about computers to know that she'll be hiding her location. No way this place, or what she's doing in it right now, is legal. The Yakuza won't want themselves associated with this, so they'll be bouncing their signal all over the world to stay hidden from the authorities, the press, the hackers, and everyone else scrambling to figure out where this is taking place and who Miley really is.

Someone will figure it out eventually. I just have to buy them some time.

Which means I need to stay conscious.

I look at the camera. Then at her.

"Go on," I say. "Tell them. Tell everyone what you think I've done."

She hesitates.

"No. This is your confession. I will not give you the satisfaction of being your mouthpiece." She grips the knife sticking out of my shoulder. "Now, tell them, or I will fucking *gut* you."

Here goes nothing.

"Fine." I stare at the camera. Take a breath. Draw on probably my last hidden reserve of strength. Spit out some blood to clear my throat. "Dear world. Um... hi. If you're watching this, feel safe in the knowledge that I'm having a worse day than you are. This isn't exactly how I envisioned my last day on this mortal coil, I'll be honest. But when your number's up, there's not much you can do about it, y'know? Ironic that by killing me, this crazy bitch is doing the same thing she's accusing me of. But anyway... my confession. Yes. I admit it. I was the gunman behind the grassy knoll."

Miley drives her fist into the side of my head. After everything my body's been through in the last few hours, it barely even registers. But that doesn't stop my brain telling me to switch off. I fight it.

"I held the camera when they filmed the moon landing in Hollywood."

She hits me again.

"I am Spartacus!"

"Enough!" She rips the knife from my shoulder and gestures with it to the camera. "This bastard killed my mother, and he will pay for it with his life!"

I tense every fiber of my body, preparing as much as I can for that knife being thrust into me again. She spins around and slashes it toward me, stopping with the blade pressing against the soft flesh of my throat.

"Your death will be slow and painful and last for hours, and the whole world will see it. Your reputation, your legacy... nothing will remain. You'll die with no dignity, and the last thought in your head will be of nothing but excruciating agony."

"Sounds... lovely."

She presses the blade harder against me.

"But you can avoid all of that. I will grant you a quick and merciful execution... *if* you confess to all of your crimes right now."

Shit.

Antagonizing her isn't going to do me much good for much longer. I can't move. I can't feel anything besides the pain wracking my entire body, and this psycho is deadly serious about killing me in front of the entire world.

I've tried to remain calm and casual about it. Figured I'd find a way out of this. But if I'm being honest with myself right now... this doesn't look good.

I try to move away from the knife as best I can. Squirming against my restraints to alleviate the pressure of the blade.

"Look, Miley... I'm sorry for how things turned out for you. Really, I am. I did what I had to do. You want a confession? Fine."

I stare right into the camera. Take a breath.

"Wilson Trent. The man terrorized the east coast for years with his corruption, his drugs, his reign of terror. The piece of shit murdered my family. I ran away. For a decade, I hid from my own fears. Until one day, I knew I couldn't take it anymore. I hunted him. I beat him. I killed him. Hell, twenty thousand people saw me do it! And I'm not sorry. I respect the law. I respect society. But I'm incredibly good at a really bad thing, and when people like him can buy the law and rule society, someone should stand up and say, 'Enough.' So, I did."

I look back at Miley.

"That's who I am. That's my legacy. And executing me won't destroy who I am or what I leave behind. So, do whatever you feel you need to do. I don't care."

"Except that isn't your legacy, is it?" she says.

I frown. "What do you mean?"

"Your legacy isn't one of justifiable revenge. It isn't one of you saving the innocent or the oppressed." She grabs my face again. Forces me to look into her masked eyes. "Your legacy is death. You focus on the big picture because it means you don't need to look at your own pathetic life. The real truth behind your *legacy*, Adrian, is that everyone you ever cared about died because of you. Your wife and daughter died because of who *you* are. What *you* did. You lost friends and loved ones in Texas because of *your* failure to act. Your best friend, Josh Winters—one of the world's most influential men—was assassinated because he was standing beside *you*."

She paces away, walking toward the camera again.

Her words sink in more brutally than her knife ever did.

She's absolutely right. All the people I've ever cared for. I've lost every single one of them because of who I am.

She turns back to me and points at the screen. Pretty sure the viewing figures have tipped into nine figures now.

"Forget about the world, Adrian. We were doing just fine before you came along, and we'll damn sure be better off when you're dead. I want your final moments to be consumed by the acceptance of the fact that every bullet you ever fired killed more than just your target."

Fuck.

I take a deep breath, which sends pain pulsing around my body. I feel a single tear roll down my cheek.

I'm a cancer to the people around me. I always have been, and I've always been too focused on justifying my actions to myself to see it.

Another tear escapes.

She's right. About everything. All those lives could've been saved if I wasn't involved.

An image of Ruby flashes into my mind. Her eyes. Her smile.

Wherever she is right now, the only chance she has of making it out of here alive is if I don't. If I live, she will ultimately suffer for it, and I can't have that. Not anymore.

"You're right," I say quietly.

Miley cocks her head to the side. "What was that?"

She marches over to me, grabs the back of my head, and forces me to stare right down the camera. "Say that again, so we can hear you, Adrian."

Each breath pushes more tears down my face. My eyes sting from each droplet.

"You're right. She's right. I'm... I'm sorry. For everything. I deserve this."

She lets go of me and faces the camera, blocking my view of the screen.

"And there you have it, folks. Justice. The man behind me has, for almost two decades, been considered the world's deadliest hired killer. And you just saw him break down to nothing. Because of me. He's a murderer and deserves to die for what he's done."

There's a moment's pause. I hear her breathing hard. Adrenaline, most likely.

"But if you want to see him suffer... that's gonna cost you extra!"

Miley storms over to the computer and disconnects the webcam.

"What... what are you doing?" I ask her, sniffing back emotion and frowning with confusion.

She approaches me, playing with the knife in one hand. She stops a few feet from me, smiling.

"Maybe you don't deserve the audience. Look at you. You're covered in blood from head to toe. Your face is a swollen and blackened mess. Your eyes keep rolling back in your skull. You're barely conscious. And you're crying, Adrian. You're fucking crying! You are completely and irreversibly broken, and I did this to you. Me. The world's greatest assassin, and you were beaten to your final breath by a nineteen-year-old girl. You're pathetic. Having the death of your legacy publicized is too good for you. You deserve to die alone. Quietly. Knowing no one cares."

I manage to smirk before the pain in my face quells any further expression of emotion. "Don't sell yourself short, kid. You're tough. Just like your mom. She'd be proud of you."

Miley growls. It's primal. Angry. She stabs the knife into the wood, inches from my head. Then it starts again. Blow after blow. Unrestrained. They connect to my face. My body. I can do nothing to defend myself. I don't know how much longer I can—

15

"Adrian? Adrian, you gotta wake up! Adrian!"

Huh? What?

I ease myself upright. Pause for a split-second before opening my good eye. I'm on the floor, beside the stage with the pole in the main room. My right hand is trembling. I try to make a fist, but it's cramping too much to allow it. My T-shirt is back on my body and stained with blood.

What the hell is going on?

"Adrian!"

Huh? Ruby?

I look around. All the doors in here are closed. There's no sign of anyone. Everything has been removed from the walls.

"Adrian!"

I look behind me. There's a pair of legs standing there. They're nice. I follow them up. Ruby is stood, tied to the

147

pole in the middle of the stage. Her dress is torn and stained with blood.

Oh, no!

I get to my feet, which is a slow and painful process. I can't physically stand up straight. I hunch over, hugging my battered and beaten torso with one arm. Gradually, I reach up with my other and start working on her restraints. Her hands are bound above her head, and it hurts as I stretch to reach them. I go up on my tiptoes and lean over, trying to gain extra height and take some pressure off my ribs. Doing so puts my head and shoulders an inch from Ruby's face. As I fumble with the rope, she momentarily rests her head on my shoulder, in the crook of my neck.

"Jesus, Adrian—you look like shit," she says.

I smile. "Thanks."

"What did she do to you?"

I manage to get her hands free. She places one gently on my face and smiles before bending over to untie her own ankles. I practically collapse back down onto the stage, thankful I'm no longer on my feet.

"Until I passed out, she was beating the crap outta me," I reply. "After that, who knows?"

She sits beside me and places a hand on my leg. "I... ah... I heard everything she said in there. Kinda hard not to. You know she was just trying to get inside your head, right? You can't believe her, Adrian. The things she said... they weren't true."

I scoff. "Weren't they? They made a lot of sense. She sure convinced me, anyway."

"Well, speaking as someone who would happily describe themselves as one of your loved ones, I can confidently say she's full of shit! You can't allow yourself to think like that. All the good you've done for this world, even when you had no reason to... she doesn't know you. Not like I do. Not like Josh did. Don't let her break you, okay?"

I smile weakly. "Thank you."

I'm not sure I completely believe her, but I appreciate the sentiment all the same.

She wipes some blood from my face. "So, were you really on camera?"

I nod. "Yup. Over a hundred million viewers last time I saw the screen." I make very weak, very sarcastic jazz hands. "Yay... I'm famous again."

"Do you know why she didn't kill you?"

"No idea. Not complaining though. But I... I think I might need medical attention."

"I think you're right." She nudges me playfully and gets to her feet. "Come on, let's get out of here. We need to lay low, regroup, figure out our next move. It's a blessing they didn't kill us, but you have to believe the entire Kazawa family will be hunting us now."

I push myself upright again, remaining slightly hunched to ease the pain shooting through my body. I see sympathy in Ruby's eyes. I see her struggling with seeing me hurting so much and not being able to help. But then I see her attention move to something else. Something behind me.

I frown. "What is it?"

"Um... we should go. We should go right now."

"Why? What's—" I look behind me. Against the wall beside the door Ruby came out of earlier are two barrels. Big, rusty, forty-five-gallon things. Stuck to the side of each of them is a block of C4 and a timer, counting down. I squint, trying to focus through my one good eye to make out the numbers. We have about eight minutes.

I let out a heavy sigh. "Oh."

"Come on!" she shouts, heading for the door that leads to the exit in the alley.

She rattles the handles, pushes and pulls against it, slams her shoulder into it...

Nothing.

It's locked.

"Try the others," I say to her.

She dashes around the room, going through the same routine with the other three sets of doors. Each time, the same result.

We're trapped.

I look back at the bomb, then at Ruby. "Wait, aren't you good at disarming these things? Remember North Carolina a couple of years ago? You literally saved my ass when your ex-boyfriend strapped a bomb to my chair."

She sighs. "Yeah, but that was two years ago. I'm a little rusty. Besides, I can see from here at least two failsafe triggers on those things. I wouldn't have a clue how to safely disarm something that complex. It's not worth the risk tampering with it."

"Well, we gotta do something!"

"Don't you think I know that? But all the doors are locked shut. I can't bust them open. You damn sure couldn't, in your condition. All the weapons have been taken from the walls. There isn't another way out. We're... we're trapped in here."

Out of habit, I look around the room, taking in every detail, doing what I can to process it in what's left of my conscious mind. A million questions all at once. A million ideas on how to get out of here.

My gaze settles on the bomb in the far corner.

Just under six minutes now.

I drop to my knees. Partly because standing is simply too

much to ask. Mostly in defeat. The realization that there's no way out of this room hits me like a wrecking ball.

Ruby crouches beside me and puts her arm around me.

"Come on, Adrian. I know you're hurt, but we have to—"

"No, Ruby."

She frowns, taken aback. "What?"

I turn to look at her, a weak smile on my face. "Don't you see? We're done."

"Hey, come on! We'll find a way out. We just need to focus."

I take her hand in mine. Squeeze it. Rub my thumb over the back of hers tenderly.

"We're done, Ruby. Look around. Miley didn't let me go. She didn't choose to leave me alive. She tortured me in front of the world and then basically buried us both beneath a building, next to a large bomb that neither of us can disarm." I hang my head for a moment. When I look up at her again, I feel a tear form in the corner of my eye. "This is where it ends."

"What? No!" She springs to her feet and starts moving around the room, looking high and low in all directions, as if urgently searching for her car keys. "There has to be a way. There *has* to be!"

I watch her, feeling more pain in my heart than I've felt in a long, long time. She turns in slow circles. Each time she faces me, I see a little more hope has gone from her eyes. I see the sad reality hitting home.

We're done.

She begins to cry. Tears flow freely down her face as she kneels in front of me, resting back on her heels and taking both my hands in hers.

"I'm so sorry..."

"What for?"

"This is all my fault. I left the race with Ko. I encouraged you to take Mia... Miley... home. This is because of me."

"Are you kidding me? This isn't your fault, Ruby. Neither of us did anything wrong here. Miley was playing me from day one. She's been planning this for five years. The other night in the bar, when I stepped in-between her and those two assholes... that was a set-up. This whole thing has been one long game to her." I think for a moment. "I guess this is my fault. My fault we're here. My fault you got hurt."

She places a hand on my face. "They didn't hurt me, Adrian. Not really. Roughed me up a bit, but I've taken much worse off better people than these assholes. Don't worry about me. But you need to stop blaming yourself. This is not your fault, okay?"

"Yeah, it is. It all comes down to me. You heard what she said. Everything I do costs the people I care about. When I was tied up, I realized I had to die to give you a chance to live. It was the only way, and I was prepared to do it. Hell, I was happy to. Because she was right. About all of it. But that doesn't matter now, I guess. Everything that's happened since I killed Trent's son has led to this moment. To us being trapped down here together with..." I glance over my shoulder at the bomb. "...three minutes to live."

She leans forward, resting her forehead against mine. I feel her shaking as she sobs. This is the most human... the most *non-Ruby* I've ever seen her.

Breathing hurts. I guess the upside is that won't be a problem much longer.

To think, my entire life, my journey of violence and death... it all led me here. Everything I've done. Everyone I've lost. It was all to bring me to this moment. Beaten beyond belief. Broken beyond repair. And right now, I'm closer to Ruby than I've ever been or will be again.

I move back and place my good hand on her chin, lifting her head, so she's looking into my eyes.

I smile, trying to show as much strength for her as I can. "For what it's worth, in my last moments, there's no one I'd rather have by my side than you. Thank you for being here for me, Ruby. I couldn't have got through the last two years without you."

She smiles back but says nothing.

"I honestly didn't think it would end like this, but then, there's something poetic about going out in a blaze of glory, right?"

"You're an idiot," she says, smiling back.

Time slows to a crawl. It's as if I can hear the seconds tick by on the bomb. I stare into Ruby's eyes. Her emerald orbs are still full of life, despite what awaits us both in the next two minutes. I see them glisten with tears waiting for permission to fall.

She takes a breath. "Adrian, I... if this is really it, I just want to say that..."

We rest our foreheads together again, kneeling in front of each other, holding each other as we wait for the end.

We part. We smile. A tear rolls down both our cheeks.

"I love you," we say in unison.

We laugh and move closer. I don't feel awkward anymore. If the last thing I ever do on this earth is kiss Ruby, I'll consider it a life lived well.

Our lips are millimeters apart. I hear her catch her breath. I close my eyes.

BANG!

Huh?

My eyes snap open again. I grimace and close my right one, forgetting the pain. We lean back, frowning at each other.

BANG!

"What was that?" she asks.

"I dunno. It sounded like it was coming from—"

CRACK!

The main doors burst open, almost tearing from their hinges. The influx of daylight from the corridor is blinding. The silhouette of a figure standing in the doorway slowly fades into focus.

"*Shinigami!*"

Holy shit!

I shake my head with disbelief. "Ichiro?"

I go to stand. Ruby jumps to her feet to help me. Ichiro rushes to my side to do the same. I glance back at the timer.

Eighty-seven seconds.

"We gotta go. Now!"

Ichiro looks at the bomb. "No shit."

With an arm resting over each of their necks, we move as quickly as we can out of the room and along the corridor, toward the hidden exit to the underground club. Ruby and Ichiro are practically dragging me.

I'm trying to count in my head.

Maybe sixty seconds left.

We make it outside. It's bright but cold. No idea what time it is. I don't know how long I was in there.

We all struggle up the steps. Turn and quick-step to the street.

About forty seconds.

Ichiro's car is waiting. Without hesitation, Ruby dives onto the back seat. I fold myself into the front. The lack of space actually helps, as I'm forced to ball up, which alleviates a lot of the pressure on my broken ribs.

Ichiro gets in behind the wheel. Fires it up. Speeds out into traffic, narrowly avoiding a collision.

Ten.

We get to the end. Take a left, running the red light.

Six.

We head down the first right, already lost in the sea of daytime traffic and chaos that flows through Tokyo each day.

Three.

Two.

One.

...

...

...

One?

A thunderous explosion rings out behind us. I turn in my seat and see a thick, black plume of smoke billows toward the sky. Cars screech to a stop. People on the streets run in mindless directions, screaming.

I glance at Ruby, who's lying across the back seat, staring blankly at the roof of the car. She's breathing fast. No doubt relieved to be alive.

I turn back around. Rest my head back against the seat. Focus on my breathing. As slow as I can. As deep as I dare.

I lift my left arm and place my hand on Ichiro's shoulder.

"What the hell took you so long?"

He laughs his trademark belly laugh as he navigates the streets, steering around cars stopped haphazardly by the explosion.

I let out a heavy sigh, ignoring the pain it causes.

I really hope we're going to a hospital.

16

I take a sip of water from the paper cup beside my bed. It tastes bitter and still hurts to swallow. I lie back and gaze at the ceiling. I take a slow, deep breath, enduring the discomfort in the hope it relaxes me.

It's been just over twenty-four hours since Kazawa's club exploded. Still can't believe I almost went up with it. People keep telling me I'm lucky to be alive.

It doesn't feel like it.

The multiple stab wounds were largely superficial, but it still sucks having a knife thrust into you more than once. Those brass knuckles Miley went to town on me with did the most damage. Cracked ribs, internal bleeding... oh, and my eye socket is bruised. I didn't even know bones *could* bruise, but it turns out they can, and it doesn't tickle. The swelling around my eye has gone down a lot overnight, due to the staggering amount of pain meds and anti-inflammatories currently being drip-fed into my blood stream.

All things being equal, I feel like I've just gone twelve rounds with a fucking steamroller.

Luckily, being in a financially secure position, I've been able to get the best healthcare available, and I have to say, this place has been great. Even my room... it's like a cross between a suite at the Hilton and something out of a sci-fi movie—everything's white and clean and sterile, but also luxuriously comfortable.

I'm in a private ward, high enough up that my view out the window doesn't even show any buildings. It's just clouds and daylight. Which would be more impressive if it wasn't so cold and miserable out there.

Ruby, thank God, is in much better shape. A few lacerations and bruises, some swelling around her wrists from where she was tied up, but other than that, she's doing okay. I swear, she's more bothered about what happened to her new dress than to her.

She hasn't moved from my bedside since we got here, other than to get coffee from the machine down the hall, which is where she is right now. I'm not allowed any, apparently, but according to her, I'm not missing much.

Ichiro dropped us both off at the main entrance yesterday and high-tailed it out of here. He's going to do some digging for us, see if he can track down what happened to Miley and Kazawa. But he wanted to keep a low profile—a luxury I can no longer enjoy, thanks to the viral video of me being torn apart by a nineteen-year-old—so he didn't want to be here when the inevitable army of authorities showed up.

I'll say one thing for all these meds—they've stopped my hand tremors. First time in almost three years my hand hasn't at least ached. The physio could've just told me to get high instead of squeezing a rubber ball all day and leaving myself open to Ruby's many innuendos.

Speaking of...

"This coffee tastes like shit." I smile weakly as she walks in, grimacing at the cup in her hand. "Seriously... one of the most technologically advanced nations on earth, and they can't make a good cup of coffee!"

"Yeah, I don't think they've quite got that right over here yet."

She sits beside my bed. Rests her feet up on the edge of it, shoving my leg away to make room for herself in the process.

"How you doin'?"

I allow my head to sink into the pillow. "I'm okay."

"Uh-huh. So, how are you doing?"

I glance over at her. She's staring at me like any mom does when they know you're lying—glaring at me through a raised eyebrow.

I sigh. "Fine. I feel like shit, Ruby."

"Yeah... me too. And all that crap crazy bitch said to you?"

I shrug as best I can. "Mind game, right?"

"Goddamn right. Remember that, okay?"

"Yeah," I say with a smile that I hope was convincing.

"So, listen, I spoke to one of the nurses out there. Apparently, the doctors have managed to delay the local authorities from questioning you, for now. And there's a shit-ton of press out there wanting your picture."

"Newspapers? Really?"

She nods. "I honestly don't think you understand just how many people saw Miley's broadcast of you, Adrian. It's literally the only thing the world is talking about. Look."

She takes out her cellphone, presses the screen a few times, then shows it to me.

"You're trending on Twitter."

I squint at the screen. "What does 'hashtag tortured hero' mean?"

She rolls her eyes. Smiles. "It means you're famous, big boy."

"Great."

I sink back into my pillow and close my eyes.

"Maybe this is a good thing?" she offers.

I lift my head slightly to look at her. "How could this possibly be a good thing?"

"Well... with so much attention, it's only a matter of time before someone IDs and finds Miley. Saves us a job."

"Yeah, but with so much attention, I won't be able to cross the street without appearing on the front page, let alone hunt down and kill an entire Yakuza family."

"Hmm, good point." She sips her coffee. Grimaces again, as if forgetting it tasted bad. "So, that's your plan? You want to go after Kazawa?"

I nod. "Bet your ass. I don't like being beaten. I don't like being a patient or a victim. I don't like people thinking they can do what they did and get away with it."

Maybe Ruby was right. Maybe it was all just mind games. Or maybe there was some truth to what Miley said, and that's why it hurt so much. I'm honestly not sure which of them made a better point. But all I know is anger makes the pain easier to deal with, so I should embrace it. Violence is my default setting for problem-solving, and it feels like a good strategy right now to stick with what I know.

"So, yeah," I continue. "I'm gonna kill Kazawa and anyone associated with him. Every last fucking one of them. Including Miley. *Especially* fucking Miley. She did something to me no one else ever has. And I'm pissed. Which means she's dead first."

Ruby says nothing. She holds my gaze for a second then looks away, staring at the floor.

"You okay?" I ask her.

She shifts in her seat before looking back up at me. "Adrian, we were *this* close to being dead. Thank God for Ichiro, but... for a while there, it looked like we were done."

"I know. But we got out."

"Yeah, and I'm grateful, obviously. But there's no way that Kazawa or his psycho girlfriend don't know we're still alive. Maybe we should..."

"Should what, Ruby?"

She sighs. "Maybe we should cut our losses. Take advantage of this second chance and move on. Start over. Somewhere quiet."

"Is that really what you want?"

"I dunno," she replies, shrugging. "Maybe."

"I don't understand. These people nearly destroyed us. We can't let that stand."

"Says who?" She gets to her feet and begins pacing back and forth at the foot of my bed. "Why do we have to take revenge on them? Pride? Principle? Jesus, Adrian, we don't have to prove anything to each other. Who else is there? Why does it matter?"

I slam my hand against the bed. "It matters because people cannot be allowed to get away with that kind of shit, Ruby! If we don't stop them, how many more people are gonna end up like us? People who can't defend themselves. People who don't know how to survive like we do. Their blood will be on our hands if we walk away now. Besides, the way I see it, if we just take out Kazawa, someone's just gonna step up, take his place, and come after us. Best way to avoid that is make sure there's no one left to assume control."

She stops pacing and stares at me. It doesn't look as if she's trying to find something to say. She's just staring at me, hands on hips.

"Look," I say, "I understand where you're coming from, okay? I do. But do you *really* think Miley is gonna let me start over somewhere else? Like you said, she must know I'm alive, because I'm trending worldwide. She's going to hunt me for the rest of her life until she finishes me. Trust me, I know what it's like to be driven by vengeance. It consumes every part of you. She won't ever stop, Ruby. Which means we won't ever be able to stop running. I don't want that. Not for myself. Not for you."

She walks over to the window and looks out. A good two minutes pass before she moves again. She turns on her heels and throws her coffee cup across the room, sinking it in the trash can stood against the opposite wall. Then she moves to my bedside. Sits on the edge of the bed. Takes my hand.

"I know you're right," she says. "But it's not every day you face your own mortality. It's not every day you see someone you care about tortured beyond comprehension. I've seen a lot of shit, Adrian, but yesterday was too much, even for me. It just makes me wonder if the fight's worth it."

I do my best to squeeze her hand with mine.

"Look, while it wasn't intentional at the time, we're in this situation because of me, and I'm sorry for that. Truly, I am. But you saw what Miley did to me. She's grown up fixated with taking revenge on me. She won't stop. Ever. This is the fight of our lives, kiddo. So, you can bet your ass it's worth it."

She takes a deep breath. When she smiles, it looks forced. The expression barely reaches her tired eyes.

"Then we fight. Whatever it takes. And you know I've got your back."

I nod. "Likewise."

We hold each other's gaze for a long moment. For the first time since waking up here, I remember what we said to each other when we thought it was over. Before Ichiro showed up. It was intense. We both thought we were about to die. Did we speak honestly, or were we just victims of circumstance? It'll need talking about at some point. I mean, we almost—

"Am I interrupting?"

Huh?

We both turn and look over at the door. There's a man standing there. Short, dark skin, a barrel chest surrounded by muscle, and an obvious power to his frame that defies his years. He's dressed in black, wearing a cream trench coat that rests just below his knees.

He smiles. "The nurse said it was okay to come see you."

"Are you a reporter?" Ruby gets to her feet and moves around the bed, so she's standing between me and the new arrival.

He chuckles. "No, I'm not. Although, there's a few of them out there, all looking for a quote from the man of the hour." He leans to the side and looks past Ruby, right at me. "How are you feeling, Adrian?"

I shrug. "As you'd expect, I guess. Sorry, you are...?"

"Moses Buchanan." He pauses to grin widely. "Josh Winters recruited me to a senior consultant position when GlobaTech bought my security firm a few years ago. When he passed away, I was chosen to replace him as CEO. My condolences, by the way. Josh was a good man and a good friend. I know you were like a brother to him."

Ruby looks around, wide-eyed, and we exchange a look of surprise.

"How did you find me?" I ask. "And why are you here?"

He steps inside the room and leans back against the doorframe. His hands are deep in his coat pockets.

"The *how* was easy," he says. "The people torturing you live on the internet weren't as good as they thought they were at covering their tracks. I'm sure a lot of people traced the signal. I'm simply better and faster than most people."

Listening to him talk, I can't help but be reminded of Josh. His mannerisms, his confidence... the way he perfectly treads the line between charming and arrogant. I see why they were friends.

"Yeah, okay."

"As for the *why*... well, I thought it only right I check up on you. It's what Josh would've done."

"Uh-huh..."

"Yeah, I didn't think you'd buy that," he says, smiling. He steps forward and extends his hand. "You must be Ruby."

She shakes it tentatively. "Yeah. How do you know?"

He looks at each of us in turn. "Honestly? Josh kept a file on Adrian under lock and key. Only accessible by whoever holds his job." He focuses on me. "It... ah... it details everything about you. From the moment you and Josh met until the moment he travelled to Rome with you."

I feel my eyes pop wide, which instantly sends a shooting pain around one side of my skull.

"Damn it!" I grimace and screw my eyes closed again. "Really?"

"Yeah. He left a note with it, saying it might come in handy."

"Right. So, why are you here, Moses? I'm kinda busy being in pain."

He takes his hand out of his pocket. He's holding a piece of paper, which he passes to Ruby.

"What's this?" she asks, taking it.

"It's a list of Tetsuo Kazawa's associates. It was too much of a risk to investigate that piece of shit personally, but I figured it's a good way for you to start looking for him."

"This is... this is great. Thank you."

"Yeah," I say. "I appreciate that. Thanks."

"My pleasure."

I shuffle myself a little more upright in bed, trying to get comfortable. In doing so, the bed cover slips a little, revealing the multi-colored patchwork of bruises on my torso.

"Ouch..." says Moses, gesturing to them.

"I'll live," I reply. "So, at the risk of appearing ungrateful here... what do you want from me?"

"Who says I want anything?"

"Really? The CEO of the biggest company in the world flies five-and-a-half thousand miles to do a favor for a guy he doesn't know, purely out of the goodness of his heart? I respect the fact Josh trusted you. That goes a long way with me. But don't bullshit me. You show up here rocking the Nick Fury look and expect me to believe you don't want anything? Try again."

He holds my gaze. His polite and cheerful exterior visibly hardens. His eyes narrow for a second. Then he nods and smiles again.

"Fair enough. I came here because of who you were to Josh. I came here because no one should have to go through what you just did. Especially in front of the world. The people who did this to you should be brought to justice. But they're Yakuza, and it's not something I want my team or my company to proactively get involved in. We're very visible too, and there are political ramifications to every decision I make. Plus, I figured you would probably want to handle it yourself." He nods to the piece of paper in Ruby's hand. "That's a peace offering, of sorts. A gesture of good faith between you and me."

"Why?"

He lets out a taut breath. Glances around the room and over his shoulder. "Because I've been around long enough to know when shit's about to go sideways. I know the signs. Trouble's coming, Adrian, and I figured it wouldn't hurt to have someone like you owe me one."

"What kind of trouble?" asks Ruby.

"Right now, the manageable kind. But the world's on a knife edge. That could easily change."

"Is Jericho still working with you?" I ask.

Moses nods. "He is."

I smile. "Say hi for me."

"I will. Although, I think he's still a little unsure about you." He laughs as he moves to the doorway again. "I'll let you rest up. Both of you. Take a couple of days. Get your strength back before you go looking into that list, you hear me? Tetsuo Kazawa isn't someone to take lightly."

"We know."

He steps out into the corridor and looks back. "Oh, yeah, I almost forgot. I took the liberty of leaving you a little gift in your apartment."

"Flowers and grapes? You shouldn't have..."

"Not quite," he replies, chuckling. "Just a few things to help you with your Yakuza problem."

He nods a silent farewell to each of us and disappears out of sight.

Ruby turns to me. "Well, that was weird."

"Yeah, just a bit."

"What do you think's going on?"

"Nothing GlobaTech can't handle, I'm sure." I gesture to the paper. "What's he given us?"

She looks at it again. "Just a list of three names and addresses."

"Well, now we know where to start."

"Yeah, but I think we should take his advice. Lay low and rest up for a couple of days. Minimum."

My instinct is to argue, but I stop myself. I can't even stand, let alone wage war on half of Tokyo. I made my point to Ruby about us needing to fight, but I admit that resting sounds pretty good right now.

I nod. "Yeah, okay. We should get a good forty-eight hours of peace in this place. But you'll stick around, yeah? I don't want you out there on your own. Not at the moment."

She smiles. "I'm not going anywhere. Don't worry."

She sits back down beside me. Puts her feet back up on the bed, shoving my leg aside again. Starts tapping the screen on her phone. I watch her for a moment, then lie back in bed, focus on the ceiling, and try to relax.

I'm coming for you, Miley. You and your asshole boyfriend. But you'll keep for now.

17

The doors of the elevator slide open, quiet and smooth, revealing our apartment. It feels good to be home. I walk gingerly toward the sofa. Ruby is next to me, linking my arm. She's trying to pass it off as being nice, but she's actually doing it to hold me up, hoping I don't notice.

I sink heavily into the familiar comfort of the cushions and lean back, exhausted. Ruby sits down beside me, resting the backpack she was carrying at her feet. It was a parting gift from the hospital, containing pain meds, bandages, and a face mask for me.

That was a strange one.

Because of the bruising to my eye socket, the doctors said I need to protect it until it heals fully. I had a fitting for this light-gray mask they give to athletes to wear over their eyes. It's made from carbon fiber and covers the top half of your face. When I tried it on, I looked like Batman, but without the pointy ears.

I even asked for it in black.

"How are you feeling?" asks Ruby.

"I'm all right," I reply, without moving. "Was going stir crazy in that goddamn bed though."

She laughs. "Yeah, I know what you mean."

I sit up and gesture to the coffee table in front of me. The black sports bag from Buchanan is sitting on it.

"Shall we open our 'welcome home' gift?"

"Not just yet." She gets to her feet and looks down at herself. "I've been wearing this dress for nearly three days. I need a shower."

"Sure thing."

"Don't do anything stupid while I'm gone, okay?"

I raise my eyebrow. "Like what?"

"Like get up to make a coffee or something. I'll be ten minutes, then I'll be back to look after you."

We hold each other's gaze for a long moment. I smile and look away, keen to avoid it becoming awkward.

"You got it, *Mom*."

She sighs. "Kids today..."

She winks before disappearing upstairs. I look down at myself. I'm wearing the same clothes I had on when I first entered The Golden Tiger. My T-shirt is ripped and stained, the holes and patches of dried blood resting neatly over my healing wounds. I look like I've been dug out of a grave.

Meh. One thing at a time.

I lean over and open the backpack. I take out a small sponge ball and begin squeezing it methodically in my right hand. Since lowering the dosage of meds, the spasms and aches from my old tendon injury are back with a vengeance. Not to mention the multiple cuts and bruises decorating my body that I'm suddenly more aware of. Even breathing tugs at the stitching in my gut.

I reach back into the bag and rummage around for the meds. I feel the small, plastic bottle under some bandages. As I squeeze the ball in my right hand, I hold the bottle up in my left. The label is printed in Japanese, so I've no idea what it says, but the doctor at the hospital said it was Oxycodone. He said something about taking one every twelve hours to help with the pain, but for no more than three days. Squeezing the ball is getting harder to do. The aching intensifies, which I know is a sign of a spasm waiting to happen.

Didn't miss this when I was high on meds...

It's also not the greatest thing to have to deal with when you're gearing up for war. My strategy, such as it is, very much revolves around being able to hold and shoot a gun.

I open the bottle and pop two tablets, swallowing them dry.

That should hold me for a while.

10:24 JST

I feel a hand press gently on my shoulder. I jolt awake. My eyes snap open, remaining wide with surprise. Ruby is standing in front of me, leaning over, smiling. Her hair's wet, dampening her thin top.

"Hey there, sleepyhead," she says before moving to sit beside me.

"Hey. Guess I must've dropped off for a sec there."

"How are you feeling?"

"Restless, more than anything." I slowly flex my hand. No aches or tremors. "You?"

"Better after that shower. Drink?"

"I'm good for now, thanks. I want to see what GlobaTech has left us."

She smiles. "You're like a kid on Christmas morning!"

I clap rapidly. "I hope it's that train set I always wanted!"

"You idiot!"

She kneels beside the table and unzips the black bag. She stares inside, then looks over at me.

"Holy shit..."

I sit forward and take a look myself.

"Holy shit!"

Talk about a jackpot. Ruby begins emptying the contents onto the surface of the table. Handguns, ammo, grenades of all kinds, an assault rifle, a pair of SMGs, a shotgun, night vision goggles, trip mines...

"What's that?" I say, pointing to a black wooden box at the bottom of the bag.

She takes it out, studying it closely with a curious frown. It looks expensive. High-quality finish. The GlobaTech logo is embossed in gold in the center of it.

She opens it, lifting the lid slowly toward me. After a moment, she closes it again. There's a warm smile on her face.

"So, what is it?" I ask her.

Her smile widens, touching her eyes, bringing them to life. It's a beautiful smile.

"I think it's for you," she replies as she hands it to me.

I spin it around on my lap and lift the lid.

I smile. My heart beats a tiny bit faster.

"Sonofabitch..."

Inside is lined with a cushioned red velvet. Resting in the middle are two handguns. GlobaTech-issue nine millimeters. Raptors, I think they call them. They're gorgeous weapons. A long, silver barrel with oak-effect panels on the butt. Engraved on each one in gold is the GlobaTech symbol again, sitting inside a pentagram.

I take each one out in turn, holding it briefly to familiarize myself with its weight. It feels sturdy but not cumbersome at all. Sleek but deadly. Similar in design to my old Berettas, but with GlobaTech's trademark futuristic-looking twist—curves are replaced with an almost hexagonal frame that surprisingly doesn't take away from the aesthetic.

Underneath them is a small note. A piece of thin, cream card folded once. I place the guns beside me and read it. I instantly feel a tear form in my eye. This time it's a good thing, and I embrace the moment. It escapes down my cheek as I smile.

Ruby frowns. "Adrian, what does it say?"

I laugh, slightly embarrassed. "It, ah... it says, 'If anything should happen to me, see these find their way into Adrian's hands. He'll know what to do.' Signed J.W."

She puts her hands to her mouth as tears instantly well in her eyes too.

I shake my head, unable to stop smiling. "Sonofabitch..."

I pick up one of the guns again and hold it in both hands, admiring it. Even after he's gone, Josh is still looking out for me. And not just as a voice inside my head, either. That guy was something else.

"You okay?" asks Ruby, sniffing back tears.

"Yeah..."

"What are you thinking?"

I look up at her. My jaw tenses. "Honestly? I'm... I'm a little scared."

She frowns and moves beside me, sitting with a leg brought up beneath her. "Of what?"

I gesture to the gun. "Of this. Of what I can do with it."

JAMES P. SUMNER

"Adrian, I'm not following you."

I let out a heavy breath, then turn my body to face her. "Look, I haven't been Adrian Hell for a long time. As far as I'm concerned, I retired him in Texas and buried him when The Order faked my death. He was a persona that became synonymous with everything bad in my life. For a long, long time. When I killed Wilson Trent, that was pretty much it. My crusade was done. My journey was complete. My family were laid to rest. But that was a dark time, Ruby. If Josh were here, he'd tell you just how dark it got for me."

She places her hand on my leg. "I know, but you have me now. I'm not trying to replace him or anything, but you know I've got your back, just as you have mine."

I smile. "I know, but that's not what I mean. Okay... imagine an alcoholic who's been sober for two years. He's been getting by because he was able to replace beer with non-alcoholic beer, so he felt he was getting the hit he needed without actually getting the hit."

She smiles back, half-confused, half-bemused. "Right..."

I hold up one of the Raptors. "Now imagine that same person has just been given a bottle of whiskey."

She holds my gaze for a moment. Then her expression softens. She smiles. "I understand what you're saying."

"I... *we*... have to wage war on a family of Yakuza. On their turf. That isn't a choice for us, Ruby. It's the difference between life and death. Simple as that. Now, factor in that crazy bitch, Miley, who has managed to give me a thirst for violence so bad, I can't remember a time when I felt like this. So, yeah, I'm scared. Scared of who I'll become. Scared I won't be able to quit again."

She takes the gun from my hand. Lays it on the sofa behind her. She holds my hand and squeezes gently.

"Look at me," she says.

I stare into her eyes.

"You have my word, Adrian. I won't let that happen to you. We're in this together. We'll finish it together. Then we'll get back on the wagon together. Do you hear me?"

I nod. "Yeah, I hear you. Thank you."

...

...

...

Uh-oh.

It's gone silent, and we're still staring at each other. My heartrate has picked up again. I think hers has as well. It doesn't feel awkward, but I'm suddenly very aware of how restless and vulnerable I am.

"Can I... ask you something?" says Ruby.

"Um, sure."

"Back at the club, before Ichiro rescued us... it didn't look great for us, did it?"

"Heh... not really, no."

"We were both convinced we were about to die."

"Yeah."

"And... well... it got a little tense there for a second. Between us."

"Yeah, I guess it did."

"Adrian, what you said to me... did you mean it?"

I take a breath. Stare into her eyes. Examine her face, taking in every inch of her.

"Every damn word."

She smiles. So do I. We both lean forward, our foreheads resting together, like they did during what we thought were our final moments. We laugh together nervously. As we part, I place my hand on the side of her face, using my thumb to caress her cheek.

"Every word," I say.

We kiss as if it's the end of the world. Her lips are soft. Her skin sizzles. My heart thumps against my chest.

Right now, nothing else exists except her.

...

...

...

We part. A lifetime of emotion passed in just a few seconds. It felt amazing. It felt—

"Ugh! Dammit!"

I wince as her knee accidentally digs into the stitching on my gut.

As I recoil, she gasps with apology, putting a hand to her mouth.

"I'm so sorry! Are you all right?"

I smile. "Yeah, I'm fine. Just battered and bruised. And rusty."

Her wide eyes soften. Her smile becomes a laugh.

"Well, it *has* been a while for you, hasn't it?"

I roll my eyes. "Oh, don't start that again!"

I stand, which takes considerable effort.

"Where are you going?" she asks.

"I need to freshen up too." I step around the table and head for the stairs. "Besides, I could probably use a really, *really* cold shower right about now."

I smile, which she reciprocates. Then she shifts on the sofa and kneels, facing me.

"You don't *have* to have a cold shower right away."

We lock eyes again. My heart begins to beat faster. I've always been the first to admit that Ruby is arguably the most attractive woman walking the planet, but I've never looked at her... y'know... in *that* way. Not seriously, anyway.

Until right now.

Never mind stopping traffic, she could stop time.

I shake my head, clearing the distracting—though not unpleasant—thoughts from my mind.

"Probably best to focus on staying alive for now. We can celebrate after we've killed everybody."

She grins mischievously. "I love it when you talk dirty!"

I chuckle. "Okay... *that* doesn't make us sound like a pair of sociopaths at all!"

I head upstairs. This shower needs to be like ice.

18

Ruby and I are sitting in Ichiro's car, which he was kind enough to leave for us, should we need to get anywhere in a hurry now that he's dropped off the grid. We're parked in a wide backstreet, deep inside the maze of Tokyo's daily chaos.

"Are you sure you're up to this?" she asks me. Her voice is laden with concern, as well as the hint of apology. She probably feels bad for even asking.

I look over at her. She insisted on driving. She's sitting half-turned in her seat, with a hand resting casually on the wheel.

"No question," I reply as convincingly as I can.

"Adrian, you can barely stand."

"I'm fine, honestly. I feel better than I look. Promise."

Her eyes narrow with inherent and justified doubt. Finally, she nods her acceptance and gestures out the window with a flick of her head.

"This definitely the right place?"

I look out across the street at the tattoo studio opposite. The main window is half-covered with large decals of Japanese symbols, which I can only assume say the name of the place. The door to the left of it is closed. Even from here, I see the wood rotting away in places. There's movement inside.

Open for business.

"This is the address Buchanan gave us," I confirm. "The guy he suspects is working for Kazawa's family should be inside any time after ten-thirty, according to his intel."

"How do you want to play it? He might not be alone."

I look back at her. "If I had a spare shit, I still wouldn't give it. The more of them, the better. Saves time."

She smiles back. Polite. Understanding. "You need to pace yourself. You're in no condition—"

"Miley could've cut one of my goddamn legs off in her little live stream, and I'd still easily take out a handful of these bastards. Besides..." I pull my jacket open to reveal one of my new Raptors holstered beneath my armpit. "I've got my guardian angel with me."

"Okay, then. Let's do this."

She moves to get out of the car, but I reach over and place a hand on her arm.

"No. I need you to stay here."

She looks back at me. Her brow furrows. Her eyes narrow. Her mouth opens.

"Why?"

I hold her gaze. Set my jaw. Become the evil that festers inside of me.

"Because you don't need to see what I'm gonna do to this guy to make him talk."

Her hand slowly releases the door handle. Her expression softens. She stares into my eyes and sees the familiar monster looking back at her. She nods without a word. She's seen the look on my face before. Knows what it means. Knows there's no point arguing.

I climb out of the car, turn my collar up as I hunch against the cold wind, and walk calmly across the street. I reach inside my jacket. Take out my Pilot and clip it in place. Same with my Ili.

I make a fist with each hand in turn, testing myself. I take a breath and feel the familiar sting of my war wounds. I cast a momentary glance over my shoulder to make sure Ruby isn't looking—which she isn't—before taking out the pain meds the hospital gave me from my jacket pocket. I pop one and swallow it dry.

That should hold me.

I can't afford to show any sign of weakness now. Not for one second. So much of my world is about perception. Not too long ago, even knowing I was in the same time zone would scare the crap out of people. I need Kazawa's people to believe I'm indestructible. It's the only way I'll survive long enough to get to the sonofabitch.

And to Miley.

Oh, I've got a bullet with her fucking name all over it.

I tap the butt of my gun through my jacket for one last piece of reassurance as I reach the other side of the street. I push the door open without breaking stride and step inside the parlor.

I'm greeted by the high-pitched whirring of a tattoo needle, coming from behind a black curtain ahead of me. There's a musty smell too—a cocktail of sweat and stale air. A makeshift counter stands against the wall to my right. A young woman leans casually against it, chewing gum. She's wearing dark eyeliner and bright purple lipstick. Her sleeveless black tank top has a skull on the front, clinging to the shape of her chest. Her exposed arms are covered in tattoos. She looks up at me.

"You lost?" she asks, her voice translated and digitized in my ear.

I smile politely. "I'm looking for someone I understand is a customer of yours."

"That right?" She pauses to look me up and down. *"We don't give out personal information without warrant. You got warrant?"*

I shake my head. "No. Do I look like a cop to you?"

She shrugs. *"You look like asshole to me. A real stupid asshole. You know who own this place?"*

"I can guess." I hold my hand out flat, level with my head, just below my eyeline. "Is he about this tall? Bad haircut... total dick... poor choice in women?"

She laughs but not because she found me funny. The expression didn't reach her eyes.

"You in wrong part of town, asshole." She reaches down and produces a large handgun, which looks out of place in her delicate grip. She rests it ominously on the counter in front of her. *"You go. No come back. Or you no see tomorrow. Clear?"*

I take a quick look around. The studio is effectively divided in two. Where I'm standing is the waiting area. There are seats under the main window; a low, wide coffee table with magazines scattered across it in front of them; some horrific music that sounds as if it's being played at double speed blasting from a radio on the floor in the corner; and, of course, our friendly hostess here.

An archway leads to the back half of the building, which

has four defined areas. Each contains a reclining chair, a rolling cart of tattooing accessories, and a curtain rail. Only one of them has the curtain pulled closed, signaling it's occupied. That must be my guy.

Beyond that is a fire exit door. No other sign of life.

Target. His tattooist. The goth chick with the over-sized gun.

Three people. No realistic threat.

I look back at her.

"Listen, *Twilight*, I'm not in the mood for your misplaced confidence or idle threats. I've had a shitty few days, and what patience I have is wearing thinner than the ice you're skating on." I brush my jacket apart, revealing my own gun. "I need to speak with the piece of shit getting some work done right now. So, either go get him... or go home."

She stares at me with disbelief for a long moment before placing a hand over her mouth and gasping behind her palm. Her eyes ping wide.

I'm guessing she's just realized she's addressing an overnight internet sensation.

She moves for the gun. Before her hand is even halfway to grabbing it, mine is drawn and raised, aimed steadily at her head.

I shake my head slowly from side to side. "I wouldn't, if I were you."

Her gaze alternates between me and the door. She takes a deep breath, glances at the black curtain, then bolts around the counter and out onto the street, quickly disappearing out of sight.

I smile to myself.

Still got it.

Keeping my gun held low by my side, I make my way

through the studio, toward the drawn curtain. The buzz of the needle is getting louder, which is good—neither of them are likely to hear me approaching.

I take a deep breath. No sign of the all-consuming pinches of pain from my history-making ass-kicking. Damn... those meds don't mess around!

Without warning or hesitation, I yank the curtain back.

What the...?

I see the tattooist first. It's another woman. Can't be much older than the one who just ran out the door. She has what I actually think is a nice design covering half her face. It's a tribal-style piece running right down the center, dividing her nose and mouth. She snaps her head around to look at me. Her eyes are wide, but she's frowning, as if offended by the intrusion.

I stare at her, emotionless.

"Leave. Now."

She looks quickly back and forth between me and her client, then springs to her feet and backs away toward the door.

I focus my attention on the guy in the chair.

Fuck me.

I'm all for freedom of expression, but this guy must have some serious self-esteem issues.

He's topless, displaying a chiseled physique that's covered almost entirely by one large, intricate tattoo that must've taken years to complete. But the thing about him that stands out the most are his eyes. The pupils are bright red, like hellfire. But his orbs are black, not white. I'm pretty sure... yeah... his eyeballs are tattooed!

The second thing that's hard to ignore is that the corners of his mouth have been surgically cut, maybe half an inch on both sides, allowing his mouth to open slightly wider than normal. And his tongue... Jesus Christ! His tongue has been split from the tip, forking it like a snake's.

He also has multiple piercings on his face, including two nose rings.

He glares at me, flicking his tongue and flexing his jaw open, like something kind of human desperately trying to intimidate a predator.

He jerks his body toward me, clearly intending to tackle me, then either fight or run. But he doesn't get chance. As soon as he sits upright in the chair, his forehead rests against the barrel of my shiny new gun.

"Sit down, dipshit," I say.

No sign of a Pilot on him, so I wait for the Ili to translate. He looks at the gun. Then at me. Then he sits back in the chair.

I smile. "There's a good dipshit. Now... I need your help."

The staring at each other while I wait for the translation is a little awkward.

"Do you know who I am?" he asks. *"You a dead man."*

I can't help but roll my eyes. "I don't care who you are. But I do care about who you work for. Tetsuo Kazawa. Where is he?"

He stares at me much longer than he needs to. I see the cogs at work behind his eyes.

"You Adrian... Hell. Yes?"

"Alive and kicking."

He smiles and flicks his tongue at me again. *"Not for long, you American asshole!"*

"You might be right about that," I reply, shrugging. "But before my time's up, I'm gonna bury your boss and everyone associated with him. A little bird tells me you might know where that piece of shit is hiding."

"Even if I did, I wouldn't tell you." He makes a slow and deliberate gun gesture with his right hand, firing at me and smiling. *"So, fuck you, Adrian Hell. You want to find Kazawa? Find him yourself."*

I lower my gun and smile back at him. In part, it's to hide my disappointment that he didn't just tell me what I wanted to know. Not that I really expected him to, but still—a guy can dream. But mostly, when a guy with a gun starts randomly smiling at you, I've found it can be quite an unnerving sight. And judging by the change in his expression, I see this time is no exception.

He holds my gaze for as long as he dares, but after a minute, he starts to look nervous. His eyes narrow and begin looking in any direction that isn't mine. His breathing gets slightly faster. He shifts uncomfortably in his seat.

"Y'know... there's a small part of me that's kind of glad you're not being helpful. Don't get me wrong—it's annoying, and before we're done here, you *are* going to tell me everything you know about where I can find Kazawa. But I think we all know I've not had the best few days. I'm feeling a little... cranky. Like I need to blow off a little steam. You understand?"

He nods slowly. Fearfully.

"The problem I have is... how do I torture you? I mean, look at you. You've done all that shit to yourself! What could I possibly do to you that you wouldn't simply think of as fashionable?"

I suppress a smile when I see him shrug, as if he's given it some genuine thought.

I continue. "But it occurs to me that perhaps the way to get information out of you isn't to torture you, necessarily, but to... undo all this work you've had done. For example..."

I snap my hand forward and pinch one of the nose rings

between my thumb and index finger. I pull on it slightly, feeling it resist against the skin of his nostril. His eyes widen with panic. He gestures wildly with his hands, waving them as a desperate plea for mercy.

Not today.

With a short, sharp motion, I yank my hand away, bringing the nose ring with me. I hear it tear effortlessly through the thin flesh. He clutches his nose as a thin stream of blood begins trickling down his face. He screams with pain.

I study the small item of jewelry for a moment before discarding it with a subtle flick.

"Now, that looks like it really sucked. What you need to remember from here on out is that shit's going to keep happening, and it's only gonna get worse for you." I jab his forehead with the barrel of my gun. "I want Kazawa. Tell me where he is, or tell me where I can find someone more helpful than you."

His head is lowered, his face partially covered by his blood-soaked hands. He looks at me through his eyebrows, boring a hole into me with a gaze laced with instant hatred. I stare into his dark orbs, seeing them flicker with indecision. My guess is he's thinking of the best way to make it out of here alive.

Spoiler alert: he's not going to.

It's fun watching him though. Even in the Yakuza, where loyalty is as natural as breathing, only a select few will ever choose their family over self-preservation. You just need to know which buttons to press.

"Fuck you, Adrian Hell. I don't know where Kazawa is."

I nod. "Fair enough. So, who does?"

He shakes his head. *"I don't know. Word is he's gone to ground. That little bitch of his caused big problem, putting you online."*

Hmm... dissension in the ranks, perhaps?

"You not a fan of his girlfriend?"

He finally looks up at me. His nose is a mess. I feel bad about that.

I'm sure I'll get over it.

He starts gesturing wildly. *"No! Ever since she come along, Kazawa been thinking with wrong head. She hurt our family."*

"So, tell me where I can find them, and I'll make sure she leaves you all in peace."

"No one heard from the boss since Golden Tiger get destroyed. Our Kyodai say to sit tight. So, we sit tight."

Annoyingly, I believe him. Guess it's back to Buchanan's list. I'll try one last thing with this cock-weasel.

"What about Ko? You know him?"

He pauses for a moment, then shakes his head. But I spotted the glimmer of recognition on his face.

I press the barrel of my gun forcefully into his forehead, pushing him back into his seat.

"Yes, you do. Don't lie to me. It'll hurt you."

He squirms under the pressure. Urges me to back off with panicked movements of his hands.

"Okay. Okay!" He shifts in his seat, composing himself. He flicks his forked tongue over his mouth, lapping up some blood from his nose. *"You know Octopus Bar?"*

"No, but I can find it. Why?"

He sighs, casting a thin spray of blood toward me in the process. *"Ko practically lives there. Him and his crew. Place open at ten. You find him after eleven."*

"That's actually helpful. Thank you."

He nods urgently. *"So... so, I can go?"*

I grimace with fake apology. "Yeah, about that..."

I pull the trigger. At this range, most of the back of his

skull is removed by the bullet. It hits the wall behind him with a dull crack, surrounded by a pink and crimson cocktail.

No way he would stay quiet. The fear of being punished for his loose tongue would be too great. He would tell whoever asked exactly what he told me, which would kill any element of surprise I have over Ko. So, this guy had to die.

It's that simple.

I holster my gun and turn to leave but catch sight of the tattoo needle resting on the rolling cart as I do. I look at it for a moment, then glance at the fresh corpse on the chair. I smile to myself.

No harm in sending a little message, is there?

...

...

...

Five minutes later, I climb back inside Ichiro's car. Ruby looks at me expectantly.

"So, how did it go?" she asks.

"No luck on Kazawa's location," I reply. "But I have the next best thing."

"Miley?"

I shake my head. "Ko."

Her eyes light up. The emerald menace in them sparkles with life.

"Perfect! I owe that piece of shit."

"Exactly. So long as we get Kazawa's location first."

"Where is he?"

"Some place called Octopus Bar. You know it?"

She nods. "I do. It's a karaoke bar just across the river."

I roll my eyes. "Karaoke? Really? For fuck's sake..."

She laughs as she starts up the engine. "You're going to love it!"

"Yeah, only because I get to shoot whoever's singing for once."

She pulls away from the curb, turns out of the alley, and we're soon lost in the hustle of a midday Tokyo.

19

I spent most of the afternoon asleep on the sofa, recharging my batteries after the exertion in the tattoo studio earlier. Ruby, for the most part, left me in peace to rest, but I'm guessing she's now bored.

How do I know?

The TV is blasting out, and she's just sat down heavily on the sofa beside me, jolting me back to the land of the living.

Let's be honest. She's not exactly subtle, is she?

I shuffle upright and crack my neck.

"Oh, are you awake?" she asks with a wry smile.

I turn to her, raising a tired eyebrow. "Apparently."

"Can I ask you something?"

I shrug. "Sure."

"That guy in the tattoo parlor earlier that you *obviously* killed... did you, by any chance, do anything out of the ordinary while you were there?"

188

"Um... such as?"

"Such as tattoo 'FUCK YOU KAZAWA' on his forehead, using your bullet hole for the O."

I laugh, embarrassed. "How did, ah... how did you know that?"

She looks at me with mock disappointment and points to the TV. I look over at the screen. It's a news report showing a police cordon outside the tattoo place. Subtitles are flashing across the bottom of the screen. The name of the guy is displayed beneath an image of his body that's dominating one corner of the screen. There's a warning to viewers about the graphic content. The reporter is saying police suspect it was a Yakuza-related hit.

I look back at her and shrug. "Thought it would be nice to say hi, that's all."

She rolls her eyes. "Don't you think that was a little reckless?"

I laugh. "Come on, Ruby. You're the last person on Earth to question any reckless behavior."

She looks dejected. "I'm not reckless..."

"Besides, only Kazawa is gonna know that was me, which is the point. He won't know what, if anything, that ass-hat told me before I killed him, so we still have the element of surprise. No harm done. If we're lucky, it might just piss him off enough to come up for air... at which point I can smash his fucking head off his shoulders."

Her expression softens, and a smile creeps across her face. "Yeah, okay. I'll let you off."

"Gee, thanks..."

"Are you feeling okay?"

I shrug. "Yeah, why?"

"You're sweating, despite the fact it's October. Just worried you might have a fever or something."

I run a hand across my brow. It's soaking. I still feel really drowsy too, despite being asleep for... what? Four hours, almost? Christ.

"Huh. No, I feel fine, honestly. Maybe a little dehydrated. Could you grab me a glass of water?"

She smiles patiently, then gets gracefully to her feet, running her hand faintly over my shoulder as she does. "Yeah, of course."

She glides into the kitchen. I sink back into the sofa.

Man, I feel like crap! I'm still half-asleep, but my heart seems to think I'm running a marathon. I bring my right hand to my face, massaging my temples for a second. It then starts to shake.

Oh, for crying out loud... not *this* again.

I look around for my Oxy-whatever-it's-called. They always help with the tremors, as well as take the edge off everything else that's hurting right now.

Where are they?

Oh, yeah, my jacket. I get to my feet and take one step toward the coat hook on the wall over by the door. I need to—

...

...

...

"Whoa!"

I land heavily on the floor, my head narrowly avoiding the corner of the coffee table.

"Adrian!" Ruby appears, rushing over to me and kneeling at my side. She places her hand on my chest. "What happened? Are you okay?"

That's a very good question. What *did* happen? I got up, and then the floor came rushing toward me.

"I... I think so. I must've tripped or something."

"No, Adrian—you fell. Like, passed out. Collapsed." Her tone is full of concern but also a hint of anger. "You're not well. You shouldn't be going after Kazawa in your condition. You should rest."

"I'm fine, honestly." I roll over on my side and prop myself up with my elbow. "I just need to get a little more rest, and I'll be good to go."

I push myself up to one knee. Try to stand. I make it halfway upright before toppling over again, this time onto the sofa.

"That's it," says Ruby, firmly. "I'm calling the hospital."

"No!" I crawl onto the sofa, lean back, and turn to face her. "Just... stop it, Ruby! Stop it! Stop... smothering me. You're not my fucking mother! I'm fine. Just listen to me. I'm fine! Do you understand? I don't need you..."

My words trail off. I don't know how I managed to stop myself from talking. I just vaguely realized I *was* talking, yet I have no idea what I was saying. I look at Ruby. The color has drained from her cheeks. Her eyes are wide and glistening with tears.

Shit.

"Look, I just need to... I need to..."

Oh, man, I think I'm going to—

I twist quickly to my side, just in time to vomit over the arm of the sofa. It feels like everything I've eaten in the last twenty years just decided to leave my body.

What's wrong with me?

I look back at Ruby. The image of her is blurry. The color is leaving my surroundings. I don't feel so good. I feel myself falling again. I really don't—

18:02 JST

It feels as if I have a dumbbell attached to each eyelid. I try to open them, but they seem weighted closed.

"Adrian?"

That's Ruby's voice. I'm on something comfortable and soft. I remember blacking out, and there's no way she'd be able to get me to my bed on her own, so I'm guessing it's the sofa.

I try to answer her, but my throat feels full of sand. I hear an illegible murmur, which I think came from me.

What the hell happened to me? I haven't felt this bad since that time Josh took me to a bar to watch a soccer match and insisted we drank pints of Guinness—which I remember had the look, consistency, and taste of tar.

Something cold and damp rests on my forehead. It feels good. I'm so hot, it's making me short of breath.

"You're okay, Adrian," says Ruby's voice. "Just try to relax."

It takes me three attempts to swallow and clear my throat.

"W-what happened?"

She sighs patiently. "You were sick—which was all kinds of gross, by the way—and then you passed out like a little girl."

I manage a small smile. Her own special brand of sympathy.

"And for the record," she continues, "I'm not cleaning that up."

I nod. "Fair... enough."

"Come on. Sit up and drink some water."

I feel her tugging on my arms. I do my best to assist, and

before I know it, I'm sitting upright, leaning back into the soft, worn sofa cushions. A cool glass is thrust into my hand. My arm is then raised by a gentle push on my wrist. I take a couple of sips and try once again to open my eyes.

Blurry light materializes in front of me. I blink rapidly to clear the fog and focus. I see Ruby's face. She's smiling, but it's more from sympathy than happiness, I think. She's crouching in front of me. Her hands rest on my legs for balance.

It's good to see her.

"You good?" she asks.

"Been better. Been worse."

"Yeah... I know. Listen, Adrian, I'm gonna ask you something now, and I need you to be honest with me, okay?"

I nod slowly.

"I mean *actually* honest, numbnuts. Don't just shrug away my concerns or lie and say you're fine. I want the truth. I deserve that. You *owe* me that."

This sounds serious...

I nod again. "Okay. Shoot."

She holds up my bottle of pain meds. "How many of these have you taken?"

I think about it. I'm not hesitating because I don't want to tell her. I genuinely don't know. Not for sure.

I shrug. "Enough that nothing hurts. Why?"

She slowly unscrews the cap and tips the bottle up, emptying the contents into her palm. I look down. I see two pills in her hand.

"You're supposed to take one every twelve hours. That's two a day. This bottle was supposed to last you three weeks."

"Okay..."

"Adrian, it's almost empty after three days! Do you have any idea how dangerous this shit is if you O.D. on it?"

I wave her away. "Ruby, please. I'm not—"

She reaches over and slaps me hard across the face. My eyes snap open with surprise. I stare at her, shocked. My cheek's stinging. She has a good left hook.

"Don't you dare dismiss me, you sanctimonious sonofabitch!" She waves the empty bottle in front of me. "These things will fucking kill you, Adrian! Do you understand that? Are you listening to me? We did *not* go through everything we've been through for you to kill yourself like some low-life fucking junkie. You're better than that! You deserve better than that! How dare you..."

She trails off as she starts sobbing uncontrollably. She buries her face into my lap, her body shuddering with heavy whimpers. I feel her tears gently soaking my legs.

Does she... does she think I did this on purpose or something? How could she think I would ever try to kill myself with pills? She knows better than most, if I ever got to the point where I'd had enough, I'd eat a bullet.

Pills?

No. That's crazy. I just need to take the edge off. I need to appear strong. I need to *be* strong to go after Miley and Kazawa. Plus, these things stop my tremors, which is a bonus, given I intend to aim my gun at lots of people before this war is over.

I just needed help pushing through the pain. That's all. Miley did a real number on me. There's no denying that. If I didn't have a little help, I wouldn't have made it out of hospital, let alone tracked down Ko.

No... Ruby is just emotional. She's not thinking straight. We've both been through a lot. Maybe I have neglected her a little. I've been so caught up in how everything that's happened has affected me, I've not thought about how it's affected her. She just needs me to—

I swear to God, if I could, I'd slap you!

Josh?

Yes, it's Josh. Satan's here too, but he can't talk right now because he's so fucking angry at you.

I must be losing it. The voices in my head are reprimanding me.

You're goddamn right we are, asshole! Look at her. Look how upset she is. You think she's pissed at you? You think she's being overly sensitive? You're a jackass.

I don't understand.

...

...

...

You know you have issues when you can actually hear the voices in your head face-palm themselves with frustration.

She loves you, you freakin' idiot! And you've hurt her because yes... you are a low-life junkie!

No, I'm not. Don't start with me. I'm not in the mood. I just needed—

Oh, you just needed... Sounds a lot like an excuse to me. You know who else makes excuses for upsetting people close to them when they get caught? Drug addicts!

No, they don't...

Think about it, asshole. The extra painkiller here and there for your tremor. Hiding the fact you were taking more of the Oxycodone than you should've been. You knew it was wrong—why else would you hide it?

Crap. I have a point.

Fine.

I place a hand on the back of Ruby's head and gently stroke her hair. She looks up. Her make-up has formed dark streams down her cheeks. Her eyes are glazed with tears.

She stares at me with total vulnerability, as if she has no control over her emotions. I know she would never allow herself to be like that in front of anyone.

Except me.

We have a bond very few people could ever understand. Forged in conflict. Strengthened by tragedy. And I've abused that bond... that trust, by taking it for granted and lying to her. I know I can rely on her for anything. Why couldn't I admit to her I wasn't ready for this? Why couldn't I say I was struggling?

"Ruby, I'm sorry."

She sniffs back her tears. Straightens her body and rests back on her feet. Crosses her arms defiantly.

"For what, exactly?"

"What do you mean?"

"I mean, what, precisely, are you sorry for?"

I go to speak but stop myself. This is the kind of thing I need to get right. Say the wrong thing here, and I'll push her away even farther. Maybe forever.

I take a deep breath. It hurts, but I ignore it.

Here goes nothing.

"I'm sorry for not being straight with you about how much I'm struggling."

She holds my gaze for a long moment.

"Struggling with what?"

"With... everything. Take your pick! Breathing, blinking, moving in general. Miley damn near killed me, Ruby." I hold up my right hand. "This hasn't been the same since Dubai. I struggle holding a gun in my dominant hand. Not a great problem to have for someone in my line of work. Especially now. I need to be at my best. I need to be strong. I need to be Adrian Hell. I can't do that in my condition. Those pills, whatever's in them... they help. They keep the pain and the tremors and the doubts at bay. They allow me to be who I need to be."

"Yes, Adrian, but at what cost? Look at you. I did a little research while you were out cold. It wasn't exactly hard to find. Everything you're feeling right now, they're side effects of these pills. They're what happens if you become addicted and then try to quit."

I frown. "But... at the risk of making myself appear worse, I'm not trying to quit. I'm trying to take more."

"Exactly. You've overdosed on them to the point where they're affecting you in the same way. You have so much of this shit in your system right now, it's beyond belief. These tablets will kill you, Adrian. They say to take one every twelve hours for a damn good reason."

"Yeah... I'm beginning to see the flaw in my logic."

"Why didn't you just tell me you were struggling?" She leans forward again, resting her forearms on my legs. "We've been through so much together. We're both still here because we're good at what we do. Because we're smart. Picking your battles is not a sign of weakness, you know? We lost this one. Our enemy was crazy prepared for a fight we didn't know we were having. There's nothing wrong with biding our time before we retaliate."

"Except we can't, can we?"

"Why not? It's the smart thing to do, Adrian. You're good. Even at fifty percent, you're twice as good as most of the professionals out there. But you're not at fifty percent. You're in single digits, and that's being generous. Going up against an entire Yakuza family out of pride at this point is suicide. We both know it."

"But we don't have a choice. We both know that too. Just because I'm not ready to fight, do you think that will stop them coming after us to finish the job? Do you think Miley's gonna sit there and say, 'Hang on, let's leave it and give him time to recover—fair's fair?' We either do what we can now and take the fight to them, or we die licking our wounds. I can promise you, Ruby—they're coming for us. They might be lying low for the moment, but wherever Kazawa and Miley are right now, they're getting ready to finish the job. I can't sit here and wait for the inevitable. We have to fight. War isn't convenient. It doesn't work around you. It is what it is, and you better be ready to step up when your enemy comes for you."

She looks away. Wipes a tear from her eye. Take a deep breath.

"Why is this fight so different?" she asks. "I don't understand. All the shit you've been through. The shit we went through together. You took all that in your stride. You did what you had to do, but you never once took an unnecessary risk."

I smile, mostly to myself. "I think Josh would disagree with you there."

Ruby rolls her eyes. "No, he wouldn't. Because he knew you better than anyone. Certainly better than me, but even I know you play a part. This reckless... devil-may-care approach you have to any situation. The shoot-first-never-ask-questions mindset. You know I see right through it, don't you? Just like Josh did."

"I don't know what you mean..."

"You're one of the smartest, bravest, most violent and caring people I've ever met, Adrian. There's a reason you've enjoyed the reputation you have for so long. You don't even take a breath unless you've calculated every possible repercussion of it."

I lower my gaze. "That's not true..."

Her hand squeezes my knee. "Please. Who are you talking to, jackass?"

We exchange a small smile.

"So," she continues, "tell me why this is different. Tell me why you're willing to sacrifice yourself to win this fight. Why not play this like every other job, every other conflict you've ever had?"

"Because this isn't like anything else I've been through. Look at me. Miley Tevani has spent the formative years of her childhood focused on nothing except killing me. She's highly trained—perhaps more so than her mother was. She's aligned herself with one of the most powerful Yakuza families in Japan. And at the risk of blowing smoke up my own ass, she single-handedly managed to neutralize the best assassin who ever lived. But she still failed because I'm still alive. I saw it in her eyes, Ruby. When she was saying all those things about me. When she was beating on me. I saw the same look I saw in myself in the early years after my family was killed. The same darkness that consumed me has consumed her. I know what it's like to have someone that driven... that passionate... that sadistic hunting you. And she *is* hunting me. Hunting *us*. Right now. If you play it safe, you die. End of story."

Ruby gets to her feet and starts pacing back and forth in front of me. I watch her, content with the silence. Each time she turns and walks slowly toward the windows, she glances at the black bag of goodies left by Buchanan. Finally, she stops in front of the TV. Folds her arms across her chest. Cocks a hip. Looks at me.

"So, get your ass up. Let's fight."

I nod. "Only way that's happening is if I take the edge off. That's the sad truth. If I go anywhere feeling everything my body's going through, I'm no use to anyone. I can't protect myself. I can't protect you."

She raises an eyebrow and screws her face up, unimpressed.

"Do I look like I need protecting?"

I shake my head. "No, but then, I didn't say you did."

"You literally just said—"

"Just because you don't *need* protecting, that doesn't mean you're not *worth* protecting."

She grins at me. Her eyes search my face.

"If you didn't have a little bit of vomit on your chin, I would kiss you right now."

I bring my hand up quickly, embarrassed.

"You're kidding me?"

She points to her own face, tapping the area just below the corner of her mouth with her finger. "Just a *tiny* bit of sweetcorn, right there..."

"Ah, Christ."

I hate my life.

20

The sidewalk vibrates beneath my feet. The rain-glazed road perfectly reflects the neon luminance of the city's nightlife.

Ruby and I stand side-by-side, staring at the Octopus Bar directly opposite. There's a large fluorescent graphic of an octopus above the double doors of the entrance. Different legs light up bright pink in sequence, giving the impression it's waving at me.

Stood on either side of the doors is a man wearing a fitted suit. Hands crossed, held low in front of them. Professional. Alert.

I turn to Ruby. She's staring intently ahead, focused.

After I wiped the puke from my face, I grabbed a shower, tried to freshen up a bit. We talked about the best way forward. She suggested I dose up on regular painkillers and caffeine. I argued I was already screwed, so those last two Oxycodone aren't likely to do much additional damage, compared to the upper hand they would give me over the course of the next hour or two.

She slapped me again before flushing them down the can.

So, three cups of coffee, a handful of painkillers, and a hot shower later, here we are. We stand together, facing what is hopefully the final stop on our journey to Kazawa.

But inside this karaoke bar, protecting Ko, is likely to be a small army of Yakuza foot soldiers. Not to mention a whole bunch of innocent people. This isn't going to be easy.

We're both dressed in black, head to toe. I'm wearing black denim with a black T-shirt, underneath a black coat that hangs down to my knees. At my back, both Raptors are holstered, ready should this shit go south.

Ruby's idea of discreet differed slightly from mine, although you have to give her points for trying. She's wearing a black skirt that comes barely halfway down her thighs and leather boots that come to just above her knees. Her black top clings to her chest but leaves her midriff bare. Her coat runs to her ankles and is tied together at the waist, concealing the belt of throwing knives and the silenced SMG over her shoulder, tucked around her back.

We're also both wearing black neck gaiters with half a skull imprinted on them.

Ruby turns to me. "So, how do you want to play this?"

"We go in, identify Ko, and get as close to him as we can before people realize who we are and start shooting. Ideally, we can secure him and use him as a shield to get back out of there. We get him to tell us where Kazawa is hiding, then we kill him."

She nods. "Good plan. And do you have another plan if *that* plan doesn't work?"

"A back-up plan, you mean?" I pause. "Nah. Where's the fun in that?"

She laughs. "No, really—what's plan B?"

I look over at the building, squinting in the pink neon glare. When I look back at Ruby, my heart rate is steady and slow. I'm as at peace with what comes next as I'm ever going to be.

"We kill everyone. Hope Kazawa comes to us."

She nods again, slower this time, more reluctant. "Okay..."

I'm not sure if she can tell if I'm being serious or not.

I look up and down the street before setting off across the road.

For the record, I am. *Deadly* serious.

We approach the entrance without slowing. No reason for these two bouncers to suspect anything. We're just two people entering a nightclub. No one else would hesitate or feel conspicuous, so why should we?

They both turn as we near them. Naturally, their attention is drawn to Ruby. The guy on the left steps slightly to the side—a small gesture to allow her into the club while subtly checking her out. I look at the guy on the right and give him a courteous nod as I follow her through the open doors.

So far, so good.

Inside the main entrance is a small vestibule. Another set of double doors stand between us and the inner arena of the club. The music, such as it is, is much louder here. The bassline still obscures any real tune, but it gives a clear indication of the atmosphere within.

It's loud. It's busy. Which means there will be a lot of people—potential targets and otherwise—to contend with.

A booth dominates the left side, made of Plexiglass. A

woman stands inside it, blowing bubbles with some gum. Her dark hair is styled into pigtails with bright pink streaks in them. Beside the booth is another man, wearing a similar suit to the guys outside. This guy, however, has a visible earpiece.

There's a hierarchy in all aspects of Yakuza life. Even in places like this. The guys outside will be the lowest-level members. No earpieces, so no contact with the more trusted security inside. They're simply there to look intimidating and to make sure the wrong people don't come in.

A fantastic job so far...

But this guy's connected. One wrong move here, and everyone inside will know to prepare for trouble. Ruby and I steel ourselves, running the same routine as before. As we near the doors, the guy steps in front of us, holding up his hand as a silent instruction for us to stop.

He points to the booth and says something I don't understand. I give him the universal gesture of tilting my head to the side and tapping my Pilot.

...

...

...

"Ten thousand Yen entry fee."

Christ, that's extortionate! But whatever.

We both turn back and approach the booth. I pay our entry fees. The girl inside the booth stares impassively, apparently numbed by the routine and mundanity of her job.

"Hands."

We each hold out a hand in turn. The girl stamps the back of them with a pink Octopus.

I look at it for a moment.

"This shit better wash off," I whisper to Ruby.

She rolls her eyes. "Yeah, *that's* the thing to concern yourself with right now. Dumbass."

"What?" I reply, shrugging.

We head for the doors once more. The guy looks us up and down, glances past us at the bouncers standing outside, then nods and steps aside, gesturing us to head further inside.

Ruby and I push open a door each and step inside the club.

...

...

...

Jesus!

We're hit by a wave of music that makes my ribcage pulse. Which, given my injuries, actually hurts. A random dance song is playing I've never heard. Easily a hundred people are crammed into the space, moving to the music. This place is packed!

Wide steps lead down to the main floor, where three large blocks stand with glass casing resting on them. Each one contains a samurai sword. Possibly decorative. Possibly real. Hard to tell from here.

The floor itself is shaped like a horseshoe, bordered by a waist-high counter with bar stools around it. In the center is a raised platform that has a large screen and a microphone stand on it. Someone's standing with their back to us, singing. Sort of. It's more like screaming. Actually, it's more like the sound a cat makes if you stand on its tail. But everyone here seems to be enjoying it.

I glance quickly at Ruby. She's discreetly nodding her head to the rhythm as she concentrates.

Figures.

Along the side walls are several single doors leading to

private karaoke booths. The glass is mirrored, so I can't see inside. I assume they're all occupied. Halfway along both walls are staircases leading to the upper level—a wider horseshoe with seating overlooking the club.

At the far end of the room, built into the curve beneath the balcony, is the bar. Dozens of bottles of spirits line the wall behind the counter. A crowd of people three-deep is stood waiting for their next drink.

"What do you think?" I ask, shouting over the noise.

"I think this sucks," Ruby replies. "I count over a dozen security guards, all armed. And that's just down here."

"Yeah, I counted fourteen for sure. God knows how many are up there. Let's find Ko and get the hell outta here."

We walk down the steps, standing either side of the central plinth. I take a look at the case. The sword inside is a beautiful weapon. Pretty sure it's real. The blade is like a mirror, and the hilt is fashioned as a green dragon with red jewels for its eyes. I reckon it would—

"Adrian?"

I look over at Ruby. She's staring ahead, looking up at the upper balcony. Her eyes are narrowed with focus.

"Yeah?"

"I've found Ko."

I follow her gaze. Leaning on the balcony, dead center, surrounded by men in dark suits, is Ko. He's dressed as he always is—casual, as if he's heading to the beach. Even from here, I see the expression on his face. A mixture of surprise and disdain. He's pointing right at us.

I let out a heavy sigh.

It was all going so well.

21

We both stand, frozen to the spot, staring up at Ko. A million things are running through my head right now. This definitely didn't go the way I had hoped. There's still a lot of real estate between us and him, and the fact he's already seen us doesn't bode well at all.

My priority is wrapping my hands around this prick's throat and punching him until he gives up Kazawa. A close second is making sure no one in this place gets hurt who doesn't deserve to—which isn't going to be easy, given it's hard to tell who's Yakuza and who isn't. A place like this, it won't just be the suits who have ties to a family. For all I know, every single person in here could be gunning for us.

Another growing concern is how weak and ineffective regular painkillers are. My right hand is aching. A familiar throbbing is gradually spreading across my entire palm, a sign that a painful tremor isn't far away. Not ideal, given my current situation.

I glance to my left.

Ruby is also a slight worry. Her legs are rigid, and she's rocking forward on her toes, like a sprinter in the starting blocks, waiting for the gun. Her fists are clenched tightly, draining the color from her knuckles. Her eyes are unblinking, transfixed on Ko.

I can't imagine what Ko and his friends subjected her to before I arrived at the Golden Tiger, but I *can* imagine the way Ruby feels right now. I know the look. That thirst for revenge. She will be salivating at the prospect of beating the holy hell out of him, which makes her a liability. I can't worry about her staying focused while dealing with everything else.

I place a hand on her arm, spinning her toward me.

"Listen, I need you thinking straight here, okay?"

Her eyes narrow. "Are you seriously lecturing me on restraint right now?"

"No. God, no. In fact, I'm doing the complete opposite." I cast a quick look up at Ko. His security guards are flooding toward the staircases on both sides of the room, flanking us. "I need you at your most lethal... your most crazy... your most Ruby-like. But I also need you thinking clearly. Don't get blinded by your obvious and understandable lust for vengeance, okay? We need to stay on mission here."

She's breathing fast and deep, evidenced by the prominent rise and fall of her chest. I see her eyes dart in all directions, taking in what I saw a moment ago. Assessing the battlefield. When she looks back at me, the focus remains in her eyes, but her expression softens slightly.

"He'd be so proud of you, Adrian," she says with a small smile.

I return the gesture and shrug. "His boy's all grown up, right?"

"Something like that."

We turn back to face the room. A line of suited Yakuza security guards appears from either side of the room, forming a wall that blocks our access to both stairwells. In the center, the crowd of people seems oblivious to what's happening, lost in their own world, dancing like they'll die if they stop.

The men all brush their suit jackets aside, revealing handguns tucked inside their waistbands. I look back up at Ko, who is still surrounded by a dozen men. He's standing with his arms folded across his chest, arrogant and tall, confident in his preconceived victory over the two of us.

I take a deep breath, then move a hand to my back, reaching for one of my Raptors. I see Ruby do the same behind me.

"Tell me we're going to get through this, and I'll believe you," she shouts to me, her gaze never leaving the sea of enemies before us.

Before I can answer, the person stood on the raised platform steps down, replaced by a young man wearing a sleeveless vest and ripped jeans. The background music fades as his song of choice begins. The familiar sequence of chords blasts out as "Thunderstruck" starts to play.

Weirdly, I catch myself thinking that's a brave choice of song for someone who probably isn't proficient in the language. But I'm not complaining. I sing it to myself as the guy starts.

Thunder!

I reach inside my coat and take out the protective carbon fiber mask the hospital gave me. I slide it over my head and adjust it on my face for comfort. Then I turn to Ruby and smile. She looks back at me and frowns. I mouth the words again, this time to her.

Thunder!

She rolls her eyes.

I smile wider and nod.

"We're going to get through this, Ruby," I shout back. "You know why?"

She shakes her head. I point generally to the roof just as the man singing says, "You've been... thunderstruck!"

I pull the neck gaiter up over my nose and mouth. Ruby does the same and nods once, signaling she's as ready as she's ever going to be. I draw my Raptor. I'll keep things left-handed for now. I tilt my head to the side slightly, a silent *here we go* to Ruby, then I take aim and start firing. Now isn't the time for diplomacy. You shoot first or you die first.

The first three rounds find their targets, dropping the first three men on the right. I set off running toward them, emptying my gun at them, more as a deterrent for them to retaliate than to hit anyone specifically, although I do catch another guy in his shoulder as I near the stairs.

I hear gunshots to my left, signaling Ruby is taking the same approach.

She'll be fine.

There were seven guys on the right in total. Three are definitely dead now. One's injured and out of action for the time being. I close in on the remaining three, stepping toward the middle guy first.

Keeping stride, I swing a stiff right hook, half-expecting him to duck under it. It was thrown mostly as a distraction, as my intended next target is actually the guy on the left. Getting the middle one to duck temporarily takes him off the board in terms of physical threats. Not much he can do if he's crouching. I'm too close for him to get a proper shot off, and if he goes for the uppercut, I'll see it coming in plenty of time. Meanwhile, the guy on the left won't assume

I'm coming for him, because of the punch I threw, leaving him off-guard.

The middle guy just threw a wrench in the works though. He didn't duck. Instead, I connected solidly on his jaw and sent him crashing to the floor. It killed my momentum and left me side-on to the guy on the left, who, in turn, is now much more prepared for me. As Middle drops, Left raises his arm, reaching out, seemingly intent on grabbing my throat. I bring my left arm up to meet him. The difference is that's the hand I'm holding my gun with.

His eyes snap wide with horror as the barrel presses against his forehead. I pull the trigger before he can react. A thin spray of dark crimson mist bursts out behind him, covering a small group of people stood nearby.

Whoops!

The noise in here is such that I don't think anyone had noticed the skirmish and gunfire up until now. But one of the young women in the group is now screaming, her face streaked with a dead man's blood.

This might be a problem...

I quickly turn my body a hundred and eighty degrees, shooting the remaining guy first in the stomach, then in the head. He drops like a stone, redecorating the wall behind him on his way down. I watch him all the way to the floor before turning my attention to the guy I punched. He's slowly climbing back to his feet. I shoot him at close range in the back of the head as he makes it to one knee. He slumps face-down on the floor, finished.

I look back at the crowd. I need to assess and prepare. This is about to get very—

Uh-oh.

When we first stepped inside, I estimated around a hundred people were in the middle of the dance floor surrounding the podium for the singers. Based on that estimate, I would say around eighty of them are currently running around in a blind panic, desperate to remember the way out. The remaining twenty are standing still, expressionless and suddenly out of place, staring right at me.

This is a goddamn Yakuza field trip!

I look up at Ko. He's still smiling. Still standing there like a king surveying his kingdom. Unwavering in the belief he's untouchable.

Oh, I'm going to choke that smile right off your face, you smug little bastard.

I stand my ground, catching my breath. On the other side of the crowd, I see Ruby dispatching the last of her wall of security. Our eyes meet over the dance floor. Half the Yakuza there turn their backs on me, focusing on her.

Shit just went sideways faster than a crab on cocaine.

I may need the other Raptor.

I draw my second weapon as I turn and run as fast as my body allows up the staircase. The music has finally stopped. I hear the hurried movements of people following me, mixed with the screams of the innocent civilians still scrambling to find a way out.

I hope Ruby's doing the same. I don't want to deal with whatever's waiting up here on my own if I can avoid it.

The staircase turns twice, first to the right, then to the left as it opens up at the edge of the upper horseshoe. A dull pink hue covers the floor and the furniture. I cast a glance to my left and see Ko gesturing wildly in my direction. A frontal assault would be unwise, despite how appealing it is. No... I need cover.

Ahead of me are two low, wide tables, covered with empty glasses and bottles, sitting haphazardly in front of seating that runs around the curved border of the upstairs seating area.

They'll do nicely.

I run toward them and jump, twisting in mid-air and landing roughly in the seat, both guns raised and aiming without compromise at the stairwell. A heartbeat later, the first three men from the dance floor appear.

I fire multiple, alternating shots in quick succession, instinctively targeting any movement. The three men drop quickly, flailing backward and disappearing out of sight down the stairs.

That should make them think twice. It buys me some valuable—

"Shit!"

The cushioned seat beside me explodes in a concentrated plume of smoke and padding as a bullet punches its way through, mere inches to my right.

I look over to where Ko is standing, but he's obscured by a mob of Yakuza security. They clamber over one another to get to me, no doubt eager to impress.

I empty both magazines into the crowd indiscriminately. I clip a couple of them but nothing fatal. They scatter and take cover behind chairs and alcoves. I look down at the Raptor in my right hand. I missed almost everything with this gun just then. My hand's no use to me right now, meaning neither is the gun. I quickly holster it and reload the one in my left.

I reach over one of the tables and grip the edge, pulling it toward me and tipping it over. I crouch behind it, completely hidden. It might not offer much protection from a coordinated onslaught, but these assholes seem reluctant to shoot, so I should be okay. I just hope Ruby's coping on the other side.

I take some deep breaths to keep my heart rate in check. Now isn't the time for panic or doubt. Now is the time for violence without hesitation.

I peek over the top of the upended table. The group of men who were protecting Ko are fanning out in front of me, over by the stairs, maybe twenty feet away. The remaining men from downstairs are coming up too, merging with them, adding to the wall forming before me. I count fourteen in total. All wearing suits. All holding handguns. All looked pissed at me. The line blocks access to the stairs and to Ko. No way through.

I look down at my Raptor. I was so overwhelmed when I first opened the box, I never really paid attention to the gun itself, beyond the shape of it. The craftsmanship is stunning. These things probably retail at twenty grand a piece. Death has never looked so beautiful.

From the other side of the room, I hear the faint sound of a man screaming, followed by a muted thud. My guess? Someone just tried to attack Ruby, and she threw him over the balcony.

I look back at the Raptor and smile.

I stand corrected.

In my mind, I visualize the line in front of me. Study the position of each man, burned into my brain from the glimpse I took a moment ago. I pick my targets. Four of them. Let's not be greedy. Four seems reasonable. I have a full mag—eighteen plus one in the chamber. Left-handed. That's... what? A required success rate of almost twenty percent?

Easy.

I pop up, quickly resting my hand on the edge of the table to steady myself. Everyone is where I remembered them. With rapid, unrelenting squeezes of the trigger, I empty my gun and duck back behind the table as they begin to return fire. I hear the thick wood splinter around me, but so far, it's keeping the bullets at bay.

I reckon I got six then. Maybe. Definitely five. Not bad.

As I reload, I hear shouting. I tilt my head, hoping the Pilot will pick up what's being said.

…

…

…

"Throw a grenade! Kill the bastard!"

Oh, shit!

I leap to my feet again and quickly scan the platoon of enemies before me. I count eight. My gaze rests on the guy standing to my right, two from the end. He has a frag grenade in his hand. A crazed, angry look on his face.

I take a breath and narrow my eyes, focusing on my target. It's roughly the size of a pear. From this distance, to me, it's as if I have the barrel resting against it.

"Sayonara, dickwad."

I snap my arm up and fire, aiming with my eyeline, relying on muscle memory and training to do the rest. I drop to my knees immediately as the explosion roars around the club. The force of the blast sends the table flying into me, carrying me backward and slamming me into the barrier of the upstairs horseshoe. I stop, hard, but the table keeps going, shattering as it crushes me. I grunt with pain as the air is punched from my lungs and already-cracked ribs receive a fresh dose of physical trauma.

Fuck me!

I cough up thick blood, spitting it to the floor in front of me. I gasp for breath—a painful and difficult process I'd gladly not have to do right now.

The air around me is misty with smoke and debris. I

push shards of broken table off me and shuffle to one knee, pausing only to expel more blood from my mouth. I look around.

A chunk of the floor and barrier near the stairs has disappeared. What's left is covered in blood and littered with body parts wrapped in torn clothing.

Well... while I perhaps didn't consider the consequences of shooting a grenade from distance, it seems to have evened the odds quite nicely.

I stagger to my feet and wave my way through the cloud of dust. As the air clears, I see Ko crouched underneath a table, his hands and forearms covering his head. Standing in front of him in a low stance, waving their guns around aimlessly, are two security guards. They mustn't be able to see clearly. I'm not exactly hiding, but they're not trying to shoot me.

I squint in the lingering haze. Try to aim at the nearest guy. My arm feels heavy, and raising it sends a stabbing sensation through the middle of my torso.

Goddammit.

I limp forward, my right hand held across my body, comforting my ribs. Both men turn to face me as I lock eyes with Ko. They raise their guns.

Ah, shit. I'm too weak to fight them both. I can't raise my gun. I just hope they don't—

BANG!

BANG!

I screw my eyes closed and twitch with shock, waiting for the bullet wounds to register.

...

...

...

I open one eye. Look around.

Nope. Still alive.

I open the other eye and stare blankly ahead as both men fall to the floor like felled trees. Ko is shaking underneath his table.

Huh?

I look to my left. Ruby's standing there, breathing heavy. A thin film of sweat coats her brow, glistening in what's left of the pink neon hue. Her arm is raised and straight. Smoke whispers from the barrel of her SMG.

She must've set it to fire single shots. Nice. Efficient. A gunfight on a budget.

She glares at me. "You shot a grenade, didn't you?"

"Yeah..."

She lowers her gun and walks toward me. "What kind of idiot shoots a fucking grenade when they're standing near it?"

I raise my hand and smile weakly before grimacing.

She shakes her head. "How have you survived this long? Seriously..."

"What can I say? Maybe I'm lucky." I nod toward her chest. Her top is stained with what I can only assume is blood. "You okay?"

She looks down at herself and shrugs. "Oh, yeah... it's not mine."

We turn to face Ko, standing shoulder to shoulder.

"So much for your protection," says Ruby. She aims her gun at him. "Now... if you wanna see the sun rise again, you'll tell us exactly where your boss and his little bitch are."

His bottom lip is quivering. His eyes are wide and glazed with tears. He looks at Ruby, then turns to me, silently begging for my help.

I shrug at him. "Hey, don't look at me, asshole. The lady asked you a question."

"I don't know!" he whimpers.

Ruby sighs and turns to me. "You smell that?"

I nod, pretending to sniff up. "Yeah, there's a vaguely familiar odor in the air."

"Hmm, I thought so. Now, what is it?" She taps her lips with her finger, as if pondering a deep question. Then she points upward in a Eureka moment and looks back at Ko. "Oh, yeah—that's it... bullshit!"

Ko shuffles out from under the table and kneels in front of us. He holds up both hands, praying for mercy.

"N-no, please! I can't tell you. He'll kill me! She'll kill me!"

I frown. "Well, they can't both do it, so be thankful."

"You've just gone from not knowing to not being able to tell us," observes Ruby. "So, I was right? Bullshit."

"Please! I'm sorry, I—"

"Okay, enough," I say as I crouch in front of him.

I muster every ounce of strength I have left to raise my gun and look as intimidating as I can. This guy's about to crack. He just needs one final push. I press the barrel of my Raptor to his forehead, dead center on the bridge of his nose, separating his eyebrows.

Christ, this hurts! But it'll be worth it.

"Look, I get it, okay? You're scared of what will happen to you if you talk to us. That makes sense. I've met Kazawa before. And Miley. I know they can hurt you in ways you likely can't imagine. But if you tell us where they are, we will kill them both. Which means there won't be anyone left to come looking for you. So, you'll be in the clear."

He looks at me. I see the fear etched onto his face.

"You promise you let me live?"

"I promise you that Kazawa and Miley won't come after you if you talk." I glance at Ruby. "And neither will we."

Ko looks at us both in turn before getting awkwardly to his feet. He nods.

"Come. I show you."

"No tricks," says Ruby as she steps aside.

Ko heads for the stairs on Ruby's side of the upper level. She follows closely, her gun trained on him. I shuffle wearily behind them.

We walk down the stairs and across the dance floor, toward the three glass cases and the steps leading to the vestibule outside. If he's going to try anything funny, it'll be when he's near those swords...

He climbs the steps without hesitation.

Huh. Pussy.

We follow him through the doors. The girl in the booth has gone. So has the guard with the earpiece. The main entrance is standing wide open and unprotected.

Ko turns to us, beckoning us both outside.

"Come. This way. I show you. I show you."

Ruby quick-steps in front of him and heads outside, turned so she can aim her SMG at him from a safe distance. I stay behind him.

Once outside, he stops on the sidewalk and points along the street. We track his gaze.

"There."

He's pointing toward a large skyscraper, towering over the rest of the city, silhouetted in the night sky, visible only by the pinpricks of light from the thousands of windows. If I could guess, I would say it was at least a mile away. Maybe a mile and a half.

"Kazawa's in there?" asks Ruby.

Ko nods urgently. *"Whole building owned by Kazawa. Many companies we control based there. Top floor—all Kazawa's. His... penthouse."*

Even from this distance, I need to crane my neck to see the very top of the structure. A mast disappears into the low clouds, attached to the peak of the pointed roof. That must be fifteen hundred feet. Maybe more.

Fuck that.

Ruby looks at me. "Makes sense he would hide out in there if he needed to lay low. No one can see him. No one can get to him."

I sigh. "Agreed. I don't like it, but it makes sense." I shove Ko's shoulder. "And Miley will definitely be with him?"

Ko nods again. *"Those two never apart. Where she goes, he follows."*

"Excellent. I appreciate your help, Ko."

He turns to me, putting his back to Ruby. *"And your promise?"*

I smile. "I gave you my word. We'll see to it Kazawa and Miley don't come looking for you. And neither will we."

He smiles back and rolls his eyes with relief. A moment later, he begins laughing.

I take a small side-step to my left.

Ruby whips her SMG up, bringing the barrel level with the back of his head.

She pulls the trigger.

His body lurches forward, hitting the concrete hard. Blood gushes from what's left of his face, pooling on the ground around him.

"Feel better?" I ask Ruby.

She stares impassively at Ko's body for a long moment before looking up at me with a satisfied grin on her face. "Much. Thank you."

I glance up and down the street. Anyone who fled the club has long since run away. There's no one around, as if word quickly got out this place was toxic and people should stay away for their own safety.

I hear the faint symphony of sirens.

"We should go," I say, gesturing toward the skyscraper in the far distance. "We've got work to do."

We holster our weapons. I remove my protective eyewear and pocket it. We lower our scarves. We cross the street calmly, putting quick and easy distance between us and the massacre inside the club.

The sirens get nearer as we disappear into the night.

22

It's freezing inside our apartment. I'm standing over by the window, leaning against it with my back to the city sprawling below. Ruby is sitting on the sofa, her legs crossed and tucked beneath her, huddled under a blanket she keeps draped over the arm. Facing her, stood in front of the TV, is Ichiro.

Ruby called him shortly after we fled from the Octopus Bar, on my request. I understand why he wanted to lay low after the nightmare at The Golden Tiger and fully respect it, but with Ko out of the way now, we're on the home stretch. With Kazawa and Miley Tevani dead ahead, we need all the help we can get.

"And you believe him?" asks Ichiro, referring to the information Ko gave us in his final moments.

"I do," I reply, nodding. "He didn't tell us anything under duress. He believed he was walking away from this on the condition he helped us. He knew who we are, and he knew we'd find out if he was bullshitting us, so he had no real reason or incentive to lie."

Ichiro thoughtfully strokes his thin, gray beard, staring absently ahead. I exchange a glance with Ruby in the silence, smiling weakly. She returns the gesture. It was part mutual reassurance, part recognition of mutual exhaustion.

"So, what's your plan, *Shinigami*?" he asks, finally.

"I don't know yet... but I know I don't wanna go up that fucking skyscraper."

"Really?" Ruby raises an eyebrow. "Why?"

I stare at the floor as the memories of Chicago and San Francisco and Dubai run through my mind like a demented slideshow.

"Because nothing good ever comes from me trying to reach the top of tall buildings," I say with a humorless smile.

Ruby gets to her feet and begins pacing a slow circle around the sofa. She traces a hand over the tops of the cushions as she passes behind it.

"So, let me get this straight. You go through Hell at the hands of your enemy. You risk your own long-term health and well-being mounting a frankly *ludicrous* crusade of revenge, convincing me and anyone else who will listen that it's necessary in the process. We go through all that and *finally* get some intel that will allow us to end all this if we're smart, and now you turn around and say, 'Actually, I don't want to do this because I'm scared of heights.'" She stops and faces me, crossing her arms over her chest. "Are you fucking serious?"

I push myself upright and square to her, putting my hands in my pockets. "First of all... I forgot you knew about my fear of heights. Secondly, it's not about that anyway. Thirdly, yes, I'm fucking serious, Ruby. Me and you taking on a building full of Yakuza is a stupid plan."

She gestures wildly at me, her eyes wide with anger and frustration. "No fucking shit! But so was going into that tattoo parlor half-cocked. So was strolling into a nightclub we knew would have an unknown number of Yakuza inside, on a slim chance the guy we wanted would be in there. This whole thing has been a stupid plan! You should be in the hospital right now, you stubborn lunatic."

Huh. Been a while since someone gave me a real dressing down. Josh used to do it all the time, when the situation arose for me to have my head extracted from my ass, but since he died, I've not really had anyone to put me straight. Ruby has, to an extent, but never like this.

I can see her point too. I understand I might be coming across as a little hypocritical, having dragged her through the trenches this far, only to stop and start thinking like she's been telling me to all along.

And honestly, yes—that skyscraper does change things a bit. I wouldn't want to go in there if I was a hundred percent. I certainly don't want to attempt it in my current state. There are limits to the *screw the world* approach to problem-solving, even for me.

I might not want to admit it, but I'm struggling. Getting to Ko wiped me out, to the point where a hospital sounds like a really good idea right about now. But I know I can't sit this one out. I know I don't have time to rest. The enemy is ruthless, relentless, and vastly outnumbers the two of us. We have to keep going. If we stop now, we die.

That being said, I will concede that, so far, the way I've gone about things... while entertaining and successful... might not have been the most efficient. I'm paying the price for it now, and that's on me. But it doesn't change the fact I need to adjust my approach, which means thinking instead of shooting.

Ha! It's only taken you how long to figure this out?

Shut up, Josh.

"You're right," I say to her. "I should be in the hospital. The way we've done things so far has worked, but it's slowly killing me. I can't do it anymore. Kazawa isn't going to stop. Especially if Miley's whispering in his ear. But this fight is getting beyond me. I need another way of winning."

Ruby sighs, shrugging her shoulders and letting her arms fall to her sides in the process. She shuffles across the room and takes my hand in hers.

"I'm sorry. I know this must be difficult for you, especially after everything you've endured so far. I'll always stand beside you, Adrian. You know that. I just... I dunno—I just have a bad feeling about this, and I don't want this fight to be your last."

I place my hand gently on the back of her head and pull her into me, wrapping my arms around her shoulders. I feel hers snake around my waist. I kiss the top of her head.

"You've known me long enough to know I'll find a way to finish this," I say, trying to reassure her. "And thanks to you, I'm nowhere near as stupid as I look anymore."

We part and exchange a smile.

Ichiro clears his throat. "If I may..."

Ruby steps away and turns so that we're both facing him.

"You are both among best in business," he continues. "That is not in doubt. But even best of us need help sometimes. And you, *Shinigami*, sometimes forget you are not one-man army. You have powerful friends. Ask them for assistance."

I frown. "Who do you mean?"

He points to the black bag, still resting on the coffee table, surrounded by its contents. "Global Tech."

I smile faintly. He can never say their name correctly.

"I think they've done enough already, Ichi. Besides, like Buchanan said himself, GlobaTech can't be seen getting involved in shit like this. They are who they are, and they have responsibilities that go along with that. They can't just start fighting Yakuza for no reason. They have shareholders to answer to. And a President. And NATO."

Ichiro shrugs. "Then give them a reason."

My eyes narrow. "I don't follow..."

Ruby places a hand on my arm. "He might be onto something. Maybe make the call, ask for help. If he's reluctant, dangle a carrot for him."

"Like what?"

"Like... the only thing better than having Adrian Hell owe you one is having him owe you two."

She smiles. I smile back and take out my cell. I stare at it a moment, realizing I don't have his number. Then I call Josh's old office number and hope for the best.

...

...

...

Ruby looks at me quizzically. I move the phone away from my face.

"I'm being transferred now."

A moment later, the line clicks through.

"Hello, Adrian," says Buchanan.

He doesn't sound surprised to be speaking to me, but his tone is firm and professional.

"Sorry to call at this hour, Moses," I reply.

"This hour? It's a little after noon."

"Oh. Right. Time difference. Well, it's four a.m. here, and believe me, I'm really sorry *I'm* awake."

He chuckles. "Fair enough. Everything okay?"

"Yeah. Your intel paid off. Thank you. We tracked down

a guy we were looking for anyway, and he told us where Kazawa is hiding out."

"Uh-huh. Was this guy at the... Octopus Bar, by any chance?"

I frown. "Yeah, how did you know?"

"CNN."

"Ah. Yeah... sorry about that."

"No need to apologize, Adrian. It's nothing to do with me."

"True. Although while we're on the subject, I could use your help."

"The guns not enough?"

I notice a slight edge in his voice, but I ignore it.

"The guns worked just fine. The problem I have is I've found Kazawa, and I can't get to him. I was hoping you could lend a hand?"

Buchanan sighs heavily down the line. "Adrian, as I said to you in the hospital, GlobaTech can't get involved in the personal disputes of an assassin. We have a good relationship with the Japanese government. I'm not going to jeopardize that by sending in my troops to clean up your mess."

I pace away from Ruby, moving slowly back and forth by the elevator doors.

"I'm not asking you to clean up anything. I just need a little assist."

"Adrian, I—"

"The only thing better than having me owe you one is having me owe you two."

There's silence on the line. I glance back at Ruby and shrug in response to her questioning expression.

"What do you need?" he asks after a few moments.

"Well, this prick is holed up at the top of a skyscraper with the girl who tortured me online. Whole lot of real estate between him and the street, filled with guns. I could use a hand with the... logistics, I guess."

"I see. And, in return, you owe me... *two* favors, right?"

"That's right."

More silence.

Man, this guy likes his dramatic pauses. No way Josh taught him that. You couldn't shut him up.

Hey!

See?

"Okay," replies Moses. "An operative will be airborne within the hour. He should be with you by nineteen-hundred on your clock."

"Wow, really? Thanks, Buchanan. I appreciate it."

"No problem. It's only because I fully understand your value. Just... don't make me regret it. This company has spent enough time on CNN over the years."

I chuckle. "Don't worry. If I make it onto TV again, it's more likely to be Cinemax."

I hang up and pocket the phone.

"Well?" asks Ruby impatiently.

I nod to Ichiro. "Good call, my friend. A GlobaTech asset will be with us this evening."

He smiles but remains silent.

"That's great," says Ruby. "So, now what?"

I stretch as much as my body will allow and crack my neck. "Well, I don't know about you, but it's been a long night. I'm going to bed. Ichi, feel free to grab a sofa."

He places his palms together and nods a quiet thank you.

I head for the stairs. Ruby follows. We both stand on the first step and look at each other, grinning like kids who didn't get caught. Her hand slides into mine. Our fingers interlock.

"Are you really tired?" she whispers.

"I reckon I could stay awake a little while longer," I reply.

We ascend the stairs, heading for the nearest bed, which happens to be hers. Behind me, I swear I hear Ichiro laughing to himself.

We'd best keep the noise down.

19:42 JST

I'm sitting beside Ruby on the sofa facing the TV, with an open laptop on the table in front of us. We all slept most of the day, waking a couple of hours ago. We grabbed a bite, showered and changed, then started working on a plan— although we're mostly drawing blanks.

Ichiro is standing over by the window, looking out at Tokyo as it gradually lights up with the artificial pulse of its nightlife. The sky has already darkened—a combination of time and poor weather. Rain batters the side of the building relentlessly, sticking to the glass and distorting the view.

He hasn't said much since we slept. I feel bad putting him in this position. He's spent years cultivating a new repu- tation, positioning himself as respected and untouchable to all Yakuza families. But I've needed to drag him into this because he's the only friend I've got in the city with a prac- tical knowledge of what I'm up against.

"When's this GlobaTech asset meant to be getting here?" asks Ruby after a sigh of impatience.

"Buchanan said seven p.m. our time," I reply, nodding at the clock on the wall above the TV. "So, they're late."

Ichiro paces across the room toward us, his hands

clasped behind his back. Whenever he moves, it's like he glides. He's silent, like a shadow. He stops in front of us and drops on the spot, landing cross-legged on the floor.

"Adrian... is this worth it?" he asks.

He must be serious. He didn't call me *Shinigami*.

I raise an eyebrow. "How do you mean?"

"Going to war with Kazawa over a girl. Is it worth it? Really."

"Ichi, you make it sound like some conflict of the heart out of Romeo and Juliet. This isn't about Miley. Well... it is, but that's not why I'm going after Kazawa, and you know that."

He shrugs. "I just think... you two... you have money, you have skills. Honestly, neither of you want to be found, you won't be. This is a fight you perhaps cannot win. What is American saying?"

He glances to the side, his eyes narrowing as he tries to recall something.

"Ah, yes!" he exclaims. "Is the juice worth the squeeze?"

I smile. That's a good saying.

I feel Ruby turn in her seat to face me. I look over at her. She smiles at me. It's a smile that says, *you know I've got your back, but he has a point...*

I take a deep, painful breath.

"You know it is, my friend. I'm sorry to bring you into this, but I don't have a choice. She blames me for her mother's death, and despite the fact I saved her from the men that kidnapped her as a kid, she's spent the last five years training to kill me. A nineteen-year-old tracked me halfway across the world, made connections with a Yakuza family, and executed a plan—almost to perfection—to kill me in front of everyone. Can you honestly sit there and tell me you *don't* think she'll pursue me wherever I go?"

He shakes his head but remains silent.

"Exactly. And it's not just me. It's Ruby too. What kind of life would we have? Besides… you're not the only one with a reputation on the line, Ichi. I might be beaten up and semi-retired, but I'm still Adrian Hell. I start running now, how long before other people start giving chase, huh? I'm a nice guy, but I've made a lot of enemies over the years. Enemies who are too afraid and too smart to come looking for retribution. But I let a fucking kid take me down… you think they won't smell blood in the water?"

I feel Ruby's hand on my leg. She squeezes it gently. I place my hand on top of it and run my thumb gently over the back.

"For the last time, you guys, we have to fight. It won't be easy. Hell, it's borderline-impossible, I know that. But we gotta do it. I have to stop Miley, and if that means taking out Kazawa and his entire operation in the process, then goddammit, that's what we're gonna do. Okay?"

Before he can reply, the elevator whirrs and rumbles into life, beginning its descent to the first floor.

Ruby and I exchange a look and spring to our feet. Well, she does. I ease myself up off the sofa, making that low groaning noise everyone's grandpa makes to help him get out of a chair.

Without a word, we move with purpose, grabbing a weapon and taking up position facing the elevator doors. I stand directly in front of them, a Raptor in my left hand, held low and loose, ready for action. Ruby is behind the kitchen counter, aiming my other Raptor with unwavering skill at the doors. Ichiro is off to the side by the TV, the shotgun from Buchanan's gift bag held by his hip, ready to cut whoever steps out in half.

"I thought this elevator was private?" says Ruby.

"It's supposed to be," I reply.

"Then how come everybody without a key seems to be able to use it?"

I glance over at Ichiro, who simply shrugs.

"What? I am special."

I roll my eyes, then nod to the display above the doors as it counts steadily upward. "Not that special, apparently."

"This could just be Buchanan's asset," observes Ruby.

"Yeah, maybe," I say. "But if it is, wouldn't they just buzz up?"

"Good point."

The elevator is halfway back up to our apartment. Whoever it is will be here any minute. Miley knows where I live. Christ, she's slept in my bed! It's not crazy to think they might have sent some men over here, like a warning shot across the bow or something.

Two floors to go.

One floor.

The elevator dings and the doors slide open.

The man inside is wearing jeans and a zip-up hooded sweater. He has a backpack slung over one shoulder. His eyes meet mine. They pop wide as he notices my gun. His arms shoot up, palms facing me.

"Whoa!" he yells. He edges slowly out of the elevator. He sees Ruby first. Then Ichiro. "Jesus, Adrian! Helluva welcoming committee ya got here."

I lower my gun and smile.

"Sonofabitch…"

I step toward him and extend my hand, which he shakes tentatively, keeping a trained eye on the other guns in the room. I nod to Ichiro and look over my shoulder at Ruby.

"It's okay, he's a friend."

Ichiro lowers the shotgun. Ruby appears beside me a moment later.

"Is this the GlobaTech asset?" asks Ruby. "Do you know him?"

"I do, actually." I move to stand beside him. "Ruby, Ichiro... meet Ray Collins."

23

The four of us stand in a loose circle around the coffee table, each holding a near-empty bottle of beer. After briefly explaining who Ichiro and Ruby were to Collins, he had asked for a drink, saying the flight was long and he needed something to keep him awake.

And here we are.

"Damn... this is good beer, buddy," says Collins, taking a grateful swig.

"Asahi," I reply, smiling. "It's the only thing worth drinking here."

"Amen to that."

Ruby sighs. "Okay, so who are you, exactly? You know us, but... why send you?"

Collins looks at me. "Does she know about... y'know... Belarus?"

I nod. "She does."

He turns to her, his grin lighting up his face. "Listen,

234

sweetheart, I'm the best GlobaTech has, okay? You should be lucky to have me here."

"Oh, no..." I mutter. I hang my head and begin massaging the bridge of my nose between my finger and thumb.

Ruby puts her beer down hard on the table and takes a step toward him.

"No, *you* listen, dipshit. I don't trust people I don't know." She points to me, then to Ichiro. "I trust these two without question. But just because you were Adrian's chauffeur for an hour a couple of years ago, doesn't mean you get a free pass with me. Are we clear?"

Collins holds his hands up playfully but takes a very serious step back. "Hey, whoa... okay, darlin'. Okay."

"And another thing... call me 'sweetheart' or 'darling' one more time, I'll kick you in your balls so hard, they'll come flying out of your ears. *Comprende*?"

He stares at me, wide-eyed and confused.

I shrug back at him. "Hey, don't look at me. I know better."

He smirks, takes a patient swig of his beer, and smiles back at Ruby as if every word she just said fell on deaf ears.

"Don't suppose ya got a sister or a cousin or something called Julie Fisher, do ya?" he asks.

She frowns. In fact, it's more like a grimace. As if a bad smell has caught her nose.

"What?" she demands. "No. Why?"

Collins shrugs casually. "No reason. Ya just remind me of someone I know. The two of ya would probably get on great, thinkin' about it." He pauses to finish his beer, then places the empty bottle down on a coaster. "Foreplay aside, lady, I'm part of an elite unit in GlobaTech that answers directly and only to the man in charge. There are three of us. Josh Winters brought us together. Moses Buchanan inherited us. We're the people they call when it's a difficult or delicate situation that they would rather keep quiet, ya know?"

Ruby relaxes a little. She takes a small step back, seemingly appeased by Collins's eventual sincerity.

He approaches me and places a hand on my shoulder. "None of us have had the chance to say this, Adrian, but we're all real sorry about Josh. He meant a lot to all of us, but to no one more than you. He was a helluva guy. We all fought for him without question."

I nod. "Appreciate it. Thanks, Ray."

He steps away and takes a long moment to look me up and down. His eyes narrow. He scratches absently at the stubble along his jawline. "No offense, but... ah... ya look like shit, buddy."

I smile. "I know. Thanks."

"We... ah... we all saw... ya know... what happened to ya."

"I think a lot of people did."

"Aye. You're one tough bastard. I'll give ya that."

"Doesn't feel like it right now, if I'm being honest."

"I can imagine. When Moses said ya needed a hand, the three of us started arguing over who would make the trip. We all wanted to have ya back."

I raise an eyebrow. "Even Jericho?"

Collins laughs. "Aye, even the big fella. Truth be told, I don't ever think he'll be fully sold on ya, but he respected the hell outta Josh after everything he did for him. He would back you up just to honor his memory, if nothing else."

Memories of Colombia flood back into my mind. The one and only time I met Jericho Stone. The man was—and probably still is—a monster. Built like a tank and twice as stubborn. Damn good soldier, though. I saved his life back then. I'm not sure he'll ever forgive me for it.

"So, how did you manage to get the short straw?" I ask.

He shrugs. "Well, Jules and Jerry are both damn-near impossible to argue with, but when I explained me and you go way back, Moses chose me. Said it might go more smoothly with a friendly face."

"Your teammates not that friendly?" asks Ruby.

Collins shrugs. "They are once ya get to know them. But they're not as forthcoming with strangers as I am. Ya see, love, I'm a people person."

Ruby lets her head roll back and sighs heavily at the ceiling.

"I swear to God..." she mutters.

Collins laughs and looks back at me. "Okay, buddy, I'm here. What do ya need?"

Ichiro thrusts a new beer in front of him. "Long story. You might need this."

"Jesus Christ!" replies Collins, jumping almost out of his skin. "When did ya go to the fridge? I didn't hear ya move!"

I smile to myself and take a sip of my own drink.

Ichiro winks at him. "Be like water."

Collins turns to me. "Who's this guy again?"

"He's a friend," I reply. "A friend who prefers to remain a mystery to people who work for GlobaTech. No offense."

He shakes his head. "No problem. No one would believe I met a goddamn geriatric ghost ninja anyway..."

Ichiro and Ruby share a laugh as we all take a seat.

"I'll bullet-point it for you, Ray," I begin. "Tetsuo Kazawa runs one of the largest and most powerful Yakuza families in Tokyo. He was the brawn behind my much-publicized ass-kicking. He's currently relaxing in the penthouse suite of a skyscraper he owns in the city. He's surrounded in all directions by loyal, well-trained, well-armed Yakuza street soldiers, and he's pissed at me. I, in turn, intend to put a bullet right between his fucking eyes."

Collins lets out a low whistle. "Jesus, Adrian, ya don't half pick 'em. I get why ya want him dead, but even *you* have to understand ya can't win a fight this one-sided, surely? Ya don't have a tank now, sunshine!"

"He has a girl with him, Miley. She's the brains. A little over five years ago, I saved her from a gangster named Jimmy Manhattan. She was kidnapped as leverage because her mother, an assassin, had been hired to kill me and didn't really want to. She's pissed at me because she blames me for her mother's death."

"Okay. And did ya kill her mom?"

I shrug. "I didn't pull the trigger, but I'd never deny my part in it. It was kill or be killed, just like it is now. That's the world we live in."

"I see."

"Young Miley has spent her formative years training to kill me and has used the small fortune her mother left her to make alliances with the Yakuza. She's the one who did the torturing in the home movie you saw. She won't stop... ever... until I'm dead. Kazawa does what she wants; ergo, neither will he."

"So, your thinking is that ya have to take the fight to them because they'll hunt ya down if ya don't."

I shrug again. "Pretty much."

"And ya main problem is getting to the bastard?"

"It is."

"Okay." Collins takes a long drink of his beer and gets to his feet, dangling the bottle between his fingers as he paces idly back and forth in front of us. Finally, he stops and looks at me. "Ya know the boss won't let me break any laws, don't ya? Like, I can't just start shooting at people because *you* tell me to. I've gotta be all respectable and whatnot nowadays."

I nod. "I know. And of course, you can't break the law by taking part in an assault on Japanese citizens without just cause."

"Ah... yeah, right."

I look over at Ruby. "Show him."

Ruby leans forward on the sofa and spins the laptop around on the coffee table, so the screen is facing him.

I point to it. "There's your just cause."

Collins crouches by the table and starts reading.

In the absence of a clear way forward, Ruby and I spent the day looking for alternative ways to hurt Kazawa. We can't get to him to shoot him, so we looked at his family's enterprises, legitimate and otherwise. It turns out one of the many corrupt pies Kazawa has his fingers in is firearms trafficking—selling and using stolen weapons. More specifically, stolen *GlobaTech* weapons.

"Sonofabitch..." says Collins as he finishes reading.

"Well?" inquires Ruby. "Good enough for you?"

He nods. "I'll be able to convince Jules and Buchanan there's enough evidence here to go official. But still..." He looks at me. "I can't go in guns-a-blazing, like I assume you want to."

"No one's asking you to, Ray. But if someone happens to start shooting at you..."

He shrugs. "Then the dumb bastards are fair game."

"Exactly." I look at everyone in turn. "Assaulting Kazawa's building is plan B. It's stupid and next-to-impossible, but if all else fails, we kick his front door down and spit bullets at whatever moves. Whoever dies first, loses."

"That's a real shitty plan B, buddy," observes Collins.

I nod. "Correct. Which is why I'm hoping plan A works."

"What's plan A?" asks Ruby, confused.

The truth is, I didn't get all that much sleep today. Ruby played a small part in that, for which I'm eternally grateful, but mostly it was because my mind was running nowhere fast, trying to think of a way to end all this. I fell asleep with half a plan. I woke up with a full one. Like most things, I'll need a little luck, but it's a sound strategy. I think.

I smile at her before looking over at Ichiro. "What do the other families think of Kazawa?"

He strokes his long, thin beard with patient and deliberate movements, taking deep breaths as he ponders my question.

"No one like him," he says, finally. "No one respect him. They all think he... douche... bag."

I smile to myself. His attempts at American slang never cease to amuse me. "And has word travelled that he was bankrolling my humiliation and all-round torture?"

Ichiro nods. "That was not well-received, *Shinigami*. He dishonors all Yakuza with such things."

Collins raises his hands. "I'm sorry... Shini-what now?"

"It means 'Grim Reaper' in Japanese," answers Ruby.

He nods. "Ah, okay. Nice."

"What are you thinking?" asks Ichiro.

I take a sip of beer. "I'm thinking we ask for some help."

"From who?" asks Ruby, pointing at Collins. "We have G.I. Jamesons over here... who else is there to ask?"

Collins furrows his brow with mock offense. "Hey!"

Ichiro locks eyes with me. His gaze narrows. His head begins shaking with the smallest of movements.

"You cannot be serious..." he mutters.

"Oh, I am," I reply, smiling.

"Can someone tell me what's going on?" demands Ruby.

I turn to her. "If the other Yakuza families hate Kazawa

as much as us, maybe they'll lend a hand. Even up the odds a little. The enemy of my enemy... and all that."

Now Ruby's eyes narrow. I recognize the look of disapproval and doubt on her face from a thousand times before.

"Who, exactly?"

"There's only one family powerful enough to start a war with Kazawa," says Ichiro.

I nod. "The Oji-gumi."

Collins shakes his head. "Okay, can ya please stop making up words?"

Ruby puts her beer down impatiently. "Adrian, didn't you..."

I nod again. "Yup."

Collins sighs. "Oh, come on! Stop speaking in bloody riddles here, would ya?"

I look at him. "About a week ago, I killed a guy named Santo and three of his bodyguards. He was a lieutenant of Akuma Oji, the head of the Oji-gumi Family."

He nods. "Let me get this straight. The only people who *can* help *also* happen to want you dead? Jesus..."

"Not necessarily..."

"It is unlikely they know it was you who carried out hit on Santo," says Ichiro. "But still... this is dangerous game you playing."

I shrug. "Maybe. But it's our only shot. If I can convince the Oji-gumi to start a war with Kazawa, it'll flush him and Miley out. Their soldiers can kill each other. We'll watch from the sidelines. I'll take out Kazawa and Miley when the time is right. Everyone wins."

"Adrian, when is it ever that simple?" asks Ruby.

"It'll be fine," I say to her. "Trust me."

"Famous last words," she mutters.

I walk over to the kitchen area and retrieve four more

beers from the fridge. I line them up on the counter, pop the top of each one, and look up at the others.

"This is what we're gonna do," I begin. "First thing tomorrow, Ichiro and I are going to have a sit-down with Akuma Oji. Ruby, I want you and Ray to run recon on Kazawa's tower block. We need to know how many people he has with him and how many civilians might potentially be in the crossfire."

"Are we expecting some collateral damage here?" asks Collins solemnly.

I shake my head. "I don't *want* any, obviously, but we can't rule out the possibility this piece of shit will use innocent people as a human shield. The building he owns is used by many businesses. Not all of them are Yakuza. Not all of them are illegal. If we're going to bring the fight to his front door, we need to know how many people we'll be putting in danger, so we can work around them."

Collins approaches the counter first, followed by Ruby, then Ichiro. They line up in front of me, each taking an ice-cold bottle in their hand.

"This is some large-scale crazy," says Collins. "Kinda wish I'd let Jericho come now..."

"If this goes how I want it to, we'll all be nothing more than spectators in a Yakuza turf war. Your strategy and firepower are a welcome asset, Ray. Plus, you lend legitimacy to any involvement on our part that might get noticed."

Silence falls. We all raise our bottles, tilting the necks so they meet in the middle. A quiet salute to the insanity agreed upon.

"I must go," announces Ichiro. "If we are to do this, I must make arrangements for meeting tomorrow, Adrian-san."

I nod. "Thanks, Ichi. I appreciate it. Watch your back out there, okay?"

He walks backward away from the counter, his arms held out slightly to the sides, a big, crazy smile on his face.

"Please! I was *Shinigami* long before you were." He laughs his trademark laugh, then turns and walks over to the elevator. The doors open. He steps inside and turns to face us. "Be outside tomorrow. Eight a.m."

The doors slide shut. The display begins counting down.

"Now what?" asks Ruby.

I shrug. "Now we drink. Tomorrow, we go to war."

I walk around the counter and head for the sofa. Ruby follows me.

"Hey, can I have the old guy's beer?" asks Collins.

24

Fuck me, it's cold.

The sun's only just starting to climb behind the thick, gray cloud that dominates the sky. The temperature's in the low fifties. I'm huddled into my coat, the collar turned up against the wind, my hands deep in the pockets. I'm shuffling on the spot—a futile gesture to stay warm. A storm is forecast to hit in the next day or so.

They're not wrong there...

The sidewalk outside my apartment building is quiet. In this part of town, it doesn't get too busy this early. There's a daytime bustle once work begins, but the bonus of living somewhere so expensive is there aren't many others who can afford to join you.

Ruby, Collins, and I sat up until the early hours last night, drinking, catching up, and sharing stories. We all took it easy with the beer. I'm taking standard pain medication now, and I need it to be as effective as possible—which means keeping alcohol to a minimum, despite the temptation to do otherwise.

My wounds are getting easier to manage. The bruising and swelling around my face have reduced, although I still have my protective mask with me, just in case. The minor cuts and bruises that cover my body are largely unnoticeable now. My hand's still giving me grief, but nothing new there.

I'm far from a hundred percent, but I'm a lot nearer to it than I was a couple of days ago.

Ruby and Collins are going to wait for the city to hit its stride before heading out to recon Kazawa's tower. Easier to blend into the chaos.

I breathe out heavily. The thin stream of air from my lungs manifests in front of me before evaporating just as fast.

Come on, Ichi. I'm freezing my—

Ah. Here he is.

Ichiro pulls over in front of me in his tiny car. I hate it, but it beats walking.

I quickly climb in beside him, and he sets off again, narrowly avoiding the car approaching from behind. His hands are tight on the wheel. I notice the color has drained from his knuckles. His mouth is little more than a thin line, hidden inside his beard. His eyes are intensely focused on the road.

"Everything okay?" I ask him after a couple of minutes sitting in silence.

He sighs a taut breath. "We have the meeting with Akuma Oji, as requested."

"That's good, right? Where is it?"

"In park by Tokyo Dome, overlooking the Shinto shrine. He goes there every morning without fail."

I roll my eyes. "It couldn't have been indoors..."

He navigates the steady traffic with aggressive and angular movements of the wheel.

"This was only way, Adrian. I had to..."

He trails off. His tone was short and sharp, as if he's pissed about something.

I frown. "You had to... what?"

"Nothing."

"Ichi..."

"To secure the meeting, I had to give up noodle bar. I had to declare my property and my street for Oji-gumi family."

"What? You had to hand over your business for a simple meeting? That's a bit extreme, isn't it?"

Ichiro shrugs. "That is Akuma Oji."

Oh, shit.

"Ichiro, I'm so sorry. I know what that place meant to you. Is there any way—"

He shakes his head. "No. It was that, or no meeting."

"If I'd known, I never would've—"

"Don't say it, Adrian. Okay? Just... don't. We need the Oji-gumi on our side. This was only way. It is right thing to do. Kazawa will continue to bring dishonor to the streets of this city. He must be stopped. If it wasn't your war, sooner or later, it would be someone else's."

We stop at a set of lights, and he looks over at me.

"You have no... how you say? *Agenda*. Your reason for this fight is personal, not political. You live here couple of years, yes? I live here whole life. This is *my* city, Adrian. I fought for it and bled for it since I was child. I retire. Leave that life with respect of every family. That bar... that street... holy ground here. *My* ground. But I had to give it up for your war. I had to pick a side. Like it or not."

We set off again and turn right, putting the river behind us and the Tokyo Dome a couple of miles dead ahead. The ominous structure is faded by distance but still dominates the skyline.

Silence has fallen inside the car. It's actually a little awkward. I'm staring out the window, watching the monochromatic world pass us by. I feel terrible.

"I do not blame you, *Shinigami*," continues Ichiro, as if reading my mind. "This is just what needed to be done. No one has sacrificed more than you to this cause. We are friends, you and me. I want to help. I want this fight to be over. For all of us. You deserve peace."

"I'll do what I can to make this right by you," I reply. "When all this is said and done, I'll buy back the noodle bar from the Oji-gumi. Business is business to them, right?"

He smiles. "Thank you for offer, but you cannot promise that when you cannot promise to survive."

"Gee, thanks for the vote of confidence!"

He laughs his deep, crazy laugh. A moment later, I join in. The atmosphere lightens. The mood changes. I won't forget what he had to give up for me, but for now, what's done is done.

We pull into the parking lot of the Dome. It's mostly deserted. We climb out. I stretch gently, trying to loosen up after being cramped into that small car. Ichiro sets off walking for the exit. I follow, putting my Pilot and my Ili in place quickly, so I can stuff my hands back inside my pockets.

The sidewalk is much busier here. I twist and turn my body as I weave through the sea of people, who all seem to be going the opposite way to us. I'm glad when we turn into the park.

The Koishikawa Korakuen Gardens surrounding the Tokyo Dome are beautiful. The vibrant, earthy colors are more prominent against the dull backdrop of the day. The wide path is clean and quiet. The noise from the street is instantly muted, replaced with birdsong.

"Let me do talking," says Ichiro. "This will be... delicate conversation."

I scratch absently at my chin, which is in desperate need of a shave. "Yeah, I can imagine."

We follow the path for a few minutes until the Shinto shrine appears on our left, floating on its own little island in the middle of a small lake. Up ahead, I see four men wearing suits, standing guard and forming a tight, square perimeter around a stone bench facing the shrine. There's one man sitting down.

Akuma Oji.

As we approach, the two guards facing us turn their attention our way. They instinctively reach inside their suit jackets, presumably wrapping a hand around a gun. Ichiro holds his hands up slightly.

"*We are here to see Mr. Oji,*" he says. "*He has agreed to meet with us. We are not armed.*"

The guards don't break their formation. We walk to them and both lift our arms. We're quickly frisked, which I would usually take issue with, but this probably isn't the time. I doubt I could effectively take these four guys out in my current state anyway.

Happy we don't have any weapons, they allow us to step between them before relaxing back into their position.

Ichiro and I stop in front of Oji and face him. He's not what I was expecting at all. He's wearing a long, dark overcoat and a scarf, which does nothing to hide the powerful frame beneath. A charcoal-gray suit is visible underneath it. His passive expression hides his years. I believe he's in his late fifties, but he doesn't look any older than me. He appears calm and collected. His position of power has bred a lifetime of patience. Beside him on the bench is a take-away cup. Steam is rising from the hot beverage inside it.

Ichiro bows slightly. *"Mr. Oji. Thank you for agreeing to meet with us on such short notice."*

Oji doesn't move his head. He simply adjusts his gaze, so it's directed at him. *"No need to thank me. You paid for it. Make it quick."*

His voice is deep and deliberate. I can see how this guy could be intimidating to the people around him.

Ichiro takes a moment to compose himself, shuffling on the spot. I've never seen him this shaken before. There's a fine line between respect and fear. He's treading it carefully.

"Mr. Oji, you are no doubt aware of what Tetsuo Kazawa and his organization did to my associate here," he begins, gesturing to me with his hand. *"A bold and reckless move that joins a long list of dishonorable practices that family has brought to our world."*

Oji doesn't move. He betrays no emotion. If he was wearing sunglasses, I'd swear the guy was asleep. The only sign he's paying any attention was when his gaze briefly flicked to me.

"What is your point, Ichiro?" he asks.

"I believe it is time to re-establish the honor and traditions of the generations before us. I believe Tetsuo Kazawa's time is at an end."

The corner of Oji's mouth curls with the slightest of movements. *"You believe, do you? This is your opinion, yes?"* He looks at me. *"Not his?"*

I'm trying not to take offense at his tone and overall demeanor. Too much is at stake for my principles to ruin it now. But still... he's a bit of a dick.

Ichiro clears his throat. *"Mr. Oji, I can—"*

Oji raises a hand, instantly silencing him. He takes a slow sip of his drink, crosses his legs, and looks at me.

"Our mutual friend is this city's diplomat," he says to me in perfect English. "I have genuine respect for him, but diplomacy often gets in the way of desire. So, tell me, Adrian Hell, what brings you here? What is it *you* desire?"

I glance over at Ichiro. His eyes are bulging in their sockets, silently screaming at me to not say anything that might get me killed and thrown in the lake behind me. I take a long moment to think about my response. Perhaps I should tread carefully. Apply a modicum of diplomacy, as Ichiro would. I need this guy's help, after all.

Then again, he did allude to not being a fan of diplomacy. And I'm certainly not. Besides, what's he going to do if I offend him? Kill me? Huh. Without his help, I'll be waging war on a Yakuza family pretty much by myself... I'm dead anyway.

Screw it.

I look Oji dead in the eye and shrug. "I want Tetsuo Kazawa dead and his business in flames. And I'd quite like you to help me do it."

Oji nods and takes another sip of his drink. He looks idly at the surroundings before briefly closing his eyes, seemingly to relish the freezing wind as it washes over him.

"I saw what happened to you," he says finally. "Most people did. I hear things. I knew Kazawa was behind it. I knew his little plaything was the one in the video, torturing you. I can understand you wanting revenge, or justice— whatever you feel better calling it. And with your reputation, Mr. Hell, I suspect your retribution will be something to behold. But why would I wish to get involved? Kazawa is a stain on this city, but he is a powerful and stubborn one. I did not get where I am today by starting fights with powerful enemies unnecessarily."

I shrug. "I could give you the logical, diplomatic argument, if you'd like?"

Oji smiles. "Sure."

"You like to think of your family as number one in this city. And you have a pretty good claim to that top spot. You have more legitimacy than any of the other families. You have more police and politicians in your pocket. You have the respect of almost every other organization in Tokyo. Except Kazawa. He's in the number two spot. Maybe. See, I think the two of you are closer than you care to admit. I think you're threatened by him because he doesn't consider himself bound by the same code as you, which makes him unpredictable. This is your opportunity to get rid of the competition without getting your hands dirty. It's a win-win for you."

He nods, processing my, frankly, brilliant case. "You are correct, Adrian Hell. You have an impressive grasp on this city's political landscape."

I shrug. "I don't know politics, but I know criminals. No offense."

"So, that was your diplomatic reason, yes? What's your honest one?"

I look over at Ichiro again, but he's given up. He's standing tall, but his shoulders are slumped forward, and his gaze is fixed on the ground at his feet. He looks like a man who has resigned himself to the fact he's about to die.

I look back at Oji. "Honestly? You already knew the diplomatic reason, because you've already tried to have

Kazawa killed. He inadvertently took out one of your business partners, and you couldn't believe your luck, could you? A legitimate reason to go after the sonofabitch. But that didn't work out. I'm giving you another reason now. I'm gonna rip that bastard's heart out. I'm gonna burn his empire to the ground, and this city along with it if I have to. Sure, I'll probably die in horrible and bloody fashion, but not before Kazawa and his girlfriend do. That's a cast-iron guarantee. You get your only real competition taken out, and it doesn't cost you anything except a few men and a friendly request to your pet police officers to stay out of my way. This is good business, Mr. Oji. Plain and simple."

He sips his drink. Points his finger at me. "Answer me this, Adrian. What makes you think I've tried to have Kazawa killed before? That would be a risky move, especially if people found out I was behind his demise."

I take a breath. Set my jaw. Clench my fists inside my pockets. In for a penny...

"I know because your man, Santo, tried to hire me to do it."

Oji stares at me. His eyes are hard, like stone. The wind has stopped. Complete silence surrounds us, as if the air itself is frozen with horror. Only the penetrating cold remains, gnawing at my face.

"Santo is dead," he replies.

I nod. "I know."

He shifts a little in his seat. I feel the men around me bristle.

"And how do you know that?"

"Because someone else hired me to kill *him*. He didn't know that when he requested a meeting with me. I put a bullet between his eyes." I pause, quickly checking the four guys haven't moved. "Sorry."

Oji stands and squares up to me. He's a little shorter than I am. Probably the same build though. "You come here under the guise of a friend, ask for my help starting a war, and then tell me you killed one of my best men? I didn't take you for a fool, Adrian Hell."

"If Santo was one of your best men, you have bigger problems than Kazawa. The guy was a cowardly piece of shit with delusions of grandeur. He loved playing gangster but didn't want to get his hands dirty. He would've bent over for the highest bidder and sold you down the river in a heartbeat. I know the type. I did you a favor."

Oji snaps his fingers. The four men rush to his side. I'm suddenly faced with a line of very angry-looking Yakuza soldiers. I take a small step back and raise my hands slightly.

"Hey, you wanted honest..." I say.

Oji nods. "I did. And I respect you for providing it, despite your situation. Some may think you foolish. But I see honor where they would see stupidity."

"Umm, thanks."

"As a reward for your candor, and out of respect for your reputation, I am willing to let you leave here alive."

He holds my gaze for a long, painful, awkward moment before walking away. His men follow, forming a box perimeter around him as he heads in the opposite direction from where we came in.

Ichiro and I exchange a confused look.

"So, will you help me?" I call after him, knowing I'm pushing my luck.

He doesn't look back.

"Enjoy your war, Adrian," he shouts. "I can't wait to see how it ends."

I let out a heavy sigh and watch him go until he's out of

sight. Ichiro moves in front of me, his eyes wide with shock. "What now, *Shinigami*?"

I shake my head, partly in disbelief and partly because I have no real answer for him. "Now, my old friend, we are fucked."

25

It hasn't been a good day.

After breaking the news to Collins and Ruby that Akuma Oji essentially told me to go screw myself, they debriefed me and Ichiro on what they had learned from scoping out Kazawa's skyscraper.

The lobby is apparently teeming with street soldiers, poorly disguised and obviously armed. There are also multiple innocent civilians, as we suspected. He rents the building out to local businesses of varying sizes—everything from start-ups with a three-person call center to multinational banks. Which makes it the perfect place to hide in, because he has thousands of human shields if need be.

It's a real dick move, but I guess it's the kind of thing you have to take into account when dealing with cowards.

So, it's almost impossible to even get in the front doors with hostile intent, and if you somehow do, every target is hidden behind an innocent life. Convincing anyone that a full-frontal assault on a building like that when you're this outnumbered is the best option isn't the easiest sell. I had a hundred ideas about how to do it, and almost all of them would've ended badly. That included scaling the outside of it. I'm in neither the physical nor mental condition to take the *Fear Factor* approach.

Collins had a few suggestions, but they ultimately relied too heavily on GlobaTech reinforcements, which we can't guarantee.

In the end, we all agreed on a simple strategy: find a good vantage point, bring lots of guns, try to lure the bad guys out a few at a time, and pick them off until we can make it inside. Then, sweep floor by floor until I have my hands around Kazawa's throat.

Not the best plan. Not the easiest plan. But it's the only one that made sense. Patience and violence will prevail.

Sadly, I was only blessed with an abundance of one of those things.

The skyscraper itself stands on the point of a large intersection in one of the ward's busiest districts. A circular street with six offshoots. The two opposite the building, at four and eight o'clock, lead south, away from the heart of Chiyoda and back toward the river. The roads at nine and three o'clock do much the same, with the left spoke taking you to Shinjuku City and the right leading you away toward the river, as the others do. The roads at ten and two o'clock form a triangle as they meet in the middle, and it's at this junction where Kazawa's skyscraper towers ominously over the streets.

The four of us are standing directly opposite, huddled behind Ichiro's car, parked discreetly in the shadows of a wide alleyway between two buildings that border the intersection to the south. The rain has been relentless most of the day, battering the city and forcing the temperature down at the same time. It's wet and freezing, and, all things being equal, I'd rather be in Hawaii.

"Is this gonna work?" asks Ruby, shouting slightly over the combined noise of the weather and the steady flow of nighttime traffic.

I glance across the street at the two men guarding the main entrance to the lobby. Both stand almost against the wall, well under the canopy that juts out above the doors, presumably to shield themselves from the rain as much as they can.

"I have no idea," I reply, perhaps a little too honestly. "But it's the only plan we've got, so we gotta make the most of it."

"And why didn't the Oji family want to help us again?" asks Collins. "Surely, it's just common sense?"

I shrug. "To you and me, it is. But apparently, pride takes precedence over logic in these parts. What can I say? At least *he's* not trying to kill us as well."

"Which is a goddamn miracle, by all accounts. Why 'fess up to killing his man?"

"A show of good faith, I guess. I figured it was best to be honest with him. Apparently, I was wrong."

Ruby and I are dressed as we were when we attacked the Octopus Bar two nights ago: head-to-toe in black. Long coats conceal multiple weapons. My face mask is in one of my pockets.

Collins paid a visit to the Tokyo branch of GlobaTech earlier. Buchanan had seen to it that he was given whatever he asked for without question. He had returned wearing dark fatigues with a modern, digital camouflage pattern on them. The GlobaTech logo is displayed over the left breast.

He also brought with him more guns than I've seen in quite a while.

I wasn't too bothered, as I'm more than happy with my matching Raptors. Ruby, however, was ecstatic. It was nice to see her acting more like her old self again. Less restraint. Less responsibility. The last few years have changed her. Mostly in a positive way, but I always felt she had lost some of the spark from her eyes. They used to glisten with life, like emeralds in firelight, whenever she was faced with danger. I remember seeing it when we first met, when I busted her out of that nuthouse.

Christ, that feels like a lifetime ago.

She's been through a lot since then, as we all have. She's grown. Mellowed, even. But you put her in a room full of guns and tell her to take and use whatever she wants... she's like a kid at Christmas.

Ichiro is also dressed for combat. Gone are his flamboyant robes and loose-fitting pants. He's wearing his own all-black ensemble, and it makes him look half his age. He's been very quiet all day though, and even now, he's gazing into space more than he's contributing to any conversation. I suspect telling him he looks good will be little compensation for losing his livelihood for ultimately no reason and returning to the life he had left behind.

Still, he's armed to the teeth, so I think he's made peace with it all.

I look at each of them in turn, waiting for the nod of confirmation.

Collins.

Ruby.

Ichiro.

I take a deep breath, holding it for a long second before exhaling slowly. I let my head roll back, sending my gaze skyward, allowing the wind to spray the rain across my face. The building is illuminated, like a beacon in the night sky.

Somewhere up there, obscured by low, dark clouds, is the enemy. Tetsuo Kazawa and Miley Tevani. Those two have come closer to killing me than anyone before them, and they've beaten me down in a way I've never experienced in all my life.

And yet, here I stand.

Sure, I ache like hell, I'm bruised pretty much everywhere, and bits of me are still broken that I never knew could break. But I'm still here.

Ruby isn't the only one who's mellowed. I'm not getting any younger—no secret there. But since Josh died, I haven't had the same desire... the same *passion* I once had for dealing death to those who deserved it. I put it down to being tired. I told myself I was finally doing what Josh had spent years begging me to do, which was enjoy the fortune I've amassed over the years.

But that wasn't it.

The truth is, I've grown complacent. I was long overdue for a wake-up call, and fuck me, did I get one! Well, the fires are stoking once more. The demon that lay dormant for too long is now awake, locked behind my door and pacing impatiently, desperate to be unleashed like the caged animal he's always been. And these two pieces of shit have been banging at that door constantly for almost a week.

I think it's about time they saw what was on the other side.

I take out my face mask and slide it into place. I turn to Collins and smile.

He smiles back but not to lighten the mood. His eyes are wide. His hands fidget and twitch. He's nervous.

"What?" I ask him.

He shakes his head. "Nothing. I'm just remembering what happened the last time I saw ya wear a mask."

Ichiro frowns. "What happened?"

I direct my smile at him. "I'll tell you when we're done here. Over a nice, cold beer and some rock 'n' roll."

He holds my gaze for a few seconds before laughing. It's the old Ichiro laugh. From the belly and a little unnerving. "*Shinigami!*"

I look at Ruby. She's holding a shotgun low by her side. Gripping it tightly with wet hands that are rigid and pale. She curls one side of her mouth into a fiendish grin.

Yeah... she's ready.

"Okay, boys and girls," I say to them. "I'll be right back. Be ready."

"For what, exactly?" asks Ruby.

I look back at her as I stride around the car. I smile but don't offer a reply. There's no need. She knows me well enough to know how I intend to make my presence known.

I pick my gaps in the traffic and navigate my way across the street at a steady pace. I reach the sidewalk and stare at the handful of steps leading to the entrance of Kazawa Towers. I've not registered on either of the guards' radars yet. The few people walking the streets give me a wide berth. Most of them have umbrellas up, so seeing someone without one in this weather must be strange enough to make them think I'm worth avoiding.

The lights of the city reflect in the puddles on the ground. I take a moment to stare into them, watching the faint image distort with raindrops. I'm up to my eyeballs on painkillers, but many of the aches and pains have gone. Or, at least, they're no longer registering. I believe the time for suffering and feeling sorry for myself has come and gone.

Never seen you channel your Inner Satan from this side

before. It's probably scarier than when I was alive, watching from a safe distance!

My Inner Josh seems to be on board, which is comforting. The last thing I need is my own mind doubting me.

I take a step forward, placing a boot firmly on the bottom step. I look up and stare at the guy to the right of the door, waiting for him to make eye contact. After years of winning every psychological confrontation I've ever found myself in, I know I can look intimidating when I need to. Dressed all in black, this face mask on, and...

I draw both Raptors from my back and hold them out to the side, nice and visible, with my fingers resting gently on the triggers.

...these bad boys.

Yeah. That should do it.

The guy on the right finally looks at me. Then he looks away. His gaze is nothing more than a fleeting survey of the area, not paying any attention to—

His head snaps back. His eyes are wide, transfixed like an animal in the headlights of an oncoming car with nowhere to go.

There we go.

Believe it or not, I do most things for a reason. Dressed in black... trench coat... mask... guns—all part of the plan. Of the image. Of the character. Channeling the Brandon Lee vibe. I would bet good money that this guy just shit in his pants when he saw me.

He starts shouting and pointing. His friend looks over. Then he starts shouting and pointing too. They draw and raise their guns, keeping a comfortable distance between us by staying close to the door.

I climb another step and keep my eyes locked on his. With his free hand, the guy on the right snatches a radio from his belt and mutters into it. A moment later, two more guys appear from inside. They're dressed in similar suits, holding similar weapons. They fan out into a wide line of four, their guns trained on me with unsteady hands.

I keep looking at the guy to my right. The guy with the radio.

"You got a direct line to your boss?" I ask him, shouting to make sure I'm heard over the noise of the rain.

I take a patient breath, letting my Ili do its job.

After a moment, he shakes his head.

Shit.

Okay. Plan B.

I look along the line, allowing my gaze to settle for a moment on each of the men standing before me.

"Any of you got a direct line to Kazawa?" I ask.

The guy on the far left takes a miniscule step toward me.

"I... I do," he replies, his voice quivering.

I smile. "Good. That means you win."

I whip both Raptors forward and squeeze both triggers twice. The first bullets to explode from each barrel hit the guy second from the left and the guy on the far right respectively, burrowing effortlessly into their foreheads like a railroad spike being hammered through a pillow. Their heads snap back, and their bodies lurch away from me, crashing unceremoniously to the ground.

The second bullets plant themselves decisively into the chest of the guy who was standing second from the right. One center mass. The other just below the throat. He joins his friends, lifeless and bloody in front of the doors.

No more than three seconds start to finish.

I holster one of the Raptors and aim the other at the remaining guy, who's visibly shaking on the spot—and not,

I'm guessing, because of the low temperatures. I suspect what just happened hasn't fully registered with him yet.

"Get Kazawa on the line and pass him to me," I say to him, almost spitting the words out as I stare, unblinking, through my eyebrows.

The Ili translates, but it doesn't replicate the tone, so it's important to get that right so the urgency of the request isn't overlooked.

Without even having to ask, he slowly crouches, placing his gun on the ground. He reaches into his pocket and retrieves a cell phone. He dials a number and holds it out for me without waiting for it to ring.

I climb the remaining steps and casually brush his gun away without breaking stride. I take the phone and hold it to my ear, pressing the barrel of my gun to the top of his skull as I do. I shuffle to the side and outstretch my arm, putting safe distance between us, should he get any silly ideas.

The phone is answered.

"What?"

I recognize Kazawa's voice instantly. The light, arrogant tone, brimming with confidence.

I pull the trigger. The guy crumples into a bloody heap at my feet. His blood quickly forms a thick river that flows begrudgingly down the steps.

"*Kon'nichiwa*, douche-nozzle."

There's a pause.

"Adrian Hell."

"Tetsuo Kazawa. Been a while. Man, I haven't seen you since... what? Last week, when you tried to kill me?"

"You're a lucky sonofabitch. But that luck won't last forever. You're a dead man walking."

I turn a slow circle, making sure I'm still alone. I see everyone standing over by the car, watching intently.

"I think you and I have *drastically* different opinions as to what constitutes luck, but that's a discussion for another day. Tell me, why have you been hiding up in your ivory tower for the last week? Miley not given you your balls back yet?"

He laughs. "You're trying to get a reaction out of me. Pitiful. It was unfortunate my club was destroyed for nothing, but no real loss. However, I am a smart man, Adrian. Business comes first. There are a lot of police on my payroll, but I still needed to lay low for a while, given the media coverage the explosion drew. There's no shame in that, so fuck you."

"Which is fine, except it wasn't the explosion that garnered the attention, was it? It was the torturing and attempted execution of yours truly at the hands of your psycho girlfriend on YouTube."

"Nothing less than you deserved!"

I can't help rolling my eyes. "Oh, please! You had no issue with me before *she* came along. This vendetta is hers. You're just going along with it so you can get laid."

"Think what you want. The fact is you're on borrowed time. I run the most powerful Yakuza family in all of Tokyo. And you... even though you're still breathing, I doubt you resemble anything close to being alive. Young Miley did a real number on you!"

He starts laughing to himself. Prick.

"No need to tell me," I say. "I was there. But I think you're underestimating my resilience. See, she might be the Harley Quinn to your Joker, but the truth is bigger and better people than either of you have tried to kill me before, and I'm still here. I'm not saying it didn't hurt. I'm not saying it didn't piss me off. I'm just saying you should check my resume. After you take on the president and get away with putting a bullet in him, everyone else just seems… insignificant, y'know?"

His laughing stops. The silence on the line is claustrophobic. It seems to affect the world around me, as even the rain has fallen quiet.

"Still trying to get a reaction out of me?" says Kazawa after a couple of moments.

"Yeah. And y'know what? It's working."

"Fuck you!"

"See?"

"Your day will come, Adrian. Very soon, you'll find yourself face-down in the dirt, and no one will even remember your name."

"Meh… you first, sweetcheeks."

"And how do you figure that?"

"Because I'm outside your front door, surrounded by the bodies of your dead men, and I've got a bullet each for you and your prom queen. Be seeing you, asshole."

I hang up before he can speak and pocket the phone.

He'll call back.

I holster my Raptor and head down the steps, back over to where everyone's waiting. Halfway across the street, I realize something doesn't feel right. I stop in the center of the intersection and look around. The traffic has disappeared. The sidewalks are empty.

Hmm. That might be why it felt quieter just then…

I understand the gunfire scaring the pedestrians. Word will travel fast. People will avoid the area. Authorities will be called. But that won't suddenly block the roads off in all directions, emptying the entire intersection. Not yet. And this isn't Kazawa's handiwork. I just got off the phone with him. His pet cops aren't psychic.

I turn around and look back at the building. I hear a

noise, a low rumbling, distant and incoherent. I take a step closer, my hand reaching behind me and gripping a Raptor for reassurance.

What *is* that?

Then I see it. The doors burst open, and a sea of dark suits and white shirts emerge. They flood the entrance area and quickly flow down the steps, spreading out across the sidewalk. There must be twenty... no, thirty men, easily. Some have handguns. Some have SMGs. I even see a couple of shotguns in there.

I'm right in the middle of no man's land, positioned between the horde of new arrivals and my friends. I let go of my gun, bring my hands around, and hold them out to the side. No sense in even trying to draw. But the fact they didn't shoot on sight is promising. It perhaps means—

The cellphone in my pockets starts ringing.

I breathe an internal sigh of relief and answer it.

"You've reached the home of the Whopper... what's your beef?"

"Cute," says Miley.

"Oh, it's you. I'll be honest, I was kind of hoping something horrible and painful had happened to you."

"I'm afraid not. Sorry to disappoint."

"Don't be. I'm used to it. I mean, look how you let me down last time we spoke. There I was, hoping to finally get some peace, and you couldn't even kill me when I was tied up and strapped to a bomb. God, you're pathetic."

"Fuck you, Adrian! Fuck... you! I've been waiting years for this. Your death is inevitable."

I frown. "Well... yeah. Isn't everyone's?"

"I'm going to end you."

"No, you're not. You've already proven you can't. Now put your boyfriend on the phone. The grown-ups need to talk."

Silence again.

I take a moment to survey the small army standing before me. I trust Ruby, Collins, and Ichiro with my life, and I respect their abilities more than anyone, but there's no way they could save me if someone decides to start shooting.

"How is the welcoming committee?" says Kazawa.

"I've seen better."

"Best I could do on short notice," he replies. "Give it a couple of minutes."

As if on cue, the slow wail of sirens drifts in on the wind. I look down the street in the direction of the noise.

"Oh, yeah. Those your cops playing my tune?"

"They are. In a few minutes, you'll have half the Tokyo PD and another fifty of my best men surrounding you. Any last words?"

"A few, actually, if you have the time?"

He chuckles. "Be my guest."

"D'you know what? Put me on speaker. I want Miley to hear this too."

There's a crackle on the line. It sounds hollow and spacious.

"She's listening. Go ahead," says Kazawa. "And make this good because you're about to die."

"Oh, I will." I begin slowly walking backward, pausing after each step, trying to make my retreat more discreet in case these two dicks can see me. "You see, the thing is... I didn't come here alone."

Miley laughs. "Aww, did you bring your sister-slash-girl-friend to watch you die? How cute."

"Yeah, Ruby's here. She says hi, by the way. Oh, and FYI —sister and girlfriend are only the same thing in Arkansas. But no, I don't mean her. I brought an old friend who works for GlobaTech Industries. You've heard of them, right?"

I don't give either of them chance to reply.

"Of course, you have—it's GlobaTech! Anyway, long story short, they've *somehow* managed to obtain evidence that you're selling their weapons illegally. Tetsuo, you naughty boy! Remember how they replaced the old U.N. Peacekeeping Force after 4/17? Well, it turns out, they have the authority to arrest and detain when laws have been broken on foreign soil too. And they're here for you. Now, you can shoot up the street all you want with your local Yakuza wars, but you haven't got the stones to start an international incident."

There's a long pause.

...

...

...

"You're bluffing," says Kazawa confidently.

"No, I'm really not."

"Japan doesn't have its own ATF," adds Miley. "And the U.S. doesn't have jurisdiction to get involved in our business here."

"Very true, but GlobaTech does. Their authority isn't bound by borders. Plus, it's their weapons you're selling, so it's kinda personal to them."

"You're bluffing," says Kazawa again.

"Believe me. Don't believe me. I don't really care. But the fact of the matter is this: if you open fire on me or my Globa-Tech friend, you'll be attacking a U.N.-sanctioned operation. You said you were smart... how bad would *that* be for business, do you think?"

I hang up.

Your move, asshole.

I step away slowly, walking backward until I make it to

Ichiro's car. I lean against it, keeping my eyes locked on the men in front of me.

"So…" says Collins. "How's it going?"

"Perfect," I reply without looking around.

The sirens get louder.

"Erm… Adrian?" says Ruby, just as ten police cars screech to a halt in front of us, five from each side. The cacophony of doors opening, boots hitting the wet ground, and weapons being drawn and aimed fills the air, drowning out the increasingly heavy rain.

That's easily another twenty guns in Kazawa's pockets that are now pointing at us.

She turns to me, eyebrows raised questioningly. "You were saying?"

I smile awkwardly. "Heh… it'll be fine." I look over at Collins. "Ray, GlobaTech has the authority to uphold the law in countries other than America, right?"

He looks at me with narrowed eyes, as if he can't tell whether or not that was a serious question.

"Adrian, we can't uphold laws *anywhere*. Including America. We're not a law enforcement agency. We develop weapons and technology for the highest bidder. We also outsource our own military force to the U.N., as you know, but not in a lawful capacity. For all intents and purposes, we're not affiliated with any country. We're just kinda… here to help. We're peacekeepers."

I nod slowly, processing his answer. It turns out I *was* bluffing…

"Okay, well, let's hope Kazawa doesn't use Google in the next five minutes."

"*Shinigami*, this is very bad," says Ichiro. "This is small army. This is a hundred guns against four. This is very bad."

"I know, all right?" I say with a sigh. "I know."

"Why aren't they shooting?" asks Ruby.

"I think Kazawa's trying to prove a point," I reply. "The ultimate show of strength. Miley wants to beat me mentally. She wants me to die broken."

"She sounds like a real peach," says Collins.

"Oh, she's something, all right..." I mutter as I scan the crowd before us.

Ichiro was probably right on the money when he said a hundred guns. This... this didn't go as well as I hoped. I'm not—

I hear tires screeching. Engines roaring. In the distance and closing in fast.

More cops?

Christ, Kazawa! There's proving a point, and then there's just showing off...

A fleet of black cars rush through the narrow gap left by the Tokyo PD to our right, sliding to a halt on the wet road. Five... six cars now. Windows blacked out. Nothing more than huge shadows in the street. They form a thick, semi-circular wall in the middle of the intersection, separating us from the crowd of Kazawa's men, directly ahead of us, and the two platoons of Tokyo's finest on either side.

They're definitely not cops. And no one's emerged from the vehicles since they stopped, so they can't be Kazawa's. The engines idle, revving occasionally.

The four of us exchange looks of confusion. I look out at the ever-growing battlefield and notice both Kazawa's men and the cops look just as bewildered as we do by the new arrivals.

Whoever they are, they're definitely not with Kazawa.

So, who the hell are they?

26

Every door of every black car suddenly opens with impressive synchronicity. The combined sound of twenty-four locks being released in unison is loud and impressive. Men and women emerge, dressed in matching suits—black jacket and pants with a white shirt and black tie. The mechanical rustle of machinery can be heard over the noise of the rain as they produce and ready their weapons.

Oh, shit.

The four of us have literally got our backs against the wall. There's no way out from here. If these newcomers open fire, we're done for. I just hope they—

The shuffling and splashing of boots on wet ground interrupts my train of thought as everyone in front of me takes aim...

...

...

...

...at Kazawa's men and the cops!

What?

I exchange a sideways glance with Ruby, sharing the same expression of relief and confusion.

"What's happening?" she hisses.

"I have no idea..." I reply.

Then someone else steps out of the back of one of the cars. I hadn't realized only twenty-three people had appeared.

The last man out is Akuma Oji.

He emerges slowly. Deliberately. Like he has all the time in the world. He looks around casually. Not one of Kazawa's men, or the cops, move an inch. I'm pretty sure they're all holding their breath, stunned by the new arrival.

Oji looks over at me, then glances at my companions. He gives me the slightest of nods.

Well...

Fuck me.

I turn to Collins. "Logic prevails."

He shrugs back. "Who knew?"

I walk over to greet him, ignoring for a moment the warzone in front of me.

"I didn't expect to see you again," I say to him.

Oji holds my gaze. It's the best poker face I've seen in a long time. "Likewise."

I raise an eyebrow. "So, not wishing to sound ungrateful or anything, but why exactly are you here?"

He sighs. Not heavily but enough to express his reluctance.

"You're not forgiven for killing Santo. That's something we will address at a later date, and there *will* be a blood debt for you to pay. But what you said to me this morning made sense."

He gestures to Kazawa's skyscraper with a sweeping, yet subtle gesture of his hand. "Tetsuo is a cancer to our way of life. He needs to go, but I was avoiding a direct war with him. It took the counsel of a wise, old friend to remind me that the enemy of my enemy is my friend. At least... temporarily."

I smile to myself and look over my shoulder at Ichiro. He's smiling back at me.

That sneaky sonofabitch.

"Well, Kazawa's gonna love this," I mutter, turning back to Oji and taking out the cell phone again. I re-dial the last number and place it to my ear. I look into his dark, emotionless eyes. "You wanna say hi?"

He shakes his head slowly, a small smile betraying his stoic expression.

"Want to know why your men haven't started shooting yet?" I ask Kazawa when he answers. He doesn't respond. "Can you even see the street from all the way up there?"

"I can see fine," he replies quietly.

"Outstanding. That means you can see all these black cars that have just arrived, right? There are some people here who would argue your claim as the most powerful family. Care to guess who?"

More silence.

...

...

...

"Fuck you," he says finally.

I laugh, exaggerating it to provoke him. "Yeah... you know. Bit more interesting now, huh? Your men and his men will kill each other. And the police... well, I wouldn't bet money on any of your cops opening fire on your behalf now. I think it's a safe bet that at least half of them are on

Akuma's payroll too. So, you know what this means, don't you?"

There's a pause.

"Enlighten me."

"It means you and Miley better put some coffee on, because I'm coming for both of your asses."

Kazawa's frustrations are so loud, he can be heard as I Frisbee the phone toward his building, not caring to hang up first.

"You are an infuriatingly effective man," says Oji. "Do you know that?"

I smile at him. "Thanks."

"Not really a compliment."

I shrug. "Yeah, but I'll take it."

There's movement across the street, which distracts me. I direct my attention to the steps and the lobby of the skyscraper. Kazawa's men have begun shuffling among themselves, exchanging glances and generally looking twitchier than they did a moment ago.

I've got a bad feeling about this.

There's an all-encompassing silence surrounding us, somewhat eerie in its totality. Beside me, Oji takes a deep breath, swelling his chest and standing to his full height, no doubt keen to show his own people he fears nothing about the situation.

On either side, the cops stand still and ready. The ones I'm close enough to see don't have their fingers inside the trigger guards of their weapons, so they're clearly in no rush to involve themselves, as I suspected.

The tension in the air is palpable. No one wants to make the first move. I assume Kazawa's given the order for his men to engage, but the fact they haven't yet highlights the influence Oji has on the proceedings.

Everyone here is on a hair trigger. The slightest nudge will start the dominoes falling, then this whole place will turn into a battlefield. I need to get to Kazawa, but I have to let this play out first. I can't kill him if I'm dead.

...

...

...

A single gunshot echoes around the deserted streets.

The sound trails off in slow motion. I hold my breath. I can feel everyone around me do the same.

Then one of Oji's men at the front of the group drops to one knee before slowly falling forward, landing face-down on the ground.

The first casualty of battle.

The atmosphere begins to sizzle with electricity.

Oji screams, fierce and disciplined.

Bullets start to crack and rattle, seemingly in all directions.

I turn and sprint toward Ichiro's car, gesturing wildly at my friends.

"Get down!"

I slide over the hood and land in a crouch behind it. Ruby, Collins, and Ichiro dash around to join me as the bullets fly relentlessly. Dull, hollow *thunks* sound out as the car is peppered with ammunition. Even the bricks of the wall behind us splinter from the impacts of poorly aimed shots.

All four of us ready our weapons and take aim, resting on the car while trying to remain covered behind it.

I look at each of my friends in turn and shout, "We're all professionals, so for the love of God, whatever you do, don't shoot Akuma's people by mistake."

"Your pep talks suck," replies Collins.

I shrug. "That's all I got. Sorry."

With measured, professional shots, we all begin firing back, trying to pick off as many of Kazawa's men as we can from back here. Visibility is poor because of the weather, and there's so much going on, it's hard to focus. Still, I manage to drop a few over to the right of the mob occupying the opposite side of the intersection.

"Reloading!" yells Ruby as she ducks back behind the car.

I join her, quickly slamming two fresh mags into my Raptors before resuming my position, leaning on the roof of the car. I notice Akuma Oji himself is crouching behind an open car door, returning fire. Impressive. Kazawa could learn a thing or two, if he wasn't locked in his penthouse suite with his shitting pants on.

The cops on either side still haven't moved or fired a single shot. Hard to know which ones are in Kazawa's pocket, which belong to Akuma, and which are genuinely police officers here to stop a turf war.

A few of Akuma's men are down. A decent number of Kazawa's men are too, but our combined forces are barely making a dent in the small army guarding the entrance to the building.

I look over at Collins, my expression firm and frustrated.

"This ain't gonna work, is it?" I say rhetorically.

He shrugs. "Christ knows, matey. I've seen stranger things, but I wouldn't put money on it, if I'm honest."

I nod slowly. "Shit."

I turn to Ruby and Ichiro, who have both ducked back into cover. Their gaze is laser-focused on absolutely nothing, and their breathing is rapid. They're taking a moment to manage their adrenaline. I've seen it a thousand times before.

Ruby glances at me. Her eyes narrow, then her brow arches. A silent question, demanding to know what the hell we're doing here.

I wish I had an answer for her.

I wish—

What the hell is that?

I stand slowly, keeping hidden enough behind the car that I won't get shot, and scan the chaotic scene before me. The cops are all getting back inside their cars. There's shouting among themselves. Engines are turning over. Lights are flicking on, bathing no man's land in a fluorescent spotlight.

Unbelievable!

But that's not what made me look around. There was something else. A sound I didn't expect. A sound that's out of place here. But I can't find the source of it with everything that's going on.

...

...

...

I finally turn my gaze skyward.

Through the low, thick gray cloud, I see the undercarriage lights of a helicopter moving slowly away from the roof of the skyscraper. Pinpricks of light edge out, forcing their way through the evening gloom.

Sonofabitch! I turn to Collins. "The piece of shit's running!"

He frowns before following my gaze upward. "Ya gotta be kiddin' me!"

I remain transfixed on the sky. I can't believe, after all this, he's taking off again. I don't understand it. I'm all for picking your spot, but he and Miley have had multiple opportunities to try and finish the job in the last few days, and yet... nothing.

I actually feel disappointed. I can't believe he's fleeing like a little bitch.

...

...

...

Except he isn't.

The lights of the chopper are getting bigger and brighter. It's descending.

I quickly analyze the significance of that in my head. I ask a hundred questions all at once. I try to understand why he would come down here in a chopper instead of flying away to guaranteed safety.

There's only one reason that makes sense.

I wish I was wrong, but I know I'm not.

This is about to get very bad.

I look over at Ruby. "We need to move right now!"

Ichiro hears me and looks around. "Why?"

"We've got incoming!"

The two of them gaze to the sky as the full shape of the chopper comes into focus. It's a standard civilian helicopter. You could probably get four people in the back. It's jet-black, sleek, and smooth. The noise of the twin blades drowns out everything else going on around us. It's descending fast. The draft swirls litter and water all around.

Kazawa's and Oji's men alike stop shooting to shield themselves against the fresh onslaught of elements. The cops are making a hasty retreat—J-turning and accelerating away from the gunfight with haste.

The four of us stand, weapons held to our sides, staring with unavoidable awe at the chopper. It's now hovering directly overhead, low enough I can see through the windows. One pilot up front. Two passengers in the back.

No prizes for guessing who.

It swings around so that it's side-on. The rear door is thrust open. Kazawa rests one foot out on the ledge and produces a light machine gun. A cylindrical, multi-barreled weapon that resembles a fucking cannon.

Instincts take over, replacing everything else I could possibly think about in this exact moment—pain, fear, concern, anger... none of it matters now.

My body starts moving before I get chance to tell it to.

"Run!"

As a unit, we dash to the left, around the hood of the car and over to the far side of the intersection. The same moment that we clear the alley, the seamless, high-pitched roar of LMG fire rips through the night. I don't look behind me. I already know the initial burst would've torn through Ichiro's car like wildfire through a dry forest.

With everyone following my lead, I rush for the left side of the entrance to the skyscraper—my thinking being to put Kazawa's men between us and his chopper in the hope he won't mow down his own employees.

The blood-red stream of gunfire sweeps across the intersection, cutting off the path in front of me. I dive instinctively away from it, landing hard on the ground before letting my momentum roll me away behind a parked car. I sit against the rear wheel, holding both guns up, the barrels no more than an inch from my face. A quick look to my left reveals Ruby and Collins did the same thing and are now hidden behind the next car along.

Where's Ichiro?

Shit!

I risk a peek around the truck, glancing out across the

street. There's no sign of him. The chopper has positioned itself above the middle of the intersection, forcing Akuma's men low behind their own vehicles. What I can see of Kazawa's people have regrouped at the edge of the steps and are simply aiming at either us or Akuma.

I survey the area again. Where the hell has he—

I see him!

He must have doubled back because he's knelt behind one of Akuma's cars, close to the alley where we started but a little to the right of it. Our eyes meet, and he nods, signaling he's okay.

I lean back behind the car and close my eyes, allowing myself a brief moment of reprieve and relief.

Okay. Fuck this.

I pop up from behind the car and empty both Raptors toward the chopper. As best I can, I aim my left hand at the cockpit and my right hand at the rear door. Sparks fly as my bullets ping off the blades and the bodywork, ultimately causing nothing but superficial damage. Still, it bought us a few seconds. The pilot banks away as both hammers thump down on empty chambers.

"Go!" I shout over to Ruby and Collins.

They jump to their feet, weapons raised, and sprint past me, toward the west side of the skyscraper. They duck down again behind one of the large planter boxes that border the stairs there. Kazawa's men open fire at the movement, but Akuma's men do the same, quickly subduing them.

I start sprinting right, back over to Ichiro. I need him to—

"Shit!"

I bring both arms up around my head in a futile gesture as a fresh burst of gunfire slices across the ground in front of me. I stumble away from the intersection and find myself behind the car Collins and Ruby just left. The whirring of the LMG is relentless, and the stream of bullets cuts effortlessly into the bodywork of this car. It won't offer me much cover for long.

I go to reload but realize I only have one magazine left. I holster one of the Raptors and reload the other, quickly racking the slide back to chamber a round.

The firing stops, and I instantly look round to reassess. Kazawa's ducked back inside the chopper. He must be out of bullets. As the chopper begins to climb, I see Miley appear, holding the handle of the open door as she leans forward. She points at me and makes a gesture of firing a gun with her hand before slamming the door shut. The chopper continues to rise, peeling away from the scene.

As the noise of the chopper fades, gunfire rings out once more as Kazawa's men resume firing at Akuma's. I scramble to my feet and sprint back over to Ichiro, blind-firing a few rounds to deter anyone from aiming at me. I slide behind what's left of his car, placing a hand on the wet, gravelly road to stop myself beside him.

"You okay?" I ask.

He nods. "Yes, *Shinigami*. Do not worry. I simply could not run as fast as you youngsters."

I smile. "Been a while since anyone called me young."

"I meant the other two. You... you are old. But you also crazy, which is why you keep going."

I go to reply but decide against it, instead choosing to smile at the fair point.

After a moment, I say, "Ruby and Collins are over to the left. You stay here and help Akuma's men."

He frowns. "What you are going to do?"

"I'm gonna follow that chopper. There's no way I'm letting either of them get away."

"On your own? Adrian, that is insane... even for you! You don't know where they're going. Or how many people will be there when they arrive. Let them go. Focus on this fight. It is far from over and could deal significant blow to their numbers."

I shake my head. "No way, Ichi. I'm done letting them dictate the terms of this. They come at me and the people I care about, then turn tail and run, choosing to hide until they decide to come at me again. And I'm supposed to... what, exactly? Just sit back and give them chance after chance to finish me? No. This ends tonight. One way or the fucking other."

Without giving him chance to reply, I get to my feet. I keep low as I move along the fleet of black cars until I reach Akuma. I kneel beside him.

"I need a car," I say.

He looks at me with no obvious expression. No surprise. No anger. No objections.

He nods and moves away from the car we're crouching behind, gesturing me inside the open door.

"You kill that bastard, and your debt to me is cleared," he says.

I nod. "Easiest debt I ever paid. Thank you."

I dive across the seats and shuffle into position behind the wheel. Outside, Akuma slams the door shut before moving out of sight, presumably to join one of his men behind another car.

I start the engine, yank it into gear, and accelerate away, taking the two o'clock exit past the right side of the skyscraper. I lean forward, looking up through the windshield, searching the night sky for the lights of the chopper. I soon see them, parallel to me, just ahead.

I stamp my foot to the floor, causing the engine to rev

harder than it's meant to. I reach the cordon placed around the area by the police—plastic barriers positioned across the street, with abandoned police cars on either side. The gap between them looks wide enough for me to fit through.

Maybe.

I brace myself, locking my arms straight. I grip the wheel until the color drains from my knuckles. I burst through the barriers like they weren't even there and fly through the narrow gap, clipping the police car to my right. I see the sparks of metal on metal in the wing mirror but pay little attention.

I struggle against the flow of adrenaline to keep my breathing calm and my mind clear.

"No running from me this time, asshole. This ends tonight."

27

I drive as fast as I dare, splitting my focus between the chopper and the road ahead. Thankfully, it's remained quiet since leaving the Yakuza warzone. The sidewalks are practically deserted, and the roads have nothing more than a light scattering of cars and scooters. Luckily for me, everyone's driving sensibly enough that I can navigate through the traffic at speed with little issue.

I'm trying to work out where Kazawa and Miley would be heading. Whether they realize it or not, there's nowhere big enough or secure enough to effectively protect them from me. And they just left Tokyo's equivalent of Fort Knox, which arguably wasn't their smartest move. If I'm being honest with myself, there was next-to-no chance of us breaching even the lobby of that place, let alone all the floors separating us from them.

So, why leave? Where's better to regroup than a mile-high fortress? Did he know I would follow? Is he leading me into—

Shit! A red light!

I slam the brakes on and turn the wheel quickly, throwing up spray from the road and smoke from the tires behind me. I fight to retain control as the car fish-tails. I narrowly miss the car in front of me by sliding clockwise around it, then immediately move counterclockwise around an overly eager pedestrian who is halfway across the street.

I steer into each slide, working with the angles instead of against them until I clear the intersection. I hit the gas again, powering the car straight as I resume my pursuit. Seeing the road immediately ahead of me is clear, I glance up at the chopper.

Oh, for fuck's sake...

Where is it?

I crane my neck to check as many directions as I can to find it, but the buildings lining this particular stretch of road are tall, so they're obscuring my view of the clouds.

"Come on, come on... where are you, you sonofa—"

A gap appears in the skyline thanks to a run of low-level restaurants, offering a glimpse of the night sky. The rain-clouds are outlined by the eerie, artificial glow from the signs beneath them.

I squint in the neon glare, desperately searching for the familiar pinpricks of light.

"There you are."

In the distance, I make out the faint illumination from underneath Kazawa's chopper. It's peeling away to its right, putting even more distance between us.

"Shit."

I stamp hard on the brakes and take a sharp right, desperate to get back on their tail. The buildings around me begin to change. Restaurants and offices and stores disappear, replaced with warehouses and factories. A road sign flashes past me. The needle's pushing ninety, but I made out the image on it. I'm heading for the docks, which can only mean one thing.

The piece of shit has a boat.

I need to reach him before he boards whatever he has anchored here. Otherwise, I've no way of going after him.

The haunting outlines of large cranes form on either side of me up ahead, hiding in plain sight against the night sky. I'm already trying to work out what lies ahead—a dock-yard, warehouses, stacks of shipping containers. Potential dock workers as well.

Innocents are the last thing I need to deal with right now. All that matters now is that I stop them before they—

An explosion of breaking glass forces me to stop thinking. Instinctively, I duck low behind the wheel.

"What the fuck was that?" I yell out to no one.

I glance over my shoulder to see a million tiny fragments of what used to be my rear window covering the seats. The back windshield is gone, shattered by the gunshot from the guy leaning out the passenger side of the black sedan that's now chasing me.

"Are you kidding me?" I mutter. "Like I don't have enough to fucking deal with."

More gunshots.

Knowing I have little ammunition to retaliate with, I sink further behind the wheel, to the point where I can barely see over it. What remains of the wing mirror on my right vanishes with a high-pitched ping. I instinctively lean to the left.

I think it's safe to assume these assholes are Kazawa's men. They probably followed me when I left the party back there. So, now I have to keep an eye on Kazawa's chopper, the road ahead, *and* watch I don't get shot from behind.

Talk about there being no rest for the wicked.

I speed up, taking advantage of the near-empty road stretching out before me. The car behind keeps pace; its dark frame dominating my rearview mirror. The shooter has ducked back inside, presumably to reload.

I need to get rid of these pricks soon. I've got more important things to worry about. Sooner or later, my luck's going to run out, and they're going to hit something significant. Like a tire. Or the fuel tank. Or me.

Come on... think, Adrian!

Up ahead, cars are parked on either side of the street, probably belonging to workers on the night shift in one of these warehouses.

I check the mirror again. The shooter is leaning back out of the window, preparing to fire. Whatever I do, I need to do it now.

...

...

...

I know!

I hit the brakes again, screeching to a long stop on the wet surface. The car behind me closes the gap down to nothing in seconds. I watch through the rearview, running through my next move over and again inside my brain, simulating the execution, playing out the calculations and the math. I see the eyes of the driver pop wide in shock as he rapidly approaches the back of my car. He swerves at the last second, moving instead to draw level on my passenger side.

Wait for it...

Wait for it...

Now!

I hit the gas, forcing my tires to spin as they battle for traction on the rain-soaked blacktop. I accelerate forward as the sedan with Kazawa's men inside it begins to pull ahead. As the trunk passes my hood, I turn hard, smashing into them.

The slippery surface of the road works to my advantage. The driver loses control, forcing them to spin away at the exact moment I pass a mid-sized truck parked by the side of the road. The sedan's front-end smashes into the large rear compartment. The sound of the chassis crumpling against the stoic truck is like an eruption, amplified by the night sky, drowning out the sound of the heavy rain.

I speed away, glancing in the rearview just in time to see what's left of the sedan careen back across the street and collide with another parked car. The momentum and severity of the impact causes it to flip. All four wheels leave the ground as it rolls over the car, seemingly hanging in the air for an eternity before smashing into the low concrete wall surrounding the nearest building.

Well, that worked.

I check the sky again. The chopper's banking left, coming across my field of vision. It's also getting lower. I need to get to them before—

Shit!

Dead end.

A chain link fenced gate stands defiantly ahead of me, blocking my path. Beyond it is the dockyard and, some-where, Kazawa's chopper.

...

...

...

Ah, screw it.

I slam my foot to the floor, revving the engine harder that it sounds like it was built to. I grip the wheel until my knuckles lose their color and lock my arms straight, bracing for an unknown level of impact.

I burst through the closed gate like a bullet through a wet newspaper, tearing it from its hinges on either side and dragging it through with me, trapping it beneath the car. I hit the brakes and turn, sliding to a long halt in the middle of a wide-open work yard. The door is open before the tires stop smoking. I step out, quickly scanning my surroundings.

Warehouses all around form a network of avenues to help navigate the docks. The cranes loom over everything like metal guardians. A few dock workers stand around, dumbfounded and uncertain, looking at each other, seemingly unsure whether to approach me or run away.

With my back to the newly exposed entrance, I see a clear path at my ten o'clock that leads to the loading bays and the pier. That has to be where they are.

I reach behind me for my loaded Raptor and check the magazine. I have five bullets left and no spare ammunition.

Screw it. I only need two—one for Bonnie, one for Clyde.

One way or the other, somebody isn't leaving these docks tonight.

I break into a light jog, careful of the wet ground and my own physical limitations.

Everything is bathed in a sickly yellow fluorescence by floodlights. Ahead, out over the water, the half-moon is shielded by low clouds. Its faint glow is nothing more than a token gesture in the all-consuming night.

All around, the sounds of the dockyard carry on the wind. Though it's unlikely to be as busy as it is during the day, there's still a low symphony of whirring machines, accompanied by the shouting of foremen to their subordinates. But it's the growing noise of the water I find unnerving. Already turbulent from the storm, I see high waves breaking against the side of the docks, crashing like cymbals in this dreadful orchestra, drenching the pier ahead.

I move past a fork-lift and take a left by a stack of crates seemingly positioned to direct me that way. The turn brings me onto the pier itself. To my left is a long line of low buildings. Storage facilities, I presume. To my right lies the Pacific Ocean and—

"Holy shit..."

That has to be the biggest yacht I've ever seen in my life! It completely dominates my field of vision and towers over the pier like a floating city. I see Kazawa's chopper on the helipad near the stern. Lights form a perimeter around the outside edge, still flickering in a clockwise circuit. The blades are still spinning but silently slowing down, the noise drowned out the ever-increasing storm.

Beneath it is a block of cabins. The middle of the deck is lowered—an open space with a small crane and a speedboat stored there. Below is a long run of interior space, probably more cabins or a hold of some kind. Beyond that, slightly shrouded by darkness, is the bow. Another block of cabins stands tall and proud, with what I assume is the bridge and helm on top of it, mirroring the helipad above me.

I see movement—faint outlines of silhouetted bodies moving with purpose in every direction. Moments later, I hear the engine fire into life. The muffled, bubbling roar of unfathomable horsepower explodes like someone converted a volcano into a jacuzzi. Almost immediately, I hear the yacht's engine revving. The deck is bathed in pale luminesce. I catch myself staring in awe at the size of it. Standing here, I don't think there's ever been a time where I've felt more insignificant. This thing is easily two hundred feet long. Maybe thirty wide. The equivalent of three or four stories high.

It begins to move slowly forward, inching away from the pier. The movement snaps me out of my trance. I'm standing almost level with the back of the boat, but nearly the full width of the pier separates us.

In my peripheral vision, I see a few more people standing around, staring at me like I don't belong. But they don't concern me. My mind is engaged, running through all available options open to me.

I have to find a way onto the boat.

But how?

And what I am going to do when I'm on it? I make out several people patrolling the decks. You could fit a couple of hundred people on there. How do I know that's not exactly what he's done? It would be the smartest thing he's done in the last two weeks if he has.

My window is closing. It's moving farther and farther along the pier and already halfway in its turn to pull away.

If I get on that boat, there's every chance it's a one-way trip. There's no exit strategy. No safe way off that thing. It's the middle of the night, and the water is fatally freezing. Right now, I don't see a way back. All I know is Kazawa and Miley must die. Nothing else matters.

When your back's against the wall, the only place to go is forward.

My vision blurs as my mind shifts itself into a state of intense focus. A level of functioning I've spent most of my adult life refining. A place inside my head where I consciously switch off all regard for my own well-being.

Something I've had to do more times than I would've liked over the years.

Shit.

Shit, shit, shit!

I sigh. Clench my jaw until my teeth ache.

Ruby would want to be here for this. She owes these two bastards almost as much as me. If I die taking them out, she's so going to kill me!

Ahem.

Huh?

While you're standing here having a moment with yourself, you know the boat's getting away, right?

My vision re-focuses in time to see the stern of the boat drawing level with the pier.

"Oh, crap!"

My Inner Josh flicks the final switch inside my head. Autopilot engages. My Inner Satan's cage is unlocked.

I tuck the Raptor into the waistband behind me. I take two measured steps back. My gaze locks on the wide gap at the stern that's revealed itself as the boat creates more distance from the pier. It's got to be twenty feet wide, easily. A platform almost level with the water. I'm guessing it's where people dive from or climb onto jet skis. On either side of it is a curved stairwell, leading up to the main deck and a metal door leading inside the cabin area beneath the helipad.

One deep breath.

I lunge forward, accelerating as fast as my old and beaten body will allow. I stomp each sprinted step down, searching for every ounce of grip I can get from the wet ground beneath my feet.

I cut across the pier, toward the edge, ignoring the pain in my chest from the exertion. All that matters is getting on that boat.

The edge approaches. I can see the water now. The stern

is maybe six feet from the pier. Maybe the same again ahead of me.

I grit my teeth until my jaw aches. I suck in deep, painful breaths.

If I never do anything again, I need to do this.

I flick a glance up ahead. I'm running out of pier.

I'm running out of time.

I will myself to ignore the insanity of what I'm asking my mind and body to accept. My foot plants down on the edge. There's nowhere left to run. Without hesitation, I push off and fly forward, my arm stretching out in front of me, desperately reaching for something to grab a hold off.

I hold my breath, frozen in mid-air.

...

...

...

Shit!

28

I land heavily on the platform. My shoulder takes the brunt of it as I slide across the wet surface, coming to an abrupt stop as I collide with the wall beside one of the staircases. The impact momentarily knocks the wind out of me.

I lie still, my head propped awkwardly against the corner, breathing fast and deep to stem the flow of adrenaline and regain my composure. I stare out at the expanding sea and the shrinking pier of Tokyo's dockyard.

Fuck me.

...

...

...

Okay, now what?

A quick physical assessment tells me my ribs and shoulder took a knock and my face is hurting like hell, but other than that, I'm in one piece.

For now.

I shuffle upright and shift so that I'm crouching on one knee. I reach behind me, feeling for the satisfying and lethal comfort of my gun. I'd best keep that for emergencies. I've no idea who knows I'm here... if anyone heard or saw me. I'll assume they didn't until I see evidence to the contrary, which means I need to stay out of the lights, move quietly, and stealth my way around this thing until I reach my target.

Ha!

Kiss my ass, Josh. I can be stealthy.

Really? Give me one example of when you even tried *to move unseen, let alone succeeded?*

That's not the point. Or the time to question things.

I smile to myself.

I need that—his voice in my head. It keeps him with me. In times like these, he would be in my ear, offering advice or lightening the mood—whatever I needed to complete the mission, to take out the target. It keeps things feeling normal. Plus, it keeps my Satan company.

If I ever spoke to a shrink about all this, I suspect they would say my Inner Satan is nothing more than a manifestation of the worst part of myself. That separating the evil inside me and giving it an identity somehow helps me disassociate myself from all the bad things I've done.

They would probably be right too. But now isn't the time for disassociation. Now is the time for very bad things.

I've never been on a boat like this before. I have no idea of the make or model. Or if boats even *have* a make and model. I don't know the layout, beyond the glimpse I caught from the pier. All I know for sure is I'm currently at the rear, about as far back as you can be without getting wet.

When your back is against the wall, the only place to go is forward.

If I'm going to do this, I need to figure out where Miley

and Kazawa are holed up, then find the quietest route around this boat to get them.

If I were a six-foot sack of crap and a teenage whore with anger issues, where would I be?

...

...

...

I would be surrounded by as many of my disposable foot soldiers as possible. It doesn't really matter where, at this stage. The trick is going to be actually getting to them on a borderline level playing field.

I'm probably better staying inside where possible. Moving around outside, even in the dark, leaves me too exposed—to bullets and to the elements.

Roughly ten feet above me is a railing. It's probably waist-high, standing in front of a door that leads inside the area directly beneath the helipad.

As good a place as any to start.

I slowly stand, remaining pressed against the wall, and listen for any movement. It's a struggle to filter out the plethora of noise from the world around me, but after a few long moments, I'm happy I'm alone.

I crouch and make my way up the curved staircase beside me, hugging the near wall as best I can without limiting my movement. I pause at the top, half-covered by the low wall, half-obscured by the railing. In broad daylight, I would be completely visible, but in the pitch-dark, I should be fine.

I peer around, staring along the starboard side of the deck. No sign of life. I can just about see where it opens out, where the speedboat and crane are. There's a pinprick of blurred light beyond that—presumably the bridge at the bow, but honestly, it could be anything.

Happy I'm in the clear so far, I step out and move forward, stopping just around the corner, hidden from the door near the railing. I press myself against the wall again, feeling the metal rivets push against me through the material of my coat. My right shoulder is level with the edge.

Lightning cracks in the sky, followed almost immediately by a roar of thunder. The wind is strong, forcing the rain sideways as it assaults the boat—and me—like a billion tiny bullets. Impressively, however, the boat remains steady.

The rapid pitter-patter of the rain on my protective mask sounds amplified by the darkness. I'm not sure if it's actually loud, or if it just sounds like it to me because it's on my face, but my paranoia gets the best of me. I quickly remove it, sliding it into one of the inside pockets of my coat.

I wipe the excess moisture from my face and take a quick peek around the corner.

No movement.

The boat's picking up speed. The noise of the engine, while barely audible over the weather, will further conceal any sound from my own movements.

Here goes nothing.

I move around the corner, remaining pressed against the outer wall, heading for the door. I make it three steps before it swings open and hits the wall with a loud, metallic bang. I freeze and catch my breath, dropping to one knee. Thankfully, the door swung toward me, so I should be blocked from the peripheral vision of whoever steps out.

I wait.

A few seconds pass before one man appears, wearing a dark poncho with the hood pulled up tight around his head. He's carrying a gun, possibly an SMG, loosely in his hands, the strap over his head and left shoulder. He paces idly forward, stopping at the railing and looking out at the ocean behind us.

I feel an involuntary smile creep onto my face.

The first casualty of war.

Moving slowly, I shuffle along the wall until I reach the open door. Now behind him on his seven o'clock, I take a couple of slow breaths, steeling myself and planning my next moves.

This needs to be swift and decisive.

I stand and move toward him. In stride, I step through and down, stamping my right foot through the back of his left knee. He crumples down to his left almost immediately, unprepared for the attack. On his way down, I swing my left elbow and forearm clockwise as hard as I can. I time it perfectly, connecting with his temple as it reaches the ideal height. The impact has a whiplash effect on his neck, and he drops to the deck like a bag of rocks.

I unhook the gun from his shoulder and use my foot to shove him under the bottom bar of the railing. I apply as much force as I can. I watch as he drops the ten or so feet to where I was moments ago. The force of my kick and his own dead-weight momentum cause him to roll away as he lands. A second later, he disappears over the edge, lost forever in the dark waters beyond.

I quickly check the weapon. It's an SMG, as I thought. A full mag but no spares. Still, it's better than the five bullets I had to my name before. I hook the strap over my head and arm, so it's rests on my shoulder, and push it behind me. I take a final glance around to make sure I didn't attract any attention, then step inside, closing the door gently behind me.

In front of me is a short corridor. It appears to open out ahead of me, but there is a door on either side before that.

With careful steps, I continue on, stopping just before the door on the left side, which is standing open. It's much quieter inside, so I listen for any signs of movement. Happy there isn't anyone there, I pop my head inside.

It's a maintenance room, by the looks of it. No windows. Artificially lit by a single strip light on the ceiling, encased in a metal wire frame. A couple of all-weather jackets hang in the corner facing the door. The room stretches back along the corridor behind me. There's nothing noteworthy in here, just three walls of metal shelving that have boxes and tools stowed on them.

I move to carry on but stop myself.

Actually...

I step inside the room, paying closer attention to what's on the shelves. I scan the array of tools until my gaze rests on a flat-head screwdriver—a thick, black, non-slip handle and a long neck, maybe seven inches.

That will do very nicely.

I head back out into the corridor, directly in front of the doorway opposite. I look inside and see a narrow, precariously twisted staircase descending into a room below.

Hmm.

I navigate the steps, using the wall for balance, and make my way down. I come out in a small, claustrophobic area, maybe twelve-by-twelve—if that. Standing upright, I'm six-one. There's perhaps three inches of room between the top of my head and the ceiling.

I look around and see two large pieces of machinery,

seemingly identical, encased by a metal railing. I'm no expert, but these look like engines.

Very interesting.

I head back up the stairs and along the corridor until I reach the doorway at the end. There isn't much room on either side of it for full cover, but I press myself against the wall as best I can and look inside.

There are a couple of windows on the left wall. On the wall directly opposite is a notice board and various pieces of health and safety information. There's a door on either side of it leading, presumably, to the open deck and speedboat. Along the right wall is a modest-sized kitchen area. It looks fully functional and kitted out in much the same way I envision most restaurants are.

There's a seating area that dominates the middle of the room, which is where I see two men talking, both with their backs to me. I'm guessing one is the helicopter pilot, given he's wearing a light gray jumpsuit. The other looks similar to the guy I disposed of earlier. Same thick jacket. Same gun that I now have.

They're close to each other and maybe eight or nine feet from me. The buzzing fluorescent lights will be shining out onto the port side deck, so whatever happens next will be visible to anyone who might walk past at the time.

This needs to happen quickly.

I spend a second debating whether or not the pilot is innocent. My gut's telling me he probably isn't. That he's Yakuza, just like the rest of them. But unfortunately for him, it ultimately doesn't matter one way or the other. If he's alive, that's a potential way off this boat for someone, and I can't allow that. I would prefer this not to be a one-way trip for me, but it definitely has to be a one-way trip for Kazawa and Miley, so he's got to go, I'm afraid.

As before... as always... I plan my attack and run through the execution in my head before moving an inch. Temporarily disable the pilot on my way to killing the armed foot soldier. Then kill the pilot.

Easy.

I grip the screwdriver and hold it upside-down, so the long neck is hidden and pressed against my inside forearm. That way, they won't see it until it's sticking out of them.

Here we go.

I step over the threshold and move with purpose into the middle of the room. The guy with the gun notices me first and turns, revealing a brow furrowed with confusion and a mouth hanging open in disbelief. The pilot hasn't reacted by the time I draw level with them.

Same approach as before, with an added step this time. Like building a deadly dance routine.

I smash my foot through the back of the pilot's knee. As he buckles, I produce the screwdriver and jab it with powerful and lethal precision into the armed guy's throat. This works well for two reasons. The first is that the initial blood loss is significant, which both weakens him now and makes him easier to finish off later. The second, if you get it right, is that it damages the vocal cords enough that he can't scream. He drops his weapon, clutching desperately at his throat.

I turn back in time to catch the pilot's head in both hands on his way down. Using gravity to my advantage, I quickly position my hands so one's on the base of his skull and the other is cupping his mandible. A quick twist results in a clean break of the neck and an instant kill.

I refocus on the remaining guy, whose eyes are currently bulging with a recognizable fear. I step behind him and place my left hand over his mouth, pinching his nose in the process. I then reach over his shoulder with my right, yank the screwdriver from his throat and slam it into his chest between the fourth and fifth ribs on the left side, puncturing his heart. I hold it in place for a few seconds until the struggling stops, then lower his body to the floor.

Two more down.

I retrieve the screwdriver, wipe it down on my sleeve, and stash it in one of my pockets.

I look to my right at the kitchen layout. All the utensils are stored away in drawers and compartments. Various pans hang by their handles on hooks high on the wall. There are preparation surfaces on either side of a large, two-door oven with a six-point gas burner stovetop.

Hmm.

Gas.

I glance at the ceiling, reminding myself I'm underneath the helipad right now.

Interesting.

I move over and open the cupboards underneath the surface on the left of the oven.

Shelving. Plates stacked and clipped in place. Paper towels. Cups, glasses... nothing exciting.

I move to the one underneath the right surface and open it.

Bingo!

Three large compressed gas canisters, all fixed securely in place, with rubber piping feeding into the oven through a hole in the side. I reach in and loosen the clasp holding the piping in place on the middle of the three canisters, just enough to create a small pinprick of a gap, so the gas slowly escapes. I close the cupboards again.

Let's call that an insurance policy.

I stand and make my way over to the door in the opposite corner, which I'm guessing leads back outside. This is going to be the tricky part. There's a lot of wide-open real estate between here and the bow. Those two douche-monkeys are either underneath it somewhere in a cabin, or on the bridge. Whichever it is, that door's my only option.

I reach for the SMG, flick the safety off and get a comfortable grip on it. Adrenaline is keeping the host of aches and pains off my brain's radar right now, which I'm thankful for. Even my hand is holding steady.

I move to the side of the door and rest against the wall, gripping the handle. I close my eyes for a second. Preparing. Focusing.

Come on, Adrian, you've got this. It's time Kazawa and your crazy stalker realized exactly who they were fucking with.

I twist the handle and slowly push the door open.

Whoa!

I wasn't prepared for the elements outside. The storm is raging to full effect, and the crosswind tore the door from my grip, slamming it open against the side.

I walk through and stop dead in my tracks.

The speedboat is ahead of me, with the small crane off to the right. There's a small stack of crates to my immediate right, just next to the slightly raised platform the door opens out onto.

There are three guys by the speedboat. Another two by the crane. One by the port side barrier. Two more starboard side.

They're all holding weapons. They're all staring at me.

Well...

Fuck.

29

_____

Time doesn't even have the decency to stand still. There are eight guys in a wide semicircle in front of me, and I have nowhere to go.

Luckily, I'm holding my gun ready to shoot. These guys are holding theirs simply to keep them off the floor, which isn't the same thing.

Plus, I'm me, and they're not.

They're dead men.

I apply a simple formula in my head. A tried and tested calculation I worked out very early on in my life:

Instinct plus adrenaline, multiplied by confidence, equals unparalleled violence.

That basic equation has solved every problem I've ever had. And the good thing about math is that it's universal. It works every time.

I squeeze the trigger, firing a short burst to my left as I slam the door shut behind me. I dash right toward the crates

—my only option for cover. I drop the first guy stood by the port side railing. I slide behind the boxes and lean out to the right. Another quick burst drops the nearest guy by the railings on this side. His friend seeks cover of his own by the crane.

Two down. Six to go.

I'm maybe down a third of the mag already. I can't afford for this to turn into a long, drawn-out firefight—I don't have the ammunition for it.

I need to be economical.

I move back to the left side of the crates, ducking momentarily as a short hail of bullets splinter the wood above my head.

I poke my head out, not even for a second, to catch a glimpse of my next target. It's small, but I have a clear shot. Three guys on the left have sought refuge behind the speedboat. Rookie mistake. The first rule of a gunfight: never take cover behind anything flammable.

I switch my weapon to single-fire mode, pop out, and fire two rounds at the speedboat's exposed fuel tank.

The explosion is instantaneous and deafening. I turn away, screwing my eyes tightly shut so as not to ruin their adjustment to the dark. The brilliance of the blast is rivalled only by the scalding devastation it's created. The ferocious roar even silenced the raging storm around me.

I look over.

Huh?

Where is it?

I look around and see nothing.

That's weird.

Then I hear something that makes me look up, and—

"Oh, shit!"

I dive right, out from behind the crates. The blackened,

burning remains of the boat lands on the deck, a little bit nearer to me than it originally was. The blast must have catapulted it skyward. The impact did what the weather and the turbulent tides have so far failed to—the yacht rocks and sways uneasily in the water, and for the first time since getting on this damn thing, I'm momentarily unsure of my footing.

Jesus!

Well, I think it's safe to say the three guys who chose to hide behind it are regretting that decision now.

The repeating stutter of automatic gunfire pings off the railings around me.

Fuck! Forgot about them...

I move left, back into cover. The heat from the flaming wreck nearby is overpowering, making it harder to breathe as it burns the oxygen from the air.

Beats being shot, though.

I chance a peek out of cover. I can only make out two guys by the crane now, ducking behind it at the far side, near the starboard rail. Can't be a hundred percent, but it looks like I took out one of the three over there with the speedboat, which would be a nice bonus.

I need to think about this for a moment. I can't move left and go around to flank them because of the burning wreck. There isn't anywhere to move to the right unless I want to get wet, so my only option is to move forward and engage. But they have a tactical advantage; in the far left and right corners from where I am are stairwells leading down to the lower deck. There, they can potentially restock their ammunition and get help from their friends. Being lured down there would be suicide. Too much cover for the enemy. Too easy to get trapped.

Unless Miley and Kazawa are down there, in which case, what choice do I have?

One problem at a time.

I fire a couple of blind rounds to force them behind cover, then move out. I quickly turn and raise the gun to check above me, making sure no one was hiding out by the chopper.

Clear.

I turn back and move toward the crane. Crouched, purposeful steps. The gun is trained dead ahead, always following my line of sight, as if linked by invisible string.

Movement.

One of the guys was ducked behind the railing that overlooked the stairwell. My gaze snaps to him. My arms and weapon follow.

BANG-BANG!

A double tap. Instinctive. Rapid, like snapping my fingers.

I reach the crane and pause behind it for a moment. No sign of movement. Did the other guy make it down the stairs?

I move around and continue, aiming for the stairs. As I draw level with the opposite side of the crane, I see a blur of movement, mostly concealed by the night.

Shit!

Uh!

No... he didn't go downstairs.

Rookie error, Adrian.

The guy was crouched behind the crane. He popped out and clocked me with the butt of his gun, right in the side of the head. I dropped and slid across the soaked deck, colliding with the railing that borders the stairs.

That shook the cobwebs loose. Jesus...

He races toward me, raising his gun, refining his aim with each step.

Fuck this. I'm not getting taken out by some no-name, low-level Yakuza.

I scurry to my knees and lunge forward, pushing both his thighs with my hands as he reaches me. His legs fly out from under him, and he falls forward, head-first and rigid. I allow my own momentum to carry me to the deck, so the guy falls on top of me.

Except he doesn't.

His head catches the top bar of the railing on the way down. I heard the dull, hollow *dink* as it connected. Sounded painful.

I roll away, turn, and push myself up to one knee in time to see his face slide over and off the top railing and flop down onto the second. The angle of his body is enough to hold him there. His hips are almost flat to the floor, but his back is being held up at an angle most yoga instructors would blush at. His chin is hooked over the middle railing, keeping him in place.

Oh, dear.

I ease myself to my feet, stretch and crack my aching bones, then bring my leg up and stamp my foot down hard on the back of the guy's neck. I feel his throat give against the stubborn metal railing. Pretty sure I heard a snap too.

His head slides off the railing and hits the floor, finally letting him rest flat.

I quickly crouch and take the mag from his gun. Put it in my pocket. Then I stand up and turn a slow circle, surveying the carnage now engulfing the deck of Kazawa's yacht. No more signs of life, although if there are more guys below me, I'm pretty sure they know I'm here now.

Just need to find—

Oh.

Hello.

I finish my turn staring ahead to the bow and the bridge that stands upon it, level with the height of the helipad at the opposite end. It has windows on all sides, offering whoever's inside a three-sixty view of the boat and the ocean.

Standing side-by-side at the window, looking out at the flames and the dead bodies, are Miley and Kazawa. The glare of the fire illuminates the glass enough for me to see their faces inside.

His eyes are wide. Shock? Probably. Fear? Maybe. If he's not scared, he fucking should be.

Miley's a little easier to read. She looks pissed.

I stand my ground. Square my shoulders. Take a deep breath. Relax. A sigh of relief this particular battle is over.

Then I wave at them and smile.

I see Miley slam her hands down and turns to Kazawa. I can't see her mouth moving, and I can't lip-read even if I could. But a blind man could see she was shouting at him.

Excellent. My work here is done.

See you soon, assholes. I'm going to—

Huh.

...

...

...

That feels a lot like a gun barrel pressing against my head.

I glance over my shoulder and find myself staring at the barrel of a handgun. It's pointing directly at my head, held steadily in place about an inch from me. Looks like a Heckler and Koch USP. Pretty sure the Japanese version of a

SWAT team uses that. Makes sense that some of Kazawa's security detail are cops, I guess.

I shift my focus beyond the gun, to the person holding it. Somewhat surprisingly, it's a woman. She's not as tall as me, but the look of determination in her eyes, coupled with the understandable confidence she has, tells me now isn't the time to resist. There are three men standing right behind her, all with their weapons trained on me.

"Drop the gun," she says.

I do, allowing it to hang loose on my shoulder. Immediately, one of the guys behind her moves around to my side and takes it from me, discarding it across the deck, toward the fire. He stays there, shoving my shoulder, directing me forward.

I throw him a look that tells him if he touches me again, it'll be the last thing he does. No need for words.

"Let's go," orders the woman, pointing to the stairs.

Looks like I'm being taken below.

As I reach the top of the stairs, I look back over at the bridge. No sign of Kazawa, but Miley is there, laughing at me.

Shit.

30

Below deck is surprisingly spacious and far more luxurious than above. This likely justifies what I imagine is an extortionate price tag for these things.

The corridor we descend into is much wider than the one below the helipad. A similar set of steps are visible ahead of me at the opposite end, presumably leading up to the bridge. The flooring is made from a non-slip material; I feel the extra grip tugging on each step I take, yet it still looks really expensive, designed to resemble marble tiling.

My new friends have maneuvered themselves into a box formation, putting two in front of me and two behind. We double-back on ourselves and head toward the stern, along the starboard side. There are three doors on the wall to my right. The first door we pass is half-open. I catch a glimpse inside as we pass, but that's all I manage, as the woman with the gun gives me a heavy tap with the butt on the back of my head.

"Eyes front, asshole," she barks.

I wince from the impact. But that's okay. I saw enough.

I saw the arms of two men, and I saw a metal rack full of weapons.

It was the armory.

Good to know there is one.

We carry on and stop outside the second door along. One of the guys in front of me opens it and steps aside, signaling me to go in. I glance around and see no one is making any attempt to follow me.

I step inside, ducking slightly under the frame.

I let out a low whistle.

This place is nice!

The floor is wooden—a light beech that immediately brightens the room. The ceiling is off-white and much higher than in the rooms above. High enough for a couple of chandeliers, anyway. In front of me, dominating the room, are two wide, semicircular sofas. They look like white leather. There's a narrow gap between them at each end and a circular table in the middle. The layout reminds me of the symbol you see on the power button of any piece of equipment. They're sunk into the floor, one step down. Ahead of me is a wide, panoramic window looking out into the night.

To my left is a four-poster bed, this time raised up by two steps. There's a closet built into the wall on either side. The whole area is illuminated by spotlights in the floor.

To my right, there's a mini bar against the near wall, some computer equipment set up in the opposite corner...

And Kazawa.

He's holding a bottle of beer in one hand, with his other in his pants pocket. His suit jacket is open. Shirt, no tie. Hair a little ruffled but still styled. Casual, like there isn't a care in the world.

Prick.

He's smiling at me.

I hear the door close behind me. I glance over my shoulder to make sure no one followed me in.

They didn't.

I make an exaggerated point of looking around before directing my gaze at him.

"You're either mighty brave or mighty stupid," I say.

He takes an easy sip of his beer. "How so?"

"Shutting us in a room together. Is Miley nagging you so much that you just want to die for the peace and quiet? Thought you have to be married for twenty years to reach that stage..."

He laughs but not with any humor. "The queen of my empire allowed me some time alone with you, so I can have my fun... and take my own revenge."

I raise an eyebrow. "If, by saying that, you're insinuating you're the king, how come you're only here right now because your queen allowed it? Sounds to me like she's the real power behind your family. What did she do to make you hand it all over to her? No way you were swayed by her winning personality. She must be dynamite in the sack."

"Say what you want, Adrian. You won't get inside my head. Not this time."

"Whatever you say. But come on, I'm curious. What did she bring to the table when she recruited you to help her get to me?"

He pauses for a moment, then shrugs. "What the hell... you're dead anyway. She approached me eighteen months ago. She had money and training and a detailed plan to get to you. She also had the promise of more money. A little over three weeks ago, she transferred sixteen million dollars into my holding account. Additional funding to help get her plan off the ground. I couldn't say no."

"She wasted her mother's fortune, if you ask me. She's clearly capable of coming after me on her own."

"That depends on perspective, Adrian. Money well spent, in my opinion. Oh, and for the record... yes, she *is* dynamite in bed."

His smug smile suggests that is supposed to make me jealous in some way.

I grimace. "Hey, do you mind? I'm already fighting back seasickness here. But whatever works for you. Anyway, what do you mean, *your* revenge? For what, exactly? You only have a problem with me because she does. Hell, someone in your organization hired me a while back."

He points a finger at me. "You're responsible for one of my biggest sources of income going up in flames. You're also responsible for the deaths of many of my men. I fucking owe you."

I'm genuinely baffled by his logic. "You need to lay off your own Kool-Aid. First of all, *you're* responsible for your club blowing up, not me. You set the bombs and left me trapped inside. You could have just put a bullet between my eyes. Being honest, you *should* have. So, that's on you. Secondly, your men tried to kill me first. Well, most of them. I'm claiming self-defense there. Thirdly, the only reason you're still alive is because I turned down the job to kill you. Something you still haven't thanked me for, by the way, you ungrateful dick."

He takes another sip of his beer, looking on impassively. "Ah, yes. A smart move, siding with Akuma Oji. How did you get him to help you?"

"Honestly?" I shrug. "I just asked him."

"Really? Huh..."

"Yeah, turns out trying to find people who fucking hate you isn't all that hard."

"His involvement is irrelevant. He's had his time. Japan is ready for a new era of Yakuza. *My* era. I'll deal with that old prick later. But for now, I'll focus on making you suffer for a little while, before my darling Miley can have her vengeance."

"I'm gonna be honest with you, Tetsuo—can I call you Tetsuo?—I'm done suffering."

I take a couple of steps into the room, casually pacing toward the bed, away from the door.

"See, I've had a pretty shitty couple of weeks. You know that, because you're the main reason for it. We both know Miley's nothing more than a hormonal teenager with daddy issues. She tried to sleep with me, albeit as part of her act. She apparently *is* sleeping with you, which is gross. We're both old enough to be her father. So, no... the real brains behind this is you. Has to be. And I've gotta hand it to you, man—you've pushed me farther than anyone ever has. You know who I am. What I've done. But you still managed to surpass everything and everyone that's come before you. You beat me. You damn near killed me. You even made me believe I was going to die. Made me accept it."

He makes a theatrical gesture with his hand. It's half-shrug, half-impatience. "What's your point?"

"My point is that after all that, I'm still here. You don't get it, do you? Somewhere out there, there's someone who has my number. Someone who is just *that* much better than me that I have no hope of surviving them. But Tetsuo... it ain't you."

He smiles. "Really? Are you sure? I mean, you're on *my* yacht... surrounded by *my* men... unarmed and trapped in a room with me. Your body is broken. You are tired and weak. You will die today, Adrian. You will die very, very soon."

I start laughing. For two reasons. One, it's unnerving as hell when an enemy starts laughing at you for seemingly no reason. All part of the psychological warfare. And two, because he's confirmed to me everything I need to know about this situation. His mindset. His arrogance. His... naivety.

This is too easy.

He's glaring at me. Frowning. Confused. He throws his near-empty bottle across the room. It smashes against the wall, just beside the mini bar.

"What's so funny, asshole?" he asks, unable to mask the frustration in his voice.

"You really haven't been paying attention, have you?" I reply, still smiling.

He's no longer relaxed. He's shifting his weight back and forth between each leg, stationary but restless, unsure whether to run at me or keep me talking.

"What do you mean?"

"Like you say, it depends on your perspective. Take a look at your big, fancy boat. Half of it's on fire! You're also... eleven men down, by my count. I did that. Me. Adrian Hell, broken body and all. Also, I'm not actually as stupid as I look, despite overwhelming evidence to the contrary. What? You think after everything I've done tonight—not just on your boat, but back there outside your little penthouse... after all that, do you honestly think I'd be blindsided by four of your security guards? I'm exactly where I want to be, asshole. See, you got it all wrong."

I quickly draw the Raptor from my back, which his amateur foot soldiers didn't bother to check for, and aim it unwaveringly at his head.

"I'm not unarmed at all... and I'm not trapped in here with you—you're trapped in here with me."

His eyes bulge wide with an indecipherable cocktail of emotions. I see anger. I see frustration. I see fear. I see realization.

Yeah... back there, when I was waving at the bridge, I had an inkling more people would be heading my way from below. I was running out of bullets and energy to fight them off, so I gambled on the fact that if they came for me, they would capture me and deliver me to one or both of these assholes. I could bypass any more fighting and head straight for my target. That's why I made a point of showing I was relaxed, or making it look like I was paying no attention to the stairs behind me.

Sneaky bastard!

Thanks, Josh. Glad you approve.

I'm also now standing far enough away from Kazawa that if he runs at me, I have plenty of time to get a shot off. And we all know I only need one. Plus, I've positioned myself on the other side of the door, so when it inevitably opens, it will be pushed toward me, shielding me from view as the people outside file in. It will be like shooting fish in a barrel.

That's... impressive.

Appreciate that, Satan. The pair of you have taught me well.

The look on Kazawa's face tells the full story. His eyes dart in all directions, perhaps seeking a way out of this. His body language is becoming increasingly restless. Using just a couple of steps to pace subtly back and forth. Flexing and clenching his hands. Visibly breathing faster.

He's panicking.

I look on with a mixture of fascination and satisfaction.

JAMES P. SUMNER

Here's the guy who was behind the near-surgical destruction of who I am. A man in a position of unfathomable power and influence in Tokyo. And I broke him in less than five minutes.

I almost feel sorry for him.

Finally, Kazawa unleashes a visceral scream, releasing all of the emotion that was consuming him moments ago. Then he charges me. A desperate move that will only end one way. And I think he knows it.

I allow him two steps before I pull the trigger.

The bullet strikes between his eyes. Dead center of his forehead. His skull snaps back as a thin plume of crimson mist erupts behind him. His body's momentum carries him forward, though, and he falls heavily through the gap between the sofas, landing lifelessly in front of the table.

"I know you were probably looking for a long, drawn-out fight," I say, more for my benefit than his at this point. "But you were right. I'm tired. I need to save my strength for your girlfriend. Sure, you pissed me off, but I never regarded you as a serious threat. You were never more than an obstacle. A means to an end. You simply didn't matter enough to me. You deserve nothing more than a quick bullet. But I can promise you this: your empire dies with you tonight."

The door flies open.

Ah, showtime.

Two of the men from outside rush in, because Kazawa's body would have been the first thing they saw as the door opened. There's no consideration for where I am at all. These guys are amateur hour.

With all the time in the world, I line up my next two shots.

BANG!

...

...

...

BANG!

Headshots. Both men are punched to the floor.

I move closer to the wall, a little farther out of sight behind the door. The other two should be right...

The woman steps into view, her movements more cautious than her colleagues.

...there.

As she turns to look at the room, she sees me leaning against the wall, my gun aimed at her head. Her eyes pop wide a split-second before I squeeze the trigger. The impact of the bullet sends her toppling over the back of the sofa nearest to her. She rolls off it and lands awkwardly on the floor, trapped between the sofa and the table.

One bullet left.

The last guy is probably a little apprehensive to come in, but I doubt he'll leave to fetch back-up. I examine the door. Specifically, the thin gap between the edge and the wall, caused by the large, metal hinges. I see him move to stand directly behind it, preparing to pop out and surprise me.

I take one step forward and kick the door, thrusting my leg as hard as I can with the intention of going *through* the door. I hear the grunt as it slams into the guy on the other side.

Dumbass.

I move around to see him sprawled across the corridor, his face blank with disorientation. I glance left and right to make sure there aren't any reinforcements heading my way, then holster my gun. I reach down and drag the guy up by his collar, then deliver a short jab to his nose. Not hard enough to break it but sturdy enough to make his eyes water. I take his SMG from around his neck and toss it aside.

Holding him by the throat with one hand, I quickly frisk him, searching for any handguns or spare ammunition.

Nothing.

Shit.

I look him in the eyes. "Well, you're useless, aren't you?"

I then use both hands to grab his collar again. With more effort than it would normally take, I hoist him over the railing and watch as he plummets into the dark ocean below.

I pick up the SMG and step back inside Kazawa's cabin. I know there are at least two more guys on this boat between me and Miley. Possibly more. I need to take the fight to them before they figure out what's happening.

I do a quick sweep of the dead bodies and grab what spare ammunition I can find. Nothing for my Raptor, annoyingly. But I'm more than prepared for what's next. There can't be that many guys left now—the boat isn't that big.

I check the mag in my SMG. It's full. I reload it, work the slide, and chamber a round. I set it to fire single shots. Safety's off. My trigger finger is extended, resting against the guard. That's my safety. Only touch the trigger when you want to squeeze it.

I head out into the corridor again. Logic would suggest Queen Miley is on the bridge. So that's where I'm heading.

This ends now.

31

I slow as I reach the door to the armory, remembering the two guys I saw in there earlier. Holding the SMG in one hand, keeping it low, I pin myself against the wall and edge forward, stopping as I reach the doorway. I place a hand on the door and slowly push it open, leaning around as the gap widens, ready to shoot if necessary.

The room gradually reveals itself. Racks of weapons— assault rifles, submachine guns, pistols... even an RPG. Jesus! No sign of life, though. I bring my gun up as I step inside, immediately turning to look behind the door.

The room's empty.

I take a moment to look around. This place has everything! Maybe Kazawa leaving the safety of his penthouse to come here wasn't such a stupid idea after all. Well... it *was*, clearly, but at least his logic was sound.

As I turn to head back outside, I see a belt of grenades resting on a small table in the corner just inside the room.

Interesting.

I leave and continue along the corridor, heading for the stairs at the far end I presume lead up to the bridge. I have the SMG held ready, keeping it low, by my hip. As I begin the climb, I turn and move backward, allowing me to see behind the stairwell above me, and to the sides, making sure no one is waiting to blow my head off.

It seems clear.

I turn slowly as I reach the top, looking around the room as I—

Oof!

Ah!

Whoa!

...

...

...

Shit!

I fall back, losing my grip on my weapon. There was a guy to the right of the stairs, set back just ahead of me. He kicked my gun hand away and got a couple of solid shots to my body before I even realized I was in a fight.

Bastard.

I forget the gun. I scramble to my feet in time to block another kick aimed at my left side, just above the hip. I leaned into it, bending my arm so he kicked the point of my elbow.

Still hurt, but had it connected properly, it would've dropped me for sure.

I'm assuming this guy is one of the two from the armory. I need to remember he has a friend somewhere.

He swings a wild left at my head as he retracts his leg. I move right, ducking under it and countering with a right hook. The guy leans back, and I hit nothing but air. As I follow through, I feel a short uppercut connect with my ribs, which staggers me back again.

Fuck me...

Either this guy's lightning fast, or I'm just slow and tired. Or both.

Whatever the case, I can't waste my time and energy fighting him.

I'm down on one knee, nursing my chest. He's a few feet away, composing himself and smiling like someone who knows he's winning.

I take a quick look around as I suck in one painful breath after another. This is an open area, which I'm guessing is used for navigational purposes. There's a large table dominating the left side of the room, parallel to the stairs, with an assortment of maps and paperwork spread across it. Behind the railing that surrounds the opening of the stairwell is a door that must lead outside. On the opposite side is another door, stood open, with a small corridor beyond that doglegs left.

I assume that's the bridge.

The main issue I have is this guy standing in my way.

I slowly get to my feet and step back into a loose fighting stance. His smile broadens, like a shark smelling blood in the water.

I try to block out the pain. Urge my brain to ignore it and focus on something useful. Like my training. Which is extensive and lethal.

What do I know?

This guy likes his kicks. His punches are effective but less disciplined. Both require space to throw them. Which means I need to close the gap.

I look him up and down.

He's light on his feet and has a confident fighting stance.

JAMES P. SUMNER

His guard is competent, suggesting training. No gun, which is strange but a blessing. He's shorter than me, younger than me... definitely faster than me. His power comes from technique, not from brute strength. If I can take away his ability to execute his technique...

I step toward him. He moves to meet me but hangs back, clearly looking to maintain the distance he needs. But this time, I skip a couple of paces and close the gap, leaving just a few inches between us. He drops his shoulder, preparing to throw a hook to my left side. But this time, I'm close enough that he'll miss if he swings it. I don't know if he's realized that, but it doesn't matter now. I'm too close. Speed and technique mean nothing if my hands are around your throat.

As he throws his hip into the punch, I lean into him, grabbing his throat with my left hand and pulling on the back of his jacket with my right. He loses his balance as I push and pull him into position against the railing of the stairs.

I force him back, causing his spine to bend over the railing by applying more pressure to his throat. Then I bring a knee up, slamming it into his stomach. He wheezes as the air leaves him, but the position of his body makes it hard for him to catch his breath.

I knee him again, this time allowing him to keel over. I drop to one knee, smashing the point of my elbow into the base of his skull on my way down. He flattens out on the floor. I'm breathing hard from the exertion, but I can't stop now. I need to finish this, to make sure I have one less enemy to worry about.

I reach down and drag him upright with both hands. He's barely conscious, and it takes a lot of effort to hold him steady. I place one hand on his head and grab a fistful of jacket with the other. Then, with every ounce of strength I can muster, I slam him face-first into the railing.

The crack of his cheekbone smashing is sickening.

His face immediately swells, discolored from the impact.

I toss him unceremoniously over the railing. He lands headfirst on the metal stairs before rolling into a motionless heap at the bottom.

I breathe a heavy sigh of relief, which hurt way more than it should.

That took more effort than I realistically had the strength for, which means dealing with Miley will now be that much harder to do.

I focus on my breathing as I try to regain some composure. It doesn't matter though. She has to die tonight. No one does to me what she did and gets away with it. I need her gone, so I'm not running and fighting for the rest of my life. I need her gone, so Ruby isn't, either. But I have to admit, this is feeling more and more like a one-way trip right now.

I turn to head for the doorway I'm hoping leads up to the bridge and see another guy pacing with vicious intent toward me.

My shoulders slump forward with momentary resignation.

Christ.

I look him in the eye. I see a knife in his hand.

Well, *you* can fuck off.

I take one step toward him and swing my leg out as if kicking a forty-yard field goal. I connect so completely with his balls that his pelvic bone hurts my foot.

Probably not as much as he's hurting right now, though.

He stops dead in his tracks and drops the knife. His eyes bulge. He leans over and vomits, then sinks to his knees, clutching his groin with both hands. I wince out of sympathy before taking another step and smashing my knee into his face. I feel the thin cartilage buckle beneath the impact. He slumps to the side, unconscious and bleeding from what's left of his nose.

I take a quick look around, but the lighting is poor in here. I can't see the SMG I dropped anywhere.

Screw it. I have one bullet left. Luckily, it's got Miley's name all over it.

I walk over to the doorway opposite, climb the few steps, and follow the short corridor around to the left. No more than a few feet, and I see the bridge in front of me. There's no door, just a threshold. From here, it appears empty.

Huh.

I move to the doorway and take a look around. There's a door directly opposite, which leads outside. On my left is the large window that overlooks the main deck. The remains of the speedboat are still burning nicely. The flames cast a flickering, hellish glow across the boat, highlighting certain features while enhancing the shadows around others.

No sign of movement that I can see.

On my right is the helm—a large, chrome wheel surrounded by a dashboard and control panels with a walnut finish. Another large window looks out at the ocean ahead. Despite the light flooding from the front of the boat, visibility is poor. Nothing but a vast expanse of dark.

I don't know where Miley is, but—

Huh?

Oh, fuck!

...

...

...

Ooof!

Ah, shit...

What the hell was that?

I'm on my back, out in the short corridor, hurting everywhere and looking up at the doorway to the bridge as Miley drops down.

She must've had herself pinned flat up there, just above the doorway, where I wouldn't have picked her up in my peripheral vision. She swung down and planted both feet firmly into my chest, the impact of which, coupled with the surprise, sent me flying backward.

Christ. She's like a fucking ninja.

She stands over me, staring down with a sick smile. She's still wearing her black catsuit with heeled combat boots. She has a utility belt around her waist but no visible weapons.

I scurry backward, so I can use the wall to get myself back up to a vertical base. I've experienced her wrath when I was at full strength, and it nearly killed me. Right now, I'm operating at around twenty percent, and that's being generous. I have to figure out a way to stall her and survive long enough to find an advantage. I just need to—

She shrieks with fury as she lunges at me.

Holy shit!

I just about manage to get my arms up to protect my face as she lands, knee-first, on my chest. I grunt as she presses all her weight down on me. She screams again—a guttural, primal cry of fury—as she rains down blow after blow, overwhelming my body and arms with vicious punches. She has a strength that doesn't belong on her frame. Her body is slight, toned. In another life, she could be a model. Yet, when she connects with a punch, it has the power of ten people behind it.

She's starting to break through my guard. A few have landed and done some major harm. I don't have my mask on. My face is already broken, which means it won't take much to do some permanent damage.

The top of my head is resting against the wall. She's straddling my body but sitting high up, almost on my chest. One knee is tucked beneath her, digging into me. Her other leg is outstretched to the side for balance. My hips are mostly free.

This is going to hurt, but...

I buck with my waist, thrusting up as hard as I can. The pressure on my back is immense, but it works. She wasn't expecting it and is thrown forward. Her head connects with the wall, and she rolls away, allowing me a moment of reprieve.

I grant myself one deep breath.

I scramble upright and dash onto the bridge. I hear her quick steps behind me. As I make it into the middle of the room, I don't bother checking first. I simply spin around, counterclockwise, swinging a Hail Mary right haymaker. I didn't expect it to connect; I just wanted to give her something to think about.

Well, it didn't connect.

Huh?

She leans back and catches my arm in both hands at the wrist. As she does, she jumps and brings both legs up. One rests easily on my left shoulder. The other snakes around me, just under my outstretched arm. I feel her cross her ankles behind me as she leans back farther.

I adjust my front leg for balance. She's now hanging upside-down by her legs, pulling on my arm. I immediately feel the pressure on my carotid artery. A wave of dizziness hits me. I'm wrapped in a hold similar to a rear naked choke, which puts people to sleep.

I can't afford to lose consciousness. If I do, I'm never waking up.

I plant my feet and clasp my hands together, using my back and my arms to try and pull her up.

...

...

...

Gah! Fuck!

I haven't got the strength left.

My vision is starting to blur. Breathing is harder. I feel my cheeks flush.

I stare into Miley's eyes. She stares back, her wild gaze laced with rage. I see the focus and commitment of someone who is dedicated to a single task.

Killing me.

Well... not today, bitch.

My breathing becomes short and fast. I'm willing myself to lose control. To let the usually well-managed flow of adrenaline burst through the barriers and consume me.

...

...

...

I bend both knees a little. Not enough to lose my balance but enough to give me a boost.

I close my eyes. Clench my jaw. Tense every muscle until my body is wracked with pain. Then I keep tensing until the pain stops registering.

My eyes open. I stare at her again. This time, her gaze relaxes. Replaced by concern. Concern because I know what the look in my eyes right now is like.

Through gritted teeth, I snarl and grunt and unleash

every ounce of strength I have left. My body might never forgive me, but I can live with that.

As long as I live.

In one movement, I push up with my legs, pull with my back, and lift with my arms...

...

...

...

I yell out as I finally hoist her up, holding her for a long moment, frozen in a violent, almost erotic embrace. Then I spin around and slam her against the window.

The thud of her back and head connecting with the unforgiving glass is almost sickening. She doesn't relinquish her grip, but I feel it loosen. I step back and lunge forward again. Same impact.

This time, she relents.

As her feet hit the floor, I wrap a hand around her throat and slam her head against the window again. It cracks, sending a spiderweb shooting out around her like a deadly halo.

I stagger backward, resting on the helm. Miley drops to one knee, dazed. The glass around the epicenter of the crack is blood-red.

"You won't win," she says, practically spitting the words at me. "You're going to die. I've spent too long... too much... I won't lose now."

I manage a weak smile. "Miley, you lost days ago."

"What? What do you mean?"

"When you left me and Ruby trapped in that club with a bomb. That's when you lost because you showed me you don't have what it takes to kill me."

"Yes, I do! I'll end you right now, you bastard!"

I shake my head. "No, you won't. You can't. If you could,

you'd have done it on your live stream, when I was tied up and helpless. I'm not saying you don't want to. I'm not even saying you're not physically capable of it. I'm saying you just can't. You don't have that thing inside you that allows you to take that final step over the line and finish it. You're too... human."

"What? Shut up! Just... shut up! Stop it!"

"Your mother had it. She was a good assassin. I respected Dominique a lot. She was cut from the same cloth as me. But you... you've got too much to live for to leave such a dark stain on your soul at your age."

"Shut the fuck up! You don't get to say her name, do you hear me? Don't you say her fucking name!"

I lean forward, resting my hands on my knees, catching my breath. When I look over at her again, I can see her eyes starting to go. The slightly vacant stare. The struggle to stop them rolling back in her skull. The head wound is taking its toll on her. Weakening her.

Thank God.

I stand straight, focusing on my own struggle to not waver on the spot. I feel warm blood pulsing down my face. I feel the pinch with every breath that suggests broken ribs —either fresh ones or recurring injuries. I can't even tell anymore. I'm a mess, and I feel unsure how far away from death I actually am.

But this isn't over yet.

I meant what I said. I don't think she has it in her to kill me. But that's not to say she won't pursue me forever. She'll just hire someone else to finish me off. And when that person fails, she'll hire another. And another. And another. It won't ever stop, not as long as she's breathing.

She gets to her feet. Her own equilibrium works against her as she rocks back and forth on the spot. I move around, putting my back to the door that leads outside. She follows suit, moving to block the other doorway.

I drop back into a fighting stance. I lift my arms up to resemble a guard, but it won't be as effective as I need it to be. It's merely a formality, I guess. See, I realized something in my moment of respite back there. While there's no denying her strength and ferocity, she's still a slim girl who's not old enough to drink. Science dictates that, physiologically speaking, I'm simply bigger and stronger. She beat the holy hell out of me just then, opening up a lot of wounds she herself caused only a few days ago. But with one brutal impact, I did just as much damage to her.

Imagine what I'll be able to do when I'm not supporting her entire body weight.

There's a part of me that doesn't feel good about it. She's just a kid. But you reap what you sow. She dedicated years of her life to learning how to kill to me. Then she spent a considerable amount of money executing an elaborate plan to do just that.

If you want to play the grown-up's game, you have to be prepared to lose as well as win. You don't get a medal for participating in the real world.

She charges at me, wild and screaming, winding up a blow with her right hand that, if I'm being honest, I probably wouldn't get up from if it landed. But she's injured and slow, and it's going to get her killed.

As she nears me, I step toward her and throw a punch of my own. She doesn't see it coming, blinded by her own purpose. I connect with the side of her jaw about as hard as I've ever hit anything in my life—even with my injuries.

Her head snaps back. I see the lights go out in her eyes. She falls to the floor, rigid and finished.

I let my head roll back. I look to the ceiling and let out a heavy sigh.

It's over.

Now, I need to get out of here.

Ever since I left the hospital, I've been convinced that this was only ever going to end one way. That me and Ruby getting out of that club before it blew was simply delaying the inevitable. For me, at least. But now I'm here... Kazawa's dead, Miley's done... I realize I don't actually have a way off this boat. I never thought I would survive, so now that I have, I'm a little screwed.

I move to the helm. I've never sailed a boat in my life. I have no idea what half of these dials and buttons and levers do. I see a handle that looks like it might be the throttle, but I don't particularly want to go any faster.

If I can find a cell phone, maybe I can call Ruby or Ray, see if they can...

I hear a noise. Confused, I look around.

You have to be kidding me...

Miley's not dead. She's lay on her back, raised slightly, aiming a gun unsteadily at me.

I sigh. "Look, kid, don't be—"

She pulls the trigger. The impact of the bullet hitting my right shoulder registers almost instantly. I stagger back, quickly losing my footing. I don't feel anything from the gunshot. Time has slowed to a crawl, which is usually my spider sense telling me I'm missing something important. Maybe the fact I can't feel anything is a bad sign.

Maybe this is it. Maybe I've finally been beaten down enough that I can no longer fight back. Maybe I'm done.

As I fall back, I reach behind me for my Raptor.

Well, if I'm done, you can bet your ass I'm taking her with me.

I aim as best I can and pull the trigger as I hit on the floor. The landing jolts my body, and the gun flies from my grip. My breathing is shallow. I lift my head and look over to see if I hit her.

I see the rapid rise and fall of her chest. She's holding her hand up to her head.

Did I... did I get her?

I shuffle my body around and use my left arm to push myself up on all fours. I crawl toward her, pausing every couple of feet to press my hand to my shoulder in a feeble attempt to heal myself.

I reach her and stare down into her dark eyes. They're wide and full of fear. Her breathing is fast. The right side of her head and her shoulder is drenched in blood. There's a thin but significant spray behind her, covering the floor. Her hand is clamped to the side of her neck.

I reach down and lift her hand away, to see the wound.

Damn...

It wasn't the best shot I've ever taken. I should've put it between her eyes. It went through and through, but appears to have nicked an artery on the way.

I place her hand back over it.

"Keep pressure applied to it, and you'll slow the bleeding," I say to her. "Move at all and you'll bleed out in a minute. Maybe two."

Miley reaches over and grabs my arm with her left hand, just below the fresh bullet hole in my shoulder.

"This... this isn't... over, Adrian," she manages.

I calmly remove her hand. "Yes, it is. You tried playing a dangerous game with the most dangerous player, and you lost. Now you get to lie here and think about that for the rest of your life. All thirty minutes of it. Goodbye, Miley."

I push myself up, holding my right arm close to my body

as I apply my own pressure to the bullet wound. I shuffle back over to the helm, aware that the adrenaline is subsiding and I'm starting to feel every single thing that's happened to me in the last twelve hours with mind-blowing clarity.

I need to find a way off this boat.

Miley coughs and splutters. I look over to see her staring at me.

"No... Adrian. It's not... over." Her gaze shifts to the door behind me that leads outside. She smiles, which looks more like a grimace. "Fuck... you."

I raise an eyebrow.

That doesn't sound good.

I move over to the door and look out the small window.

It's dark. I can't see shit. I can barely make out the ocean around us. I can tell it's still stormy. Not sure if it's raining or if that's the mist from the sea all over the windows. Thunder is still rumbling, though. And lightning. Just seen a flash in the sky, behind the clouds. It lit up the ocean for a long moment. I could see—

"Fuck me!"

I look back at Miley. She's laughing.

There are two boats docking with the port side of the yacht. Big things, like mini hovercrafts. There was at least six people on each one. Maybe more—I only caught a brief look.

I can't fight them all. I can barely move.

Shit.

I look back out. It's too dark to see anything again now, but I reckon I have no more than a couple of minutes before they swarm the bridge.

I stare at the floor until my vision glazes over. I'm running through every option I have.

What have I got? What have I done? What do I need? What can I do?

...

...

...

I refocus as the only path I have left to walk becomes clear. I think, subconsciously, I knew it would always come to this.

I scoop up my empty Raptor and holster it behind me. I turn and stride past Miley, not even bothering to look at her as I leave the bridge and head back in the navigation room. I walk with haste. What I must do now isn't something I'm happy about. I know that if I slow down at all, logic will take over, and I'll stop completely. I can't afford for that to happen.

I don't want to do this, but I do want to live. I want to see Ruby again. I want to be happy. And all that trumps the insane thing I'm about to do.

I quickly descend the steps down to the starboard corridor and duck into the first room. The armory. I ignore the guns. I don't have the energy for a firefight with a dozen more Yakuza soldiers, even if I do have the bullets. I grab the belt of grenades and head back out, taking the steps up the main deck.

I have to be quick and quiet here. I can't afford to—

An orchestra of gunfire erupts over the noise of the storm. Countless muzzle flashes flicker in and out of existence, seemingly all around me.

"Fuck me!"

I crouch, pausing for a split-second as I consider retreating back to the armory.

No.

I'm done. Whether this works or not, I'm done here.

I take a deep breath. And another.

I look over at the door to the rec room and kitchen, illuminated by the persistent flames of the wrecked speedboat. It's maybe twenty-five, thirty feet...

The gunfire isn't even pausing for breath.

Here goes nothing. Or everything. Whatever.

Grenade belt in hand, I set off running as fast as my body will allow. I get a slight boost from the incentive of not wanting to be torn to shreds by bullets, but I'm still nowhere near as fast as I can be.

Bullets pepper the deck beneath my feet and ricochet off everything around me that's metal. I raise my arm to cover my head, as if that will make any difference.

"Fuck, fuck, fuck, fuck, fuck, fuck!"

I make it to the crates, but I don't stop or even slow down. I jump onto the raised platform and throw the door open to the rec room.

Jesus!

I stagger slightly, hit by a wave of gas. The smell collides with me like a brick wall.

Didn't think I made the hole in the piping that big...

I take one deep breath, which makes me feel a little woozy, drop my head, and continue running at full speed across the room. As I reach the door on the other side, I pull a pin from one of the grenades and throw the belt down into the engine room as I sprint past.

Three seconds, max.

I run along the narrow corridor.

Three...

I push through the door at the end, shoulder first, bursting out onto the walkway overlooking the stern.

Two...

Without breaking stride or concerning myself with

whether I can physically do it, I place a hand on the railing. I jump up onto it, planting my feet for balance.

One...

I push off as hard as I can. The height helps me clear the loading space below, where I first boarded. I bring both arms up in an arc, so my hands meet above my head. I reach the apex of my dive when—

BOOM!

The explosion behind me sounds like nothing I've ever heard before.

The noise and the power behind it are terrifying.

The force of the blast throws me farther than I ever could have jumped. I twist in mid-air, milliseconds before I hit the water, in time to see the rec room and the chopper parked on top of it disappear in a small mushroom cloud of fire and devastation.

I land in the water shoulders-first, plunging into the icy depths.

The trick in cold water is to not panic. The more you move, the faster you bring on cardiac arrest from the shock to your system. You have to remain calm and keep movement to a minimum.

Not an issue for me. I couldn't move anymore, even if I wanted to.

The heat from the explosion feels as if it's boiling the ocean around me. I lie motionless, holding on to the last breath I think I'll ever take. A rippling haze of orange and yellow dominates the world around me.

I feel myself floating. An overwhelming sense of peace floods into my body.

The world grows dark.

I told Kazawa that, one day, I knew I would meet the person destined to take me out. Perhaps today was that day, after all. I feel nothing. No pain. No suffering. Just... sweet, peaceful nothing.

The world seems mostly dark now.

I feel myself smile.

Not a bad way to go, I guess.

...

...

...

I see a bright light above me. Brilliant and white. They say that's what you see, at the end. That you should move toward it. Well, it seems to be moving toward me, but given I'm probably drowning, maybe some higher power is taking pity on me and helping me out a little.

It's more than I deserve.

An image of Ruby flashes into my mind. I see her floating in front of me, as clear as day. Her smile. Her laugh. Her green eyes.

If she's the last thing I ever see, I can leave this world a happy man.

You'll be okay, Ruby. I promise. You'll be just...

...

...

...

...fine.

32

"There he is," says a familiar voice. "How ya doin', buddy?"

I frown, mostly because I'm confused, but also to squint against the bright light assaulting my eyelids.

What the hell is happening right now?

Am I dead?

If I am, Heaven sounds a lot like Ray Collins.

God help us...

I tentatively open my eyes, keeping them screwed narrow until I'm sure they won't be singed out of their sockets by the light.

My head's resting to the right. The first thing I see is Collins's face, smiling down on me.

I swallow hard, trying to get enough moisture to allow my mouth to work, but it feels like someone's scraping razorblades around my throat.

"Please tell me I'm not dead," I say to him.

Blowback

He laughs. "Far from it, my friend. I mean, ya look like shit, but you're definitely alive."

I breathe a sigh of relief.

Hang on...

"How, exactly?"

"Because your friend here is almost as bat-shit crazy as you are," answers another familiar voice. This one sounds softer, more comforting. Better looking.

I turn my head to the left and see Ruby. Her eyes are like jewels, wide and happy and glistening, but I see the concern behind them. Her smile is as much out of relief than anything else.

I move my hand up to her face. As I hold her cheek, she places her own hand on mine and leans into my palm slightly.

"Where am I?" I ask her.

"In a private medical facility just outside Tokyo," she says.

I look around. Everything's white and clean. Lots of technology. A couple of nurses at the opposite end of the large room.

"GlobaTech?"

She nods and gestures to the room. "Who else?"

I smile. "Yeah. So, are you okay?"

She shakes her head. Her smile broadens. "I'm fine, you idiot."

"W-what happened?"

"Hey, all in good time, fella," says Collins. "I think ya need to rest up some more. Ya went through a hell of a thing."

He steps away, but I reach out to make him stop.

"No, wait. I need to know." I shuffle up the bed, ignoring the massive amount of discomfort as I prop myself semi-

341

upright against the pillows. "What happened to the boat? To Miley? How did I get here?"

Collins chuckles. "All right, slow down, partner. One thing at a time."

He nods to Ruby. I turn to her expectantly.

She takes a deep breath. "After you took off from the warzone outside Kazawa's building, more cops showed up. Actual cops, by all accounts. A lot of Kazawa's men were arrested. Some of Akuma's people were too."

"And Akuma?" I ask.

"He took off in the chaos. I think Ichiro went to see him yesterday."

"Yesterday? How long have I been out?"

"About thirty-six hours," says Collins.

"Jesus..."

Ruby continues. "So, as the scene was diffused, Colin Farrell over here made a call to his GlobaTech friends and got a chopper to come and pick us up. Figured it was the fastest way to find you."

Collins laughs. "Farrell? I'll take that! Thanks, sweetheart."

She sighs. "Ray, I swear to God..."

I roll my eyes. "All right, the pair of you, quit flirting. I'm awake now."

We all share a moment of laughter and respite.

"What happened with you?" Ruby asks me.

"I made it to the docks, where Kazawa's chopper was landing on the biggest yacht I've ever seen. I managed to jump aboard as it was pulling away. I swept through it and took out his security detail."

"How many?" asks Collins.

I think for a moment. "Um... thirteen, plus Kazawa and Miley."

"Christ…"

I shrug. "It was them or me. What can I say? So, how did you find me?"

Ruby laughs. "Adrian, sweetie, when you blow up a two-hundred-foot luxury yacht, it's kinda hard to miss."

"Ah. Right. Got you."

"How exactly did you do that, by the way?"

"On my way through, I created a small gas leak in the kitchen, which was right by the engine room. After I finished Miley off, two boatloads of back-up arrived. I figured I couldn't take them all out as well, so I ran back through the boat and threw a belt of grenades I borrowed from their armory into the engine room on my way past. It seemed to get the job done."

"Bloody hell… I'll say!" laughs Collins.

I look into Ruby's eyes. "I thought I was finished. When I hit the water… I just knew I was done for. It felt even more real to me than in the club. I felt at peace. I'm sorry."

She frowns. "What are you sorry for?"

"For giving up. For leaving you."

"Honey, you didn't give up. You were blown up—there's a difference. And you didn't leave me. I'm right here."

"Can I ask…" says Collins. "What was it like? Ya know, feeling that… peaceful. Thinking it was the end an' all."

"It was surreal. I saw the bright light and everything." I look over at Ruby. "I saw you, clear as anything, right in front of me. It put me at ease. Helped me accept it."

Her eyes mist over, and she squeezes my hand tightly.

"You thought that was you dying?" she asks.

"Well, yeah… I did."

"Oh my God…"

She smiles as a tear escapes down her cheek. She leans

over and kisses me. Soft and passionate. It floods my body with warmth and joy and comfort.

She moves away, still smiling.

Collins clears his throat. "So... I'm getting the impression ya not interested in a bit o' the Irish, babydoll?"

I fail to suppress a laugh. Ruby throws him an evil glare that lasts a few seconds before giving way to a smile. We share another moment of reprieve before Collins claps his hands together.

"Right, I'm gonna leave the pair of ya to it. Honestly, watching the two of ya is kinda makin' me sick anyway."

I smile and extend a hand, which he shakes firmly.

"I can't thank you enough for your help," I say to him. "You heading back to the States?"

"Tomorrow, maybe. Need to head over to the local branch here, fill out some paperwork, and write up a report for Mr. Buchanan. Who, I imagine, will want a chat with ya at some point."

I nod. "Of course. I owe him. Twice."

He looks over at Ruby. "And you... look after our fella here, all right?"

She smiles and moves around the bed toward him. She puts her arms around his neck and gives him a hug and a kiss on the cheek.

"You're an asshole," she says. "But you're my kind of asshole. Look after yourself, partner."

He smiles and nods. "Always."

He gives us both a casual salute before leaving the room.

Ruby sits down on the edge of the bed and takes my hand again.

"Just so you know," she says. "That bright light you saw, it wasn't the afterlife. It was the floodlight of the GlobaTech chopper Collins borrowed. And the image of me giving you peace at the end... that was actually me pulling your dumb ass out of the water."

I laugh, mostly from the relief of discovering I wasn't quite as finished as I thought. "Really? Damn, that's... that's amazing. I owe you my life."

She rolls her eyes. "Are you kidding me? That doesn't even bring us close to being square. I'm just glad you're safe."

We share a moment of comfortable silence.

"So, what now?" I ask her.

"Now, you stay here and rest. Your body has a lot of healing to do. It'll take time. And for once, time is what you got."

"Yeah, I guess so. What happened to Kazawa's yacht?"

"Local authorities are still investigating the wreckage, with a helping hand from GlobaTech."

"I thought they can't get involved?"

"Usually, they can't. But given the evidence we provided to Collins, they had a way to justify offering their assistance."

I think for a moment, almost afraid to ask.

"Is there any sign..."

"...of Miley? No. They're still recovering bodies. Collins gave me a de-brief earlier, while you were still out. Said they've found Kazawa and a handful of others, but there's a lot of debris to sift through. They confirmed additional wreckage of a chopper and two speedboats though, which ties in with what you were saying about the back-up."

"Yeah, I guess so."

"Adrian, it's fine. Honestly. It's over."

I smile. "Guess I'm just not used to having no war to fight."

"Well, you don't. Not anymore. Neither of us do. And if

you ask me, once you're back on your feet, we should leave Tokyo and settle down somewhere else. Somewhere new."

"Sounds like a great idea."

"And let's both try and leave the business behind this time, yeah? Actually retire and just... rest."

I go to speak, but a phone ringing stops me.

I look around, confused. "Is that you?"

She shakes her head. "No, it's not my ringtone." She looks over at a bag resting on a nearby chair. "Wait, it might be yours. I brought some things from the apartment yesterday, for when you wake up."

She moves over it and rummages inside, producing a ringing cell phone a second or two later. As she hands it to me, I look at the screen. See the caller ID.

I close my eyes as I feel my heart sink.

"What is it?" she asks, seeing my reaction.

"You know that whole retirement plan of yours?"

"Yeah..."

I show her the screen of the phone. I watch as her heart sinks to meet mine.

"I have a feeling that's not gonna happen." I answer the call and place the phone to my ear. "What can I do for you, Mr. President?"

THE END

EPILOGUE

The car pulls over outside Narita International Airport. The drive took just under an hour from the apartment. It felt longer for me because I was folded into the passenger side of Ichiro's Suzuki Roller Skate. He was kind enough to bring us here.

I'm well on my way to recovery, which I guess I have Ruby to thank for as much as the fine folks at GlobaTech Tokyo. If it wasn't for her threatening me with violence if I so much as breathed in the direction of the door to my hospital room, I wouldn't have rested up half as well as I have.

The three of us stand in a loose triangle on the sidewalk outside the main entrance. The sky is gray and harmless today. The weather is cold without being particularly bad, despite the time of year. Ruby and I have an overnight bag with some essentials inside. No point in having anything other than carry-on baggage for the flight.

It's been a week since President Schultz called me. I'm well enough to travel, so we're heading to D.C. in a couple of hours.

I extend a hand to Ichiro, which he shakes gladly. "Thank you, my friend. For everything."

He laughs his trademark, slightly insane belly laugh. "*Shinigami*, it has been honor!"

"At least you'll be kept busy and out of trouble," says Ruby before embracing him and kissing his cheek. "Now you have your noodle bar back."

He laughs again. "Busy, yes. Out of trouble? Never!"

I smile. I'm going to miss him.

"It was a nice gesture from Akuma, handing back control of your business," I say. "I'm really happy for you. I felt terrible that you had to give it up in the first place."

"A necessary evil. And the right choice. Good deeds breed good deeds."

I smile. "Fortune cookie wisdom?"

He smiles back and taps his chest. "Ichiro wisdom."

"And our slate is definitely clean?" asks Ruby.

Ichiro nods. "Akuma Oji was very clear. The blood debt Adrian owed for Santo was paid by taking out Kazawa."

"That's good," I say with a sigh of relief. "I guess with Kazawa out of the picture now, a lot of Tokyo is in a state of flux. You look after yourself, Ichi."

"Quite the opposite, *Shinigami*. I suspect word got around that Akuma paid you to wipe out Kazawa. The Oji-gumi are back on top. Everyone else back in line. Peace on the streets."

"Uh-huh. That's worked out very nicely for everyone, then. How, I wonder, did that slightly dramatized version of what happened travel around so quickly?"

Ichiro shrugs and remains silent.

I let slip a small, knowing smile. "I suspect whoever did it was experienced enough and smart enough to know what would happen if such a story got out. How it would benefit everything the way it has."

He shrugs again and winks at me.

"We'd best get going," says Ruby.

I grab my bag and sling it gently over my shoulder.

"When will you be back?" Ichiro asks me.

I shrug. "I honestly don't know. Ryan wasn't exactly forthcoming with information. I'm not sure what he wants me for, but I'm hoping whatever it is doesn't take long. I need a vacation."

He laughs. "Stay out of trouble, *Shinigami*. You too, *Shi No Tenshi*. See you both when you return."

That means Angel of Death.

Ruby blushes. I think she's happy she has her own nickname.

Ichiro nods a final farewell. He gets back in his car and drives away, leaving Ruby and I standing side-by-side, looking at the entrance to the airport.

"You ready for this?" she asks.

I shrug. "Does it matter?"

"I suppose not. Presidential orders an' all that. So, are we?"

"Are we what?"

"Coming back here?"

"I don't know. Would you want to?"

"I don't think so, no. You?"

"Honestly? As long as I'm with you, I couldn't care less where we are."

She smiles and takes my hand in hers. We walk into the airport, immediately swallowed up by the sea of people as we prepare to head back to the States.

Back home.

A MESSAGE

Dear Reader,

Thank you for purchasing my book. If you enjoyed reading it, it would mean a lot to me if you could spare thirty seconds to leave an honest review. For independent authors like me, one review makes a world of difference!

If you want to get in touch, please visit my website, where you can contact me directly, either via e-mail or social media.

Until next time...

James P. Sumner

CLAIM YOUR FREE GIFT!

By subscribing to James P. Sumner's mailing list, you can get your hands on a free and exclusive reading companion, not available anywhere else.

It contains an extended preview of Book 1 in each thriller series from the author, as well as character bios, and official reading orders that will enhance your overall experience.

If you wish to claim your free gift, just visit the website below:

linktr.ee/jamespsumner

You will receive infrequent, spam-free emails from the author, containing exclusive news about his books. You can unsubscribe at any time.

ACKNOWLEDGMENTS

This book has been a long time coming!

I began writing this mid-2018, excited by the fact I had been planning this particular chapter of Adrian's life for almost four years.

Sadly, life has a bad habit of getting in the way sometimes. Honestly, it felt like something was telling me I shouldn't write this novel. I had to deal with a divorce, severe mental health struggles, and a trip to the hospital with stress-related chest pains. I almost gave up.

But I didn't. Writing has always been my one true love in life, and I wanted to get back to being me. To being happy.

And so here we are, two years later, at the end of what I consider my strongest novel to date.

I worked hard to overcome what I did, but I didn't do it alone. The people that helped me along the way deserve recognition.

Claire - one of my oldest friends and my surrogate big sister. She supported me through the tough times and shared in my joy during the good times that came after. I would be truly lost without her in my life.

Adam - my brother from another mother, who's been a consistent part of my life for many, many years. As much a part of my family as anyone, he is the consummate distraction for when times are too tough to face.

Alexis - a strong and beautiful soul I've known almost twenty years. Having her to talk to about things that affect my mental health is invaluable, and I love her unconditionally.

Rick - a guy I've known since I was eight years old. We reconnected a couple of years ago and have become very close friends. I'm incredibly proud of him for being on the front lines in recent times as a nurse. He understands the troubles I've been through all too well, and he has always been there to pick me up when I've been down.

Coral - my long-time <u>editor</u> who, yet again, has taken a good book and made it great. Her work is on another level, and I couldn't be happier having worked with her once more. She is also much, much more to me than an editor, and her personal love and support has helped me focus and find happiness again.

Finally, to my readers. I wouldn't be here if it wasn't for your dedicated and continued support of me and my work. I genuinely love each and every one of you, and I want you all to know... I'm back.

This one is for all of you.

Thank you.

POST-CREDITS SCENE

"Is it done?"

"Yes. Kazawa's dead. His organ trafficking business along with him."

"Good. And the assassin?"

"Should've landed in Washington a couple of hours ago."

"Hmm. He got the call sooner than we had expected."

"Is that a problem?"

"No. We'll just have to bring a couple of things forward."

"What do you need me to do?"

"For now? Nothing. Keep a low profile, rest up, and wait for my call."

"I thought you wanted me to go after your next target?"

"Not yet. Besides, he's proving difficult to track down. When the time is right, we may need to go straight for plan B."

"The woman?"

"Yes. You find her, he will find you."

"I'll await your call."

The line clicked dead.

Miley Tevani looked out over the Tokyo skyline for a moment longer before moving over to the sofa and sitting down heavily. She felt frustrated but knew better than to question her orders.

She pressed gently at the extensive bandaging covering her neck. The stitching had begun to irritate her. She gazed absently around the penthouse, trying not to think of the night she spent here a couple of weeks ago.

But she knew he wouldn't be back. There was no reason for anyone to think she was alive. She had been careful to cover her tracks. But even if anyone did, no one would think to look for her in Adrian Hell's apartment.

Here, she could bide her time and fully recover. Yes, she had her orders, which she would obey without question. But she also had her own agenda. Her own mission.

Make Adrian Hell suffer.

Made in the USA
Columbia, SC
15 August 2023